A Matter of Temptation

A Matter of Temptation

USA TODAY BESTSELLING AUTHOR
STACY REID

The Duke's Shotgun Wedding
Copyright © 2014 by Stacy Reid

Entangled Publishing, LLC
644 Shrewsbury Commons Ave., STE 181
Shrewsbury, PA 17361
Visit our website at www.entangledpublishing.com.

Amara is an imprint of Entangled Publishing, LLC.

Edited by Stacy Abrams
Cover design by Bree Archer
Model Photographer Chris Cocozza
Cover art by FairytaleDesign/Depositphotos and
Shutterstock/Von Dmitry_Tsvetkov
Interior design by Toni Kerr

Print ISBN 978-1-64937-096-9
ebook ISBN 978-1-64937-224-6

Manufactured in the United States of America

First Edition July 2022

AMARA

ALSO BY STACY REID

THE SINFUL WALLFLOWERS

My Darling Duke
Her Wicked Marquess
A Scoundrel of Her Own

WEDDED BY SCANDAL

Accidentally Compromising the Duke
Wicked in His Arms
How to Marry a Marquess

SCANDALOUS HOUSE OF CALYDON

The Duke's Shotgun Wedding
The Irresistible Miss Peppiwell
Sins of a Duke
The Royal Conquest

Du'Sean, always and forever.

CHAPTER ONE

The only way to satisfy
temptation is to yield to it...

Miss Wilhelmina Eleanor Crawford—Mina to her friends and family—deeply inhaled the aromatic soup which she stirred in the large iron pot, her mouth aching for a taste of the thyme-infused dish. "The smell is divine, Mrs. Bell," she said with a grin, blowing at the tendril of hair which escaped her cap and tickled her nose. "Adding onion and thyme was a stroke of genius on my part, you must admit it."

Their portly cook smiled, using the back of her hand to wipe at the sweat matting the hair curling atop her forehead. The large stone kitchen was rather hot, but it was preferable to the blistering cold that had been infused in each grayscale stone earlier.

"I hate to see ye laboring so, Miss Mina. 'Tis not the work of a lady to be cooking in the kitchen."

"*Nonsense*. I love being your helper and keeping your company."

Mrs. Bell harrumphed, but her bright hazel eyes gleamed with affection for her young mistress. Mina had started assisting their cook out of necessity after their family fell on dire straits and they had become unable to pay their servants' wages.

A shout echoed from outside and Mina went over to the windows to peek out, grinning when she saw little Tommy perched on a willow tree branch flying a kite—the kite she had given him only two weeks past for Christmas. Mina laughed when his curses drifted on the air as the harsh wind tried to rip his tiny body from the limb. Thankfully there was a soft mound of snow covering the ground, enough to cushion him if he fell from that height.

"That one has the mouth of a sailor on him," the cook said, "and he curses using all those fancy words you've been teaching him. He has ideas now that he'll stop being a stable lad someday and will be a physician! I never heard the likes of it." She shook her head with a harrumph. "Ye shouldn't encourage him so, Miss Mina. Soon he'll be getting those airs, too, the ones of an impossible dreamer."

"I believe in him, though! Little Tommy can be whatever or whomever he wants to be, and I shall help him," Mina said, pressing her nose to the cold window. The yearning to be outdoors stirred inside of her. "Oh, look at him fly that kite!"

"Why don't you go out there? Anyone with eyes can see ye badly want to join him."

With that soft urging from their cook to do something as simple as fly a kite, Mina was suddenly acutely reminded that once she had dreamed of impossible things, and they had soared inside her heart, pushing her to reach for dizzying adventures. "I am not a young and reckless girl anymore," she said softly, that familiar wrench twisting through her heart. *I have not been for six years*. Brushing aside the loneliness that tried to creep over her body, Mina straightened and turned around.

Cook shook her head again. "It ain't reckless to climb a tree around these parts—no one to mutter about it. I do not see why ye keep denying yerself simple fun, Miss Mina. It ain't natural for a lovely girl such as yourself to be so buried down in the country-side and having no enjoyment of life."

A door slammed in the distance, saving Mina the necessity of a reply. Cook frowned and said, "It sounds like the young master is home. He is always closing that door with too much force."

Concern curled through Mina, and she lowered the wooden spoon onto the small plate before her on the stone counter. There were days she could read her brother's mood simply from how he entered his country manor. Without the benefit of a butler to see to such needs as opening and closing doors, he managed the task himself, one greatly aided by his emotional ups and downs.

Gently removing the cap from her hair, she muttered, "I will see if he will eat with us, Mrs. Bell."

Mina hurried up the stairs leading from the kitchen, down the servants' staircase, and into the lower floor hallway that was no longer lined with grand paintings. The sweet melody of a sound being played on the pianoforte rode the air, and her concern grew. Whenever Anthony was troubled, he turned to the comforting solace of music, especially Beethoven. Did this mean he had been denied the loan by Drummonds bank?

She all but ran to the sparsely furnished music room and pushed open the ajar door. Anthony's fingers faltered at her entry, and he shifted on the bench to face her. Mina stopped, her breath catching at the wild look of fear in his dark green eyes before her brother shuttered his expression.

"Anthony, what is it?" She took a few more steps

into the room. "Please, just tell me whatever it is. We will work it out together."

He inhaled a shaky breath and released it heavily. "The bank denied our loan. They would listen to none of my plans."

Mina gripped her fingers until they ached. This was a disaster indeed. "Did they say why?"

"The last two loans are still being paid on, and they do not believe I have the confidence to manage a third," he said with a harsh laugh. "Though I am Viscount Crawford, no heiresses are lining up to marry me for my title. The bankers are aware of this. One of them even went as far as to say agriculture is dead, it is all about manufacturing now, and we do not have the tools or men of the trade to venture out from farming."

Mina and her brother had spoken of it at length before he made the journey to London. Still, though they had prepared for a rejection of their application, Mina had not really envisioned the consequences of that rejection. Mrs. Bell had not been paid a salary in almost a year, and the lone footman and stable boy had their own families to care for and feed. They needed to be paid. Their manor was also in dire need of repairs and proper staffing and supplies of food and other necessities to see them through for the rest of the year. The larder and pantry were almost empty.

"I still have Mama's necklace. We can pawn it for a tidy sum to see us through this year until we come up with another plan," she said staunchly. "We will practice greater economy and retrench even further—"

"Retrench further? Mina, we are barely holding on. What more can I do? Whatever income we have goes into paying off loans and debts."

Guilt clawed at her with raking talons. Before their father had passed away five years ago, there had been a plan to help the family replenish their coffers, but Mina had destroyed it with her reckless impetuosity and ruined herself spectacularly and irrevocably by eloping.

She'd naively wished for a grand sort of adventure. Well, the future would be an adventure, indeed. Mina's heart clenched at the uncertainty that gripped her.

"I have to leave in the morning," Anthony said suddenly, unable to meet her eyes.

"Where do you go?"

"Perhaps to London," he said with a bitter twist to his mouth. "The season will start in a few weeks. Do you remember Lord Phineas Moulton? He recently married an American heiress, and his estates were saved. Perhaps I might do the same for us."

A desperate hope when Mina could not imagine who would extend any invitations to their family. "Where will you stay? Our townhouse in Mayfair was recently let."

Anthony tilted his head to the ceiling and pinched the bridge of his nose. She hated seeing him like this. Loath to think about how she had failed her family by running away with a gentleman she had thought herself in love with, she slowly removed the apron. Realizing her fingers shook, Mina took a calming breath. There was an air of desperation about her brother; it informed her that more than the bank denying them the loan had happened. "Anthony, why don't you sit down and tell me everything from the beginning? Please."

His lips flattened, and he shook his head. "I got myself into this mess. I cannot burden your delicate thoughts—"

She made a wry sound of disbelief that cut him off. "My delicate what now? I assure you they have long been hardened by necessity."

"Mina—"

"Anthony!" She fisted a hand at her hip. "We do not lie to each other since…" *Since my idiocy.* "We do not lie to each other. We agreed. Please, inform me what is plaguing you. I can tell there is more to it than the loan."

His throat worked on a swallow, and she watched with mounting anxiousness as he struggled. What did her brother believe so difficult he could not tell her? "Did you kill someone?"

"For God's sakes, Mina, nothing so grave."

Yet he still could not meet her eyes. "Did you—"

"Well, not yet anyway," he added, briefly closing his eyes. "I am to fight in a duel," he rushed out.

"A *duel*!"

He eyed her warily. "Yes."

Bewilderment rushed through her. "What you say makes little sense. What do you mean you are to fight in a duel? Is this why you are heading to London?"

He grimaced. "No, I plan to go back to London after the duel. I must leave soon, or I will be branded a coward. We would be irretrievably ruined with no way forward if I am to develop such an indecent reputation."

Mina padded closer to her brother, a tight feeling of panic gripping her. "Anthony, this is absurd.

Dueling is *illegal*! If I recall correctly, they were made illegal many years ago. Just participating in a duel is a crime, and the risk to your person cannot be so lightly dismissed. How did you get involved in such a matter?"

He gave her a long-suffering glance. "There are secretive, underground duels, Mina. Gentlemen have not stopped taking part in honor challenges because it was made illegal. Sometimes your naivete frustrates me."

"It is yours that bears the frustration. You very well know it is a criminal act, and you still intend to take part in one? Why would you do so?" she demanded, aghast. "Have you no thought about the consequences?"

"I have no other choice," he said tightly.

"Who are you to duel?"

There was the slightest of hesitation, then he said, "Simon Loughton, Earl of Creswick."

Mina recoiled as if she had been slapped. While she had never met the earl, his reputation preceded him, and even buried in the countryside for the last six years, Mina had heard tales of Creswick's political shrewdness and ambitions.

Her father had been an admirer of the young earl's brilliance and cunning. Though the many articles Mina devoured in the past spoke of the man's ruthlessness, they also referenced his honor and the excellent motions he argued, first in the Commons and since gaining the earldom in the House of Lords. Arguments that had swayed the passage of bills that affected the realm and helped reshape the very fabric of their country and further afield to the United

Kingdom's commonwealth.

"Why would the earl do this and risk his reputation? It is ill-judged," she said faintly, sitting on the edge of the chair. "*Why*?"

"I was invited to an intimate card party at the earl's house in Hertfordshire," her brother said, misery and regret lining his handsome countenance. "I wish I had not gone, Mina. But I thought this was a great opportunity to form lasting and noteworthy connections, and…" He scrubbed a hand over his face and blew out a harsh breath. "I had hoped I could perhaps leverage some connections for investment loans. But then…there was talk of-of cheating and…"

"And that *knave* challenged you to a duel," she cried. "Has *he* thought about the consequences? I… What can we do to avoid this? I've read that an apology will fix—"

An indecipherable expression settled on her brother's face. "Mina, I cannot apologize! I am the challenger."

She stared at her brother as if he had grown horns. "*You* challenged the earl?"

"Yes."

Mina was so astonished, she laughed. "Is this a poorly conceived jest?" At his silence, she said, "Whatever could you have been thinking, Anthony? Even if the earl cheated at cards, the best thing would have been to hold your head low and let it pass. It's only cards, for heaven's sakes. Why should the matter be so serious?"

There was a deep look of shame in his eyes that scratched at her chest. "I was the one who tried to cheat at cards, Min."

Mina stilled, dread pooling low in her belly. "I do not understand."

"I suspect Creswick knew I had some cards hidden in the sleeve of my jacket. I could see the knowledge in his unflinching stare, and I... I damn well panicked and accused him first of cheating."

Mina dropped her face into her hands. *This is a disaster*.

Nor was this her brother. He was her twin. She knew him better than everyone. Anthony was a *good* man with a strong sense of honor, fairness, and refined sensibilities. To have attempted to cheat at cards with such influential gentlemen at the table was inconceivable, and then to have accused another of a falsehood? Then, with a burn of sorrow, she realized desperation had driven him to act so foolishly. "What was the pot, Anthony?"

"Five thousand pounds."

She flinched. Such a fortune to be laid on a private gambling table, a desperate lure for Anthony when there seemed to be no solution from the straits that blighted their family. He had inherited debt and a crumbling estate, and a sister whom he loved but one who could not marry herself to help their family.

Tears burned her eyes and throat when she recalled her father asking her if she could bear the consequences of falling in love with a man who could not financially provide for her or assist their family with any noteworthy connections.

"Yes, Papa, for we love each other!"

How sure and passionate she had been. *How silly!* For she had never envisioned such a consequence of her brother dying on some cold, empty field because of a decision she had made six years ago. "How did you end up challenging the earl, Anthony?"

He looked so deeply ashamed, she almost wept for him. However, Mina stiffened her spine and held his gaze, forcing him to tell the truth.

"He was so coolly amused at my wild accusation. Everyone at the table fell silent, and he laughed, Min." Anthony tossed the cushion into the wall with his strength as if it allowed the shame and frustration to leave his body. "Then the earl said that I was not worth his time. I felt as if his dismissive calm would show that *I* had something to hide…and God, Mina, I am not sure what the hell I was thinking. I got angry and challenged him to a duel. The duke laughed and said we were not to get ahead of ourselves, but before I could say anything more, the earl accepted my challenge."

"How did everyone else respond? Surely they intervened."

"Only silence blanketed the room." He raked his fingers through his hair. "Then there was no more opportunity to step back; the die was cast."

Mina could only imagine the shock her brother had felt. His bluster to cover his own failings had been called upon. "Do you…must you have seconds? Will there be a doctor present?"

"The duke simply mentioned I am to present myself to Norbrook Hall, the earl's estate, at dawn tomorrow. There was no mention of seconds or anything. I was even given a choice to pick the weapons to use. An offer made by the earl in that damn indifferent tone of his," her brother said with raw frustration. "It is normally the person being challenged who gets the choice of weapon, and he offered it to me."

Dueling had been outlawed. What rules could be applied? Mina felt like a fish floundering on dry land. "We have no dueling pistols," she said, for they had sold the last pair of Mantons some weeks back. A pair of dueling pistols many had called antique and priceless.

"That is why I picked the rapier. I am not too bad."

Hope unfurled like a flower in bloom at the first touch of spring inside Mina's chest. "The rapier?"

"Yes."

Anthony was correct. He was good at fencing...but Mina was exceptional.

Her father had fondly called her his fencing master. Did she dare contemplate such a thing? The idea that she could duel in her brother's stead felt frightening, preposterous, but also right. "Anthony?"

"Yes?"

"I will fight for you."

He inhaled sharply, clearly shocked. "What do you mean?"

"Do you recall as children I used to dress in your clothes and climb trees with you? Even our parents had difficulty telling us apart," she said, warming to her wild idea. "We *are* twins, and our features are remarkably alike. The same eyes, face shape, and hair color. Yes, I know you are a bit taller than I am and a bit heavier, however—"

He slashed a hand, cutting her off. "Have you lost your good senses, Mina? Fight Lord Creswick for me? I fear you are unequal to the task. I have been more about than you, and I fear you are not aware of his reputation as well as I am. Though he is only three years above our four and twenty, the earl is…he is rather shrewd, incomparably clever, *and* ruthless. I could never risk you so lightly and send you in my stead to be run through!"

Her heart shuddered violently inside her chest. "You believe he means to end the duel in *death*?"

Anthony's throat worked on a swallow. "I do not know what to think anymore, Min."

"I fear your anxiety has allowed you to conjure all sorts of imagining," she said reassuringly, though her belly was knotted with doubt. "And that you believe Creswick can be that ruthless without any consideration for his position within society is reason enough for me to fight in your stead. Anthony, you have never beaten me. I am sorry if this wounds your pride, but you know it to be true."

For a moment, he seemed as if he wavered, then he straightened his shoulders and firmed his lips in a resolute line. "There is too much risk to you. If you were to be discovered, your reputation would be shredded and that would ruin your happiness."

"Ruin my happiness?" The idea so astonished Mina, a half laugh, more of a scoff tore from her. "What happiness?"

"Min?" he asked with an air of confusion.

Of course, Anthony had been incapable of seeing that she was discontent given the heavy duties and responsibilities on his shoulders. And a part of her job had been to ensure that he never had to worry about her well-being.

"I am not happy with my lot in life, Anthony, and I do not mean to say so for it to be a burden, but to assure you that I am not risking *anything* if more scrutiny was to befall my reputation," she said softly. "I made a mistake six years ago when I thought I fell in love. Since then I have buried all sense of myself because I believed it was my impetuous and adventurous nature that contributed to our dire state now. Pretending to be you and fighting in your stead is perhaps *more* than just saving your hide. It is a way for me to escape, even for a bit, the tedium of country living and merely just…existing."

Mina smiled at him reassuringly, hoping to convince Anthony with her truth. She couldn't quite pinpoint when she had started feeling as if merely existing was no longer for her. What had she gained from sequestering herself in the countryside and hiding away from life? *Nothing*. And that filled her with more sadness than anything else. For she had thought there was much to gain staying quiet, hiding her true self even when no one observed. That she buried her adventurous heart for so long only proved that she was as stalwart and unflagging as Papa usually praised.

She shrugged off the awkward and painful memories, for as much as she did not like her current situation, Mina was at a loss as to how to rise from it. Fighting this duel for Anthony should save him, and perhaps fill her with enough adventure to fight the emptiness eating inside her heart with a measure of something. "Anthony—"

He held up his hand to forestall further arguments. "I have already proven myself a man willing to cheat. I could not live with also being a coward who would send his sister to face death while he hid in the safety of his home."

Mina stood, hating that her knees trembled. "Anthony! What if you should lose?"

Fear flashed in his eyes, but he lifted his chin. "I cannot afford to lose, so I will not."

Then he turned and walked away, going to the library, where a pair of rapiers hung on the wall. Their father had been so proud of the pair of fencing swords, for they were gifts from King George himself. Mina fisted her hands at her sides. "Do you mean to leave now?"

"I…" His stomach rumbled, and he gave her a sheepish smile.

That smile made her throat ache, for she clearly saw he was trying to reassure her even as fear lived inside of him. She was his older sister by only five minutes, and she had failed him once. Mina could not fail him again.

A sudden movement through the open door had her whirling around. It was Mrs. Bell, and she used the corner of the apron to dab a tear from her eye. She had clearly overheard the conversation and felt a shared terror for her young master, who had treated her like family.

"Yes, Mrs. Bell," Anthony said after clearing his throat.

"The soup has been ladled, my lord. It is a bit thin, but it will fill yer bellies for the night."

Mina attempted to smile, but when her lips would not curve, she bit into her bottom lip to prevent their trembling. "We will be there soon, Mrs. Bell. Will you eat with us tonight?"

Some months ago, the distinction between servant and master overturned when Mina collected her bowl of rabbit stew and went below the stairs to sit at the table with the cook. Anthony had cautiously followed, looking uncomfortable. While Mrs. Bell had seemed ready to faint, there had been motherly compassion in her eyes, and she had remained silent, shifting over on her wooden bench to make room for them. That night the stew had tasted more delightful, and Mina had been warmed and less lonely. Even Anthony had smiled as he devoured the simple dish of rabbit, carrots, and potatoes.

"Not tonight, Miss Mina." Her bright gaze went between them. "I suspect you and the young master will want some time alone."

Mrs. Bell hastened away, and Mina faced her brother. "I need to wash up."

"I will await you before eating."

"You can start without me," she said. "I... I might be a while."

He nodded, and Mina felt his eyes on her as she departed the library and hurried to her bedchamber on the second floor. The room was cold, and she shivered, noting the fire in the hearth had burned low. Mina went to the bath chamber, where she stripped from her gown, petticoats, and undergarments, a task she had become very adept at doing herself for at least a year.

Their father had refurbished their country manor with indoor plumbing several years ago, and thankfully the water was tepid and not icy cold. She did not linger in the large bathtub but cleaned herself with economic movements, careful not to get her thick tresses wet. Once out, she dressed in a simple dark green bombazine dress with several rows of buttons to the front. The stockings she slipped on had holes, but they kept her feet warm.

Mina was putting on her shoes when a soft knock came on her door. "Yes?"

The door opened, and Mrs. Bell peeked in, astonishing Mina. The boot forgotten, she slowly straightened.

"If you aim to get going, Miss Mina, it is best you do it now. The young master's asleep."

She sucked in a sharp breath. "What do you mean?"

A pained look came onto Mrs. Bell's face. "I overheard the conversation, Miss Mina, and I... I added some herbs mixed with a small amount of laudanum to his soup."

"Mrs. Bell!"

"I gather it is sounder than whatever you planned, because I know you would not have let him go. And I suspected you would have drunk with him until he was so soused he would not have been able to sit on a horse."

Mina smiled. "It was a thought, but neither of us holds any sort of alcoholic drink well, so I would have been similarly affected. I was trying to think of another way to convince Anthony."

"Aye." Mrs. Bell smiled. "Now off you go, Miss Mina."

An ache rising in her throat, she went over to the kind woman who served as their cook, housekeeper, and always a listening ear and shoulder to cry upon. "Thank you, Mrs. Bell. Please take care of my brother until I return."

Mina hurried to her brother's chamber and changed into a pair of his older trousers that fitted a bit loosely, making quick adjustments to the belt to prevent them from falling off. Her breasts were modest enough and needed no binding, but to be safe, she wrapped them in linens. Then she donned an undershirt, a striped blue and white waistcoat, and jacket. Unpinning her hair that tumbled loosely to her midback, she picked up the scissors and took a deep breath. Mina wanted the earl to believe her to be Anthony, thereby possibly earning his respect. That respect would see Anthony a far way in the *ton* and could be the beginning of their fortunes turning around.

Still, Mina hesitated. Memories of her mama brushing her hair while singing wafted through her thoughts, bringing with it a fierce missing. With an irritated huff at her hesitation at this critical juncture, she put aside the shears and wrapped her hair in a coronet and fitted a cap tightly to her head.

Staring in the mirror, she thought her disguise perfect. The cap was pulled low enough over her brows, and as his twin, she shared the same eyes and slanting cheekbones as her brother. He was a bit taller, but they both owned a slim, elegant build, and hopefully, the earl would not notice the small differences.

A sliver of unease ghosted down her spine when she recalled the man's reputed brilliance. Pushing aside the feeling, she hurried downstairs and peeked into the library, where Anthony reposed on the lumpy and worn sofa, snoring. Closing the door behind her, she collected her coat and the rapier and headed to the stable, where they shared the lone stallion that remained stabled at their property. He had been their favorite horse, and sentimentality had prevented them from parting with Raven for much-needed money.

Little Tommy jumped down from the loft and assisted her to fit the saddle and stirrups.

"Do not sleep in the stables, Tommy," she murmured. "It might snow."

His blue eyes lit up and he nodded. "Aye, Miss Mina. Especially as Raven won't be here."

"Hurry and go on," she urged, smiling as he ran toward the main house.

Then, without the aid of the mounting block, Mina expertly hauled herself atop the horse. Norbrook Park was perhaps a couple hours of riding. She was familiar with the earl's estate, having passed it several times with her father when he'd been alive. It was one of the largest in all of Hertfordshire, sitting on over two hundred acres of prime lawns and woodlands. Still, she would ride with caution as a woman alone, especially if she stopped to water Raven.

Hopefully, Anthony would not wake and notice that she was gone before the duel ended. Even if he did, her brother had no means to secure himself a carriage or another horse to race to the earl's estate to stop her. Perhaps she should have left a letter reassuring him, but she sensed that Mrs. Bell would not leave Anthony unattended and would explain all that happened. Mina nudged their beloved stallion forward down the lane, almost afraid to look back.

Urging Raven into a gallop, she calmed her racing thoughts, filling herself with the determination to win. Her victory might go a far way in restoring Anthony's reputation and might even regain a measure of respect from those gentlemen with whom he'd wanted to form a connection. Recalling the dejected way he

held his head even in sleep, Mina was all the more
certain she had acted in the right. This *was* all her
fault. A proper marriage to a gentleman of connections would have seen Anthony's position more
secured as the new Viscount. Her decision to run away
to marry that man—she really could not even *think*
his name—had been the first card to topple in an up-
right deck.

Mina arrived at the earl's estate well before the
break of dawn and dismounted from her horse at the
manor's forecourt. She stroked and patted the stallion,
softly crooning, "Thank you for taking me safely,
Raven."

Mina led her horse toward the grand stables in the
distance, handing him over to a stable lad who hurried
out and collected her animal without any question.
Fishing for the pocket watch inside the coat's pocket,
she shone its face toward the bright moonlight, hoping
to ascertain the time. It was almost four in the morning. Mina hugged the cloak tighter around her
shoulders as a gust of wind sliced through the thick,
fog-shrouded darkness.

Walking with graceful confidence across the open
field of the earl's estate took more effort than she
wanted to admit. Her blasted knees were trembling so
badly, she had to pause for a few seconds and gather
her equanimity. Blowing a sharp breath, she ignored
the sudden fear clawing at her belly and strolled
across the cold, empty lawns, dotted with snow that
crunched beneath her boots.

There was no one outside, and the large country
estate echoed with eerie loneliness. Looking up in the
dark of a starlit night, she could see looming

cream-colored stone towers topped with small domes and crenulated portions three stories high between them. The central portion rose to four stories, and large gilded doors would give entrance to the main part of the house. The shadows gave the impressive mansion a slightly spooky effect, and she shivered as an owl hooted.

Mina sent up a swift prayer that her ruse would go off as planned and that she would not be discovered. Despite reassuring her brother that she was unafraid with little to risk, truly, she could not imagine the consequences if the Earl of Creswick discovered it was a lady with whom he dueled.

CHAPTER TWO

"Are you really to duel that pup?" the Duke of Beswick drawled from where he reposed with refined elegance by the roaring fire. "A bit cruel, don't you think, Creswick? Your technique is flawless, and you have never lost a match. Surely you saw the lad's anxiety about the entire affair. I say it took immense courage not to have cast up his accounts."

The murmurings from his friend barely pricked the attention of Simon, the Earl of Creswick, as he folded the letter sent to him by a most trusted gentleman in his curated network of informants hidden in the deep pockets of the underworld in London.

Beware. Those who were once friends are now enemies.

The message was grave, ominous, and wholly expected, considering his recent support of an earnest call for reform. Another man might be frightened by the dire warning that those opposed to his political stance wanted to harm him. Some feared that should certain motions be passed into law, they might lose money and status. Greed was a powerful motivator for murder and mayhem, and many made their money stepping on the backs of men, women, and children.

Come, he thought darkly, refusing to let such threats dictate the work he did for those who suffered the most in the realm. Many years of fighting had beaten back some of the poverty, squalor, and injustice that plagued the country's most vulnerable citizens, but these injustices were far from eliminated.

It was up to men like him to use their considerable influence to help better the world. Simon believed in that duty above all else.

"Are you to ignore us, then?" Daniel, Lord Stannis, demanded. "Come, man, now is not the time for that brooding insouciance."

"Viscount Crawford cheated at cards," Simon said, lifting his glass of whisky to his mouth and taking a healthy sip. "He is the one who challenged me. I merely accepted."

"Yes, we all suspected he was cheating, but very badly done. The viscount still lost all that he won in the early rounds," Beswick said, his green eyes cool and penetrating. "I merely thought such trivial matters were beneath your attention, Creswick. I am surprised at the consideration you are giving this matter."

Lord Stannis fixed Simon with a curious stare. "We thought you respected his father?"

"It is *because* I respected Lord Crawford that I have decided to teach his son a lesson," Simon replied with polite indifference. The viscount's father had been an impressive orator in the House of Lords, a gentleman whom he'd admired. "We know another gentleman would not have taken so kindly to having his honor impugned and being accused as a cheat by the very man who did the actual cheating. It is a good thing it was me the blasted fool accused."

His compatriots had little to say to that, and the duke even lifted his glass in a silent toast. "Try not to kill the pup. I have no taste for digging up the cold earth to bury a body."

The loud clatter of carriage wheels sounded through the open window.

"Is Crawford so eager that he would arrive early?" Stannis demanded with a gruff laugh, pushing to his feet to refill his glass from the carafe on the rosewood table between the sofas and chairs.

The duke cast him a speaking glance, and Stannis winced. Instantly Simon suspected they were up to no good. "I have a dawn appointment to keep and want no part of your debaucheries."

The earl tossed him a devilish grin, ambled over, and slapped Simon across his shoulders in a show of joviality. "Come, man, the best thing to do hours before risking your life is to have some fun."

The rich carnality lacing Stannis's tone suggested the kind of fun he envisioned for the rest of the night.

Simon smiled in derision. "My life shall not be at risk."

He was confident in his skills and even hoped it might not come to a meeting of swords if the damn fool would allow for a conversation. The young viscount had a reckless and desperate air about him that had drawn Simon's curiosity, enough for him to intervene with a lesson. Still, one must always be careful of those who wore desperation like a second skin. Some men allowed themselves to believe they had little to lose when they got to that point. Proven by the viscount and his absurd challenge—he gambled with his honor, reputation, and life.

The door shoved open, and four decadently dressed ladies spilled into the room, another of their friends, George, Marquess of Moncrieff, entering behind them, his cravat missing and his gaze heavy with satiation. George had clearly chosen the courtesans intending to satisfy the most jaded of tastes, with an evident bid to captivate Simon's disinterested senses.

"Why are these ladies here?"

Stannis clapped his shoulder once again. "My good man, these are no ladies, but courtesans of the finest qualities with cock drying skill. They will wring every drop from us before the night is out and leave us limp with exhaustion. And I assure you, we will enjoy every single moment."

The women were indeed all beauties, and if their gowns had been less revealing, they might at first glance have passed for diamonds of the *haut ton*. The tallest female with a fine hourglass figure was a dusky brunette with flashing dark eyes. She wore scarlet, and it suited her. The redhead, who leaned on her arm, was possibly slightly foxed, but her dainty figure was topped with a very nice pair of alabaster globes, which spilled out of her tightly laced green gown.

The third lady was the most modestly dressed in ethereal pale blue, and having flashed an artful glance at him, she looked down as if she were as innocent as a nun. Her pale blonde curls were the work of a master coiffeur, and she played the part of the *demi-vierge* very effectively. The fourth girl clinging to George had creamy skin, light brown hair, and hazel slanting eyes.

The library was dimly lit by a small blaze on the hearth, leaving much of the room in shadow, but the ladies' charms could not be denied.

"You started without us," Stannis drawled, ambling over to one of the women and lifting her against his body to lightly kiss her mouth.

Moncrieff grinned. "The train ride from town was boring. Our cart was private, the ladies needed a distraction, and I happily obliged."

"A distraction that carried to the carriage?" Beswick asked archly.

Moncrieff grinned. "Aye."

Though of late, Simon had been restless with a nameless dissatisfaction and perhaps needed the outlet of a night of pleasure, an irritating and all-too-familiar boredom crept over him. His friends had always encouraged him toward more sensual pursuits, but Simon found that not even the choicest companions and most delectable courtesans could hold his attention for they did not challenge his interest or his mind. These gentlemen were a good lot, but they were more interested in enjoying themselves than being useful to society.

"Oh, he is a lovely one," the blonde cooed, sauntering over to him with a sensual sway of lush hips. "I've always liked me a gentleman this pretty but also manly."

Simon grabbed the hand that lifted to caress his face. "Do not touch unless invited to," he said with biting coolness, never one to like being groped at will by others. Worse, it was something of an annoyance to be called pretty, especially when the very gentlemen in the room often acted like fools in regard to it.

The courtesan appeared momentarily uncertain, and she glanced at the other gentlemen for guidance. Simon lowered her arm and stepped away from her light floral perfume.

"Come man," Moncrieff drawled. "Tell me you are not tempted."

"Not even in the slightest."

"More for us," Beswick drawled, slipping his arms around two of the courtesans who sweetly giggled.

Simon knocked back his drink in a long swallow, appreciating the burning bite in his gut. Setting down his glass, he met their gazes. "Avail yourself of my guest chambers, gentlemen."

Simon then made his way from the library down the prodigious hallway to his private study, lit by several gas lamps and a flickering fireplace. He lowered himself into a wingback chair near the windows and peered outside in the dark. A glance at the mantel revealed it only a few minutes after four, at least two hours away from the breaking dawn. It was too late really to attempt sleep, considering Viscount Crawford should arrive soon.

Suddenly Simon was irritated with himself for having accepted the challenge. He should have simply taken the young viscount aside and given him a severe lecture on the dangerous risks of cheating, for with the wrong man he could find himself in a situation that he could never step back from. Simon had thought to reach Crawford with a language he understood. That rubbish of years past about dueling for honor and reputation might mean something to the young viscount, but a sound thrashing could likely urge him to turn away from this foolish and reckless path altogether. But now Simon wanted it to be done and over with. There were far more important things commanding his time and attention.

The shadow of a figure appeared in his vision, slim and elegant, creeping in a clandestine manner. It was damnably disconcerting to suddenly see a small face pressed against his windows. The quick image of slanting cheekbones, full lips, and a classical, elegant nose seared in Simon's mind before his gaze collided with vivid green eyes.

A quick pulse of an unfamiliar sensation darted through Simon before it wafted away. Those eyes widened upon seeing him sitting so close, and the person faltered into stillness.

Finally…something interesting.

Grabbing the rapier from off his desk, Simon went to the window and shoved it open with some impatience. His interloper jerked back, stepping into the shadows. Simon slung one foot, then the other over the sill, and into the palatial gardens. "Identify yourself. And state why you are trespassing in my gardens."

"I am Viscount Crawford, here to duel with the Earl of Creswick."

"You've arrived earlier than anticipated, Crawford. Should I be impressed with your eagerness to face your demise?"

To Simon's surprise, the sharp sound of a rapier as it hissed from its blade rode the darkness, and with shocking speed and grace, the tip pressed to the side of his throat, right above his beating pulse. *Hell*. That he had not expected.

Simon was inarguably impressed.

"Demise," the voice said, low and husky. "You mean to murder a man over cards, my lord? Where is the unblemished honor that some whisper in awe of? Perhaps it is I who shall ensure it is you who meet your demise tonight."

An unknown sort of savagery slithered at the threat at his throat. "Demise and death are not one and the same." He kept his voice flat, lest this creature before him used his cadence to try and decipher his reaction. Simon whirled left with an agility that alarmed his opponent, given the swift intake of breath. His blade was unsheathed and held pointed to the ground in one fluid moment. He felt the viscount's admiration more than saw it.

"You are very swift," Crawford murmured. "And very graceful."

"That I am."

"I am better."

That low answer had a steel of challenge beneath it, a murmur that said he stood unafraid. Simon almost laughed, surprised the lad had some mettle. "Truly astonishing you would think so," he murmured, sliding his boots through the snow-covered lawn, Simon's thoughts calculating as he circled Crawford.

"A worthy opponent," the viscount said with a soft bite that was undermined by the tremble heard in it. "This encounter will prove interesting."

Perhaps the young lord indeed wanted a fight after all. It invigorated Simon to anticipate the mettle of his opponent and the slight possibility of danger that meant he might enjoy a good bout. He did not think the young viscount would take long to deal with, but Simon could always hope that he was well trained enough to not embarrass himself too much.

"Do you agree after our duel, the demands of honor have been met?" Crawford murmured.

"Yes."

A considering silence fell.

"There are no physicians here."

"I do not plan to maim you."

"I have never fought in a duel before. I have no notion of what to expect, only what I have read about.

Where are our witnesses, my lord?"

"Are we not men of honor? Do we need witnesses?"

He felt the viscount's start of surprise. "You would still consider me a gentleman of honor?"

"Yes, only a foolish one."

Another pulse of silence that felt fraught with perilous tension coated the air.

"Then I shall fight well to reclaim your good opinion, my lord. Rumor mentioned that once it is lost, it is never to be regained."

"There might be some truth to the claim."

"Ah, then I shall endeavor to prove myself worthy of it."

"*En garde*," Simon said.

"*Allez*," the viscount said, then darted forward.

The flash of steel in the darkness was swiftly parried by Simon and the clang of metal on metal pierced the stillness of the waning night.

The viscount's fencing skill was exceptional, his form agile and graceful, even if his arms lacked the strength of Simon's. The viscount jumped forward, attacking in a flurry of moves so swift, Simon could hardly measure. "I am impressed, Crawford."

"My aim *was* to please, my lord."

Simon parried, almost flicking the rapier from the young lord's hand, but even that move had been anticipated and countered. They circled each other slowly, the mounting anticipation almost like a tethered hook into each person. A rumble of thunder sounded, and the viscount lifted his face to the sky. "I fear it will rain in a few minutes, my lord."

"I shall be done with you in one," Simon said, an

edge of boredom to his words.

"It seems I must quickly disabuse you of the mis-apprehension that you'll win. I was being indulgent," the viscount said in a low, scratchy tone.

Simon's interest was further piqued. "Indulgent?"

"Why, yes. It is honorable to allow an opponent a measure of pride in their skills when one duels."

"Awe me then, my good lad," Simon murmured, oddly amused, his earlier insouciance gone.

"Should I awe you with impunity?"

"Of course," Simon drawled. "I expect no reservation."

"I do admire a gentleman who does not own a fragile ego."

Simon chuckled. The viscount seemed different— more self-assured than he'd been at the card tables yesterday. A quick slash, a stab by the viscount was counter maneuvered, and then Simon advanced with three quick, brilliantly defended thrusts. Within two minutes of fighting, Simon knew he had met his match.

The viscount performed a feint, luring Simon to attack left, and then the man slipped under his flank in a counter-riposte. The move was so flawlessly executed, a pulse of sheer admiration went through him. This man was a brilliant fighter, and Simon was challenged to fence with the full range of his considerable skill. Three moves later, the point of the viscount's sword pressed against his chest.

"Must I draw blood?" the viscount drawled. "It would be a pity."

Simon arched a brow. They both breathed a bit raggedly, and despite the coolness of the night air, sweat had dampened Simon's forehead. "Your skill is astonishing."

"Of course it is."

That bit of arrogance almost felt charming, and a smile hitched at the corner of Simon's mouth. "I have never been beaten before."

"High praises from you, my lord. I accept them."

The hint of soft humor surprised him. The viscount lowered then sheathed his sword. Simon did the same. "I shall spread the word to those who witnessed your challenge that you won the duel fairly and well. Does this satisfy you, Crawford?"

"Yes, thank you, my lord."

Simon could feel the viscount thinking, then he murmured, "I will tender an apology for cheating at cards. It was wrong of me to do so. It was even more wrong to accuse you, my lord. I am ashamed and very sorry for it."

How curious. Why hadn't he apologized at the game itself? Or before they fought? It struck Simon then that the man had wanted to garner his respect by besting him, a gentleman the *haut ton* praised as being unbeatable in many regards. "You offer an apology, but I also require an explanation."

"Very well, my lord. I was in desperate need of funds, and the pot of five thousand pounds was a regrettable temptation, as certain investment and loan opportunities have fallen through. While my explanation does not excuse my shameful action, I hope it mitigates it and that you will pardon my mistake."

"Apology accepted."

A soft breath of release hissed in the cool air. "Thank you, my lord."

Simon reassessed his earlier opinion of the viscount. The man had mettle and perhaps only deserved a chance that circumstances of a debt ridden estate had deprived him. "Come with me inside for a drink. We shall discuss your low coffers and the investments you were seeking to make. Perhaps even a place on my team as a political ally."

He sensed the viscount's shock. "Inside?"

"Yes."

"To discuss investment opportunities?"

"That is what I said," Simon said slowly, canting his head left when the viscount shifted further toward the darkness.

Another shaky inhalation. "Regrettably, I must decline, my lord. I hastened away from my home and left my sibling frightened and uncertain about the outcome of the duel. I must return home and assure that all is well. Will you allow me to come back in the evening for this discussion?"

"Very well."

"Thank you, my lord. I bid you farewell. I shall call upon you in the afternoon around five."

Simon got a strange impression as he bowed. As the viscount was about to turn away, a light came on from a room somewhere in the palatial mansion. It cast aside the shadows in the gardens which hid the side profile of the viscount and the smile that curved his mouth.

Simon was momentarily transfixed. Something hot and uncomfortable pricked low in his belly, disconcerting enough where he snapped his head back and stilled. That smile hinted at a bit of cunning and something sweet and softly alluring. The hot dart of sensation that went through him had been fleeting, more of an elusive whisper of want, gone before he could fully examine its strangeness. But the impression it left behind was stamped upon his bones and felt like a hot brand of lust.

A most disconcerting awareness. All from the sensual curve of lush lips. And that informed Simon more than anything else that the opponent who had best him with such fearless and marvelous skill was a woman. His heart jerked, and he blew out a slow, audible breath.

Bloody hell.

CHAPTER THREE

Inexplicably, despite the danger of discovery and condemnation, dueling with the earl was the most alive Mina had felt in ages. *No, perhaps in my entire four and twenty years*. He was the best fighter she had ever crossed rapiers with, but she had won. She started to turn away, her heart beating erratically, a crackling liveliness surging through her veins.

"Wait."

Mina's breath caught in her chest at that flat command which arrested her movements. Her fingers reflexively tightened over the rapier's hilt, and not wanting to appear unduly suspicious, she paused. "Yes, my lord?"

"Who are you?"

Oh God. Her laboriously acquired composure rattled, and panic closed her throat. What had given her away? With a calmness that belied her racing heart, Mina murmured, "I do not perceive your meaning, Creswick."

"You are not Viscount Crawford."

The surety in his tone sent a primal pulse of warning down her back. Surely he could not know it, not when they were mostly in shadows. The barest hint of dawn covered the land in gray, but there was still not enough light for him to sound so confident. Mina would have to be as brazen as possible. "Your jest is in poor taste, and I have no time for games, my lord. If you will excuse my presence, I must return home without delay to my family."

There was just enough light to see the skeptical way his eyebrow lifted. Careful to not meet his gaze, she dipped into another bow, straightened, and whirled away, painfully aware of his stare on her retreating back.

Mina moved as fast as she possibly could, eager to mount her horse and ride away. The sound of approaching footsteps urged her to glance over her shoulders. She almost fainted to see that the earl prowled after her, his strides languid and confident.

Oh drat.

Nerves rioted dreadfully inside her. There was no help for it; Mina could only hope he would not chase her. She broke into a run, sprinting for the stables. She silently and virulently cursed her short legs when the earl easily overtook her, forcing her to stop. Quickly darting left, she tried to escape, but he shuffled and blocked her path. She tried to run back where she came from, and he once again easily moved past her to stand in her way.

"This is ridiculous, my lord," she cried, careful to keep her voice low. "Surely you see this!"

"You are the one running."

"You are following me, my lord, and preventing me from leaving your estate. I have never seen such outrageous behavior in a gentleman of your consequences."

"This rebuke coming from a woman pretending to be a man? Dare you really have the face to try and admonish me?"

Mina felt faint. How could he have guessed it? "A woman?"

"Yes."

Wings of indecision fluttered in her belly. "You are very wrong, my lord," she said stiffly. "It is senseless for me to be insulted when sadly, this misconception about our person is a thing we suffer in common. I merely did not expect it to come from you, considering the circumstances."

"What do we have in common?" he asked with a measure of amusement.

"You are uncommonly *pretty*, and I am slim and elegant. Surely you understand my gist."

A low, affronted sound came from his throat. "Remove your cap."

The man was like a bulldog. "And what next? My coat, my trousers? Nay, my good man, I dare not undress any part of me lest you incorrectly interpret that I am open to your advances."

"What a clever little mouth you have," the earl drawled, his eyes skipping over her like sharpened blades.

Clearly not so clever where the suggestion that he might be a catamite did not immediately shove him from her path. *God, this is awful.*

It also meant he was positively assured of her femininity. Mina could not think of how to escape the wretched man. All of the advances she had made on behalf of Anthony were crumbling because of this stubborn, vexing, bacon-brained...! She could think of no curse word that accurately fit the earl.

No longer winded, she made another dash past him toward the stables. Something snapped her neck back, and Mina's gasp strangled in her throat when she realized the blasted man had tugged the tightly fitted cap from her head. Pins dislodged and her hair came apart and tumbled over her shoulders and down to her midback.

Mina froze, unable to turn around and face the wretched blackguard.

He sucked in a harsh breath. "Your hair…even in the grayness of the breaking dawn, I can see its vibrant red color. It is remarkable."

She lifted a gloved hand to caress the tendril of hair that curled over her shoulders, at a loss at what to say at the reverence in his tone. Mina cleared her throat, steadying her nerves. "I must leave," she murmured, not liking how quivery and uncertain she suddenly felt.

"Face me."

"No," she murmured low in her throat.

"You can speak naturally."

"I'm afraid my voice is a bit hoarse."

"Ah, a lady who commits to her role wholeheartedly. Allow me to invite you inside for a spot of honey, Miss Crawford. I'm told it has soothing, restorative properties."

Miss Crawford. She closed her eyes. Of course, he would accurately deduce it was her. Mina turned to face him, alarm jolting through her when she noted how close he stood. The sun peeked from behind the mountains and clouds, and she got her first look at the vexing man. Her mouth dried. Her brother often jokingly said the earl was pretty, but Mina disagreed.

He was shockingly beautiful with his sharply elegant cheekbones, a decidedly arrogant nose, and midnight black hair. His eyes were a brilliant, striking blue. His body was lean, lithe, powerful, with no trace of softness anywhere. She took in the full effect of his form, noting his cravat and coat had been discarded sometime during the evening and his chin revealed a slight dark shadow that his valet would no doubt deplore. The silken brocade of his turquoise waistcoat must have cost more than her best gown.

She watched the earl warily. He was too close for comfort. So dangerously, enticingly close. It set her teeth on edge that she found him so terribly attractive.

"Come inside with me, Miss Crawford. I have no wish to remain longer in the chilled air."

"I do not enter the homes of men who planned to harm my brother."

He arched a brow, his mouth quirking in a shadow of amusement. "Harm?"

"Why else would you have accepted his challenge if you meant him no harm?"

The intensity of his stare encompassed her entire body, and annoyingly her heart raced.

"I can only think being discovered has scattered your wits."

Drat. She did feel dispossessed of rational thoughts. "I—"

"It was meant to be a lesson in humility, a thing your brother sorely needs."

"And who appointed you his teacher?" she asked with biting politeness, even though she knew her brother's actions were beyond the pale.

"Would you have preferred I allowed him to cheat without impunity?"

His voice had gone flat, yet those dark blue eyes bore into her as if he waited for Mina's reaction to levy judgment. That rankled her, even as her stomach pitted with a sensation of discomfort.

"What do you think would have happened if your brother had attempted to accuse another gentleman with less consideration than myself?"

"So you mean I should thank you for accepting his challenge."

"Yes."

"Very well, my lord, I thank you on behalf of my brother."

"Follow me," he imperiously commanded, turned around, and walked away.

As if he expected she would simply obey. Mina hurried after him, needing to ascertain what this meant for her brother that the earl had uncovered her. He did not seem angry. It took them a couple minutes to walk around the side of the large manor to the forecourt.

The earl opened the door himself, and they swept into a magnificent hallway. It was paneled in dark russet wood to waist height and then papered in pale cream with satin stripes and a leaf and floral repeating design. Every few feet were gas lamps, some of which were lit. At a safe distance below the lamps were landscape paintings by some excellent masters. The ceiling was high and beautifully plastered in white and gilding and also held some unlit chandeliers which flashed with cut crystal.

They padded down the passage in silence, and a long, drawn-out moan whispered through the air. Glancing around for the source of the odd panting cries she had heard, Mina gasped at the sight of two lovers entwined in each other's arms at the bottom of the staircase. The man's hand was underneath the woman's gown, and he…he had a portion of her breast in his mouth. The shocking sight almost cast her into a faint.

"Good heavens!" Mina whispered, thoroughly aghast *and* curious.

"Stannis!"

The earl's voice snapped through the scene like an icy blast, jerking the lovers apart.

"Ah, Creswick…Crawford, do join us. I suspect the duel is over?"

"Yes," Mina hurriedly said in a choked voice. "I won." There, hopefully that should prevent the earl from decrying her.

The man he called Stannis grinned. "Well done, lad. I was about to take this delectable piece upstairs. I am sure she will be happy to accommodate my friends. You deserve this reward after beating the invincible Creswick."

The woman in his arms giggled throatily and crooked a finger, beckoning them over. Stannis flicked his tongue over her breast, and she purred. Mina choked on the air, heat engulfing her body.

"You forget yourself, Stannis," Lord Creswick said in an icy bite. "You are in the presence of a—"

Mina pinched the top of his buttocks between her thumb and forefinger. Even through her gloves and his clothes, it felt like she tried to pinch a rock. The man was hard everywhere, it seemed. Mortification swamped her, and she could hardly tell the earl it was an accident. "I meant to pinch your lower back," she hastily assured him quietly. "Not your derriere." *Oh God, Mina, stop talking!*

"That you would dare pinch me at all is the cause for concern, Miss Crawford," he whispered back.

She was feeling decidedly indignant. "In my defense, I wanted to stop you from saying he was in the presence of a lady. Was that not your intention?"

"Why?"

Mina blinked. "Surely you would not want it known you fought a woman *and* that you were beaten by her!" she hissed softly, glaring up at his broad shoulders.

"Why would I not want it known?"

That curious answer deflated her hope of secrecy. "Well…you were beaten by a lady."

"I was beaten by a fighter of exceptional skill. That she is a lady has no bearing on the truth that I was defeated. "

Mina stared at him in astonishment as something frightfully warm surged through her veins. He was far more interesting than she had expected.

She looked away from him. "I do not want it to be known it was not my brother who fought you and won."

The earl frowned, but he made no reply, simply continued past the staircase and with a sigh of relief, she followed on. Thankfully the blond Adonis had taken his rakish person up the stairs with the giggling lady wrapped around him like a vine. The earl opened a door and allowed her to precede him inside a lavish library that fairly stole her breath with its elegant beauty.

The room rose two stories and there were stairs and a small balcony to access the upper level all in the same warm wood flawlessly carved by a master. Most of the books were bound in a dark blue leather, gilded on their spines with their titles and authors' names.

One side of the room held a row of long windows which were currently covered by royal blue drapes, patterned with gold. The floor was covered by a carpet woven mostly in shades of cream and gold with touches of blue. The room was furnished by several large sofas, and to one side was a desk and chair which was neatly stacked with papers and books. Two large fireplaces held banked down fires, so the large room was comfortably warm. She jolted when he closed the door behind him with a decisive *snick*, closing them inside the intimate warmth.

The earl strolled over to a large oak desk and sat on the edge, casually folding his arms across his chest and pinning her with that brilliant stare of his.

Mina forced herself not to fidget under that unswerving regard. "Are we here to discuss the investment opportunities, my lord?"

"I will get straight to the point, Miss Crawford. I am impressed with your skills."

For a brief moment, every part of her felt flushed with warmth and delight. "I…thank you, my lord." Truly, Mina was surprised at his praise. "I—"

"I had thought to offer your brother a place on my team as a researcher. Even to prepare him to argue certain motions in the House of Lords. He seemed bright and eager enough."

Hope surged through her heart. To work beside Lord Creswick would be a wonderful opportunity for her brother. The earl had finished Oxford University at the age of sixteen years, and many, including her father, had waited with a keen breath to see which side of the political spectrum he argued for. It mattered not that his late father was a part of the

Conservative party.

The young earl had broken tradition and had shown himself a brilliant early thinker, forming his own radical and wild opinions that had even caused the Queen to summon him to the palace several times to consult with over important matters, before the death of Prince Albert. It was said the Earl of Creswick had been regularly invited to events at the queen's royal residences, up until her widowhood, when she had sought isolation in her other residences.

Mina's father and the Earl of Creswick had often been depicted in the political cartoons as locking horns as a pair of bulls or stags. She had particularly laughed at the one showing her father as a shaggy Hereford bull with his opponent being a rather more vigorous Spanish fighting bull.

Mina was only in her seventeenth year at the time, but she had followed the political tracts with great interest. Papa had been a great political orator and used his charisma and glib tongue to sway those to his side when needed. Creswick, however, was more conservative in his address, yet when he spoke in that calm and collected way of his, it was reported that his words would slice through the chambers with the power and precision of arrows, swaying many to support his motions.

Or so the newssheet which she had avidly devoured had said. Mina still recalled her astonishment when she'd discovered Creswick was only a man of nineteen years. Now he was a man of seven and twenty. His appearance was still youthful and far too handsome, with his savagely elegant cheekbones and eyes so blue, they might rival the waters of the Aegean sea.

A different impression was only formed when one looked into his eyes. They seemed older beyond his years and capacity. Even now, as they watched her mull over his words, they were steady and piercing, almost frightening. There was a dangerous kind of beauty to Lord Creswick, and for the first time in years, Mina felt a slow pulse of attraction.

Disconcerted by the sensation, she briefly averted her regard. "I am sure Anthony would be most pleased—"

"That he could not face me, Miss Crawford, and fight me himself does not inspire me with confidence in his character."

Her heart jolted. "My lord, I assure you, Anthony wanted to be here. I took the choice from him because I knew myself to be the better fighter."

"I shall make the offer to you, Miss Crawford. Would you like to work with me?"

Mina stared at him, thoroughly taken aback. "*Work* with you?"

"Yes."

She felt considerably discomposed. An opportunity she had never dared dream of had been presented to Mina, rendering her speechless. She could terminate the endless days of merely existing in the countryside, waiting for life to start while believing it would never happen. That aching loneliness would be filled with purpose…with *something* other than loss, regret, and emptiness. A quiver of excitement filled her belly, and she worked hard to mask her reaction. "In what capacity, my lord?"

His gaze suddenly gleamed. "I require a secretary."

"There are no women secretaries, or if there are, I

have never heard of one." She narrowed her eyes on him, wondering if he had a more licentious purpose in mind.

His mouth quirked. "I admit clerical work is a male-dominated position. However, why does it matter if there are no women secretaries before you, Miss Crawford? I have doubts a lady has ever fought a gentleman in a duel either and bested him in such a spectacular fashion."

There was a disconcerting hint of sensuality in his slight smile that she did not want to notice. Mina got the sense the earl admired her, and the awareness of it did odd things to her insides. This man had always been described as a force of nature, a gentleman in possession of piercing wit, intelligence, shrewdness, and so handsome to justify him being considered one of London's most elusive and sought-after lords. Mina had no business feeling even an inkling of attraction toward him, especially given the disaster that had happened the last time she allowed herself to keenly admire a gentleman.

She pressed the flat of her palm to her belly, hoping to still the flurry of wild flutters. "What shall I do for you in this capacity?"

"Whatever it is that I wish. Your father often spoke of your keen ingenuity."

Mina was unwillingly enthralled. Taking a deep, steady breath, she tamped down the need and hope unfurling through her heart. Her brother was the one who deserved this chance to improve their lot.

"In a somewhat more pained tone," Creswick continued, "he also spoke about your restless, adventurous spirit. I was pleased to have seen a hint of everything today."

"Most men would have been appalled."

"I am not most men." His quiet voice held a sardonic note. "And allow me to say: you are not most women."

• • •

Miss Crawford kept her chin held high, however the slightest tremble was seen in her gloved fingers. "I must decline your incredible offer, even as I thank you for making it. My brother, my lord, must work with you. Most certainly not me."

"Very well," he said. "You may leave."

A frown marred Miss Crawford's pretty features and a spark fired in her extraordinary green eyes. "You agree, my lord?"

Simon had known the viscount's father. Admired him. Had stood toe to toe with the man on the political stage and then had sat down with him afterward and drank. Many of the man's tales had surrounded his children, Wilhelmina and Anthony. For that reason, Simon had made the instant connection that the slight and elegant figure who fought him could only be the viscount's sister.

"No. I have no interest in working with your brother."

Her brow furrowed slightly. "My lord! Please do reconsider."

They fell into a striking silence, then he said, "As I said earlier, Miss Crawford, I am not keen to have a man on my team who had someone duel in his stead."

Miss Crawford took a few steps closer to him but

still ensured she kept a considerable distance between them. That she was careful now amused Simon. Hadn't it been mere moments ago she held a rapier to his throat?

"When I suggested the switch to my brother, he refused. It was a bit of chicanery on my part why I am here. I am certain once he discovers it, he will race here to stop me."

"Chicanery?"

She looked a bit disconcerted. "Yes."

"This even affirms he is the wrong man to join my team, Miss Crawford," he said coolly. "The young viscount possesses neither cunning nor nerves of steel. You do."

"I accept the compliment," she said with honeyed sweetness, though her lovely eyes shot fire at him. "If I was confident you would compensate me as you would any gentleman on your team and respect my contributions in the same light, I, of course, would take the post since I bested you and it is clearly my mettle you admire. However, as I am a lady and—"

"Done."

She stared, a look of polite enquiry on her lovely face. "What is done?"

"You are hired and will be given all considerations as if you are a gentleman on my team."

"I beg your pardon?"

"I do not like repeating myself," he said flatly.

The fire in those lovely eyes gleamed a little bit brighter. "I fear it is a necessary evil when conversing with me. I am sure you'll survive the ordeal, my lord."

He stared at her, and she smiled.

"You will be my secretary."

"Your secretary," she repeated.

An irritating habit.

"I will compensate you two hundred pounds per month. I will not work with your brother, so you need not bother beseeching me in vain. You may accept my offer or depart my premises."

She gasped, not in delight but in affront. "That is a rate far lower than at which governesses are paid, my lord."

"It is?"

"Yes."

"You were offered a recent post?"

Her chin lifted. "Yes. I am versed in Latin, Greek, Italian, geography, and classical literature. I am also adept at running a large household. As your secretary, I suspect I would be expected to endure this…gruffness daily *and* your mercurial temper."

He leaned against his desk and shrugged. "Yes."

Her eyes widened, as if she had not expected him to admit to his temper so baldly.

"I am also a woman working alone with a gentleman."

"Get to the point, Miss Crawford."

"I must be compensated for occupational hazard."

Simon was considerably intrigued. "What occupational hazard?"

Her eyes gleamed with a hint of shrewdness and a bit of humor, a decidedly suspicious mix. "Why, *ravishment*, of course."

Simon stilled. "Ravishment?"

"Yes. You *are* a gentleman, an astoundingly pretty, er…handsome one, and I am a very delectable young lady."

"Delectable," he echoed, thoroughly flummoxed and… What the hell was that whispering of sensation wending through every crevice of his body? It felt almost like the wonder of when he discovered a new book or when he developed a new political argument and felt that surge of challenge and anticipation. She'd clearly passed the point of discretion, but he was more amused by her boldness than anything else.

Her color was a trifle heightened, but she bravely met his eyes and said, "I do not flatter my vanity to say so. It is a mere fact I am remarkably lovely."

Such breathtaking nerve.

As if she had heard his silent admonishment, an elegant shoulder lifted in a casual shrug, hauteur and confidence settling over her like a second skin. *I am not afraid*, that stare said. Simon was increasingly, unwillingly captivated.

"That we will be closely working together as a gentleman and a lady in close quarters, there is bound to be a temptation, and you might succumb to it, my lord."

An almost perverse enchantment with her audacity scythed through him. "I hardly think so," he said drily. "There is nothing about you I find the least tempting."

She looked startled by his casual dismissal. "Truly?"

"Yes. Even if I flirt around, I won't flirt with you, Miss Crawford." *Ever.*

She cast him a brilliant smile, and the sheer loveliness of it rocked him back on his heels. Simon did not like this woman and the reaction she provoked from him without seemingly trying. He scowled and she fluttered her lashes at him.

"Wonderful. I have heard many ladies who work as governesses who suffer groping from their employers. In these men of distinction and consequence, their honor should have controlled their base urgings and prevented their astounding misconduct. I am relieved that you will not have that problem despite the licentiousness I just witnessed in the hallway. There are, however, other irretrievable hazards."

Simon looked at Miss Crawford as if she was a rare creature formed from a sort of magical elixir. He held little discourse with women, but he had never heard his friends speak of any lady so oddly unconventional and sweetly alluring.

An odd feeling of alarm throbbed in the back of his mind. He had no interest in finding this damn woman alluring. "And what other hazards are these?"

"I must be compensated for the loss of reputation I am bound to suffer from working in a close, intimate space with you, my lord."

He held her stare for several beats. "Are you not the lady who was found tromping through Scotland alone at eighteen, having been suspected of being the…victim of a failed elopement? To which reputation do you refer? Do you have any?" he asked ruthlessly, uncaring of delicate sensibilities.

"Oh dear," she murmured. A hint of a flush mounted her high cheekbones, but she did not flutter with any evident nervousness.

Nerves of steel. His interest piqued to an even greater degree. Worse, she was a beauty, owning a creamy, flawless complexion. Thick lashes framed extraordinary green eyes and her lips were pink and

lush. His gut clenched and Simon felt the faint provocative stirrings of temptation.

Miss Crawford used a finger to tap her lower chin,
as if in studied contemplation. "You would allow that
more damage can be done to my reputation. I will also
make allowance that I have a past scandal and offer a
fifty percent discount on the occupational hazard pay."

She held up a hand as if she halted his interruption. "You drive a hard bargain, but I *cannot* give
more than fifty percent, my lord, and it would be a
shame if you try to negotiate for a lower percentage in
your favor."

Simon almost booted her from his home.

"I will accept payment of four hundred and twenty
pounds per month." Then she seemed to hold her
breath and wait.

"A fortune for your services," he said drily.

That breath eased from her, and she murmured, "A
mere pittance to a lord of your consequences. I dare
say far more is tossed away at the card tables and the
race tracks."

Simon realized then she was trying to regain the
pot her brother had attempted to cheat to win. Her
gall was truly astounding.

But at the same time, he quite liked that despite
the rumor of her ruined reputation that had been
rampant in society a few years ago, the lady did not
own the air of someone defeated. She was certainly
fearless, her spirit one of loyalty and bravery.

She would make a good addition to his team, and
in hiring her, he would repay her father his unselfish
and unflinching service to the realm. "Done."

Her lips formed a small moue of astonishment.

"You will compensate me five thousand pounds for the year?"

"Yes."

For a moment, she looked uncertain. "I have responsibilities that need immediate attention, my lord. I will accept a quarter pay in advance."

"Done."

Her lips parted at his capitulation, and her lovely eyes widened. "The terms of my employment, a severance package, and termination clauses must be outlined and signed by both of us, Lord Creswick."

"Very well."

Now bold suspicion glinted in her eyes. "You are awfully agreeable."

"In the right circumstances, I can be accommodating."

A small smile touched her mouth even as her gaze narrowed further. "Please remind me of these circumstances."

It was his turn to be indulgent. And he truly wanted to help her, for the mere fact that her father had been a mentor and an incredible man who gave his time and tireless efforts in service of his country. "I have more than one vacancy to be filled on my team. You would be a good fit, Miss Crawford, for the role of my secretary. You are quick witted and own unflinching courage."

A soft color dusted her cheeks. "Did you lose your last secretary to nefarious means?"

Simon suppressed the odd urge to smile. "No."

"Whatever happened to him?"

The young baronet had given up his political ambitions for love. The wife he married barely had a dowry and no connections in the *ton*. Such rubbish. Though very beautiful, his wife offered nothing to a gentleman who needed connections with respectable government officials to garner a swift advancement in his career. The difficulty would be finding a secretary who could take Fenley's place, and he did not necessarily think Miss Crawford a perfect fit, regardless of what he'd said.

Yet, he could not help recalling the air of desperation that had surrounded her brother and determined she would do for the foreseeable future. "The good fool thought himself in love," Simon found himself answering, idly wondering why he bothered.

Her eyes gleamed with bright humor, rendering her startlingly lovely. "Are you one of those addlepated gentlemen who do not believe in love, then?"

Addlepated? "Is love a concept that requires belief?"

"With parameters of confidence and trust, I daresay yes, for love encompasses trusting someone else with our feelings and thoughts and having the confidence in their character that the trust will not be misplaced."

A derisive smile touched his mouth. "Love is simply a rather overused word to express pleasure with something. I recently heard a young boy cry out that he loved meat pies. He has no trust or confidence in meat pies, just a mere fleeting pleasure as it satisfied his tastebuds and filled his belly. That love is selfish, for it only refers to the feeling the boy derived at the taste of the pie. How does one equate that love with a man or a woman?"

"I daresay there are degrees of love."

"Are there?"

"Are we to have a philosophical conversation about love, my lord?"

Why did her tone sound as if she teased him? Simon frowned. His peers did not tease him. And ladies, well, he had never allowed a woman this close for her to dare to try. He did not believe he liked the sensation.

He was abruptly and unexpectedly certain having Miss Wilhelmina Crawford working under his roof was going to be a mistake.

CHAPTER FOUR

Anthony was pacing along the thinly worn carpet in the library like a caged lion when Mina entered. He whirled to face her, his eyes scanning over her frantically. "You are in one piece."

"Yes, I am," she said softly. "I am sorry to have worried you, Anthony."

"Thank God! You were gone for several hours." He lifted a glass to his mouth and drank deeply. "My damn nerves are shattered. Mina, what were you thinking? To have conspired with Mrs. Bell to put that damn concoction in my soup! I cannot credit such mischief. You might be the older twin, but it is my responsibility—"

Gripping the latch behind her, she leaned back against the door. "I won, Anthony."

Her brother stilled. "You *won*?"

"Yes."

"Against Creswick?"

"Yes."

He shook his head as if in a daze. "The idea is inconceivable. The earl is unmatched at the London Thames Fencing Club. Why, this is marvelous, Mina!"

She took a steady breath. "Somehow, afterwards he uncovered that he fought a woman. I cannot fathom what alchemy he used, since we were in the shadows and most of my features were hidden."

"He knows he was bested by you, a lady?"

"Yes."

Her brother dropped onto the sofa heavily as if he

had been shoved. "Good God, if this gets about, he will become a laughingstock."

"I do not think the earl cares for such nonsense. He is rather impressed with me," she said softly.

At that, her brother stared at her in astonishment. "*Impressed* with you?"

"Yes. He offered me a job."

"A job?"

"Must you parrot everything I say?"

He jumped to his feet. "That blasted bounder! Does he think to make you an unflattering offer?"

"A real job, Anthony! Working as his secretary, taking his dictation, writing his correspondence, and answering his letters. Which by the way, I already saw a mountain of it piled high on a desk in the corner of his library, which is magnificent."

"You cannot work for the man," he said, aghast.

"Why not? Do not forget we both discussed me taking on a post of governess. This role might put my mind more to use, and the pay is far superior. I have negotiated for a quarter advance, and the earl agreed."

"Why would he agree to this? I fear he is up to no good."

"The earl has no design on my person, if that is what you are worried about."

"Know that if he does," her brother said ominously, "it would be to take you as his mistress. With your tattered reputation, no man would make you his wife."

She flinched, and a grimace of regret crossed his face.

"I am sorry, Min. I did not mean to say it so baldly, but I do not understand Creswick's motivation."

Her brother depended on her to be unflappable and courageous, so she smiled and buried the aching pain deep inside her heart. "I believe it might have been his acquaintance with Father. Do recall they admired each other, and I think this a kindness on his part. Do not think it charity. I will be working. We can make some much-needed repairs on our tenants' cottages. Perhaps we can make a down payment on that new agricultural machinery Farmer Johnson mentioned. He did say it will improve productivity and invariably our profit margins. Then we must pay Mrs. Bell and little Tommy their back wages and also advance them for the next year."

"How much is your advance?" he demanded.

"At least one thousand pounds."

He scrubbed a hand over his face. "Ah, Mina, I do not fear it will do that much."

"Nonsense, it is a small fortune. We will also sell Mother's necklace and—"

"No," Anthony said gruffly. "We will not sell Father's swords or Mother's necklaces."

Mina swallowed against the tight ache in her throat. "You said the necklace is valued at least three hundred pounds. We can allow—"

"That is all we have left of them, Mina, please. I will go to London. I'd asked my good friend at Cambridge, Lord Walton, to stay at his townhouse for the upcoming season. I'll need some blunt for a new jacket at least, a pair of boots, a few pairs of trousers, and some waistcoats. I mean to throw myself in the thick of the marriage mart and see if I can marry an heiress. We need more than a thousand pounds to set things to rights."

They spoke further into the night, and Mina went to bed hopeful, despite Anthony's concerns, that they might be able to turn their fortunes around for the first time in years.

This will be a new sort of adventure. Finally there was a chance for her to leave home and do more, instead of endlessly wishing for a different life. She stared up to the ceiling, thinking of Lord Creswick and the odd sensations he had evoked.

I must not be a splendid fool again, Mina silently whispered, even as she smiled, gladdened that she was receiving the opportunity to help their family and a chance to escape the lonely malady plaguing her.

. . .

The very next day, Mina knocked on the door of the palatial mansion at precisely nine in the morning. A grim looking butler opened the door, and she almost asked if someone had died.

"The earl is awaiting you in his office, Miss Crawford," the butler said. "If you will allow me to show you the way?"

She nodded, slipping from her threadbare coat and gloves and handing them over to the butler. Patting her hair to ensure the chignon was firmly in place, she walked down the large hallway to the earl's office. The butler knocked once before opening the door. Mina stepped inside, frowning, for there was no one in the spacious office. Another door opened and the earl emerged with a distracted frown on his face.

"You are late," he said flatly, not removing his gaze from the papers in his hand.

"It is nine, my lord."

"Work starts at six."

She almost choked on the air. "It is almost a two-hour ride to your estate from my home, my lord."

"And?"

"I shall be here at six," she said pertly, hurrying over to a large desk she assumed to be hers.

"There are some ground rules that must be rigidly observed, Miss Crawford."

"Yes, my lord," she said, sitting before the fine desk. She almost moaned at the well-padded chair and its lushness.

"There will be no personal callers during work hours."

"I never imagined having personal callers at your house, my lord."

"Given your brother's temperament I am certain he will show himself a few times to ensure you are not being debauched."

Mina stared at the earl, who had yet to remove his eyes from the sheaf of papers he read. "Noted, my lord."

"There will be no distracting chatter or smiles from you."

"You find my smile distracting, my lord?" *Oh dear*. She winced and fervently wished she could drag back the question. Her impulsive words finally wrested his attention from the papers and his gaze landed on her with the force of an anvil. There was an unfathomable watchfulness in the eyes that caressed over the length of her. The oddest sensation fluttered in Mina's belly.

"No smiles."

"Yes, my lord."

He looked back down to his paper. "You are entitled to an hour break for lunch."

"Yes, my lord."

"Work ends at six. Then we have supper at seven."

She sucked in a breath. "Work is from six in the morning to six in the evening?"

"Yes. I believe it will be sensible if you remain my guest for the duration of your employment, Miss Crawford. Traveling two hours to and fro each day is nonsensical. I will also allow that you may start your working hour at eight."

She lifted her chin. "I do not need that consideration, my lord. Please treat me as you would a male employee."

Those eyes lifted to her once more and a faint smile touched his mouth. "Which one don't you need?"

"Both."

"Very well." He flicked to the next page and stilled, a fine tension settling in his shoulders. Whatever he read perhaps angered him. After a few minutes of waiting, Mina realized he had dismissed her from his awareness. Looking around at her desk, she noted the several sheafs of paper, several quills, pens, and inkwell. She also noticed the mountain of correspondence that had been on his desk was now on hers.

Mina could not explain the giddy anticipation she felt at doing something useful with her days. A knock sounded on the door, and a gentleman ambled in, a briefcase gripped in his hand. He tossed her a shocked look before masking his expression.

"My lord," he said, bowing to Creswick.

"Mr. Heffner, allow me to introduce my secretary to you, Miss Crawford. She is an extension of me and is to be accorded all respect and consideration as they would be given to me."

He pushed his small wire rimmed spectacles up his nose. "Yes, of course, Miss Crawford, a pleasure."

She murmured her reply, learning that he was Phineas Heffner, a barrister and Member of Parliament of a borough in Manchester, and a member of the earl's political team. The men got down into their meeting, with the earl firing off question after question, all thought provoking enough to momentarily distract her as she listened. The barrister himself was impressive, and with a smile, Mina went to her tasks. First she counted the envelopes, shocked to find there were one hundred and nine of them. Some dating back to almost two months.

Reaching for the first envelope, she slit it open with the silver letter opener and unfolded the crisp paper, half of her attention on the passionate conversation with Mr. Heffner.

Dear Lord Creswick,

It was an honor to have you dine with us last weekend. My wife plans to hold another small, intimate gathering in March, and we would be pleased to count you amongst our guests. My daughter who has learned that you greatly admire Pleyel is keen to play one of his sonatas for your listening pleasure. We look forward to your timely response.

Yours,
The Earl of Dunford.

This letter was sent almost five weeks ago. Mina unrolled a sheaf of paper, plucked up a quill and dipped it into the inkpot. She had no idea what the dratted man would want and given the air of concentration he lent to whatever he read, Mina suspected it was not wise to disturb him.

"I have no time for frivolity," the earl said unexpectedly.

Mina glanced at him, noting that Mr. Heffner was careful not to look at her. The earl's nose was still buried in his papers, but somehow he had sensed her hesitation.

"I have no interest in balls or those invitations clearly aimed at matchmaking me with their daughters. Some political dinners might be considered. Decide the ones you think best."

"Yes, my lord."

He stood and departed the room with Mr. Heffner who was polite enough to bob a farewell. Mina steadily worked through the envelopes, first categorizing those that were invitations to balls from those that were invitations to political dinners. The ones that felt like veiled threats or bribery went into their own piles. The ticking of the clock on the mantel urged her to lift her head and she was surprised to see almost an hour had passed since the earl had left the room.

Rotating the stiffness from her shoulders, she stood and ambled over to his desk. She noted a pamphlet and plucked it up. *A Brief Summary of the Laws in England concerning Women: together with a few observations thereon* by Barbara Bodichon. A fierce blast of hope went through her to see that the earl read Miss Bodichon's work.

"Is there something that interests you, Miss Crawford?"

Taking care not to be startled, she turned around. He watched her with a hawk-like intensity that was almost discomfiting. "You are familiar with Miss Bodichon?"

"We have met," he said enigmatically.

"Do you support her cry that the married women's property laws should be reformed?"

"I do."

Mina gave him a blinding smile.

A black scowl settled on his face. "No smiles, Miss Crawford."

She hurriedly flattened the curve of her lips. "Forgive me, my lord, I forgot that rule for just a moment. Even in discussions with my father, he was not at all certain the move to grant married women greater liberty over their property the right one. We argued passionately over it."

"The plan is to introduce a Married Women's Property Bill next year in Parliament."

"Your plans, my lord?"

"It will have the full weight of my support."

Mina contained her pleasure and hurried over to her desk. Plucking up her quill, she twirled it around her fingers for a few seconds. The earl went over to his desk, seated himself, and took up a few letters she had left for his perusal. "My lord?"

He lifted his head and arched a brow. "Yes, Miss Crawford?"

She almost winced at the reprimand spied in his cool gaze. "Forgive the interruption. However, it is well known that having the ears of ladies is just as important as having the ears of the husband, especially when you want to sway the husbands to your side," she murmured. "I would not so readily dismiss balls and routs as yet, my lord. I daresay you should accept some of these invitations."

He held her gaze for a long moment. "That is a valid point, Miss Crawford. I have never before used such a strategy."

She tapped the edge of the quill on her chin. "I could not help overhearing your conversation with the barrister."

"I did not desire a private meeting. If I had I would have gone into my inner sanctuary. I meet freely where you are, Miss Crawford, so those I work with attribute your presence to a professional respect in my life and not a personal one. That will leave little room for nonsensical speculation."

Mina started to smile and quickly stopped the motion when she saw his black frown coming back. "Thank you, my lord."

"You will need to procure a new wardrobe. I will ensure London's best modiste attend to you by the end of the week."

She sucked in a breath. "My lord?"

"It is you who will accompany me to these balls and routs, Miss Crawford."

"I had not thought my duties as a secretary extended so far," she said faintly, sitting straighter in her chair.

"Of course it does."

It hovered on her tongue to suggest there would be many who recalled her scandal and might be driven to stir up the embers into a blaze. Instead she said, "From your conversation with Mr. Heffner you are also unequivocally agreeing with the conservative party that nationwide reform is needed?"

"Yes."

"You are willing to become an enemy of your own party, my lord?"

Enigmatic eyes landed on hers. "Should we allow the common man to suffer, in order to be in the favor of others?"

The earl's political alliance was evidently a Whig Liberal rather than a Tory Conservative. That he would stand in argument against most of his fellow peers with joining the call for social and economic reform was a rather bold and decisive move. Was he not afraid? Her father had often mentioned the ugly underbelly of the political world created by those driven by greed and want of power.

Mina's fingers tightened on the quill, curiosity about this man scything through her. "Why do you consider the plight of the common man? Why does it matter to you?"

Some emotion flared in the earl's eyes before his expression shuttered. "Do you speak from your place of privilege, Miss Crawford?"

"I speak from a place of hoping to understand the gentleman I am working with, my lord."

His gaze was watchful and unfathomable. "Are you blinded to the squalor that many of our denizens live within, and if they had more power through voting for their own representatives they might have a better chance of a good and worthy living existence?"

"I am not blind to it, my lord. You forget my father was a great supporter of reform and had interest in the Chartist movements of earlier years. However, do you not consider the arguments that only when the working classes have been educated they could be entrusted with the right to vote?"

"No." Something indecipherable flashed in his eyes. "Does an uneducated man not know that he suffers in squalor and poverty? Does he need education to let him know that his representatives care little for him and his family? Does he need to be able to read to know that he needs work, and he needs to be uplifted from his plight? He needs the right to vote *now*, especially given the indifference of the nation to ensure education is equal and just."

Mina rested her chin on her palm and leaned forward, keen to hear his opinion.

"There are many rotten boroughs where there are only a few legal voters, which means they are basically in the local lord's gift. Who would vote against the man who employed his family and could make sure a man and his family were not welcome to events in the country? No one. A man must protect his family and hence we cannot blame him for his vote. It is the government who should give the common man more choices. More votes and more power to the people will ensure less corruption in local representatives, and perhaps see people who are benevolent representing boroughs and uplifting the people socially and economically. A man does not have to be learned to benefit from easing the circumstances of his life. The poor must not suffer for being poor. It is for that very reason the Poor Law Act of 1834 has been so damn heinous and unconscionable."

She smiled. "Your passion does you credit, my lord."

He tossed her a startled glance before his expression shuttered. "No smiles."

Oh drat. "Even the ones without showing teeth?" To provide an example, she allowed her mouth to curve without the parting of her lips. Perhaps there was room for negotiation on this matter.

The earl stared at her as if transfixed. The notion that he might be captivated was only a fleeting impression, for an appearance of boredom settled on his face before he returned to his work. There was something about him that tugged at her senses, the feeling was almost primal and frightening. It occurred to her she was much more intrigued by his mind than his physicality, even though the man *was* astonishingly handsome.

Mina thought it prudent not to prod him too much—she could sense his force of will and personality beneath the calm veneer he presented to the casual observer. In as little as a day, she'd already formed the opinion that the Earl of Creswick was a compelling and complex gentleman. She glanced away from the earl and went back to her task.

The rest of the day passed in a blur, but by the end of it, she had responded to all his correspondence and taken dictation for nine letters from the gruff, and often impatient, man. Her fingers ached, she was more exhausted than she would have thought possible—but Mina believed it wonderful.

CHAPTER FIVE

A few days later, Mina ended her fourth working day with her employer feeling an odd surge of energized excitement. Being at the earl's estate and observing his daily meetings with land stewards, political allies, solicitors, and barristers was rather interesting and educational.

Most of those who met with the earl found it diffi-cult to keep up with his thinking. Even Mina herself often puzzled over his commands and expectations. Sometimes his communication felt cryptic, other times too complex to unravel. And the dratted man loathed repeating himself. The earl seemed to be able to easily digest large amounts of information and quickly deci-pher the value of the information provided by his team.

He had high expectations of them, and she could see that each man strove to live up to those expecta-tions. Mina enjoyed working with him thus far, even as she felt decidedly uncomfortable, for she did not under-stand the force of his character and at times even found herself daunted by his concentrated energy.

I might never be quite comfortable around him.

That evening, as she rode Raven home, there was a distinct chill in the air and thunder rumbled overhead. Mina glanced up at the sky, noting the bloated clouds and that the sun had disappeared. She had made it a habit to not wear any bustle, and donned trousers un-der her skirts to allow her to ride astride. Still, Mina did not believe she would make it home before the rain arrived.

On the heel of that thought, the sky opened up and drenched her in torrential showers.

Oh drat.

She was about an hour into her journey from the earl's estate and it made little sense to turn around. It was best to forge ahead, since it was an equal journey to her brother's abode. Cold bit at her bones and Mina darkly thought she might catch her death before she reached home. Urging Raven into a careful run, she hunched against the rain and tried to travel as swiftly as possible.

"Miss Crawford!"

She slowed the horse and wheeled around, astonished to see a large black stallion galloping toward her. Through the fine mist of the rain, she discerned the broad shoulders of the earl. Her heart jolted inside her chest when he drew up alongside her. "Lord Creswick, is all well?"

"Forgive the impropriety, Miss Crawford."

"What impro—" Mina's words died as the earl leaned across, wrapped his arms around her waist, and dragged her off her horse with strength and dexterity. "My lord!"

Surely it was some sort of divine grace that did not allow them to fall off the stallion. Or perhaps it was just the strength and care in his arms as he placed her to sit astride before him. A large umbrella suddenly opened over their heads, and the icy rain no longer pricked at her exposed face.

"You little fool," he said by her ear. "Why did you not turn around?"

"I am halfway home, my lord," Mina said. She was a shivering, teeth chattering mess. "It seemed more prudent to continue there."

"Take the edges of my coat and draw them around you."

"Draw them around me?"

"Must you truly make me repeat myself, Miss Crawford?"

Huffing out a breath, she reached for his coat and tugged it around her body. Mina was immediately swallowed by warmth, a rousing masculine scent, and shocking intimacy. The earl urged the horse back toward his home, and a quick peek over his shoulder showed that Raven dutifully followed. Mina was so very conscious of his weight behind her and the personal way she shared his coat. It was as if his vitality surrounded her, warming her more than she thought possible. Reaching up, she attempted to take the heavy umbrella.

"I have it, Miss Crawford."

"Surely your hand will tire to hold it above us for so long. We are at least an hour ride from your estate, my lord."

"We shall meet up with my carriage soon."

Mina understood then the earl must have ordered his carriage to retrieve her when he noted rain was imminent, but hadn't waited for it to be readied, simply chased after her. A peculiar warmth blossomed throughout her entire body and settled right inside her chest. "Thank you for your thoughtfulness."

A gruff sound chuffed from him. To her ear, it sounded irritable.

"What is not prudent is for you to journey back and fro daily. You will remain at Norbrook Park Monday thru Friday. Winter is still upon us, and the weather is unpredictable."

"I...I...I..." Her teeth chattered so violently it was with great difficulty she pushed the words out. "I do believe I shall consider your hospitality and choose to remain here as your guest, my lord."

"Very good, Miss Crawford."

She spied the carriage in the distance and a sigh of relief relaxed her even more against the earl's chest. They rode in silence to the carriage, where they quickly dismounted and entered the warm equipage. There were a few blankets on the seats, and he handed her one, which she wrapped around her shoulders. There was a small awkward silence in which Mina wondered if she should attempt conversation.

"You will write a letter of instruction to your servant for your clothing to be packed, and I will arrange for everything to be sorted by this evening."

She stared at him. "Thank you, my lord."

He leaned back against the squabs and closed his eyes. The earl showed no further inclination to converse, and Mina brushed aside the curtains to peek through the small carriage window at the sleeting rain. She frowned at the shadows she spied on the road, gasping when they raced past what looked like a family trudging through the mud-logged roads on foot. They were perhaps farmers. Mina squinted, noting that each person seemed as if they carried a small bundle.

"My lord!" Mina said, before she could caution herself. "Please stop the carriage."

It was to his credit that he knocked on the roof right away and arched a brow in question.

"I... There was a family in the rain. They are on foot and seem to have children with them."

He opened the door and vanished into the rain. Mina waited anxiously for his return and was about to dash outside when he lifted a little girl of about four years inside, and then a boy of about six. A man then entered with his wife, and they seemed very uncertain yet thankful as they sat in the large conveyance, shivering and huddling together.

"Thank ye, milord," the man said, bobbing his head as Mina handed him a couple blankets. "The rain fair drowned us."

The earl merely canted his head and made no reply. Mina smiled at the family reassuringly. The little girl buried her face in her mother's lap and sobbed. The sound, though muffled, was heartbreaking.

"Is she hurt?"

"No milady, it just be nerves."

The little girl lifted her head, her pale blue eyes bright with tears. "We lost Biscuit in the rain."

"And who is Biscuit?" Mina gently asked.

"Our best friend she is," replied the little boy, his lower lip trembling. "She's our dog."

Mina glanced out the window, understanding at that moment there was a dog outside in the downpour. Before she could formulate a plan, the earl knocked on the roof and the carriage clamored to a stop. The door opened and he went outside. The couple looked at each other and then back at Mina, as if they were uncertain as to what was happening. They waited for a few minutes and then the earl returned, dripping, and clutched in his arms was a very small dog.

"Biscuit!" the girl cried, reaching her hands up.

The earl took one of the remaining blankets and wrapped the puppy inside before handing it over to the child. And the entire time, the dratted man's face remained austere. Yet when his gaze met hers, his eyes gleamed with an expression Mina dearly wished she could interpret. A sharp sensation wrenched in the vicinity of her heart and Mina had to quickly look away.

The earl took the family to their cottage, much to the children's delight and the couple's palpable relief. As the man exited the carriage, he turned around and peered at the earl.

"Milord," he began almost hesitantly.

The earl settled his piercing gaze on the man, who seemed to grow even more nervous under his direct regard. "What is it?"

"Me brother who works in a factory in Manchester explains it well wot yer doing, milord, with the votes for all working folks. I just wanted to thank you, milord—the right to vote is very important to all of us."

The man held out his hand as if to shake the earl's, and realizing his blunder, he quickly lowered it and turned away.

"Mr. Thompson," the earl murmured.

The man whipped around, his eyes widening. "I wasn't aware ye knew me name, milord."

"I know the names of all my tenant farmers, Mr. Thompson."

Then to the man's evident shock, the earl held out his hand. Mina's heart pounded as she watched the farmer stare at it. Men of rank and consequence did not shake the hands of farmers. In the *haut ton*, the manner of shaking hands was just as important as deciding whose hand was appropriate to shake.

Mr. Thompson's expression was solemn when he shook the earl's hand, but his eyes gleamed with a sense of pride. The family departed and the carriage rattled toward the earl's estate. He had leaned back against the squabs, his eyes closed, his face shadowed by the carriage lamp.

Lord Creswick was even more complex and unfathomable than she'd thought. Mina allowed her gaze to linger over his features, and far too long on the slant of his sensual mouth. Her belly pitched, and soft want hummed beneath her skin, a want she had never before experienced. She analyzed it, broke it apart and came to the stunning awareness that she wanted to lean forward and press her mouth to his. What would it feel like?

"You are smiling, Miss Crawford."

"You were rather incredible with Mr. Thompson. Surely in this instance I am permitted a small smile, my lord."

The earl's eyes remained closed, but she could feel the tension that invaded his frame. "No, Miss Crawford, you are not."

Thoroughly vexed with the earl, she bared her teeth in a parody of a smile. Mina choked on the air when he chose that moment to open his eyes. A small smile, if the barely there curve of his lips could be called such, touched the corners of his mouth. Something hot and primal burned in his gaze and Mina wondered if it was a trick of the carriage lamp. Except it felt as if something shifted in the air between them.

"Even half drowned, and baring your teeth like a feral creature, you are exceedingly lovely and all too fearless."

Her pulse danced at that low murmur, and she was

so astonished, Mina did not take exception to the "feral creature" bit. The earl thought her lovely.

Unexpectedly, his regard felt peculiarly provocative and an awareness that had not been there earlier passed between them. A heated feeling swept through her, shaving away the cold. There it was again, that very nervous flutter stirring in her stomach. A devil riding her, she murmured, "Occupational hazard."

The earl's expression shuttered even more.

Mina winced. It was beyond the pale for her to tease the earl so, and her actions would bear introspection later when she was alone in her bedchamber.

They sat in silence and Mina was eager to escape the confines of the carriage and the smothering, peculiar tension. Upon arriving at his estate, he assisted her down without any word to her.

"Thank you, my lord," Mina said, hugging the blanket around her shoulders.

He did not offer a reply but walked away, his stroll as languid and graceful as a jungle predator. Staying alone under the earl's roof was still dangerous for ladies like her who had been declared ruined spinsters no decent gentleman would ever consider as a bride. Not that she could ever marry.

Still, Mina would have to be very careful, because she knew that her heart could not be trusted. She'd always owned to a wild and adventurous spirit, but she hoped that over the years she had acquired some degree of maturity and had learned how to temper the desires that beat inside her breast. What she had rebuilt of her reputation was very fragile, and it would not help Anthony if she should act irresponsibly.

But she could not deny the powerful attraction she

felt for the earl and silently vowed to herself to hide it under a veneer of professionalism from his far-too-penetrating gaze.

• • •

Almost two weeks had passed since Simon hired Miss Mina Crawford, and approximately nine days since she'd been living under his roof. She was proving to be rather interesting. Miss Crawford was loyal, erudite, clever, and too pretty. Simon wouldn't call her beautiful in the conventional sense, at least not what his male peers, such as Beswick and Stannis, raved to be beauty and considered in fashion. He had always thought that the idea that a certain style of beauty could be in fashion was illogical. But Miss Crawford was arrestingly and teeth achingly lovely, especially when she smiled. The lush shape of her body had also been expertly designed to tempt a gentleman's baser instincts.

And to his constant surprise, his were most assuredly tempted.

Simon suspected it had something to do with how carefree she seemed from society's constraints. Perhaps the lady considered herself thoroughly ruined and had little to care about being buried in the country. The door to their office opened and she ambled inside, her face buried in a book. The gentle upward curve of her lips hinted at wicked amusement with whatever was on those pages.

Sunlight came streaming through the windows in bright slashes of golden rays. Those rays lit up her hair, and his breath caught. Her hair reminded him of the russet color of autumn leaves. There went that curious stir of an unknown heat in his loins, cautious and lingering enough that he lowered the reform proposal he had been reading.

This unprovoked attraction has tossed him into an odd sort of imbalance. He did not like it. A dark, brooding mood settled over him and he tossed down the pages of the proposal and leaned back in his chair.

Simon was not a man who made mistakes. He thought of every move and countermove at least ten steps ahead as if life were a chess game. Yet he had not done so when hiring Miss Mina Crawford. He had allowed a past connection with her father to convince him and that he had then continued allowing it to happen was another source of bemusement for him.

Why?

Miss Crawford's sigh of pleasure as she closed the book had him briefly looking away. Setting the book aside, she went around her desk and plucked up the many letters that had been sent to him by would-be reformers. Her task was to read through them and select the common themes and compile them for his perusal.

There was a great call for reform demanding that bills were written so that not only would education be made available for every child, but that every man, whether they were educated or not, when they reached twenty-one years of age, were of sound mind, and were not undergoing punishment for a crime, should have the right to vote. That he was known to be open to reform had many reformists sending him their viewpoints so that he might read and prepare with his team for him to make the arguments in the House of Lords.

Simon dragged his gaze from her and considered the pile of letters she had left for him. Reaching for the one from his grandmother, he opened it.

My dearest grandson,

The most alarming rumor has reached my ears that you employed a lady as part of your team. I heard this lady to be the daughter of the late Viscount Crawford. There was a spectacular scandal surrounding her name a number of years back, so I fear I must caution you. I tried to uncover the details, but there is much mystery surrounding it, and I suspect her father had a hand in burying all known facts.

By the by, I have met the most charming and delightful woman, Lady Cassandra Farcoun. I think she would make you a most excellent wife, and I would like you to meet her. Please respond and let me know when you are coming to town — your social skills will need to be brushed up, for I am quite decided Lady Cassandra will be the next Countess of Creswick.

You need not fear that I am being rash in my choice, for I have greatly examined the current crop of debutants and also those ladies who have been out for a few years, and I considered seriously which qualities any young gentleman might seek in a bride.

A beauty, of course, though I consider that you have not displayed any particular preferences that may guide my hand. I made the assumption that a lady of good breeding and impeccable reputation is obviously required. Those were the main requisites I kept in mind. I suspect you would not want a vapid woman who could not handle ordering your staff and would be capable of acting as your hostess given your political interests.

Familiar as I am concerning your temperament, I also suspect you would not want a fiery virago, who would make demands on your time and purse beyond what you felt reasonable for your countess to be. Lady Cassandra is perfect in the regard that she is of a mild manner but also has considerable intelligence and is held to be a great beauty.

If you are not tempted by her, I have made a list of the eligible ladies of the season. Many of them are beautiful enough and own to good breeding, a few even would come with sizable dowries, even though you are wealthy enough not to need one.

Yours,
The Dowager Countess of Creswick.

The clever old bat had finally sent in the reminder of Simon's promise, twisting his arm. When he'd wanted to venture to university at the young age of twelve, his grandmother had not wanted to let him go so soon, especially when she had recently lost her only son and daughter-in-law in an accident a year prior. Simon's mind had processed grief differently, and he had simply accepted his parents had departed as part of the cycle of life and death.

That the cycle existed and was known to all should have eliminated the worry about death and the need to grieve when one died and went on to their rewards. His grandmother had not agreed with his outlook and had clung to him before using all her considerable influence to assist him in enrolling in Oxford University at the age of twelve years and three months.

A dazzling prodigy he had been called by many, but he hadn't thought of himself as brilliant, simply hungry to consume the written word. Sensing his lack of interest in worldly pursuits, she had made him promise he would go on a grand tour for at least a year after university and insisted that she would be the one to select his bride from the *haut ton*. He had quickly relinquished the right to choose his own spouse, never dreaming there might come a day when he would be interested in a particular woman's charms. He certainly had not been interested in women at twelve years old.

That day still had not truly arrived. The few lovers he had taken to his bed had been almost by rite of passage, with little personal enjoyment garnered from the entire affair. He had gained some experience in what pleased women but somehow found the concept of going through a host of ladies he knew little about and cared for less rather boring. Bedding was given too much importance by his fellow peers. And marriage *much* too much consideration by his grandmother.

Still, a gentleman must honor his word, always. Duty and honor had been taught to him by his father and were stamped upon Simon's heart. A thing his grandmother also understood about him, and clearly was using it to her advantage now.

It amused him that his grandmother thought she was twisting his arm, but he'd had recent thought that he should start considering finding a wife. His grandmother frequently impressed upon him that he not only had a duty to the realm, but to his estates and title. He would need an heir, to make sure that his dependents were properly looked after when he was dead and gone. Last month he had fondly told her he was still young, only seven and twenty, but she had only fixed him with an intent stare and smiled.

Looking at that last line again, he arched a brow.

I am quite decided Lady Cassandra will be the next Countess of Creswick.

He could feel the pen had been dripped in acid when she wrote it. Entering the marriage mart would not do for Simon. He truly had no time for courting, nor wished to indulge in those steps. His grandmother had asked him a few months ago as to the requirements he would need in a wife. Simon recalled he had said, "good breeding, good connections, an impeccable reputation," three important qualities for any gentleman in a life of active politics.

Lady Cassandra was sure to be a beauty, a good hostess and conversationalist, educated to at least a reasonable level. She might even own some musical or artistic talents. Though he did not need it, his grandmother would only select a lady with a handsome dowry, for it would be proof that her family was socially equal to his, and she would consider that an alliance without a fortune on at least one side as imprudent.

He plucked a sheet of paper and wrote,

Very well, Grandmother.
Find me a wife and I shall marry her. I leave the choice entirely in your hands, as I trust your judgment. However, keep in your thoughts the qualities I listed as important.
Your grandson,
Simon.

CHAPTER SIX

Miss Crawford strolled into the large study, appearing perfectly buttoned up and extraordinarily pretty in a navy-blue day dress with its narrow pleated skirt, long sleeves—that hugged her shapely arms, ending in white ruffles—with a matching navy-blue jacket decorated with many pearl buttons. Her skirt had only a modest bustle which he thought a ridiculous fashion idea, but she would be expected to wear them. Her dark red hair was caught up in an elegant chignon, with small wisps curling becomingly over her face.

That he noticed her in such fine details should have alarmed Simon. Still, after several days in her presence, he decided to simply accept his extraordinary reaction to her without letting it rattle his composure. In that way, in no time at all, surely he would become the master of himself and this irritating awareness of Miss Crawford.

"Good morning, my lord," she said brightly, a smile about to form.

She quickly sobered under his scowl, but the corners of her mouth quirked.

"I am to meet Mr. George Headley in Westminster tomorrow," he said. "I am leaving for London in the next hour."

"Very well, my lord. You will be missed."

Simon blinked. "You are to accompany me, Miss Crawford."

Her lips parted in surprise. "To London?"

"Yes."

"But you said you are to leave in the next hour."

"Yes, the carriage is being prepared."

"It is impossible for me to be ready in an hour, Lord Creswick, simply impossible."

"I assigned a personal maid to you, Miss Crawford; simply put the girl to work in packing your valise."

"Are we to take the train?"

"No."

"It would be much faster and perhaps more comfortable than a carriage."

"No," he snapped. "Do not make me repeat myself unduly, Miss Crawford."

Evidently startled at the hardness of his tone, she looked away from him and busied herself with several sheaves of papers scattered on her desk. There was a baffling pinch in the vicinity of his heart, and he stared at her bent head for long moments. He sighed deeply and rubbed his palms over his face. He had never found himself in the position to consider someone else's feelings before, but he did not like the idea that he might have bruised hers.

Her presence these past couple of weeks had not been the intrusion he thought it would be, and the lady was a most excellent working companion, never complaining when he pushed them even beyond six with his letters and dictations. His previous secretary, Fenley, would have grumbled all the way to the door.

"Forgive me, Miss Crawford. You did not deserve my ire. I am simply not fond of trains."

"Your reasons are your own, my lord, and you owe me no explanation," she said with only the softest hint of a smile.

Still, there was a cautious glow in her eyes that he

had never seen before. "My parents died in the Sutton Tunnel railway accident. I have not been fond of trains since, and though it is faster and more convenient to travel that way, I find that I ignore them."

Her expression softened. "I am so very sorry, my lord."

He made a sound in his throat, not at all sure what to do with the tender empathy in her lovely eyes. "There is nothing to be sorry about. Should you wish to take the train, I have no objections. I will send a carriage for you at the station in—"

"I am happy to travel with you, my lord," she said, quickly slapping a hand over her mouth to hide her smile.

An unfamiliar longing awakened inside him, and at this moment, he regretted forbidding her to smile in his presence. "Smile at your will, Miss Crawford," he said gruffly.

Though she appeared pleased, her mouth did not smile. "I shall be ready within the hour, my lord."

She hurried from the office, and to his amusement, there was a slight skip in her steps as she departed the room.

At least two hours later, the carriage rumbled along the country road to London. The journey would only take them a little over an hour or more if there were no problems on the road. Simon had been reading several of the notes Mina had made for him. Her writing was neatly elegant, and he noted that she asked in the margin why so many feared reforms. He glanced up and observed her head bent, which revealed the soft skin of her neck and the pulse beating there. The desire to press his lips to that exposed skin unexpectedly rushed through him. *Hell.*

"It is fear," Simon murmured, needing this conversation to take his thoughts from tasting Miss Crawford's skin.

Miss Crawford lowered the book she had been reading, a gothic romance, and pinned him with her startling green eyes. "What is fear, my lord?"

"I was reading your margin notes. Many powerful and wealthy people fear change and the power they will inevitably lose. Most of this fear rests within the ruling class, who truly believes it an injustice for the country and its institutions to extend the vote to people too insufficiently educated to know how to use it wisely."

Pleasure suffused her face, and with a jolt Simon realized he looked forward to having a conversation with Miss Crawford. He also found himself curious about her, a thing he had never before felt in regard to a lady. Simon canted his head and stared at her, wondering what was it about her that tugged at his senses, and how exactly he should deal with the anomaly.

* * *

Mina closed her book, a thrill going through her heart at the conversational opening offered by the earl. Working with him for the past two weeks had been most interesting, but beyond their work environment, the man ignored her most soundly. Mina even suspected he purposefully avoided her. Not that she wanted him to seek her out, but his attention was always buried in some book or letters sent from London or Birmingham even at their dinners. It was clear to her his work was important, and she admired that he was not a rake about town as so many men of consequence were reputed to be.

Mina often watched the earl in his meetings, which he held with at least three different people every day. She observed that he was mercurial, one instant his mood brooding and turbulent and in the next instance calm complacency. He could also retain an exceedingly large amount of information with extraordinary detail, and Mina had seen him read four books in one evening.

She found him rather impressive but kept the thought to herself.

Creswick set aside the papers and leaned against the squabs, his repose relaxed and a bit indolent. Mina admired how his clothes were faultlessly tailored to his lean, graceful physique. He cut quite a dashing figure in his black trousers, well-fitted matching jacket, and an exquisitely designed blue waistcoat.

Careful to not appear too obvious in her admiration, she glanced out the carriage windows at the rolling countryside. "I suspect many in the ruling class have a limited understanding of injustice," she said. "How could they have so little care that the working class is not represented by anyone who helps their interest? Do they not care that the majority of the working class earn less than seven pounds per month? I cannot comprehend how one could live on so little."

"I agree, Miss Crawford."

The earl stared at her and a small silence fell. Mina idly wondered if she should point out that his piercing regard was too unswerving and…provoking.

"Do you plan to return to your home every Friday

evening, Miss Crawford?"

"I… Yes."

"I do not mind your presence at my estate even when we are not working. You may avail yourself of all its amenities."

The pitter-patter of her heart echoed in her ears. "In the village near our manor, many of the children do not know their letters. For the last few years, they come to my home on Saturdays, and I teach them."

Admiration glinted in his eyes, and oddly it warmed her entire body.

"How many children?"

"Currently thirteen. They are so hungry to learn, and many are quick, I dare not miss a lesson," she said with a wide smile.

The earl's jaw tensed, and he looked away from her. She recalled then he did not like when she smiled, and Mina bit into her lower lip, suspecting he found her smile lovely. It was a compliment her father always paid her, and she had caught the earl more than once looking at her mouth. The idea that he might like her smile too much left a giddy feeling inside her heart.

"Do you find it fulfilling?"

"Teaching?"

"Yes."

Mina frowned thoughtfully, wanting to offer an honest reply instead of a glib one. Her father had been an unusual character, a meritocrat and quite liberal in his belief in the expansion of education for all classes and both sexes, and that belief had been passed to her. "At first I was desperate to fill my days. I had nothing to occupy my attention, as there is little to do with running a household with no servants. I do not attend balls or social events. I have read all the books in our library. I take so many long walks, my calves are rather...muscled. Some days were frightfully boring, and being around the children offered a respite from the tedium of merely existing. Then I started to understand how eager they were to learn, how proud they were to be educated, and how wonderful it was to see their eyes glow with hope they might be more than just servants."

Mina sighed. "They were like sponges, soaking up everything I had to offer. I only wish I could do more. Build a school...hire proper tutors. Grand dreams I sometimes think about when I am sitting on a branch high on a tree and looking out over the land."

"I get the sense you dreamed about more than just that, sitting on that high branch."

"Of course!"

The look he gave her was deeply considering, and Mina flushed, embarrassed at sharing so much. Despite teaching the children their letters, basic calculations, how to fish and paint and even fence—something had always felt missing from her life, and frustratingly she had not been able to identify what she needed to fill that emptiness.

A proper marriage was long off the cards for her, and Mina understood she could not hope for much with her tarnished reputation and dubious past. It was a truth she had accepted after the ordeal of running away from the man she had eloped with to Scotland.

Still, there was a loneliness that she could not hide from. And there were days when she considered she was only four and twenty with many years of this emptiness before her. She would lie in her bed and stare at the ceiling, filled with tormenting regret.

"Your eyes are remarkably expressive," he said, his face carefully composed.

Something unknown darted through her heart, a wonderful sense of thrill. "I—"

The carriage jolted, and she lurched forward, gasping as she tumbled off the seat. The earl caught her, and somehow she ended up perched on his lap and held tightly against his chest. Another lurch, and their heads butted together.

"Good heavens, what is happening?"

"You are in my lap, Miss Crawford."

His voice sounded strained, and his fingers dug into her hips.

"Not by design, my lord."

"You could return to your seat."

Deviltry darted through her, and she grinned. "I might be tossed about if I do. Perhaps it is safer if I—"

Her words broke off on a gasp of alarm as the earl all but tossed her back into her seat. Mina softly laughed at the black scowl he sent her. She suspected it was not wise to tease the earl beyond the limits of his forbearance. "My lord, I—" They both stiffened at the sound of a pistol. "Are we being robbed?"

A dangerous gleam had entered the earl's gaze, and he withdrew his own pistol from the pockets of his coat. The carriage came to a shuddering halt, and she watched in astonishment as he reached under the seat and brought out a walking cane. He tossed it to her, and she deftly caught it.

"These men might not be highwaymen. There is a blade hidden inside the walking cane."

A few sharp retorts echoed outside.

"Your coachman and tiger are fighting them off?"

"Yes."

"Are you certain they are not robbers, my lord?"

"They could be. However, I recently got a warning from my spies in London that I should be aware of friends who are now enemies. Many are not happy with my support for reform."

Mina was aghast. "Unhappy enough that they would *kill* you? You are a peer of the realm. Surely no one would dare be so bold or reckless."

"They might only want to hurt me enough that I am unable to venture to town. My presence is needed in Westminster. Should they prevent me from attending the House, that would be a triumph. If anyone enters the carriage, run him through."

She stared at him as if he were a creature. "*Run* him through?"

Dear God, she sounded like a frightened mouse. Very unflattering, but there was little she could do about that.

"Yes," he said, then he shoved the carriage door open and hauled himself outside into the fray.

Good heavens. She gripped the handle of the cane, her heart a pounding mess. There was a shout and several other retorts. How many men were there? The earl had an incalculable influence on the political minds of the time, and clearly that made the Earl of Creswick too dangerous. Her father had spoken about this darker side of politics, but she hadn't believed it until the evidence was before her. Unless the earl had found other enemies she did not know about.

Dear lord, please let them be ordinary robbers.

Suddenly the carriage lurched off at an alarming speed. Mina was tossed about, her shoulders slamming into the door with jarring force. She cried out, gripping the blade and bracing for a crash. The many dreaded stories about carriage accidents roared through her mind, and Mina knew at this moment she might die. The fright that went through her heart left the taste of ash in her mouth.

The carriage wildly rocked side to side, and she held on for dear life. A piercing regret filled her heart at the thought that she had not lived a memorable life. She had allowed one foolish mistake to define her entire existence, and she had hidden in the country away from condemnation.

I've never kissed a gentleman.

I've never had ice cream. That felt even more painful than the lost kiss.

I've never felt the fine mist of the ocean spray on my face; I've never swum in the sea.

I've never flown a kite.

I've never had one of those Fry's Chocolate Creams.

I've never tasted passion.

Mina was suddenly filled with a desperate longing that threatened to overwhelm her good sense. Finally, she thought it: *I've never…never kissed Creswick.*

All things she had longed for, even if fleeting, at one point in her brief life. Mina moaned as the equipage careened, tilting her to the side before it slammed into something with shuddering force, but thankfully it did not turn over. Panting harshly, she sent a swift prayer to the heavens that she was unharmed. The carriage door wrenched open, and a man stood there, pointing a pistol at her.

Good God.

"My good sir, you are pointing a loaded pistol at me."

"Out," he snapped, his tone menacing and measured.

She would have asked for greater occupational hazard pay if she had known. At least another five thousand pounds.

Mina clambered from the carriage, using the cane to assist her, hating that her legs wobbled. There was no one about, not even the earl. *Oh God, please let him be safe and well.* She sent up swift prayers for the coachmen and footmen who'd traveled with the earl. Mina then turned her thoughts onto escaping with her life and virtue intact. "My good sir," she began, ensuring she infused her voice with tears. "I a-am petrified. I cannot imagine what—"

With speed the man could not have anticipated, she drew the blade from the cane and, with a flick of her wrist, sliced his arm open. He bellowed, dropping the pistol and grabbing his arm, trying to stem the bleeding.

Thank heavens Papa had insisted she learned to fence. Mina hurriedly picked up his pistol and backed away from him. "I am terribly sorry, but I had no notion if you meant me any harm. I needed to call your bluff. Hurry and tie something around—"

The cock of another pistol behind Mina froze her. A man walked into her line of vision, a sneer on his mouth.

"Ye be a clever one, ain't ye."

"I gather you are comrades," she murmured, wondering at her chances.

The sound of running feet reached her ears. "Miss Crawford!"

"I am here, my lord," she shouted, gladness surging

through her. "There is a man with a pistol!"

"Miss Crawford!"

Before she could respond, the man grabbed her, his hairy arm wrapping across her chest in a brutal band. Something cold was pressed to her throat, and her stomach dipped. Though she could not see it, Mina suspected it to be a blade. The earl emerged from the woodlands, and when he saw her, an odd, desperate fear crossed his face.

"Do not come closer," the barbarian holding her growled. "Drop yer weapon."

The earl tossed aside his pistol without a moment's hesitation.

"You will release Miss Crawford this instant," he said, with so much menace in the glance he cast upon her kidnapper that even her belly pitched with fright.

"Yer in no position to make demands."

She gasped as a sharp sting pinched her neck, and something warm wetted her collar. The earl froze, appearing like a marble effigy. His eyes went flat and hard. Before she could even think to question the change in his demeanor, his hand moved with shocking swiftness, and a flash of silver steel glinted. The hand around her throat slackened, and the man behind her dropped with a harsh *thud*.

"Do not look," he said gruffly. "And do not faint."

Mina resolutely pulled herself together, still aware of her pounding heart. "I am not the fainting sort," she said, wincing at the smallness of her voice. As if controlled by an external force, her body started to turn and—

"Do not look, Mina!"

The earl's intimate use of her name was enough to arrest her curiosity and snap her gaze to his. "Is he dead?"

"Yes," he said tersely. "Are you hurt, Miss Crawford?"

"No." She pressed her gloved fingers against her lips to stop their trembling. He reached into his top jacket, withdrew a silver flask, and handed it to her.

"To steady your nerves."

She reached for the small bottle, uncapped it, and took a healthy swallow. Her chest burned and she coughed a bit before she took another gulp of whisky.

"Do you feel steadier?"

"No." She gave him a brave smile. "Shall we continue, my lord?"

"I will meet with Hadley another day," he said tersely, coming over and taking her hand in his. He drew her away from the scene of mayhem along the beaten path. She could feel the tension in his grip as they strode along.

"Are your staff safe?"

"Yes, no one was hurt."

Thank heavens. It mortified Mina to feel that she was trembling. "I am more rattled than I realized," she said with a shaky laugh.

They stopped under a large oak tree, and she rested against it.

"Breathe slowly, Miss Crawford, and steady yourself."

Mina was intensely mindful that they were standing mere inches apart, of the earl's heat and masculine strength caging her against the trunk of a tree. Was he even aware of his actions? That she could feel his heartbeat as if it was hers? Their faces were so close together, she couldn't help admiring the sheer beauty of his. Mina cleared her throat. "My lord, I—"

Her words died away when the earl took her chin

in his hand and raised her face to his. That touch, even through his gloves, seemed to hook into her entire body, rooting her to the ground.

"You are fired."

The snarl in his voice jolted her. He had always remained enigmatic and insouciant, an exceptional fire she thought she would never be able to touch, much less influence in any sort of manner. Yet now his brilliant blue eyes burned with anger and something that looked like fear. For her.

"Why?" she breathed, gripping his forearms and fiercely holding his stare.

"Is this incident not enough reason, Miss Crawford?"

"No."

His eyes darkened, the blues of a roiling ocean on the cusp of a violent storm. The energy that leaped from him crackled and pricked over her skin, shortening her breath.

"Bloody hell, Miss Crawford, that man had a knife to your throat!"

The truth burst from her. "You prevented him from harming me; from the moment you appeared, all my fear melted away." His eyes flashed with something savage, and her heart lurched. "I am not the wilting sort. Are you, my lord?"

"You could have been hurt—"

She thrust herself forward so their lips almost brushed. He reared back, clearly surprised by her action, and she followed, smiling inwardly, for his hands had not fallen from her face. "I was not hurt. Do not forget the qualities that allowed you to hire me. I *am* fierce and indomitable and—"

"No," he hissed, his eyes darkening. "You are sweet

and soft and so damn lovely and—"

Mina mashed her mouth to his, stealing his words and breath. He made a harsh sound of surprise against her mouth, and it vibrated through her entire body and stirred an unknown heat low in her belly. All her senses became centered around the sensual pressure of his mouth against hers, the stillness of his body, the soft shudder that went through his frame.

Oh God.

Once she had begun kissing him, it felt impossible to stop. He cupped her cheeks with both hands and nipped sharply at her bottom lip. A punishment for breaking the bounds of propriety he had set between them with his distance. Then he licked the very spot he bit, a soothing balm to the erotic sting. Mina whimpered. Swirling pits of fire dropped into her belly. She didn't want to ever lose this feeling. Her knees were shaking so much, she was glad to cling to his forearms.

His mouth moved over hers with carnal thoroughness and with a sigh of want, she parted her lips. Their tongues glided together and a violent shock of heat, a burst of pleasure claimed her as he kissed her in a manner she had not thought possible—intimate, carnal, and so wonderful, her senses were disoriented.

He kissed her over and over until she trembled in the cage of his embrace. Somehow his legs had nudged her thighs wider, and she was perched atop his thighs and on her toes. Mina slid her hands through his hair, moaning. His kiss assaulted her senses with decadent pleasure.

His knees moved and she jolted to feel the hardness rubbing against a place she had never been touched. Her sex suddenly ached, and she moaned when he moved his thigh once more against her. It shocked Mina when he grabbed her hips and hauled her more against him.

She tore her mouth from his, breathing raggedly. Her mouth felt bruised and deliciously swollen. Her heart fluttered as if a wild bird were in her stomach while some undefinable sensation hooked inside her chest. His gaze lowered to her mouth, and she could feel his desperate want to continue kissing her.

The earl closed his eyes, the skin drawn taut over his elegant cheekbones as he clearly mastered his needs. And cradled as he was between her thighs, she could feel the desperate proof of his arousal.

His long lashes fluttered open, and all the swirling hunger had vanished from his gaze. His thumb feathered over her swollen bottom lip. "Kissing is rather interesting."

Mina's pulse tapped briskly in her ears as she peered up at him. Was that to say he had never kissed before? She blinked bemusedly up at him. Surely not, yet he did it rather splendidly. "Have you never kissed before, my lord?"

The sudden gleam in Lord Creswick's blue eyes was oddly unnerving, yet he did not answer her. He traced her cheekbones and the curve of her eyebrows with his thumbs. Her heart trembled until it ached inside her chest.

"You are fired, Miss Crawford." He spoke in his habitual tone of indifference. "We shall return to my home, where you will pack your bags and leave."

Bloody hell.

CHAPTER SEVEN

They had not traveled far from his main estate when they'd been accosted by the group of men. Simon managed to get them home within an hour after his coachman found the horses that had broken free from their harnesses. He closed his eyes, recalling the feel of Miss Crawford's lips on his and then her body as she had ridden before him on the stallion back to the estate. The journey had been silent, and he hated that small tremors had wracked her body. Once they had arrived, she had hurried to her room to remove the clothing that had a few sprays of blood on the back of her jacket. How she had paled when he'd informed her of it.

"My lord," Robert Beechman, his man of affairs, said behind him. "Should we discuss what happened today and come up with a contingency against attacks like this? The local magistrate and the police were already alerted, but perhaps we might make more plans for the future."

At his silence, the man cleared his throat, but Simon still did not remove his gaze from Miss Crawford, who sat in a simple day dress on the stone bench in the gazebo in the far distance. She had gone to the one the farthest away from the house, clearly to be private with her emotions.

You are still scared.

The awareness jolted him, and he lifted the spyglass to his eyes once more, directing it toward her face. She was turned away, looking out to the woodlands, but he could see that her teeth worried her bottom lip.

Parliament was to open in a couple of weeks, and that was where his attention needed to be. Not on the aching sadness on Miss Crawford's face. Simon could afford little distraction from his duties, not at this critical juncture.

"We shall resume this meeting next week," he said, feeling the man's jolt of surprise.

Simon had never canceled or postponed a meeting in…well, never. He had never done it. The uncharacteristic behavior was sure to start some manner of speculation, especially when he noted Mr. Beechman following his line of vision. What was even more surprising was the man's mouth grinning.

"Why do you smile, Mr. Beechman?"

"Ah…well, I…" The man gave him a sheepish look. "It is merely good to see you show any interest in, er…in a lady. There is already a rumor spreading about town that you are to marry this year."

Everything inside of Simon stilled. "Miss Crawford is my secretary, Mr. Beechman, nothing more."

"Yes, my lord. I shall return tomorrow for our meeting."

The man collected his papers and briefcase and hurried from the room, still with that irritating grin about his mouth. Lowering the spyglass, Simon made his way outdoors. There was a decided nip in the air, and he went back inside to collect his cloak and held it over his arm. The vexing woman had not worn a coat and would likely catch a chill. Though it had stopped snowing and was a bit warmer in the country-side, it was still winter.

She was so lost in thought that she did not hear his approach, and Simon even made efforts to crunch some twigs beneath his boots.

"Miss Crawford," he murmured.

She whirled around, her eyes wide with fright. "My lord, I—"

Miss Crawford stumbled coming off the top step of the gazebo, and he darted forward and caught her against his chest. Simon inexplicably became all at once aware of everything about her...the subtle scent of her perfume, the coldness of her nose as it brushed his jawline, the softness of her skin, the firmness of her small breasts against his chest, the hitch in her breathing and how it flowed through his body, filling places he'd not realized were empty and hungry for...for *this*.

He wanted to hold her body close and drown in her scent and taste. He steadied her with a silent curse and then snatched his hand away from her and stepped back.

Her cheeks were flushed and her eyes shadowed when she peered up at him. "Forgive me. I am not usually so easily startled." She tucked a wisp of hair behind her ear.

"You are freezing."

Her eyes widened when he wrapped his cloak around her shoulders. A sigh escaped her, and she shoved her arms inside, burrowing into its warmth. She looked ridiculous, for it dwarfed her slender frame, giving her the appearance of vulnerable femininity. Simon swallowed when she smelled the damn thing, her lashes fluttering closed.

He was tempted to ask what it bloody smelled like but wisely kept his council. "The snows are just melting," he said gruffly. "It is unwise to venture outside so sparsely dressed, Miss Crawford."

"I shall keep it in mind, my lord. Thank you. Though I fear the hem of your cloak will be ruined." She held it up to show him as it was already dragging in the damp grass.

"That is of little consequence, as long as you remain warm."

Her mouth curved. "I shall do my best to hold it up."

Simon's gut clenched, and he ruthlessly suppressed the feeling. "I wish to speak with you. Await me in the drawing room." First, he had to deal with this damnable heat enveloping his body.

"I see." Curiosity lit in her eyes. "I gather you are no longer going to London?"

"Not today."

"Is it even safe to go at all, my lord? What about the gentleman you were to meet? Could he have been the one to set up…the earlier disaster?"

He hesitated, then answered, "No. Mr. Headley needs my support. He is a member of the Reform League, and he is to inform me on how those meetings are taking place. What are the whispers about the bill and the way the tide is moving."

A small frown touched her brows. "I have not heard of this league."

"A few years ago, in December of 1863 precisely, Marquess Townsend founded the Universal League for the Material Elevation of the Industrious Classes."

Her mouth twitched. "A mouthful."

"Its main purpose was to lower the back-breaking and soul-destroying working hours of the lower classes and promote their education. Despite his honorable efforts, the marquess was a bit reserved about reform. Many departed from the league to create their own, to be the drivers of reforms more in line with John Russell's arguments in the House of Lords."

"I thought Lord Russell was a Liberal. He was the one to petition for reform last year, but according to the letters I have been reading, the call is now led by the Conservatives, namely Benjamin Disraeli."

Simon smiled. "Disraeli is a cunning one."

Her eyes widened. "You admire him?"

"I do." He waved for her to walk beside him and escorted her toward the house. "When Lord Russell put the bill forward last year, Disraeli's counter-arguments that the ruling class's interests will suffer a tremendous blow incited fear in many and split the liberal party. A more liberal Whig emerged who was supported by other radicals and reformists."

"And you are one of those?"

"If I am to be put in a box, I suppose I am. Disraeli will soon introduce his own Reform Bill into the House of Commons."

"And you are fully committed to supporting this?"

"Yes. My aim is to sway as many as possible toward voting for the bill. Reform is needed, Miss Crawford, and every man with a conscience must fight to ensure equality and justice in London and the rest of the United Kingdom. Then we will fight toward women getting that same equality, including rights to divorce, to be freely educated, to work if they wish, and to vote."

She cast him a sidelong look, filled with some admiration. It stunned Simon to feel a curl of warmth twisting through his chest. It was not tinged with desire, this warmth, but it was just as heady. He stopped. "I must go."

Her eyes widened at his abruptness, but he did not wait for her reply but walked away toward the lake in the far distance.

I should never have damn well kissed her.

Simon idly wondered what other delights between a man and a woman he had been missing out on, and his damn cock twitched because that brief but visceral flash of a woman naked atop his sheets was Miss Crawford. With a growl, he tugged off his boots, jacket, waistcoat, and shirt, ignoring the biting cold. There was no logic to deal with this damnable desire stirring through him with the violence of a storm. These desires must be erased from his mind and body. He would have to use unconventional methods to shock his body into behaving properly.

Running toward the lake, he dived in, going deep in its murkiness, beneath the remnants of the water lilies that created such a picturesque display in spring to summer.

This was a damn mistake.

The thought floated through his consciousness only a second after his body had hit the icy waters of the lake. Pinpricks of pain attacked every surface of his body, the sensation brutal in its intensity. He clawed to the surface with furious strength and swam to the embankment. Simon hauled himself up, gritting his teeth against the cold, jarring his body like brutal slams of a fist to his midsection.

Well, it had certainly killed the ache that had stirred at the base of his cock. If only he had not damn near killed himself to get the deed done.

Hurrying inside the house, he hastened down the hallway to his library and stormed past an astonished Miss Crawford to his inner sanctum, so that he might stand by the roaring fire. He heard the slamming of the outside door, and he breathed a sigh of relief.

His secretary, nay his unexpected tormenter, had left. Now she only had to permanently stay away. Simon scowled. *What is she still doing in the office?* The lady should be packing for her imminent departure. The door to his inner office flung open, and Miss Crawford rushed inside with a large blanket and the housekeeper on her heels with two more.

"My lord, you are half naked!" the housekeeper declared, turning away and covering her eyes.

"I am very well aware of it," he growled. "It is the reason I am in my *private office*."

Miss Crawford folded one of the blankets and patted the armchair seat. "Come, my lord, sit."

He went, wondering why he was responding to the damn woman's order.

"Thank you, Mrs. Basil," she said to the hovering housekeeper who looked like a worried hen. "Have the kitchen prepare some hot broth right away. Infused with thyme and scallions."

"I do not drink broths or soups," he said flatly. "Nor do I need to be fretted over."

She bared her teeth in a parody of a sweet smile. "You will today. A pot of tea as well, Mrs. Basil, and some sandwiches and cakes."

"Yes, Miss Crawford." The housekeeper bobbed, not to him, but to Miss Crawford, as if she was the mistress of the house.

He cast his annoyed glare at Miss Crawford, and the woman tossed the blankets over his head, smothering him. Then with more vigor than anyone could expect, she started to dry his hair and body. "Are you to chafe the damn skin from my chest?" he snapped.

"If that is what it takes to keep you warm and from death's door," she snapped right back at him.

Simon was…inexplicably amused.

"What could have possessed you to dive into the lake, in the middle of winter? Do you have a death wish?"

"I could have fallen in accidentally," he said drily.

"You ran and dove in. I *saw* you," she said pertly, vigorously rubbing his hair.

Some heat was beginning to seep back into his muscles. He considered where the lake was and the position of the office. "You cannot see the lake from here, Miss Crawford."

"I know," she said after a considered pause. "However, I was watching you."

"Shameless," he murmured, liking that she had felt compelled to watch him.

"I know that I am," she said, with laughter lurking in her tone. "But you must admit it is a charming kind of brazenness."

You are indeed charming, Miss Crawford.

Clearly a similar madness was claiming her, and that meant she was just as tempted as he was to explore this fine thread of want that linked them. Of course she would—Miss Crawford was the rebellious hoyden who had pressed her mouth against his without any thoughts of consequences. He shoved the blanket off his head and their gazes met. The yearning he spied in the depths of her eyes knotted his belly, and the words he'd been about to snap died away.

Simon silently allowed her ministrations, noting that she appeared worried.

Tenderly, she used the blanket and coasted it over his chest and shoulders, wiping away the rivulets of water. Simon felt somewhat scarce of breath. If only she weren't so damnably lovely. "You are fired," he said gruffly.

Her eyes crinkled at the corner. "I know."

"You should be packing. My carriage will take you home."

"I recall that it is damaged."

"I own more than one equipage, Miss Crawford."

She soundly ignored that and said, "Why did you go into the water when it was freezing cold?"

He stood, grabbing the blanket before it dropped to the ground, drying off the rest of his body with swift, economic motions. "My reasons are my own."

Miss Crawford, interpreting with fiendish accuracy the source of his discontent, smiled. *The minx*. She *liked* that he wanted her, and the awareness aroused Simon. "Have you forgotten your speech on occupational hazards?"

Her lovely eyes widened. "No."

"Then do not look at me so, Miss Crawford."

Her cheeks turned a rosy pink, and she lifted an elegant shoulder in a shrug. "Perhaps if we were to mutually agree that kissing can be delightful, then it would not be ravishment, my lord."

Bloody hell.

Those soft, provocative words ghosted over his cock, striking it with hunger. As if his manhood had a will of its own, the damn thing started to ache and lengthened. Taking a deep breath to steady himself against the reaction, he waited until his erection diminished before dropping the blanket on the armchair. Walking over, he tapped her lightly on her nose. "We shall both be thankful you are leaving in a few hours."

"Tomorrow," she murmured.

"Why not today—"

"It is raining. I do not like traveling in the rain."

A quick glance through the windows showed it to be so, and when he looked back at her, she stared up at him with an expression of amused indulgence. He wanted to kiss the smile from that lush mouth. Take his lips on a path down her throat and even lower.

"In all my years, a lady has never tempted me," he murmured.

Using the back of his fingers, he brushed his knuckles against the softness of her cheeks. A sigh left her, and she closed her eyes and leaned into his caress.

Dangerous.

Simon lowered his hand and took a careful step back. "I will provide you with my largest umbrella, Miss Crawford. You shall be fine."

A peal of laughter unexpectedly came from her, delightfully rippling over his skin. Seeing his black scowl, she slapped her hand over her mouth to contain it. "Very well, my lord, I shall pack my valise post haste. You may call for the carriage to be readied."

Still smiling, Miss Crawford turned around and hurried from the room.

• • •

Simon was not given to excesses like gambling, wagers, or drunkenness. He tried to think of the last time he'd had a woman and could not recall the encounter to mind. He had a rather predictable routine, and even a few of his friends called him dull, except for when it came to politics—then he was considered a dangerous animal few would dare contend with.

He'd never had any sort of difficulties ordering his thoughts, though, closing them down whenever he needed for important matters like sleep. Yet, Simon had lain awake in his bed for exactly three hours and eleven minutes.

All because of a damn kiss and a woman who refused to be fired.

He allowed himself to taste her in his thoughts. To lick along her neck, down to her belly, and then her sex. It was dangerous to have Miss Crawford under his roof for any length of time. He didn't want this blasted temptation or awareness of her to dig its roots inside of him and blossom. A woman had *never* been a distraction for him before. And by God, if one should prove to be so damn distracting where all he had to do was think of her and need swirled and clawed inside his belly, it should be a lady he could add to the list of candidates to be his countess.

Miss Mina Crawford was not eligible in any regard, especially given her ruined reputation and lack of connections in the political sphere. Why in God's name was he even thinking of Miss Crawford in terms of marriage? Pushing that nonsense from his mind, he sat up on the edge of the bed, blowing out a harsh breath. Sleep would elude him this night. And perhaps even tomorrow and the next and the next. As long as

Miss Crawford was under his roof, Simon would be tossed out of his normally calm and logical order. It would just not do.

To think of her sleeping down the hallway, perhaps looking softer in sleep made him feel raw, and furious, his own lust and weakness for her exposed in the way he craved to take her in his arms.

Damn you, Mina Crawford.

After leaving his inner office earlier, she had not returned downstairs. When the maid had gone to summon her for supper, she had reported Miss Crawford to be soundly asleep. Thinking of the ordeal of the day and her narrow brush with death, he had ordered for her to be left in peace to sleep and then sent word that the carriage would no longer be needed.

Simon had dined alone, then smoked a cheroot outdoors in the chilled night. On his way to his chamber, he stopped at her door and knocked. No answer had come forth, and he had continued on to his chamber. Suddenly irritated, he pushed from his bed, padded over to his door, and left his room. Simon went to her room, knocked soundly once before entering.

The large room was ablaze with light from a gas lamp and the roaring fire in the fireplace. The tempting minx who was hell-bent on haunting his good senses sat in the center of the four-poster bed, wrapped in a thick quilt and smothering a delicate yawn, her glorious hair tumbling well past her shoulders to spread around her.

"My lord," she gasped when he closed the door behind him with a soft *snick*.

"Why are you still here, Miss Crawford?"

She was not unsettled by him in the least, lifting her chin in a gesture of defiance. "Is that why you invaded my chamber in the dead of night?"

Her tone of disgruntlement bemused him. What did she have to be upset about? He was the one tossed out of disorder. "Yes."

"Well, you can ask me in the morning," she said pertly.

"Are you daring to dismiss me from your room?"

"Yes."

He barely prevented the growl rising in his throat. "It was a mistake to hire you."

She rolled her eyes, tugged the blankets to her chin, and snuggled down back into the bed. "The rumors say Simon Loughton, Earl of Creswick, is too brilliant to make mistakes. Good night, my lord."

"What kind of creature are you?" he hissed. "Have you no shame?"

"No," she mumbled into the pillow and even had the nerve to snuggle more against its softness.

"Do not be alarmed, Miss Crawford," he warned in a low tone. "I shall lift you and deposit you outside. I will suffer no screaming."

Simon suspected the wretched creature laughed from her shaking shoulders. "Do you understand I am planning to toss you from my home on your arse, and you won't be allowed back inside?"

She smothered a yawn and muttered something unintelligible.

"You are not at all frightened, are you?" he murmured, damning that slow pulse of fascination once more to perdition. "Here you are with a gentleman in your chamber, and you are not at all alarmed."

At this, she turned over, still holding the blanket to her throat.

"It takes a lot to frighten me," she murmured, a challenge sparkling in her green eyes. "Nor do I believe you are about to toss me out in the cold."

He had never encountered anyone so unmoved by his authority. All his life, either his intellect, rank, personality, or just a mixture of all had people, sometimes even his friends, act with deference around him. But here was this lady being so dismissive. Was she not aware of the ease at which he could accomplish anything he desired?

"At first, I had thought you a clever lady, but you do not seem to understand that your services are terminated."

"I thought about it, and I decided not to accept your termination, my lord."

"I will not have you in danger," he said, his mood shifting with mercurial swiftness. Now he felt restless and edgy, a dangerous mood riding him.

A hint of vulnerability flashed in her eyes. "Is that the only reason you want to fire me? You fear for my safety?"

A memory of their torrid kiss rose in his mind, but he assured himself he was a man of logic and intellect, well able to manage the baser urges that seemed to plague most gentlemen. He was not at all worried about a kiss. "I would not want to see you hurt."

"You protected me," she said softly. "Even killed the man that threatened my safety."

Inexplicably, he lingered over her features. *And I would kill dozens more if you were to be hurt.* He did not share the violent thought, merely returned her intense regard.

"Why do I need to worry when I am by your side? You carry some of the dreams of my father. It is one of the reasons I have not allowed myself to be as yet fired." Using her fingers, Miss Crawford combed back several tendrils of hair that tumbled over her forehead and cheeks. "I shall go when I am ready."

He had never heard a more outrageous statement in his life, yet it filled him with a peculiar feeling of amusement. "Only some of your father's dreams I carry?" he asked, curious about a man he had admired, a man their great nation had lost too soon.

The viscount had clearly educated his daughter beyond the standards of most men and filled her heart with the courage and daring of a lioness.

"Yes, only some." Her eyes glittered with good humor. "Papa would not dream of my lips in the way you do. It is clear that it is thoughts of kissing me that kept you awake and sent you to invade my room like a growling tiger. Were the cold waters of the lake not enough to dampen the desire, my lord?"

The words were so shocking that it took him a while to fully process them. With a scowl, he ruthlessly buried all traces of his interest, slowly calming the racing of his heart to its normal rhythm.

"Your impertinence knows no bounds."

She chuckled, her eyes sparkling with thousands of secrets. That soft laugh whispered over his skin, then danced in a swirl of sensation to land on his cock. *Hell.* Simon stiffened at that desire prickling along his skin like fire. It was then he noted the blanket had infinitesimally slipped from her shoulders, and a dark purple bruise spread from her collar bone and disappeared into the covering.

"What is that?" He walked over and stopped at a respectable distance.

She glanced at her bared shoulder and gasped, quickly tugging the coverlets to hide the bruise.

It felt like ice shards pierced his chest. "You were hurt."

That same shoulder lifted in a dismissive shrug. "Just a bit."

"Did the men hurt you before I arrived?" Damn his hide for not probing more earlier.

Startled eyes met his. "No. I even flayed open the arm of the first bounder to point his pistol at me. And you arrived just as the…just as that man grabbed me. It was the crash of the carriage that bruised me a bit."

"Where exactly are you hurt?"

"My shoulder…arm…and my back. I gather with rest I shall be fine."

A tight feeling twisted at his chest. Now he understood the exhaustion to which she succumbed to earlier. "I shall summon the physician."

Miss Crawford cast a glance at the clock perched on the wall by the fire. "My lord, it is minutes after two in the morning."

"The physician will come should I summon him," he said with a touch of cool arrogance.

She was looking at him thoughtfully. "Thank you for your care. However, it is unnecessary to pull him from his warm bed. I am not dying, my lord."

Still, he could not quiet the seething unease in his gut. "Why did you not inform me of this matter, Miss Crawford?"

"I did not believe it so dire, and I am aware you

had important matters to attend."

"Those matters were not more important than your comfort and well-being, Miss Crawford. See that this does not happen again," he said with an icy bite. "I must be appraised of any harm to your person—even if it is a stubbed toe—at once."

Her eyes had widened, but now they crinkled at the corners as she smiled. "Very well, my lord."

"There is no need to look so damn pleased with yourself. I would own this concern for any one of my employees."

"Of course, my lord."

"I will return in just a moment. Do not move."

Simon left her room and made his way down to the smaller library on the second floor, where he had some peppermint salve. Grabbing the small container, he made his way back to her chamber. Miss Crawford was right where he had left her, sitting in the center of her bed, the blankets clutched to her throat, appearing like a frail damsel.

If he had never believed it before, now he understood how appearances could deceive. The woman was a vexatious lioness…and he liked that. He held out the salve to her. "It works incredibly on bruises. Apply it liberally."

"Thank you, my lord. You may rest it on my dressing table. I shall have a maid apply it in the morning."

"It will soothe the pain and allow you a better rest. It is best to apply it now."

"I am not able to reach my back, my lord."

"I will summon the maid."

"My lord, why wake the maid from her bed when you are the one insisting I apply the salve now, you are capable of doing so yourself, and I will allow you to do so?"

He tilted his head briefly to the ceiling. Simon could feel her staring at him. Simon blew out a harsh sigh and made his way over.

Her eyes glowed with rich humor. "You are not going to the gallows, my lord."

He did not want the minx to see that he was on the verge of smiling. No, that might just encourage more teasing. A dangerous urge to succumb to the taunting temptation and ravish her slid through his veins. *Get it over with*, it whispered, and then he could dismiss her from his awareness once he had her. Simon tried to master his reaction into reasonable order.

She scooted over to the edge of the bed and turned her back to him. A few shifts and tugs and her upper back were now bared to him. *Bloody hell*. A large bruise mottled the area, distracting him from the awareness Miss Crawford might be half naked beneath the blankets. Simon opened the container, dipped three of his fingers into the salve, and liberally spread it over her skin. She hissed and jerked.

Simon froze. "I'll be gentler."

Her shoulder relaxed, and he tenderly coasted his hand over her shoulder blade and the center of her back until the edge of the coverlet brushed his fingers, luring him to slip his hand even farther. He grabbed the errant thoughts with an iron will and squeezed them until they grew smaller and smaller and then disintegrated.

A tremor worked its way through her body and her breathing audibly hitched.

"Is everything well, Miss Crawford?"

She nodded and remained silent. He quickly and as gently as possible coated everywhere that looked bruised and stood.

"I shall leave it here for your maid to assist you in the morning."

"Thank you, my lord."

His gut clenched at the husky note in her voice. Without looking at her, he asked, "What are your other reasons for not being fired as yet?"

"As it involves a considerable explanation, I would like to inform you of them in the morning, my lord."

Curiosity darted through him. "Very well, Miss Crawford, I shall see you in the morning."

He left her room and returned to his, shrugging the banyan from his body to slip naked between the sheets. Folding one of his elbows under his arm, he stared up at the ceiling, a smile touching his mouth. That lingering shadow that had been in her eyes by the gazebo had not been there just now. He was glad for it. Simon closed his eyes and simply went to sleep.

CHAPTER EIGHT

Dearest Simon,

I was appalled to receive your letter and your abrupt order to simply find you a wife, and you shall marry her. Do you not plan to care for this creature you shall marry? Once you are in town, I urge that you take some time from politics and attend a few balls, musicales, and when the weather improves perhaps a few picnics in the gardens. Court your bride to be, my dear. You will be rewarded for it. Marriage is not meant to be cold and distant but filled with warmth, passion, and a deep understanding of each other's character. And my dear, I assure you that any wife of yours will need to be acclimatized to your many facets.

You, my dear grandson, sorely lack charm, and I fear you need more of my help than I'd realized.

Yours,
The Dowager Countess of Creswick.

Simon's grandmother's letter had been waiting for him in his office when he entered a few minutes ago. Given the early hours, he suspected she had not used the regular post to deliver it but sent one of her footmen.

She had often bemoaned that his blunt mannerisms did not suit the sensibilities of English society and many of their debutantes. Many bitterly complained he was too direct and unapologetic, and his grandmother often warned him he would need to procure himself some charm to win a wife. Now it seemed she was of a mind to interfere further in his life on her quest to see him settled.

What rubbish.

A soft knock sounded on the door, then Miss Crawford opened it and entered. This morning her hair had been caught in a loose chignon, with several strands of fiery tresses curling becomingly on her cheeks. She wore a dark green dress with a narrowed skirt with pleating at the hem that enticingly hugged her small but lush curves like a possessive lover.

She glanced at him, and whatever she saw in his expression prompted her to ask, "Have you received another threatening letter?"

"Something far worse."

She pressed a hand over her chest. "Has someone died?"

"No."

"Must I pry the information from you with incessant questions?"

"It seems I am required to acquire some charm."

Her eyes widened slightly. *"Charm?"*

"Yes."

She ducked her head, but he saw the touch of a smile on her mouth. "As in masculine allure... charm?"

"There are other kinds, Miss Crawford?"

Humor brightened the sheer beauty of her eyes. "I can never tell with you, my lord." She took a sip of the tea she'd just poured. "I daresay you should call me Mina...you have been in my room while I was naked. Surely that is credible grounds for informality."

The lady was determined to shock him. "You, Miss Crawford, were mummified in a blanket."

"I maidenly held onto it so tightly because, well, I was naked beneath."

The soft rhythm of his breathing fractured. *Naked.*

Their gazes met over the rim of her teacup, and for the first time since meeting Miss Crawford, a bright yet delicate blush stole across the high ridges of her cheekbones. So the lady knew she had teased too far. He allowed himself the indulgence of imagining her body naked. How soft and lovely she would appear, her curves lithe yet richly pronounced. Simon's heart pounded, and a dormant lust stretched to life with a raw purr of hunger.

Miss Crawford rose, sliding her palms down the side of her skirts. She looked beguilingly nervous. "I shall ring for a pot of tea," she murmured and hurried toward the door.

"We already have a pot, Miss Crawford."

Her hand stilled on the knob, and she rested her forehead on the hard surface of the door. Simon stood and walked over to her, stopping only a mere breath from her. Her elusive fragrance of lavender filled his lungs. Something trembled in the air between them, forceful and intense. Without turning around to look at him, she said, "I have never had an affair before."

Sweet mercy. "Neither have I."

A fine shiver went through her body. "Are we about to have one, my lord?"

"No."

She turned and leaned against the door. "That is a pity. I would rather it be you."

"Rather what be me, Miss Crawford?"

"The gentleman I shall select to be my lover."

She bit into her lower lip, a nervous gesture, but he could see the spark of rebellion and determination in her eyes.

"You plan to take a lover," he said slowly, fighting down the alarming surge of want that leaped through him.

She looked at him, faintly cynical. That look made him curious, even filled him with considerable intrigue.

"Yes. It is not only the purview of gentlemen or widows to have affairs. I daresay already ruined ladies can, too." A lock of fiery red hair fell on her cheek. "You see, I realized something when the carriage raced away with me, and I was so certain I would die."

I am so damn sorry, Miss Crawford. "What did you realize?" he asked gruffly.

"That I had not lived, and I have no plans for my future. No hopes, no dreams, because I was led to believe because of my past...mistake, those things simply no longer existed for me. I am only four and twenty, and if I had died...I would have done so with many regrets."

Those aching words sliced him deep.

"I cannot *un-realize* it." Her voice had begun to shake. "And it is for that reason I am not as yet... fired." She appeared bright eyed and a little breathless. And teeth-achingly lovely, determined, and rebellious.

Bloody hell. He would never understand the reasoning of women as long as he lived. "I trust you will explain to my satisfaction."

She gave him a long, steady look. "Occupational hazard."

Sweet mercy.

"I was almost killed, my lord, and I cannot imagine any greater occupational hazard than that."

"I agree, that is why—"

"You *owe* me," she said in a rush. "You owe me all the experiences I wished for at the moment I thought my life would end before I…before I…"

Before she had lived. Her voice echoed with unfulfilled longings that she might never attain, and it struck him how forcefully the reminder must have been driven home yesterday.

Unfulfilled longings. A thing he could not truly understand. All his life, if he desired something, he worked toward it, even if others claimed it impossible. That word did not live within him, and he had many experiences to prove it. It was with a sense of bemusement he acknowledged the only thing he had ever denied himself after a craving had awoken was Miss Crawford herself.

And that was because he did not like the sudden chaos in his well-ordered life and that he could be so easily…distracted or be drawn to such an unusual creature. Miss Crawford braced as if she anticipated his gruff rejection or something derisive, but Simon was rooted by the look in her eyes. A knife had been pressed to her throat, the man holding it, his intention unknown but unquestionably dangerous. Forefront in her thoughts would have been her death…and biting fear. A carriage had hurtled along with her, jarring her about and bruising her shoulders and mottling them in those ugly colors.

It must have hurt like the devil, but she had not cried or screamed or descended into any sort of hysteria. Her bravery had carried her home, held up under his terse orders of termination, and even valiantly dealt with the pain of her bruises because she thought he had important work to do. She was brave and selfless.

In a word, Miss Wilhelmina Crawford was magnificent.

"Tell me what those thoughts were."

Her eyes widened. "All of them?"

"Yes."

"Before I do, you must understand that the…occupational hazard compensation I require for that most awful fright is that you assist me in making them come true."

Hell. "I will bear this in mind, Miss Crawford."

"My first thought was that I had never kissed a gentleman."

A primal surge of possessiveness struck his heart. "Never?"

"Aye."

"You eloped once, Miss Crawford."

Her eyes twinkled. "I was wise enough then to allow no liberties until I ensured I was secretly wed. Alas…there was no wedding night."

"The damn fool did not try to steal kisses?"

She shook her head slowly, her eyes twinkling. "The damn fool."

That softly mocking, yet amused whisper kissed over his skin, stirring his arousal. "I gathered you've crossed it off your list."

"Of course not, I was hardly satisfied."

He stilled. "I had not thought there was an issue, given how you clung to me, Miss Crawford."

Her breathing fractured, and a pretty flush of pink bloomed across her cheeks. Her eyes skipped over his face, searching every nuance of his expression. "Were *you* satisfied?"

And then he understood her lack of satisfaction came from the hunger that had been awakened for more before that very passionate embrace. They stared at each other, that awareness settling between them. She did not wait for his answer, but murmured, "I also want to eat Fry's chocolate cream bars. Lots of them."

"I've never had one," he said gruffly, the oddest feeling rising inside him to promise her a slice of the world.

Her lips parted, and she stared at him for a long time. "I want to fly a kite and feel the wind at my back as I race with it to make it soar into the sky."

A kite. How novel.

"I want to feel the spray of the ocean on my face... feel the sand between my toes, wade out into the water." She closed her eyes, lifted her chin, baring the delicate line of her throat to his gaze, her fingers fluttering to rest there. As if she imagined the droplets of water against her skin. "I want to eat ice cream."

A peculiar chord tugged inside of him. "It is criminal that you've never had ice cream, Miss Crawford. Simply criminal."

She lowered her lashes, as if she felt too exposed, and was hiding that raw hunger from his observation. In this moment he sensed she was a caged butterfly desperate to burst from its cocoon and spread its beautiful and glorious iridescent wings.

Her lush mouth curved, and her eyes snapped up and ensnared his. "I want more kisses, Simon. Lots more."

•••

Mina stared up at the earl, a frightful feeling of longing cascading through her. For a moment, it seemed as if he would yield to the impulse so clearly marked in his gaze. *Kiss me*, she silently entreated, wanting to feel alive. Her heartbeat danced at a swift tempo as she waited with aching anticipation. The earl mastered himself and stepped away. A soft pain of disappointment pierced her heart, and Mina wondered at her brazen attraction for him, that she would so ache for his caress and kisses.

Everything was forgotten as the earl shifted close, raising his hands to cup her cheeks. His touch was warm, reassuring, and felt so right. "I will join you."

His words sliced through her heart and settled deeply. "Truly?"

A charming smile touched his mouth. "Truly. Now get your cloak."

"My cloak?"

"Yes, and hurry."

Astonished, Mina opened the door and hastened up to her room, then gathered her cloak. Going over to the armoire, she retrieved her hat and fitted it atop her curls. She went back downstairs to find the earl awaiting her and the carriage being brought around. Mina frowned, however, it was with a sense of thrill and anticipation that she went outside in the brisk air, and allowed him to assist her up into the carriage.

Inside was pleasantly warm and she relaxed against the squabs, waiting for the earl to enter. After he spoke with the coachman and his tiger, he must have gone back inside, because when he entered he had a pistol and a walking cane with a hidden blade. Her heart lurched. "Are you anticipating danger, my lord?"

His mouth twitched at the corner. "I thought I was now Simon and you Mina?"

She stared at him, quite delighted. "We are."

"Good. I do not believe danger is ahead, as this trip is unplanned, nor are we heading to London."

"To where do we go, my lord?"

"To the seaside."

"In winter?"

"*Carpe diem*, Miss Crawford."

Mina lightly laughed, almost at a loss. "I would never imagine you a gentleman of impulse to so casually urge me to seize the day."

He stretched his legs before him and folded his arms across his chest. "I am a man of many facets."

She could not help the surge of curiosity about this man that went through her, and she recalled his earlier comment before she had unburdened on him. "By the by, why do you need to acquire charm? You are already a very handsome man."

"My grandmother does not think it enough."

"For what, if I might be bold enough to pry."

His brows lowered. "This is what you are truly worried about being bold with?"

Mina grinned. "I was being polite."

"She believes I need it for my future wife."

"You are to be married?"

"Yes."

She was considerably discomfited. "You are *en-gaged*?"

His piercing eyes gleamed, quite unnerving her. "Not as yet. There is no need to worry it will affect our kisses."

She sucked in a surprised breath. "Kisses?"

"I thought you said you wanted lots of them?"

"I…" She felt almost dispossessed of thought. "I had not realized you were of a mind to grant them."

"You implied that another gentleman might be on the end of your kisses. It is best I do not dwell on the murderous feelings I had at the thought of another putting his hands on you and falling at your feet as you allow him to ravish you," he said drolly.

Mina laughed, never imagining the man who had worn the fiercest of scowls for the last couple of weeks could be this earl. He seemed almost rakish…most devilish and charming. "I do not think your future bride would appreciate us sharing kisses."

"I hardly think she would mind," he said drily, "as I have not met this creature as yet."

Relief pierced her. Mina would not have kissed him again if he had been affianced. "It is rather astonishing we are casually discussing kisses."

"Hmm, I must also warn you that our kisses will never result in marriage for us," the earl murmured, those eyes intent on her face.

"I would never dream of it," she said lightly.

"Why not?"

"I…" She tucked a wisp of hair behind her ear. "I

am not a woman who can ever be married."

"A curious statement. Your scandal is mostly buried, and you are rather lovely."

Mina caught herself staring at him, lowered her eyes, and looked away briefly. "The very reasons you would not marry me, my lord—my lack of reputation and dowry and notable connections—are the same reasons another would not consider my hand."

"Many gentlemen might overlook such supposed flaws, but your implacable tone suggests it is firmly impossible."

That familiar ache of regret pierced her chest. "I have a secret, my lord, and that secret prevents me from ever stepping forward with another."

"I propose you are the only one who knows the secret."

"You mean to say I should lie?"

"I mean to say you should keep it to yourself. It is your own business."

"An enlightened perspective," she said with a small smile. "But my secret is also owned by another, and it irretrievably prevents me from marrying." *Again*.

He stared at her with piercing contemplation. "Is the owner another gentleman?"

"Yes," she murmured.

"Provide me his name and I shall ensure his demise."

A laugh escaped her. "I get the keenest sense you want to marry me off."

"It merely occurred to me you might have owned more dreams than ice cream, chocolate cream bars, and kisses. A husband, and children of your own, perhaps. Your past scandal would forever deny you those joys."

The carriage rocked and rumbled along the country road, and she could only helplessly stare at him. "Perhaps," she said softly, "I was the one responsible for my scandal, so I only dream of what I know is allowed. I do not think of husbands or children, my lord. Ever." Those dreams were now useless. *Through every fault of my own.*

No more, she thought, briefly closing her eyes. *What's done is done.* And she had promised herself only last night: no more regrets.

"I have read that it can be faked."

"What can be faked?"

"Your virginity, Miss Crawford."

She choked on the air. "My lord! I am scandalized."

He sent her a disgruntled look. "You only need a vial of chicken blood on your wedding night and—"

Her mirth cut him off, and his lips twitched.

"This conversation suggests that our common sense has been entirely defeated, my lord."

His eyes darkened with an emotion she could not fathom, but there was a dangerous beauty to that stare. "What did you think just now?"

"That I like your laugh. That I want to kiss you until you are soft and eager and helplessly weak with passion."

His stare dropped to her mouth, his desire to kiss her a tangible thing. Then the earl's lashes lowered, and when he glanced at her again, she saw no want, only curious indifference. How did he master his passions so effortlessly?

"There is a time for everything," he murmured, as if he had read her thoughts.

"I had always imagined passion to be spontaneous and incendiary," she mused softly. "Or so claimed all the romantic books I've read."

He made a low, curious sound, reached into his pocket, and pulled out a small book. "Like this?"

"I was wondering where I left it." Mina reached for her copy of *Persuasion* by Jane Austen. "Have you read it?"

He seemed surprised by the question.

"Or do you only read political books or those that highlight current social and economic crises?" At his arched brow, she said, "I saw the copy of *Oliver Twist*, and *Alton Locke* on your desk. I've read *Alton Locke* and found it quite despairing. The author beset his protagonist with too many vain longings and ambitions that were never fulfilled and worse, he died in the end."

"I believe Charles Kingsley's intention was to highlight the social injustice suffered by his protagonist. That his wild ambitions and expectations above those of a normal working-class man were experienced by many then in society and still today. While it is despairing, it is the reality of many."

Mina pushed back another willful wisp of hair behind her ear. "I understand this, however I would rather read a book where I am assured of a happy ending and that leaves me with a smile on my face. Reality is already far too bleak."

"We still have a way to go; let me hear your tale of a happy ending."

"You want…want me to read to you?" she stammered, feeling a bit silly at the anxiousness that seared her.

"Yes."

"Very well, I shall read one of my favorite stories to you."

He rested his head against the squabs, closing his eyes. With a smile, Mina opened the book and started to read. "Sir Walter Elliot, of Kellynch Hall, in Somersetshire, was a man who, for his own amusement, never took up any book but the Baronetage…"

CHAPTER NINE

The earl took her to Southend-On-Sea, a wonderful seaside resort that was made popular several years past by the visit of Princess Caroline of Brunswick. Living in Hertfordshire, Mina heard of it but had never taken a day to visit. A realization that seemed so silly now. Southend-On-Sea beach stretched for several miles along endless dark golden sands, with a wooden pier that seemingly ran never-ending out into the ocean. The sea was an icy blue-gray, moving in small frothy waves that dashed against the beach. It looked chilly and not very inviting but reached as far as she could see, where looming dark clouds hovered. Near to the pier was a railway station that appeared to have little to no passengers passing through today. Her boots sank into the wet sand as they strolled closer to the incoming waves.

"We are the only foolish ones by the sea today," she said, tugging her cloak tighter around her and peeking at the overcast sky.

"Nonsense. We are the only *brave* ones."

The sea breeze rolled over the land with a distinct nip, and the wind bracing her was fresh and invigorating. Unexpected delight cascaded over her senses. Mina held her arms open and turned her face to the sky. Though the rays of the sun were barely felt, it was still a glorious sensation. They strolled along the beach without speaking, each to his or her own thoughts, yet Mina felt contented.

Somehow, she had never realized how much she

held back from trying to live, always hesitating as a form of self-protection. A fear that she might encounter the bounder she had eloped with and had been forced to hit over the head with a chamber pot, grateful that it was one of the new enameled metal ones and so had not broken. The fear that she might venture to London and stir that old scandal and affect her brother's chances, fear that she might let loose that wild, irrepressible heart of hers once more and fall to an even greater ruin.

That fear was no longer in her heart, simply because she could have died that day.

Mina cast the earl a sidelong glance, noting that he seemed even younger than before, with no frowns of intense concentration upon his face. "Do you come here often, Simon?"

How odd it felt, his name upon her tongue.

"No. I've driven by but have never stopped."

That he would take time away from his work stunned her. "Why did you agree today?"

Silence lingered between them, and she wondered if he would answer.

"I thought you understood this was payment for the hazards you suffered while working for me. Yes," he said drolly. "You are still fired."

Mina laughed. "Am I truly?"

"Yes."

"You could have merely compensated me, Simon. There was no need for you to personally accompany me."

Say it, she silently entreated, wanting him to admit desiring to be with her as much as she wanted to be with him. He might appear indifferent and composed, but there were times she felt the burning heat of his regard.

"I am already to pay you an astronomical sum and still hire another secretary."

She faltered. "You are still to pay me?"

"Yes."

"I cannot take your charity, my lord," she said, her pride fiercely stung. "I will *not*. I shall earn that money fairly or not at all."

She looked away from his steady gaze, hating the ache of tears suddenly burning the back of her throat. Mina did not want his pity or charity. Never that.

Simon reached out and touched her chin, drawing her back to face him. "Very well, Miss Crawford, very well."

A breath shuddered from her. "Thank you."

"You should bear in mind you will be required to accompany me to town. You'll not hide from your scandal there."

His words were flat and implacable and the idea of being so exposed again scraped against her composure. "I am not afraid," she said staunchly, though her heart beat wildly inside her chest. "But my brother will need to accompany us, as a chaperone of sorts, to still those wagging tongues from sullying my reputation even further."

"Very well. The modiste I'd sent for in town should arrive tomorrow. You are to order ball gowns, at least six, new boots and dancing slippers—hats and gloves, riding habits, and day gowns. I've already sent to town an order for two new cloaks. If your pride still smarts at this, I will deduct the wardrobe from your salary."

"Not at all, these clothes are work expenses."

He chuckled and they continued strolling. Holding her cloak tighter, she went toward the beach, stopping when the water lapped at the tip of her boots. How she wished it were summer and she could walk barefoot and sink her toes in the sand.

"I believe I shall risk feeling the waters on my toes," she said suddenly.

"It is cold, Miss Crawford."

She wrinkled her nose. "I daresay if you survived a dip of your body in a lake, without any illness, my feet and my person might very well survive this." Mina stooped down and nudged off her boots, revealing her bare toes. Mina yelped at the coldness of the sand and stones. *Good gracious.*

"Where are your stockings?"

Suddenly, she felt embarrassed. Still, she did not quibble. "They had holes." A low rumble filled the air, and she glanced over at the pier, wondering if a train had pulled into the station.

"It's thunder."

She snapped her head skyward, alarmed to feel a drop of icy rain on her cheek. "It is about to rain?"

Mina was not entirely prepared for how the sky opened and immediately doused them in rain. She shrieked, and the earl grabbed her hands and sprinted with her toward the carriage thankfully parked close by.

"My boots!"

"Leave them."

Something pierced one of her feet and she stumbled with a cry. Simon glanced down and, to her shock, grabbed her about the waist and tossed her over his shoulder before breaking into a run.

Thankfully she had not worn the small bustle to widen the skirt of her gown. The speed at which he moved with her weight was impressive, if not jarring, and before she could even protest, she was slung down and caught perfectly against his chest, then urged up inside the carriage.

The earl said something to the coachman she could not discern, then hauled himself inside. His hair was damped, and the man was hardly out of breath.

"Good, you are barely wet. The heat from the warming pans will provide enough—"

Mina laughed, the light, airy sound echoing in the carriage as it rumbled away. "You are utterly deranged, and I would never have discovered it if…" She swiped away a trickle of water that ran from her hair to her cheek. "Even if all of London had witnessed it, they would still not believe that Lord Creswick tossed a lady over his shoulder like a barbarian. We even ran, leaving my boots!"

"I shall replace them," he said, his blue eyes gleaming. "Now let me see your foot."

Said toes reflexively curled on the carriage floor. Taking a deep breath, she lifted the skirt of her dress slightly, baring her ankles to his gaze.

"It was the bottom of your feet that were hurt, Miss Crawford."

She did not remind him to call her Mina, suspecting he reverted to formality whenever she tossed him into disorder.

"Was it your ankle that was hurt?"

"No."

Holding his regard, she lifted her legs and placed her foot in his lap. First Simon removed his gloves, then, retrieving a handkerchief from his pocket, he dusted the sand from between her toes and under her feet. She wriggled them and he looked at her. "I am extraordinarily ticklish. A thing my brother in the past took fiendish advantage of."

"There is a red bruise, but the skin did not break."

The earl pressed the spot almost at the center of her sole and she winced. It was rather tender. He did not release her but lightly encircled her ankles.

"Tell me, Mina, do you only require kisses?"

Something unknown trembled inside her. "No."

The elegant ridge of his cheekbone seemed to sharpen. "Good. I was remiss in my earlier statement. We will be lovers."

She felt an odd sense of fear, then scandalized delight at her daring, anticipation, nerves, and such hunger trembling and wrenching her in different directions. "We will be lovers," Mina whispered, holding that steady, unfathomable gaze.

He slid teasing fingers over her ankles and up to her shin.

Oh God. She attempted to withdraw her foot from his grasp.

"Stay."

He leaned forward, reached for her, and slipped his hand around her hips, drawing her onto his lap. Mina gasped, grabbing his shoulders as for a wild moment she thought she would have fallen from his grasp. He held her to him, pushing her skirts and petticoats upward, urging her knees to bracket his hips. The position was scandalous and evocative. Yet Mina did not think about it; she merely gripped his shoulders and pressed her mouth to his, then stilled.

Simon cupped her cheeks in his hand, and slanted his mouth over hers, taking her soft kiss to one of deep intimacy. He didn't just move his lips against hers, he nibbled and stroked, burning her with desire. Their motions did not have the ragged and furious passion of their first kiss, yet it felt more intimate and deeply pleasurable.

"God, you make a man forget his name," he said against her mouth.

Mina lifted her hand and touched his cheek, drew her finger slowly down his jaw and across his lips. She felt so sensual and adventurous—no longer a girl hiding her passionate heart but satisfying the cravings in her soul.

That these cravings should emerge with such depth for this man still left her with an odd feeling of uncertainty. Holding her stare, he slid his hand up her calf and around to her thighs, then up until he found the wet folds of her soft sex through her drawers. They both stilled, and her throat worked on a swallow. The tension building between them was thick and heated.

"Arch your neck," he murmured.

She complied, and he licked along her throat, his teeth scraping over her wildly flickering pulse.

"I have never wanted to linger over the taste of a woman's skin before." Another kiss, a mere brush of his mouth up to the underside of her chin.

Mina no longer felt warm but burned with a delicious fire.

She clasped his shoulder as that lone finger parted her folds and rubbed her with arousing delicacy. Then he stroked deeper inside her body, drawing forth an alarming wetness. A wicked kind of pleasure darted low in her belly and a whisper of a moan left her lips.

"I have never wanted to feel this tightness on my finger before and to imagine it might be my cock that is here."

Oh God.

He slipped another finger inside her sex. A cry of pleasure escaped her, and he caught it with his mouth, kissing her with ravenous greed.

"I have never wanted to stretch a woman here before," he purred against her lips, "so that she might feel more pleasure and anticipate the full feel of me when I am here."

Mina grew alarmingly wetter.

"Am I...I..." she stammered, her face burning.

"Hmm?" He kissed her mouth, a chaste brush that stood out in provocative contrast against the fingers he thrust in and out of her. The effect was sublimely provocative.

"How prettily you blush," he murmured with sensual provocation. "Tell me, Miss Crawford."

The sensual, teasing way he drawled her name sent another wild burst of heat to flow through her. His thumb found her nub of pleasure and glided against it. She jerked her hips, unintentionally impaling herself more on his fingers.

Mina moaned. "Should I be this wet?"

"Yes," Simon hissed, delicately rubbing over her sex, coaxing her to open like a flower about to bloom, then he sank a third finger inside her body, stretching her and stinging her with erotic pleasure and a bite of pain. "I never knew the delight I would feel to touch these soft, soft curls between your legs. This wetness... I have never wanted to taste it on my tongue before. I have never expected that lust could feel this exquisite."

He took one of her hands and put it between them, so her fingers curled over his manhood through his trousers. His mouth drifted from hers, touched the curve of her ear softly, tracing the shape with his lips. "I never imagined I'd feel my blood beat so violently through my cock."

Mina whimpered as arousal pierced her belly with frightening intensity. Then only silence lingered as his mouth ate at hers with ravaging greed and his fingers stroked her to a feverish pitch. Her breasts ached to the point where the simplest press against his chest abraded the sensitive tips of her nipples bound behind the tightly laced corset. His thumb glided over her clitoris, rubbing, pinching, until she was a trembling mess. Mina pulled her mouth from his and buried her face against his throat, trapping his scent deep inside her lungs. Her arousal was so intense that her body trembled, her heart hammered, and soft whimpers tore from her. She bit into his neckcloth, squeezing his shoulders as the piercing pressure in her belly tightened.

Simon hugged her even closer against his chest, driving his finger even deeper into her sex. Mina bit the cravat harder as her body shattered, and she convulsed in his arms, pleasure destroying her. She brushed her fingers over his nape and his shoulders trembled. It was then she realized this sensual power went both ways—that he could shake with desire for her, too. Mina curled a lock of his hair between her fingers.

His thumb circled her nub and she jerked, that

spot so sensitive, she almost hurt. He did it again and she moaned weakly as heat stirred again. And despite that aching sensitivity, her whole body seemed to reach for him.

He drew a deep, shuddering breath. "I am very tempted to take you now," he said, his voice rough with need.

She waited with a sort of breathless anticipation, but he only removed his fingers from her body, fished a handkerchief from his top pocket, and cleaned them. A frightful flush went through her body to see the wetness glistening on his fingers. Seeing her reaction, a low, sensual chuckle came from him, and he kissed her hard.

"I do not want to fall with child," she whispered against his mouth, knowing it to be a grim possibility for women who dared.

A hunger leaped in his eyes before his expression shuttered. He pressed the flat of his palm against her belly. "I would take care of you and any child of mine."

"I will be no man's mistress, even for the powerful and influential Lord Creswick," she said with caustic bite.

He was perfectly silent for a moment, a tiny crease between his brows. "I will protect you. There will be risk of children once we are lovers. You have no need to worry about an illegitimate child."

Suddenly their torrid encounter did not seem so passionate or romantic. Mina pushed from his lap and sat in the seat in front of him, painfully aware of the silence shimmering between them.

Be careful. Do not fall in love with this man, she reminded herself.

Brushing aside the carriage window, she peered outside, lest he saw the emotions in her eyes. They were nearing his estate and were already driving through lands he owned. She could feel the earl's regard, and when she glanced at him, he was considering her with a deeply enigmatic stare. He did not attempt to fill in the silence. The way he watched her, with such slow intensity, as if he was trying to dissect her, was nerve-wracking.

"You are staring, Simon."

"I know."

The soft heat in her cheeks had become a blaze. "Do you think me too wanton?"

"Would you care if I did?"

Her heart felt as if it was being ripped from her chest. "No." *Perhaps*.

A slow grin curved his mouth. "I think you honest. It is a rare quality in my dealings. I like it. I like you."

Mina returned his smile. *I like you, too.*

"You've never had a man," he said unexpectedly and knowingly. "Your response seemed to shock you."

"Perhaps I have, but he was a bumbling fool," she said mockingly.

"A sobering thought." Simon canted his head slightly. "No. I am your first," he said with a touch of dangerous arrogance, his eyes gleaming with rich and challenging humor.

Somehow, she did not want to give him the satisfaction of an answer. He closed his eyes, and she studied him unabashedly, knowing she would have to be extraordinarily cautious with her heart even as she tumbled into a magnificent affair with this man.

• • •

Mina's eyes remained heavy-lidded with arousal, her lips red and swollen, her cheeks flushed. A pounding ache still lingered in Simon's cock, which had hardened into a pike and strained against his trousers. His arousal had yet to subside, and he'd be damned if he took her inside a carriage. She deserved a soft, well-padded bed, silk sheets against her back, and a skilled lover who would bring her pleasure. His disinterest in bed matters before would return to haunt him. He had a vague memory of a lady crying out beneath him, with too much thrashing about, praising his stamina, before he had found release.

Hell.

That was bloody well not enough. He wanted to delight her, to revel in her sweet cries, to enslave her senses with decadent pleasure. Like just now. Lust had owned him and urged him on, and she had rewarded him with her wild and passionate response. The whimpers she'd made against his mouth undid him and everything—that elusive scent and tart yet sweet taste of her lips, felt trapped under his skin.

Feeling his stare, she once more glanced at him before lowering her eyes, her dark lashes curving against her cheeks. It was quite astonishing, the way she captured his regard, until it wasn't. Simon accepted then she would always affect him so, and it might never leave. Even after he'd had her over and over.

I'll be no man's mistress.

When she'd said that, he hadn't argued, for that was not the role he wanted her to occupy. Simon's own reasons for why he was with her at this moment even eluded him. Yes, he wanted her, and yes, he had decided that he would take her to his bed. That he had felt a violent jealousy at the idea of another man touching her made little sense to what he knew of himself. That he abandoned his work for the day when the date for convening parliament drew closer made even less sense. But there was a need inside him. To hold her and provide comfort, to shield her from the terror she had experienced, and to bring this precise look to her eyes.

Soft satiation and contentedness.

Yet he acknowledged his desire to provide this wasn't altogether sensible, and that he could lack a true sense of understanding of his own motivations annoyed Simon. In silence, he helped her fix her clothes, then settled back against the squabs. A quick peek through the carriage curtains revealed they had arrived back at Norbrook Park. The carriage clamored to a stop in their forecourt, and he descended and held out his hand to her.

She shot him a startled look of enquiry, then began to descend the steps.

"You are without boots. I will carry you inside."

Her head came up. She scowled at him. "You will not!"

"The ground is graveled," he began in a tone of acute boredom, not understanding this sudden burst of missish manners.

"Your staff will not see me in your arms." She held his eyes a moment, and then her gaze slid away.

"The footman and coachman saw me carrying you from the rain at the beach, Miss Crawford."

A faint color rose in her cheekbones. "That was an entirely different situation justifiable by the torrential rain. Now it will only give rise to unflattering speculation, and we both know the power of servants' gossips."

"Very well."

Her chin lifted high, she gingerly walked on the stones, wincing when they dug into her tender soles. Yet she did not falter or complain. The butler opened the door and wisely made no comment on her bare toes and their damp clothes. Once inside, she sighed as the heat enveloped her.

"Will you join me for dinner, Miss Crawford?" he asked, careful to maintain their formality in front of the servants. "Perhaps afterward you might continue your reading of *Persuasion*."

"Yes, my lord."

"I look forward to it."

Then she hurried away and up the winding staircase to her chamber.

Simon followed at a slower pace, smiling when he saw her twirling atop the landing and hugging her arms to her chest.

How incredibly fascinating you are, Miss Crawford.

What was even most astounding was that he felt the keen sensation as if he were coming alive for the first time in his life—for a woman who would only be a fleeting presence in his life. Would he remember her years from now, that he had met a lovely girl named Miss Wilhelmina Crawford? *Most unlikely.*

The image of how she had looked by the seaside as she lifted her face to the sky and inhaled seared through his thoughts. That wide, happy smile that had curved her mouth for such a simple thing. The dark passions in her when she'd unraveled in his arms. The fierce pride when she'd refused his presumed charity.

Or perhaps I might very well be haunted by memories of you.

CHAPTER TEN

The following morning, Mina hurried down the staircase and to the office, appalled that she had overslept. After dining with the earl last evening, she had spent almost four hours with him in his library, taking turns reading *Persuasion*, discussing the merits of Anne Elliot allowing others to influence her against marrying Navy Captain Frederick Wentworth. Of course, the earl had thought it fit to point out the fickleness of supposed love, with her arguing that it was hard to decide to live with another when family and friends were so against the union. Mina had only gone to bed at minutes after one, with a vow that she would be ready for work by six in the morning.

With a groan, she glanced at the clock in the hallway. It was already nine, and she had completed her morning toiletries as fast as possible with the help of her maid.

"Miss Crawford," the butler said, bowing to her. "I am to inform you that Lord Creswick is not at home."

It burned on her tongue to ask about his whereabouts, but she only nodded. "I see. Thank you, Milton."

"The earl informed me that you might oversleep, and breakfast was kept warming for you, Miss Crawford. You may make your way to the breakfast hall."

"Thank you."

After eating her fill of poached eggs, thinly sliced hams, kippers in cream sauce, and a few pieces of butter toast, Mina went into the office and answered some letters on the earl's behalf. The door to his inner office tugged at her attention and lowering the quill, she rose and went over. Opening the door, she examined the smaller inner sanctum that until now she had not dared to enter alone. It was only one story high but was paneled in the warm cedar wood, which she now knew was used in many of the rooms on the ground floor of the house. It had one window that looked out on the gardens, but from which the lake could not be seen. The same blue-and-gold drapes were open. Mina suspected that it was the original document room of the house, as one wall held shelves laden with scrolls, ledgers, and maps of some great antiquity. It was furnished with a smaller desk and three chairs.

A knock on the main door to the office sounded, and she hurried outside to open the door. Milton held out a silver salver. "A letter arrived for you, Miss Crawford."

"Thank you!" It could only be from Anthony, whom she had written to last week. Mina walked over to the sofa by the windows, sat, and opened his letter.

Dearest Mina,

Forgive me for only just writing since I've arrived in London. I received your letter and let me hastily assure you that I am in good health, and you need not worry. My reception in town was not as bad as I imagined. It seems the Duke of Beswick and the Earl of Stannis believe it was me who bested Creswick in fencing. I offered them my apology, which they accepted, and Lord Stannis has even invited me out for a night about town with his set. I am mindful of his "rake about town" reputation and will not be too hasty.

Mina, thank you for fighting in my stead. I admit I would never have won without your timely intervention.

That you are now living beneath the earl's roof does fill me with a measure of alarm, but I am trusting your judgment. I would caution you there is a rumor being spread about town that he is soon to marry, though society is not yet aware who is the fortunate lady. I know your adventurous spirit, Mina, and I caution you to not lose your heart to the damn man.

I have also met the most delightful girl. She is an American from New York, and her father is a shipping magnate. It is dashedly uncomfortable that she is an heiress, for I do not want her to believe my pursuit is because of her wealth, though I painfully admit it is a factor. Her name is Miss Rebecca Ashley, and she is one and twenty. Her manners are most charming, Mina, I believe you will like her.

I have been about Town, and I have not seen that wretched man you mentioned. I do not think should you travel to town, that you will encounter him. Should you do so and he accosts you, I shall plant him a sound facer. Rest assured I will protect you, Mina.

By the by, the air is electrified with talks of the possibility of a reform bill going through and there is discontent in the streets. There was a recent protest near Hyde Park, however it was hurriedly quelled by the police.

I miss your presence and I look forward to seeing you, Min.

Yours,

Anthony, Viscount Crawford.

Mina lowered the letter, stood, and went to her desk. She would need to reply right away. She sat in the comfortable chair with a soft sigh. What should she really say to him? That she was taking life more seriously or that she was planning to live each day as if it might be the last, with a grand adventurous spirit guiding her?

Dearest Anthony,
I am so pleased that you met a lovely girl and that you own genuine admiration and affection for her. I would urge you to not lie to her, even if it is by omission.

A peculiar fright pierced her heart, and her breath shuddered from her.

Mina had not told the earl or anyone the full truth of her elopement scandal. She still recalled that sage advice from her father, as he had hugged her in his arms, and she sobbed out her heart to him.

Tell no one of this, my sweet girl, not even Anthony. Promise me this. I will fix it.

Papa had done his best to help her in putting out the fires of rumors, but he had not freed her of that bounder. Then Papa had died only a few months later. There had been a time she fretted over it having been her actions that had caused his heart to give out. Her papa had scolded her and assured her he was aware of the malady for the last few years but had kept them in the dark. Then he had died only a few days after that admission, tossing them into grief and uncertainty about their futures.

Mina smiled as she thought of the earl and his lack of interest in her secret. He did not even seem to care about her scandal, elevating him in her thoughts above everyone else in society. Still, a sense of discomfort gripped her that there was so much more he did not know.

Mina, stop it, she silently berated herself. The earl was to be her lover. Though they had this burning attraction and even ease of bantering between them, she knew whatever they had would only be temporary. The earl himself owned that belief, and it was not due to her past scandal. Even if she could marry, the earl would never consider Mina with her lack of connections and reputation. He had too many fine diamonds to choose from to lower his expectations.

Mina briefly closed her eyes. *I know we could only ever be temporary, so why dream of impossible things?*

Pleasure and loving could be powerful and consuming, but eventually burn out. Then they would part. An unknown sensation wrenched tightly in the vicinity of her heart, and she pressed a palm over the top of her breast.

"There is no need for me to complicate our attachment with silly musings," she whispered. "The earl is not entitled to my secrets, nor am I to his."

Gripping the quill, she looked outside the windows, pleased to see the sky no longer had that bloated gray appearance, and the sun had peeked brightly from the clouds. Taking a breath, she returned to her letter.

I daresay you should inform Miss Ashley of your dire financial straits before you marry her, not after. It would also be a very unpleasant experience for her should she hear the rumors about town and not from you, Anthony.

I shall arrive in town soon with the earl, perhaps as early as next week. I confess there is some degree of anxiety in my heart, but so many years have passed since I was last in London, I doubt anyone would recall that I had a failed elopement. The friends I made that year have long disappeared, and perhaps I might meet new people now, but it would be a vain hope to think that my scandal will not re-emerge, or that it will not tear those new friends from me. My standing is very precarious in society, and it might only take the slightest of incidents to dig up my past, so I must be cautious in my connections.

Lord Creswick wishes for me to accompany him to balls and certain outings. I wonder at his motivations for this, as I cannot fathom how my presence at any social events might help his efforts.

It is alarming to hear of protests in the streets, but I cannot regret them happening, as I feel it is the most profound means our disfranchised citizens have to express their discontent and let their woes be publicly heard.

By the by, Lord Stannis is a reprobate. Be careful he does not lead you to acquire a reputation as a rake about town!

Yours,
Mina Crawford.

She folded the letter, slipped it in an envelope and franked it, leaving instructions with a servant to have it delivered to London posthaste. Then Mina ventured outside as a carriage clattered up the long driveaway leading to the earl's home. She watched as it drew into the forecourt, and a petite lady with dusky skin and vibrant black hair descended from the carriage.

The lady was impeccably dressed in a charcoal gray suit and cutaway jacket, trimmed in black braid over a high-necked white blouse with the effect of a cravat at the neck. The jacket's sleeves were three-quarter length and allowed the full sleeves of the blouse to reach to the wrists with lace-edged cuffs. It was definitely a professional outfit, that complimented the lady's vivid coloring. She had managed to achieve professional, stylish, and rather sensual all in the same outfit. Mina was quietly impressed and wished she had the confidence of this lady to wear her clothes with such panache.

She glanced Mina up and down, a moue forming on her lips, her brown eyes a bit reserved.

"Miss Wilhelmina Crawford?"

That jolted her. "Who might you be?"

"I am Miss Danielle Stanton. The earl has sent me down to make you beautiful," she said with an accent Mina could not place. She strolled round Mina, as if she was inspecting a thoroughbred mare.

"Oh, dear, now that will not do at all. It is totally old-fashioned and does not flatter your figure at all. What you are wearing is an offense, simply dreadful. I now understand the earl's concern. The sooner I take you in hand the better, there's no time to be lost."

Mina chuckled. "I gather you are the famous and temperamental modiste."

The lady lifted her chin quite arrogantly. "Yes. I have been paid a most handsome sum to provide you with a new wardrobe in a week! I tell him it is not enough time, and he merely tosses more money at me.

So we must see it done. Everyone in my shop will work on your clothes around the clock for the next week, and when we have finished, Miss Crawford, you will be arrayed *most* splendidly."

Mina waved her hands for the lady to precede her inside and went with Miss Stanton through the door the butler held open. Mina had mentioned to the earl that she could simply visit London and make her purchases from Bainbridge's departure store. He had merely fixed her with his enigmatic and slightly derisive stare.

Once inside, the butler led them to a large drawing room, and Miss Stanton promptly got down to business measuring Mina. She informed Mina that she was not a fan of the very wide bustles that the lady's magazine showed to be the current rage. The lady seemed to be more her personal dresser than anything else, making a notation in her small notebook to procure silk stockings, chemisettes, ribbons, lace shawls, and parasols. Her ballgowns were to be made from silk, brocade, and lace of the finest quality with the style and cut *à la princesse* with broad sashes of lace and ribbon to start from the front of the waist and form a large bow on the back.

Mina endured the many measurements and breathed a sigh of relief when Miss Stanton finished and made her departure. Shortly after, a cobbler called and stated he was there to take her order for shoes, boots, and slippers. Mina was astonished, for surely she could make those purchases in town from Harrods. She was to have a close-fitting, ankle-high boot for everyday wear made with kid leather. Evening shoes with heels, at least three pairs were to be made, and black satin riding boots.

Mina hardly knew what to think about the earl's effort on her wardrobe. It felt as if he went beyond the bounds of what an employer would do for his secretary. His keen attention to ensuring that she was arrayed beautifully and with comfort brought a rush of pleasure to her heart.

Simon, I vow to repay your unmatched kindness.

Mina had luncheon outside in the gazebo near the lake, basking in the rare, pleasant weather, and then went inside to read for the rest of the day. There was very little to do with the earl not firing dictation her way or demanding she pen a letter immediately. The pace was much slower, and that familiar boredom crept over her senses.

As she left the library at ten that evening, the rattle of a carriage drew up the driveaway. She smiled, and a sigh of relief left her. It was then Mina acknowledged she had been worried about his safety, those men who had accosted their journey an ever-present shadow in her thoughts.

She went up the stairs and into her chamber, smothering a yawn behind her hands. Padding over to the dressing table, she unpinned her hair, allowing it to cascade from her shoulders down to her back. She rang for the servant who quickly assisted her out of her gown, two layers of petticoats, and the small bustle. Mina breathed a sigh of relief when the maid unhooked the tightly fitted corset and rotated her shoulders. She took her well-worn but comfortable cotton nightgown from the armoire and slipped it on over her head. Mina lay on the bed and drew the covers up to her chin as a knock sounded on the door.

She sat up, gripping the edges of the sheet below her, her heart pounding a sudden harsh beat. Mina had not thought the earl would come to her tonight. Pushing off the bed, she took a few steps before pausing, laughing a bit shakily to see that her fingers trembled. Gathering her equanimity, she hurried to the door, opened it wide, and allowed the earl to enter.

She closed the door, turned around, and leaned against it. The earl appeared coolly remote until their gazes met. Like an instant flame, soft want stirred low in her belly. The light from the gaslamp caught and highlighted the savage beauty of his features. The harsh flatness about his mouth lessened as his lips curved in a smile, until only the piercing intensity in his blue eyes remained. Her throat grew thick with longing, and she almost reached for him.

The unfathomable force which always seemed to tug her to him terrified her, for it hinted that she might make herself and her heart too vulnerable to this man. Even now, a sense of too feminine frailty cascaded over her senses at the way he stared at her.

I want to consume you, that look said. Mina had only ever seen that intensity when he dictated to her with words that pierced with their power and intent.

"Ghastly," he muttered. "Do remind me to send a message to Miss Stanton tomorrow to provide you with newer nightdresses."

Mina sniffed. "I am certain you did not come into my chamber to disparage my nightgown."

"It was not to ravish you, either, so wipe that look from your eyes," he said caustically.

"I am not afraid," she gasped, then smiled.

"Perhaps a bit anxious."

He closed the distance between them to press his mouth to hers, a soft kiss of reassurance. Mina sighed into that embrace, leaning against him, and responding with soft passion. Before heat could kindle between them, Simon pulled away. "It is rather interesting I missed your presence for the day. I have never endured this concept of missing another before."

"Welcome to humanity, my lord."

Mina smiled when he fixed her with his unflinching stare.

She touched his mouth with two of her fingers. "You went to London."

"Yes."

"And you are back in one piece."

"There might not be another attempt. An investigation suggests those fools were desperate robbers. I am also aware that could be a story to persuade me to relax my guard. Still, the bill has garnered far more support than anticipated. Whoever was foolish enough to attack me, if they were indeed political rivals, would be idiotic to continue, as they might now need to murder at least a dozen peers of the realm to do any sort of damage."

"I am relieved to hear it, but promise me you will be careful."

"I am always careful and armed. I trust few, and I have many spies about town keeping me appraised of any whispers of nefarious plots."

"Spies?"

His mouth curved upward. "Aye. In the seedy underbelly of London *and* in drawing rooms."

"Drawing rooms?" she asked with a light laugh.

"You've invaded others' households?"

"With a few well-placed and well-paid maids, footmen, and coachmen."

"*Shameless*," she teased.

"A major part of political life is played out in ballrooms, drawing rooms, and the secret places some gentlemen travel. We must have ears and eyes in all places, hmm?"

As if he could not help himself, he kissed her mouth again.

"So you had a good day," she whispered, wanting to wrap her arms around him and just hold him to her.

The warm rush of his breath touched her skin. "I met with Mr. Headley and a few compatriots. We argued politics, drank whisky, and smoked cheroots. All in all, a good day." His mouth curved in another faint smile. "I brought you this."

She couldn't help the way her lips curled upward with delight. "Fry's chocolate cream," she murmured, reaching out to pluck it from his fingers. A sense of thrill went through her, and she tore off the paper wrapper and immediately bit into the treat. The flavors exploded on her tongue, delighting her. "Oh, my, this *is* wonderful."

"Are you to share a bite?" Creswick asked, regarding her with a little amusement.

"It depends, my lord," she said after swallowing. "Did you purchase only one chocolate bar or several of them?"

"I got you a box full."

Delight pierced her. "A large box or a tiny box?"

"A distinction that greatly matters, I see."

Mina smiled up at him and held out the chocolate

bar. "I can afford to be generous, then, even if it is a small box."

He took a bite, slowly chewing. "The taste is interesting."

She took another bite. "I want to see the box and count every single bar. I might perhaps eat a second one now. I do feel famished."

"Greedy."

Mina nodded shamelessly, and he smiled, stealing her breath with the beauty of it.

"I have much reading to do, Miss Crawford, so I shall bid you good night."

It was then she noted he held four books in his left hand. Seeing her stare, he held them up. "Books on the sensual arts so that when we come together, it is wonderful, hmmm?"

Mina could scarcely find breath. "You worry you might not be wonderful?"

His eyes gleamed with a provocative light. "I thought I was in control. The violence of feelings that have crept up on me tells me if I am not careful, I will mount you like a beast and have my wicked way with you. While I believe I would derive immense pleasure, I cannot say the same for you."

Mina could only stare at him in silent surprise, wondering at the heat twisting through her at the idea of him falling atop her and ravishing her. The earl prowled toward her and dipped, his lips drifting over her temple in the barest caress.

"Sleep well, Miss Crawford."

Then he vanished from her room, leaving that mixture of helpless want, delight, and the fear that she might already be sliding too deep.

CHAPTER ELEVEN

Simon had always had a talent for recalling with perfect clarity almost everything that he read. Nothing, however, had ever tormented his senses quite like the erotic literature he'd been reading since last evening. Closing the last book which had many graphic illustrations, he leaned back in his chair, staring outside the windows. It seemed that the simple act of lovemaking could involve many ways and techniques that he had never before considered.

The door to his office opened without a knock or an announcement, and the Duke of Beswick strolled inside. He had clearly told the butler not to bother to announce him, and as Beswick strolled over to the tray of decanters and poured himself a glass of whisky, it appeared he felt entitled to treat the house as if it was his own.

"Beswick," Simon greeted without standing. "What brings you to Hertfordshire?"

"An irate husband who found me in his wife's chamber," he said with an air of disgruntlement. "The man's anger astounds me. All of society knows he has neglected his wife for that low-born actress of his who already has two of his bastards." His green eyes glared at his whisky as if it was at fault for the cuckolded husband being irate at discovering his wayward wife with himself in *flagrante delicto*.

The duke was five years older than Simon and should have known better than to tup the wife of another peer. Beswick looked both peeved and somewhat embarrassed. His normally clear complexion was flushed red and he seemed like he had dressed in a hurry and done nothing to rectify his disarray.

"Ah, we speak of Lord Ballentine, a man whose support we desperately need when the bill is introduced," Simon remarked.

The duke scrubbed a hand over his face. "Hell! I was not thinking."

"Fix it, Beswick," he growled.

The duke nodded, then pierced Simon with a far-too-carnal look. "Did you know you have a luscious beauty outside, running across the lawns with hair like fire and sunset flying a kite? Good God, man, the image was so striking I stood and watched her for several minutes. I believe I have found my next mistress."

"Have you?" Simon asked with dangerous softness.

The duke dealt him an arrested stare and cleared his throat. "If the lady is already spoken for, I—"

"The lady is my secretary, Miss Crawford. See that you treat her with the utmost respect."

"Oh, I will," Beswick said with a suggestive sneer, "I will respect her pleasure and—"

"You will lose the hand that you touch her with," Simon murmured, as if they discussed the weather. "And I do not speak metaphorically."

"What if she welcomes my advances?" the duke said with smug assurance.

Simon allowed his mouth to curve into a small smile. "You'll still lose it."

Green eyes narrowed on him. "By God, you are entirely serious."

"I am always serious when it comes to Miss Crawford."

Beswick seemed not to know what to make of his response and Simon did not believe he owed one of his longest friends an explanation. If he declared that Mina was off-limits, then he should simply accept that. "The House convenes in two days. I will be coming to town tomorrow."

"Alone?"

"My secretary will be accompanying me."

Beswick seemed to mull this over for a minute, pinning Simon with a puzzling stare. "There is a rumor about town that you intend to marry soon."

"That rumor is correct."

"You are not the kind of man to have a mistress and a wife."

"Once again, you are correct."

The duke's eyes widened. "Is it Miss Crawford you plan to marry?"

"Of course not. I leave it up to my grandmother to select the perfect candidate. It matters not to me who will become my countess."

"A bit cold-blooded of you, don't you think, Creswick?"

Simon paused. "No, my grandmother understands the kind of lady needed to walk by my side."

"There are many talks that you could position yourself to become Prime Minister in a few years. You will all but need to marry a paragon," Beswick said drily.

An argument many had brought to him, but Simon was not yet certain he wanted to pursue such a path. "Let's discuss the salient points of the bill, not my eventual marriage alliance."

They went down to business, discussing the tensions in London and what it might mean for the country should the reform bill be tossed out. Emotions were already running high and hot, with protests happening all across England, Wales, and even in Edinburgh. Simon and the duke went over the clauses in the bill which were likely to cause the most controversy and what compromises could be made to bring more members of both Houses of Parliament to assent.

They did not speak for long, as Beswick was eager to return to the railway station and take the mere thirty-minute train ride back to town. The duke left with the promise that he would somehow fix his conflict with Lord Ballentine.

There was much work to be done, yet Simon found himself drawn to the windows, his eyes searching for Miss Crawford. He wanted to know if she enjoyed the majestic kite he'd had delivered to her from London. He recalled the delight on her face, which warmed his chest. She had invited him to venture out with her, and he had reluctantly declined. Miss Crawford hadn't pouted, merely grinned and hurried away.

Flying a kite.

So simple, yet she found it a joy. Acting on the need urging him on, he went outside and looked for her. After several minutes of walking around the estate, he realized she was nowhere to be found. Calling for his stallion, he rode along the lanes, directing his horse to the eastern lawns of the rolling estate.

It was her hair that snagged his attention. A flash of fire streaming behind her as she sprinted across the lawns, chasing the kite soaring through the sky. He had a moment of terrible weakness, a too deep longing welling in his gut, and it was all for her. Urging his stallion into a gallop, he rode toward her. The retaining strings were no longer in her hands, and they danced and bobbed in the air as the wind soared the kite higher and farther away. As he neared her, he saw that she wore male trousers, a vest, and a fitted jacket. He slowed his horse to trot beside her.

"You'll not catch up to it."

She cast him a dazzling smile. "Perhaps not. The fun is in the chase, my lord."

The sun peeked through the clouds, splashing a warm golden glow over her rosy cheeks. Her green eyes seemed brighter…happier.

"We could chase it together," he offered, surprising himself.

"That is a capital idea."

Miss Crawford reached up her hand to him, and he hauled her atop his horse so that she sat before him and astride. She wriggled against him, trying to get a comfortable seat herself, and then with a sigh she relaxed against him. Clicking his tongue, they rode away, keeping pace with the kite.

"Why did you let it get away?"

She laughed, the sound sinking deep inside of him. "I wanted to see how fast it would fly without me holding it back."

He rested the top of his chin on her head, inhaling the rose and honeysuckle scents coming from her hair deeply into his soul.

"I never dreamed the day would have been so windy or that I would not be able to catch back the strings."

"And your idea was to chase it?"

"Yes."

"That kite might never stop."

"Wouldn't that be lovely," she whispered wistfully. "That it would always soar free over the oceans and continent, exploring the world."

"You have a desire to travel?"

"Don't we all? There is a vast world out there to explore."

"I suppose there is a traveler in all of us."

For a moment they both stared up at the overcast sky, watching the large blue and yellow kite dance in lazy swirls.

"Have you ever flown one?" she asked.

"No. I did not play much as a child."

She twisted around in the saddle, craning her neck to see him.

"You should be looking at the kite, Miss Crawford."

Her eyes twinkling, she leaned in and kissed his lips in a quick peck before turning forward. He wanted to cup her cheeks and drive his tongue deep into her mouth, kissing her until she was breathless with want, and then he would drive his cock into her warm willing body. *Bloody hell*. It was hard to keep his concentration when she was this close to him and smelling so wonderful.

"I can hear your heart beating…so fast and hard."

"You did kiss me just now."

"That little peck has you rattled?"

A rough sound caught in his throat. "I might very well toss you off my horse."

"You would never hurt me," she said, laughing.

She leaned against his chest, and he liked the sigh

of contentment that lifted from her, as if she found a safe haven in his arms. His hands tightened reflexively around her waist, the sincere trust in her tone doing peculiar things to his heart.

"Why did you not play as a child, Simon?"

"The idea never appealed. I was an only child and I loved knowledge. Books were my toys."

"When did you develop your love of the written word?"

The stallion slowed into a trot.

"My mother claimed I began reading before I turned one."

"That is incredible!"

"Perhaps," he said with a lazy shrug. "My favorite place in the house was always the library."

"Had you no other pleasures that you enjoyed?"

"Fencing. None of my peers could best me."

"Until me," she said with smug satisfaction.

Simon chuckled. "Until you."

"Did you not play outside on the lawns with your parents? My father and mother often played with me and Anthony. It was…lovely."

"My mother loved riding. I would join her on her early morning rides and raced with her through these very woodlands. And I love sailing. My father taught me how, and he often took me out on the ocean."

"At what age did you lose them?"

"I was a little over eleven years," he said gruffly.

"Oh, Simon. I am so terribly sorry."

"Death is a part of life, an inevitable cycle."

"It is still painful to lose those we love when it is far preferable to live with them for as many years as possible."

"There are truths in your words." It hadn't been until he had stood by the seaside after he graduated from Oxford that he had truly felt the aching loss of his parents. He had logically argued the feeling away, but he had wished at that moment for both his mother and father to have been by his side. That he had not lost them at all. "Did you not lose your mother and father as well?"

"Mama died when I was ten, and then I lost Papa at eighteen years. My father never recovered from the loss of Mama. I cannot imagine it, loving someone with my entire being and then for that person to die."

It flashed through him then that one day Mina Crawford would not exist in his life...perhaps not in this world.

"You are squeezing the breath from me, Simon."

He worked to loosen his arms about her waist, beating back the complex jumble of sensations that had filled him just now.

"So you've never climbed a tree? Never chased a wild rabbit?" she lightly asked, as if she sensed he needed a shift in topic.

He used the side of his jaw to nudge hers and kissed the edge of her mouth. "Sounds nonsensical. What need would I ever have to chase a rabbit?"

He swallowed her mirth with another kiss. Their teeth *clinked* together, and her muffled laugh puffed breaths into his mouth. "I do not think kissing and riding a horse are compatible."

Another harsh gust of wind blew, swaying the trees surrounding them. Simon quickly lengthened the strides of his stallion into a gallop, while she shouted like a hellion for them to fly with the wind. The wind god perhaps listened, for the kite soared away from them with astounding speed and they gave chase, the icy breeze whipping against their faces, her hair blowing over his face.

Simon found himself laughing, reveling in her delight. They were one with the wind as their mad chase took them along the beaten path through the woods and up a grassy small hill and around a dangerous bend at breakneck speed. Finally, he slowed the horse to a brisk trot. The horse's sides heaved with the exertion as he settled back to an easy gait.

"Look, it has become tangled in the high branch of that majestic oak."

The tree was an ancient fixture of his grounds and its naked limbs spread far and wide and high into the sky. The wind dashed through its branches, shaking like skeletal fingers at them both.

"I see an opportunity and an adventure before us, my lord."

"We will not attempt to climb the tree to get that kite."

She twisted in the saddle to peer at him. "Simon—"

He kissed her. A deep thumping pleasure rolled through him when she parted her lips for him. Her breaths came in uneven gasps, and a slight tremor went through her.

"Are kisses always this pleasurable?" she asked.

"I've never kissed another but you."

Her eyes flew open. "Why not?"

"Because at any given moment there are at least two hundred species of bacteria in the mouth. I was decidedly against sharing another person's bacteria," he said with a faint touch of hauteur.

Miss Crawford, who had been listening with gathering incredulity, said faintly, "I did not need to know that knowledge, my lord."

"Hmm, I had the same thought after reading Antonie Philips van Leeuwenhoek's research."

Her eyes brightened with amusement. "And what age did you read this enlightening work?"

"Perhaps eight or nine."

"And your previous lovers did not complain?"

"Is this your way of asking if I've had other lovers, Miss Crawford?"

"Yes."

A small silence lingered. "They did not complain."

She surprised him by leaning in to rub her nose against his. "You are exceptional with your kisses, and I am very pleased you accepted my many bacteria."

Mina held his jaw between her gloved hands and took his mouth with hers, pulling something impossible from deep inside Simon—a foreign sensation that wrenched violently inside his chest.

"Now, about climbing—"

"No." He wheeled the horse around, unmoved by her glare, and urged them into a gallop toward the main estate, her soft laughter curling around him.

• • •

The rousing conversation Mina was having with Simon about a satirical cartoon printed by *The London Charivari* of the Duke of Beswick and one Lord Ballentine fighting over a bone dressed in lady's clothes was forgotten as she mulled over how to trap the earl's queen. After their exhilarating ride outside earlier, they had dined together before retiring to the library. He had been pleased to discover her love of chess and had invited her to play with him. Four matches later she had only won one, and Mina was determined to win this one as well. Simon was an exceptional player and that she had won a match had titillated him.

"We leave for town in the morning."

Thoroughly distracted, Mina lowered the chess piece she had been in the process of moving and glanced up at the earl. "Tomorrow?"

His attention never left the game. "Yes."

Dark blue and silver drapes flapped under a gust of wind. The earl rose, padded to the window, and closed it. "It is snowing, and from the fierceness of the wind we might need to brace for a snowstorm. We will need to leave early for town before the road becomes impassable."

Still unable to see her way out of the brilliant trap he had laid, she took one of his knights off the board. "That leaves me little time to pack, Simon."

He came back down on the floor where they had been sprawled, playing their matches and drinking whisky. Mina felt pleasantly warm and toasty, especially being so close to the roaring fireplace.

"There is no need to travel with any of the clothes you came with. As my secretary, you must represent my house. Several gowns, cloaks, unmentionables, shoes, and other fripperies are already at my townhouse in Grosvenor Square."

A moment of silence passed. "Are you not worried about the speculation that might arise with me staying in your home?"

A small smile touched his mouth. "No. However I have invited your brother to also stay as my guest."

"Ah, so it is the Crawford siblings who will be your guests."

"Yes." He took a sip of his drink. "My grandmother will also frequently stop by, and that will lend the correct air of respectability."

Mina lifted her glass to her lips, swallowing the potent drink, enjoying how it warmed her throat and belly.

"Miss Crawford?"

The way he said her name felt erotic. "Hmm?"

"Take off your clothes," he said, desire echoing in the words he uttered. "All of them."

The glass dropped from Mina's hand and crashed into the chess set, scattering the pieces about the carpet. Words hovered on her lips, teasing ones that might ease the wicked tension that suddenly thickened the space between them with such breathtaking intensity. His gaze on her felt predatory…carnal…but in the depths of those beautiful dark blue eyes, she saw the promise of pleasure. She thought of all she knew of him, how purely focused he could be when doing a task, and the idea of all that intensity on her caused a wave of fire to engulf her. Mina was…nervous and already unbearably aroused. Simply from a command…a stare.

She stood, blushing that her legs were shaky, and moved away to the center of the carpet.

He did not sit and watch her as she'd expected. Simon stood and started to remove his clothes.

Oh God.

She unbuttoned the tiny rows of buttons of the

fitted jacket of the dress, then turned her back to him. The earl brought with him a delicious heat that surrounded her like a sensual blanket. The tickle of warm breath caressed her ear, kissing over the sensitive skin of her nape. A sharp tug as he pulled at the tight laces of her corset sent a quiver through her belly. He helped her remove the single layer of petticoat she wore and unhooked the eyelet of the bustle, then she stepped from it. Mina quickly removed her chemisette and drawers before turning to face him.

A powerful heat flared in the depth of Simon's eyes. His gaze skipped over her body, lingering on her breasts, which seemed to swell under his attention, before moving down to the flatness of her stomach and the curves of her hips. Mina too stared unabashedly at him. Simon was simply magnificently formed with lean, delineated muscles that roped over his entire body. She swallowed at the sight of his manhood which hung heavy and thick between his thighs. Mina stroked her fingers over his shoulder, then moved down to the curve of muscles on his chest.

His arms encircled her waist and flushed her against his body, then he pressed his mouth to hers in a deep, open mouthed and shockingly carnal tangle of tongues. Simon swept her into his arms and laid her out on the padded chaise, coming over her body and between her splayed legs.

His kiss pulled at that wanton place inside her, and she responded with helpless arousal. That place between her legs ached to be filled with him and she rolled her hips in a languorous arch of instinctive sensual invitation. His knee slid between her legs, pressing against the sensitive slit of her sex. A small noise of pleasure broke from her throat. Ripping his mouth from hers, he bent his head and kissed her belly. Fire seared her senses. His tongue dipped into her navel in a wicked glide, and she moaned, anticipation and nerves cascading through her in equal measure.

His hand cupped her breast, his thumb teasing the nipple, as he nibbled along the soft curve of her hips. That hand left her breast and seared down her belly, brushed lightly over the curve of her hips where he lingered with his mouth, then delved between her thighs, finding her wetness. Two fingers pushed deep, and Mina whimpered, wildly reaching for him and gripping his shoulders. His fingers vanished and it shocked her to feel his mouth there instead.

Dazedly she glanced down at his dark head. *Oh God*. He licked her and pleasure twisted tightly, low in her belly. His wicked kiss against her sex offered no mercy and she slapped a hand over her mouth to still the rising scream. He destroyed her with pleasure, and she broke apart in his embrace. Simon climbed over Mina and urged her to wrap her legs around his hips. Simon held her gaze, his beautiful face harsh with lust as he started to enter her.

His inexorable invasion was painful, and a sob hitched in her throat. But then he reached between them with one of his hands, gliding his thumb over that nub of pleasure, rousing hidden parts of her that opened and wept unashamedly for him, easing his way. He started to ride her in a slow, deep rhythm that steadily increased in intensity. He stroked into her over and over, deeper and harder with each plunge and retreat. Mina became lost in pleasure, lost in his taste and scent, lost in the pleasure-pain centered between her thighs, lost in Simon. Ecstasy ravaged her until she came apart in a burst of such intense pleasure, she screamed.

He swallowed it, groaning as he rode her through the convulsion, pulling from her body to spill his release on her stomach. His shoulders trembled, and she reached for him, tenderly brushing a sweat dampened lock of hair from his forehead.

When he kissed her, it was with such aching softness that her chest squeezed. Simon pushed from the chaise and returned with a handkerchief and cleaned his release from her body. He wrapped her in a blanket and took her down with him onto the carpet. They lay there with her atop his body and her nose pressed in the curve of his throat.

"Did you learn all of that from the books you read?" she murmured drowsily.

"I believe I forgot everything I read the moment you started taking off your clothes."

He sounded bemused and she felt delighted.

"Are you happy, Mina?"

The question startled her. Was she happy? For so long she had lived each moment of her life in fear of society's rigid condemnation, with little regard for the desires she owned in her heart. Her brother's country home had become a cage, and she never allowed herself to drift too far, lest she wandered down a dangerous path. What was frightening was that perhaps she might have even convinced herself to return to that cage, if not for their carriage robbery accident.

Being with the earl was…beyond everything Mina could have wanted. He pleased her with his fight for equality for those who could not fight for themselves, the kindness he had showed her brother by not holding his dishonor in condemnation…and the kindness he had shown her from the instant he had hired her.

A delicate tendril of heat spun through her body. "I am," she murmured.

He tugged her into a sitting position, bundling her in the blanket, when a knock came on the door. The earl stood and drew on his trousers before walking over to it. He seemed to expect the intrusion and had arranged for it, for when he opened the door there was no one outside, just a tea service trolley.

Mina smiled softly, knowing he had arranged for it so to protect her reputation within his household. Simon rolled the trolley inside and over to her. Then he removed a large silver tray and set in on the carpet before her.

"Go ahead, Mina."

She lifted up the silver covering and stared at the several bowls of ice cream.

"We have chocolate, strawberry, raspberry, lemon, and cucumber ice cream."

An unknown sensation moved through her body. It was sweet, tender and…perhaps it was love. Mina was most certain she had never felt this piercing emotion for another.

She lifted her gaze to his to find his eyes intent and gleaming with emotions she could not place. "What if I fall in love with you?" she asked hoarsely.

The faintest of smiles touched his mouth. "Are you falling, Mina, is that why your eyes are now shadowed with fear?"

Mina ached with an exquisite longing. "Yes."

His expression grew intent. "Every part of me seems to always reach for you. I do not understand it, but I am not afraid of it, Mina Crawford. Should I find it disconcerting that one of my greatest pleasures is seeing you smile? It simply is what it is. I do not fight what I feel."

"Where does it leave us if your heart also falls for me? You want me...I want you...but then you are to be married to a lady who will surely be perfect for you in every respect, and whatever we have must end then. I...I..."

Long-denied yearning broke through the hardened barrier behind which she had deeply buried it. Hungry, painful swirls of wants rushed through her with crippling intensity. Tears burned Mina's eyes and throat as she admitted how alone she had felt over the years, and how frightened she had been to even dare to hope for more, knowing it would be impossible. The earl had a way of simply sucking the air out of any space with his presence. And sometimes to Mina, it felt like drowning, being this close to him, and wanting him with that painful ache.

Suddenly she felt bleak and afraid. A great pressure swelled in her chest, shortening her breath. "Stop it," she said.

"Stop what?"

"That part of you that keeps reaching for me...let it stop reaching. *Please*."

His expression flickered, and his gaze turned cynical. "If I risk my heart, that is my choice."

She slapped his chest. "What heart? You scoff at love. You are cold and brilliant and *different* than the rest of us. You do not love as we do, feel pain as we do…you do not grieve as we do. Yes, I know it, I could feel it from you. Don't you *dare* risk…risk anything on me. Take your damn heart, my lord, and tuck it away somewhere safe."

A chilling distance seemed to cloak him, yet a dangerous fire snapped in his eyes. Reaching down, he hauled her to her feet and took her mouth in a punishing kiss. With a muffled cry, she gripped his shoulders tightly and wilted against his chest, surrendering to his ravishing lips. He lifted her, and they stumbled, but he caught her to him, and she wrapped her legs around his hips to anchor herself from falling. With a strength that aroused and intimidated in equal measure, he palmed her buttocks, lifting her even higher up to him and sucked her breast into his mouth.

Mina cried out, and then her back was being pressed against a wall, her legs widened even farther as he urged her down and shoved her onto his cock. Full penetration was deep and immediate, and she shuddered under the impact of his sensual invasion, her muscles burning at the stretch that was pleasure and pain.

"Simon," she gasped.

He stilled. "Did I hurt you?"

Her heart pounding, she stared at him. "It is a good kind of hurt because I cannot bear the idea of you stopping."

Mina gasped, clutching his shoulders when he started to move.

He tossed her into ecstasy with shocking swiftness, and she arched into his arms as pleasure crested through her body. His body slid into hers with savage sensuality, as he plunged into her over and over, his expression a grimace of tight lust. Their mouths clasped, their teeth *clinked*, and their tongues tangled. Wicked pleasure rose inside her like a wave, sweeping away all doubt and fear. Mina weakly cried out when she unraveled again, flying apart with a wild cry of delight. With a curse that sounded like a benediction, he pulled from her as he found his release.

Simon lowered her legs to the floor, and she winced at the soreness felt. He carefully cleaned her, and then wrapped the blankets around her shoulders. Placing a finger under her chin, he lifted her face to his. "Did I hurt you with my roughness, Mina?"

"I only felt pleasure."

He stroked her cheek very gently, kissed her temple softly. "Are you ready to eat ice cream?"

"Yes."

His lips touched hers with a soft, sweet possession that made her heart ache and shiver. They went down on the carpet, and reached for bowls of ice cream, eating until they were full and not speaking more about any matters of the heart.

CHAPTER TWELVE

They arrived in London the following day with little fanfare, the anticipated snow suspended, so they reached the city a couple of hours after leaving Hertfordshire. The journey had been pleasant, and Mina had read while Simon studied a large sheaf of bound papers. Brushing the carriage curtains aside, she peeked outside, smiling at the bustle of people as they hurried about their business. It was the first week of February, and thankfully the cold from the previous month was already ebbing. The bright sun rays bathed the land in a warm glow, and she smiled to see a little boy of about six being held in his father's arms as the child pointed at something in the sky.

It was working men and families like these that Simon tried so hard to help achieve equality. She thought back to some of their conversations and those he had with other reformers and comrades in his office. Their strategy for change was wide and far-reaching, with future plans to reform the marriage property act to give women more rights and freedom. At times she felt a sense of awe and pride to be so close to a movement that might transform the lives of many and the very fabric of their nation. Mina wished she could do more and had plans to support women's right to vote whenever that time came.

And it would come.

She had learned to believe in Simon's implacable conviction and the shrewdness of his strategies.

"You seem lost, Mina; what do you think of?"

Pulled from her reverie, she murmured, "The future and what it might hold. I find myself anticipating it with great expectations."

A light laugh left her when he reached for her, tilted her face up and kissed her deeply, effortlessly rousing her senses. For the entirety of their journey, at times, he would briefly wrench his attention from his reading to draw her closer and kiss her with bruising hardness or at other times with soft sensuality. Then he would return to his readings. Perhaps she would have been amused if each kiss had not urged her closer and closer to desire.

Making love with Simon had been...shattering. Since the first time he took her on the carpet, and then their frantic coupling against the door, he had lifted her into his arms and taken her into his chamber. Once there, he had lingered over her body, teasing and exploring every curve, dip, and hollow with a studied air of concentration, sensuality, and curiosity. Each kiss and stroke had seemed to be a lesson following her reaction. Those wicked things that had made her gasp and arch, he'd paid keen attention to and repeated. Perhaps too keenly, for he had brought Mina to a trembling mess of boneless satiation after attaining pleasure from his tongue, lips, and hands alone four times before he had taken her with breathtaking slowness.

Even now, she blushed, recalling her loss of self at his hands.

She wanted revenge. The anticipation of having him at her sensual mercy as she learned what he liked was the keenest sort of torture itself. Simon casually glanced up at her and froze, his eyes widening slightly.

Then he smiled, the curve of his mouth wickedly delighted, the gleam in his brilliant blue eyes anticipatory.

"I look forward to whatever it is you are dreaming of, Miss Crawford," he murmured.

Drat. Even as Mina smiled, her cheeks heated. "Perhaps it is ice cream I am thinking about, your lordship. I did particularly enjoy the icy bite of cucumber and lemon."

He chuckled, and she liked that she made him laugh.

They arrived at his grand townhouse in Grosvenor Square several minutes after entering London. He escorted her inside, making some introductions to the staff, namely the butler and housekeeper, who were made to understand that she was his new secretary and a guest in his home. Despite their professionalism, Mina could feel the speculation in their gazes, especially the housekeeper; she escorted Mina to a guest bedchamber on the third floor.

To her surprise, several new day dresses, riding habits, and ballgowns were being carefully put away in the large armoire by a fresh-faced maid who introduced herself as Mary. The clothes were of the richest satins and silks, the designs exquisite. The modiste had outdone herself, and for a moment, Mina felt that surge of hunger for the glittering excitement of the *haut ton*, the lavish balls and routes, the rides in Hyde Park, the tours of the museums and sights to see. To see and be seen by those who supposedly mattered.

She shook her head at her silliness. Once, she had been a debutante in the blush of her first season, a beauty viscounts and earls had paid court to, but the gentleman she had thought to grant her heart was only the second son of a fencing master of great renown on the continent. As a girl of seventeen, Mina had been dazzled by Leonardo Peretti's vivacity, his quick ability to laugh and flirt, and the warmth in his eyes whenever he stared and smiled at her. Though he had been almost a decade older than her, he was never serious about any academic or business pursuit, seemingly living a grand life due to an inheritance from an uncle who lived as a count in Italy. He loved traveling and spoke of all the exotic places he and Mina would travel once they were wed.

Her father had wanted Mina to form a match with a viscount who had all the proper wealth and connections, and she had passionately called her father a hypocrite, for he had married for love instead of an heiress, yet now wanted to rob her of the same.

Oh, Papa, she thought wistfully, missing him until her heart ached. Closing her eyes, she recalled a moment in the past when her father chased her across the lawns of their estate as she ran with a little piglet clutched in her arms. Her mother had been there, laughing like a hoyden and shouting her encouragement.

Mina opened her eyes, letting go of the memory and the ache of loss. Calling Mary to assist her in removing her clothes, Mina blushed when the girl's curious eyes lingered on the red strawberry marks dotting from her collarbone down to the curve of her breast and belly. Marks left by the earl's mouth.

Knowing the servants might gossip despite their discretion, Mina kept her expression impassive as she made her way to the adjoining bathroom, which was a thing of beauty with all its modern conveniences and plumbing. She soaked in a long bath and washed her hair with a bar of ivory soap. Mary then assisted her in lathering her hair with egg and rinsing it thoroughly with rose water, creating a luxurious shine with a subtle scent of rose and honeysuckle.

After spending almost two hours on her bath and hair, Mina selected one simple day dress to wear. She slipped on her stockings, lightly trailing her fingers over the silky feel and tying the garters at a little above her knees. Drawers, chemise, and a new lace corset followed, then a small bustle and a two-layer petticoat. The corset sucked her waist in more tightly, and the gown as it buttoned to the front hugged her upper body like the warm clasp of a lover before flaring from her hips.

Mina stared at herself, astonished at how greatly the new clothes could enhance her beauty. With a little scoff, she instructed Mary to arrange her hair in a simple chignon with a few wisps teasing about her cheeks. Then slipping her feet into satin half boots, she headed downstairs to the library.

"Anthony," she cried upon opening the door and seeing him sitting in a chair before the earl.

Her brother stood up and turned around, sucking in a sharp breath. "By God, Mina, you look beautiful."

She wrinkled her nose. "It is merely new clothes."

"Still beautiful," he said with a grin, his green eyes bright with pleasure at seeing her. "I've missed you, poppet. So very much."

"It has only been three weeks," she said with a laugh, hurrying over to hug him.

"It is more like a month, Min!"

She realized how much she had missed him, especially their late-night chats by the fire where they had dreamed of what could be, mostly for his future.

Anthony gave her a wide grin. "Lord Creswick has invited me to dine at his home tonight and also to a ball."

"A ball?"

"Yes, to be held here in a few weeks!"

She sent Creswick a sidelong glance of inquiry.

He stood. "The Queen has been convinced to open Parliament on Tuesday. My grandmother is also to host a ball here in a few weeks, and I was extending a personal invitation to Lord Crawford."

Her brother seemed as if he was about to burst at the seams with his pleasure.

"Our townhouse is also open, Mina. Those were the arrangements I have been making. We are still not fully staffed, with only eight new hires, but we will be a far cry more comfortable than how we were in Hertfordshire."

There was a touch of worry in her brother's eyes, and she knew he was anxious about the scandal and speculation that might stir about town over her staying with the earl. She smiled reassuringly. "I shall ask Mary to assist me in packing, and after dinner, we shall depart for Russell Square."

Anthony blew out a sharp breath of relief. "Very well. I was hoping you would spend the season in town. I know you've missed town life even if you had not complained."

"Do not forget I am his lordship's secretary, Anthony. I can only remain in town if his lordship also remains in town."

Anthony grinned, appearing more boyish than ever. "Capital! There is lots of talk about Lord Creswick choosing a wife from the eligible beauties this season. I am certain…"

Perhaps her brother saw the ache in her heart reflected in her face, for his words trailed off, and he grimaced. "Forgive me, my lord, I spoke in haste about unfounded rumors."

"There is nothing to forgive, Crawford. I do have plans to select my bride this season."

Her brother nodded stiffly, sending her a careful and probing glance. Ensuring her expression remained only smooth, she said, "If you will excuse us briefly, Anthony, I must consult with his lordship about my hours of work while in town."

Her brother tugged at his neckcloth and, after a brief hesitation, departed the palatial library. Once the door closed behind him, she met Simon's eyes. There was a watchful quality in the beautiful stillness of his gaze, and she went over to him, careful to remain a respectable distance. "Thank you, my lord, for the kindness you have shown Anthony. A connection with you will see…will see previously closed doors opened to him. You have my gratitude."

A brief, fragile tension seemed to seethe in the air.

"I suspect you are leaving," he murmured, lifting a glass she had not noticed to his mouth.

Mina clasped her hands before her, her fingers aching. "Yes. My brother's townhouse is only a few minutes away."

"You need not worry about the scandal of staying under my roof. There will be no rumors."

Mina swallowed. "You believe you have the power

to squash it?"

"Of course I do," he said with an arrogant lift of a brow.

"You need not suffer undue exertions," she said with a small smile. "It is better to maintain an air of respectability while we are in town."

His mouth remained unsmiling, and an uncertain prick lanced her heart. "Shall we work today, my lord?"

"We shall."

They stared at each other, and the questions as to their affair rose in her heart. They'd had no discussion after their night of untamed loving, and Mina felt bereft and uncertain with the polite civility of his stare.

"Be here by eight each morning, Mondays to Friday, Miss Crawford."

There was a sensual rasp in the way he said her name, and for a moment, there went that gleam in his eyes before his long lashes lowered.

"I will be here, Simon."

"I might not be in residence when you arrive, but now that the season has launched, invitations will flood here and will need to be deftly handled. Tomorrow will let me know the fight we will have on our hands concerning the bills we want to pass, and your fingers might be worked to the bone daily with all the letters and proposals needing to be written. A carriage will be made available for your use. I have little confidence your brother has managed to set himself up with an equipage."

"I am ready for the challenge," she promised.

"Good."

He said nothing further, merely watched her in

that enigmatic way of his, and Mina wondered if she should ask where they stood regarding what happened last night. Then she recalled what her brother had just mentioned. The earl was to find his bride this season.

"I shall go and pack," she said softly.

"Very well."

Her heart gave a frightful squeeze when he went around to his desk and returned to his work. Mina hurried from the library, fighting back the surge of chaotic feelings stirring inside her heart. A couple hours later, when her new wardrobe had been packed away for her departure, searching for the earl to bid him a good evening revealed he had already left the townhouse for his club. Mina retrieved Anthony from the music room where he'd been idly playing and made their way from the earl's townhouse to the carriage he had made available for their personal use.

The journey home was only a few minutes as the roads were uncluttered by other carriages. Sadness, relief, and joy clutched her heart as Mina descended the vehicle and peered up at their townhouse. "It has been so long since I've been here."

"If not for your efforts, I would not have been able to open it up."

She glanced at him. "I was wondering how you managed to evict our tenants on such short notice."

"I should have told you," Anthony said gruffly, "but I could not bear for you to worry. They have moved out over six months prior."

They went inside, and the door was opened by a new butler Anthony introduced as Mr. Wilson. Their previous retinue of loyal servants had long moved on, and she glanced around, noting the changes to their home. They had been lucky with the previous tenants, who had decorated all the downstairs and much above—although Mina missed the ornaments and items of value that had been sold to keep them above water. The new decor was not to Mina's taste, but it was fresh, clean, and showed no signs of being ravaged by mice or moths.

Dinner was a simple meal of grilled fish in asparagus cream sauce, chicken cooked with curried spices and butter, thin slices of roasted meat with cream buttered potatoes and a fig pudding. Mina thought it was delicious and ate with gusto. Anthony spent several minutes extolling Miss Rebecca Ashley's virtues, but there was a deep look of uncertainty in his eyes.

Mina dabbed her lips with the serviette. "Is your courtship not progressing as you had hoped?"

"I have told her of my impoverished state." Anthony took a breath. "Since then, each time I called upon her, she is unavailable."

"Oh, Anthony, I am sorry."

"Yet there was a ball last night. When our eyes met, I could tell Miss Ashley wanted me to ask her to dance. So I did, and she accepted. There was little room for private conversation, but I could tell she was most pleased to be dancing with me."

"Perhaps it is not Miss Ashley herself who said she was unavailable."

"That is what I am afraid of," he said with a grimace. "If her parents do not approve of our match, I would not be dishonorable and try to convince her to marry me without their consent."

She smiled at him. "You are a good, honorable

gentleman, Anthony. You are also a viscount. If Miss Ashley loves you and you love her, I am certain you will both be able to convince her parents of the match."

He seemed surprised at her praise, and then he flushed. "Thank you, Mina."

They ate in silence for a few minutes, and when she felt his stare upon her, Mina glanced up.

"Are you in love with Lord Creswick?" Anthony bluntly asked.

"Do not be silly."

"That is not an answer, Min. You are deflecting."

"I own to some feelings for him," she said quietly, "but I do not know if it is love."

"He seems very considerate of you," Anthony carefully said. "It is clear he cares for your comfort, and that matters."

"The earl is simply a kind man."

"I think it's more than that, Mina. There was something about his eyes when he looked at you. I believe you matter to him. And that is incredible. Many mention him to be a cold and aloof man, not given to sentiments merely because his mind is so elevated above messy emotions. At least that is what Beswick and Stannis say. That Lord Creswick could be this different with you is…interesting, is it not?"

Hating the surge of gladness that squeezed her chest, she said, "He'll not marry me if that is what you are hoping."

"You are the daughter of a respected viscount and—"

"One who has an awful scandal in her past and no dowry!" *And secrets*. "I eloped, Anthony, with a man society would not approve of in any regard. Even if that was six years ago, it would take little effort to stir those rumors to life. I am not—"

"You are also kind and beautiful," he insisted stubbornly, "and a lady who is intelligent enough to match a man of Lord Creswick's wit and shrewdness. You are loyal and…and lovely, Mina. Surely he will see it, too."

She stared at her brother, an ache in her throat from the words hovering on her tongue, words that would spill her secret so he might set aside that foolish hope. Still, she could not say it, and it was more than just because she had promised her father to never speak about it to anyone. Mina could not bear to rehash everything she had left in the past.

What's done is done.

And while she would use what had happened to inform her decisions of the future, she did not want to revisit how naïve she had been or the pain and fear she'd endured when the person she had thought she was falling in love with turned on her with violence. Mina deftly changed the conversation to the events they might attend for the season instead, laughing and chatting long into the night.

• • •

The following morning, Mina arrived at Grosvenor Square forty minutes before the required time. She informed the butler there was no need to announce her, and then she handed over her coat, bonnet, and scarf. Taking a deep breath to brace her heart against seeing the earl, she padded down the long, elegant hallway to the library. She knocked and opened the door after waiting a minute. The earl was seated before his desk, his head bent over papers. Mina stood there for several minutes, studying the shape of his jaw, the way his brows furrowed in intense concentration, the stillness as he absorbed whatever he read, the way he would use his fingers to pinch the bridge of his nose. Last night as she had tried to sleep, memories of their time together had stirred in her mind, keeping her awake for long hours.

I am such a fool to be falling in love with you.

Mina's heart squeezed and trembled and ached. It felt strange, raw, and frightening, this feeling that writhed inside her chest for Simon. She must have made a sound, for he glanced up. Mina almost gasped at the raw emotions that leaped into his eyes, stamping want with savage hunger and something infinitely tender on his face before his expression shuttered.

"Don't, please," she burst out, pressing a palm against her belly.

"Don't what, Miss Crawford?"

"Do not hide from me what you feel…when I feel so much for you." The words were a whisper and with shaking hands, she tugged off her gloves and tossed them onto the sofa's arm. Simon stood, his motions controlled as he went around his desk and came over to her.

Mina stood, lifting her face up to his.

Oh God.

His eyes swirled with intense emotions, and he grabbed her about the waist, hauled her into his arms in a move that was at once fierce and tender. Then he claimed her mouth in a kiss that left her trembling. Mina helplessly responded, slipping her arms around his neck and kissing him with passionate urgency.

"I thought you only meant for us to have one night," she gasped against his mouth, closing her eyes as he feathered kisses down to her jaw and the section of her neck exposed about her collar.

"Is one night enough for you, Mina?"

"*No.*"

Gripping her hips tightly, he closed his eyes briefly. "I want more than one night. I *need* you for more than one night. I do not think an affair will ever be enough."

That shocking admission almost felled her.

"Why that fright in your eyes?"

Her heart knocked painfully against her ribs. "Because I only have an affair to give you," she whispered.

"I am not yet asking for more," he said.

Not yet? *Oh God.*

Simon kissed her again for several long minutes until her lips were delightfully swollen.

"Come, we have a lot of work to do. I will present my speech tomorrow, and I need to read it over once more."

"You have it?"

"Of course I do."

Mina nodded and went to her desk, lowering herself into the chair.

But as she drew forth several letters that had only just arrived and set about her work, a smile hovered inside her heart.

More than one night.

CHAPTER THIRTEEN

Simon ruthlessly finished his thorough review of the speech he intended to give on the morrow before the Queen at the opening of Parliament. He outlined points to emphasize and scratched out those that might negatively influence the lords with undue fears. The arguments had to slice with enough depth to penetrate those with hardened hearts but not enough to fill them with fear. After setting aside his speech, Simon had gone through all the estate ledgers with his stewards, and everything seemed to be in order. He did not feel like reading or any other of his usual activities at present.

"You are nervous," his lover's soft voice said.

He drummed his fingers on the surface of the oak desk. "I am not a man prone to nervousness."

"Then what are you thinking about?"

"Everything that can go wrong tomorrow, everything that might go right."

"I daresay there are many good and honorable gentlemen in the House."

"Honor and goodness have little to do with politics. If those 'good' men feel as if their interests, especially their great wealth, are threatened, they will vote against reform."

She lowered the quill and leaned back against the high winged back armchair, looking more lovely than she should. "Don't you feel an inkling that your interests are threatened? You are a lord of the realm like they are."

"No. And even if they were, we would still move forward. It is a lesson I learned firsthand from your father and mine."

Her eyes widened. "My father?"

"Yes."

"I was not aware our parents knew each other," she said wonderingly.

At the hunger he saw in her eyes, he ceased tapping his fingers and considered her. "They were on different sides of the political spectrum, but they had many political dinners at our home, especially during the fight to repeal the Corn Laws."

Her brows puckered as she delved into their history to recall the point he mentioned.

"Those were the laws, tariffs, and other trade restrictions that prevented imported food and corn from entering the United Kingdom," she murmured. "I believe it was successfully abolished in 1846."

Simon greatly liked Mina's educated mind and that he could freely discuss history and politics with her. She was never afraid to reveal ignorance, and should he explain a particular matter, she grasped it with impressive alacrity. "Yes."

"You would have only been six years of age at the time, my lord."

His mouth curved. "I was already reading books by Charles Dickens at age six and had a greater understanding than most men of their content. My father had me at his side, teaching me even at that age, for he understood my advancement and was even proud of it."

Her eyes were bright with admiration and something infinitely tender. "The Corn Laws blocked the import of a reasonably priced corn that the people could afford."

"Yes. Even though there was a dire food shortage throughout all of England, for many could barely afford the food here, laws were put in place to make it virtually impossible to import food from abroad. The great famine had started in Ireland, and even then, many seemed unmoved by the starving plight of thousands when cheaper imports of food would have alleviated or stopped that great tragedy. Do you know why that happened?"

Her extraordinary eyes flashed with fire. "Because the Corn Laws enhanced the profits and political power associated with land ownership."

"Precisely." Simon surged to his feet and walked over to the windows overlooking the gardens. "Many lords' wealth was rooted in the land and as agricultural proprietors. If the Corn Law was repealed, your father and even my father stood to lose a good portion of their wealth. The viscount more so than my father, who had diversified his holdings. Still, Lord Crawford fought for it to be repealed because he believed the poor and those most vulnerable had to be protected. Even at the cost of his wealth."

"Thank you," she said softly, coming to stand beside him. Mina peered up at him, and her eyes glittered with fierce pride.

He lifted his eyes to her. "I did nothing."

"It was a side of my father I never heard about before. I miss him and I… Thank you, Simon."

Their eyes met, and she smiled. He felt like he was tumbling and falling and couldn't quite catch himself.

"Say you will break for lunch with me."

He normally worked through the luncheon hour he gave her, but at the warm invitation in her eyes, he nodded. "Yes."

Delight lit up her eyes, and for a moment, Simon couldn't seem to draw his breath quite deep enough in his chest.

"I was thinking we could have ice cream."

"Ice cream?"

"Yes. I heard you earlier when you informed the housekeeper that they should have a ready supply of ice cream made daily with fresh fruits." She peeked at him rather adorably from beneath her lashes. "However, if you would like to have something else, we could. Then we have ice cream after."

He barely recognized the feeling knocking around his chest. It took Simon a while to realize it was pure contentment. That there would be nothing wrong if he spent the day simply basking in Mina Crawford. And he did not mean inside her quim. But inside her presence, to be a part of the way she laughed, to smile because of how her lashes fluttered when she ate.

The lady loved food and was not shy about it. He enjoyed that about her. She also liked music. He had caught her yesterday in her break playing with passion on the pianoforte. When he'd complimented her, she'd told him her brother was the piano master and she the fencing master.

Simon was about to kiss the smile from her mouth when an imperious knock sounded, alerting him to who stood on the other side. He turned around as the door opened, and his grandmother framed the doorway. He made a mental note to start closing and locking the door to the library whenever Mina was inside with him.

The dowager countess was a small woman, stiffly laced all in steel gray, which exactly matched her hair. Her fashionable bustled gown was austere in its simplicity, totally unornamented except for a large oval opal brooch ringed with small diamonds. The fingers of her hands were covered with rings and seemed clenched in front of her as if in fury. Her eyes shot her grandson with a gimlet stare and her face wore an expression of stern disapproval.

Simon courteously bowed. "Grandmother, I had no notion you were coming to visit today."

She sniffed. "Was your outrageous letter not an invitation?"

Her dark blue eyes landed on Miss Crawford, who had dropped into an elegant curtsy.

"Grandmother, permit me to introduce to you Miss Wilhelmina Crawford, Viscount Crawford's daughter. I recall him to be a gentleman you admired. Miss Crawford, my grandmother, the Dowager Countess of Creswick."

His grandmother softened only slightly but pinned his lover with a suspicious stare.

"Your Ladyship," Mina said, dipping into another respectful curtsy.

"Your father was a great man, Miss Crawford. It is good to meet his daughter."

"Thank you, Your Ladyship."

Then with practiced deliberateness, she turned her gaze upon Simon. "Your fiancée will call upon us here at one in the afternoon. You should make yourself presentable to see her."

Mina visibly flinched, and that telling reaction sent a lance of discomfort through his chest. He considered her for only a moment, ensuring he did not linger on her expression that was carefully composed. Despite that icy loveliness radiating from her face, her eyes burned with emotions.

"As I have not yet met…whoever you chose as a suitable bride and have yet to make any offer, I am not yet affianced," he said mildly. "See that you remember it."

Narrowed eyes assessed him. "Your letter did say whoever I selected would become your future countess. As I know you are not a gentleman who goes back on his word, you will be delighted to call Lady Cassandra your fiancée soon. I believe we should make the announcement to society at the ball I will host in a few weeks' time."

His grandmother was not the kind of person to speak about their family matters so casually before someone she had just met. That left Simon to presume this gesture was precisely for Miss Crawford's benefit. It was designed to prick at her vanity and to wound her heart if she held any affection for him. A coldness moved through him, and so he stared at his grandmother with polite indifference. He truly did not take kindly to those who wanted to hurt Mina without cause.

Simon paused. Even if they had just cause, and believed her to be a villainess, the primal urge to crush those who dared still resided inside his chest.

How interesting.

For a moment, his grandmother looked uncertain,

then she lifted an imperious brow in his direction.

Mina stepped forward with a lovely smile. "If you will excuse me, my lord, Your Ladyship, I am on a break, and there is a delightful book I have been meaning to read."

His grandmother hardly spared her a glance, and Mina hastened from the room, closing the door behind her with a small *snick*. The dowager countess sauntered forward and sat on one of the sofas. She tilted her head, the plumed feather bobbing with her motion. "Your letter, my boy, was beyond the pale."

Simon was suddenly, inexplicably bored. The precise feeling that always crept over him whenever his grandmother spoke about some debutante she wished him to meet or discussed his eventual wedding. "Was it?"

"You informed me to simply pick your wife as if you were shopping for a horse. Allow me to correct myself. You would give more consideration to whichever stallion you purchase by visiting a stud farm directly or at Tattersalls!"

"I have too many important matters on my mind to concern myself with courtship. If you would have waited until I have the time to attend the matter myself, I am certain you would be satisfied," he said drily.

"Don't you dare, my boy! You and I know that if it were up to you, there would always be something more important."

"Nonsense. I know my duties to the title, my estates, and tenants. My father informed me of them by the time I was two years old."

An exasperated sigh left her. "My dear, I assure you, should you enter a marriage with little feeling between you and your bride-to-be, you will not be happy." She held up a hand to forestall his reply. "I know you are not a gentleman given to sentimentality, but you'll not know if you own to those feelings unless you explore them."

Those feelings. And what blasted feelings were those? He could not help but think they were the very ones he endured whenever he thought of Mina Crawford or the ones that lingered in the shadows of his heart and took little effort to emerge and haunt him. This morning when he had realized she was in the library, they had burst forth from their cage, raking at him with clawing talons of longing. And what had he longed for? To hold her and kiss her, to walk with her by the seaside as she dipped her toes in the water, to kiss her…to take that taste with him for the day, only to return home and kiss her again.

"If you will excuse me, grandmother, I have a meeting in Westminster to attend."

A gasp of outrage sounded. "Lady Cassandra will be calling with her mother, the marchioness, at one!"

"You made those arrangements without consulting with me over what I have on my calendar," he said calmly. "While I will not object to your arrangements, do not mistake that as meaning you can order and control my life. If you consult with Miss Crawford when I am gone, she will share my calendar for the next several weeks. I will not object to meeting this paragon of yours, but now is not the time to be thinking of courtship. I daresay sometime in spring with all those balls might be a better idea."

Though she huffed, his grandmother did not object, and Simon made his way from his townhouse, regretful that he had not sat in his conservatory and eaten ice cream while a pair of enchanting green eyes conveyed their delight at him.

• • •

The opening of Parliament was underway, and the Queen looked upon everyone crammed in the chamber. Lords presented their speeches on the issues affecting the realm and their proposed bills on how to fix said issues. Many speeches delved in length on the problems the nation would need to address over the coming months. A few notable lords touched briefly on the need for reform, the ravages of cholera on the country, and that a commission of enquiry needed to be established. Others proposed to establish more favorable dealings of the crown with trade unions and organizations that supported the working-class men.

A fine tension went through the chamber when Simon stood, no papers in his hand, for he had committed his speech and arguments to his memory. He could feel the surge of anticipation that went through the chambers.

"The question has been raised whether there is to be a Reform Bill or not," he began. "It must be admitted that the present time is unquestionably favorable for its consideration. I am sincerely convinced of the absolute necessity that a reform is needed. My arguments are in favor of a judicious, cautious, and temperate Reform, and I will use my time to inform why this is a necessity and why we as representatives of Her Majesty must be so moved that we must bring this reform into existence, whether we be Liberals or Conservatives."

Simon touched upon many aspects of the bill, detailing the benefits that should accrue for the citizens and the nation itself. He spoke, his voice strong and determined as he sought to persuade his fellow peers of the importance of bringing about necessary reform to strengthen the nation and further the good of the commonwealth. He spoke with dignity and conviction and Simon thought that he had won over many of those whose support was uncertain.

He sat, and several more speakers rose to deliver their speeches. A few hours later, Simon left Westminster after conversing with many other peers and made his way to his carriage.

"Creswick!"

He paused as the Earl of Stannis walked over to him. "Tonight, we drink and wench. Join us."

"I am not interested."

He waggled his brow suggestively. "Come man, most of the men you want to discuss politics with will be there. There is nothing like good conversation over a bottle of whisky, cheroots, and cunny."

Simon was momentarily amused. "I should only be bad company for you and Beswick. I regret that I must decline and beg to be excused," he mildly said.

Stannis scowled and Simon smiled. Turning to

stroll away from the earl, he went to his carriage and hauled himself inside. There was a restlessness upon him that Simon could not dismiss. There had been as many speeches today opposing reform as those that supported. The real work would now begin, and the upcoming months were crucial for the scales to be tipped in the balance for reform. Simon needed to lobby many of his party to ensure sufficient support for the bill when the time came for it to be voted on. He would have to work hard, even insidiously if necessary, to achieve the outcome best for the nation.

Upon reaching home, he went upstairs to strip from his robes and clothes, then padded below stairs. He went to his exercise room and to the sandbag he used to practice his boxing. Wrapping his hand with thin leather strips soaked in vinegar, he started to pound away at the bag, ruthlessly working out the restless edge eating at him.

He did not like feeling unsettled. This was not his character, and worse, he did not understand in this moment what drove him. A sound made him pause and he turned around, breathing deep when he saw Mina framed in the doorway. She held two white bowls in her hands with spoons sticking out in the middle.

She lifted one of the bowls to him. "Ice cream?"

Simon chuckled as that restless feeling somewhat quieted. "I am beginning to think you believe ice cream has curative and restorative properties."

She padded into the room, and he took the bowl from her, dipping the spoon into the cold yet sweet treat to shovel a spoonful into his mouth. The sweet, creamy flavor burst on his tongue. "Strawberry."

"Yes, and if you dig deep enough, you will find chunks of the strawberry, and below that layer mangoes."

He took another spoon, finding some of the fruits she mentioned.

Her eyes crinkled at the corner. "Do you like it?"

"Yes."

"I made it myself." A wide smile bloomed on her mouth and her eyes glittered. "I convinced your cook to allow me the liberty to invade her domain. I think she quite enjoyed showing me how to make ice cream."

Conscious of his sweat slicked skin, he sat on the floor, leaning back against the wall, not at all surprised when she joined him. They sat right there on the floor, eating ice cream in companiable silence. She sat with him in the stillness of the night, shared the silence with him, and even offered some of her ice cream when his finished.

Simon smiled. Even now that both bowls had been emptied, they did not speak to each other, and Simon leaned his head against the wall, at peace with the silence, yet feeling the restless energy once again brewing in his gut.

Mina stood and made her way from the room, only to return several minutes later dressed in boy trousers and a white shirt that dwarfed her frame and looked remarkably like his. *Sweet Mercy*. He could tell that her small, yet firm breasts were unbound beneath the loose shirt, for the overlarge neckline draped, revealing her pale neck and upper clavicle. Her fiery red hair also tumbled down her shoulders in waves to her back and her toes were delightfully bare.

The restless energy stopped as if it had slammed into a wall, and curiosity instead stirred within Simon. Mina tossed something to him and as he caught it, he realized it was a rapier.

Ah, Miss Crawford.

Simon released a slow breath and rose, unsheathing the blade and holding its point to the ground.

Mina regarded him soberly. "I can feel the restless energy thumping from you. I can also tell you have no wish to speak about it."

He grunted noncommittally.

"Ice cream and my lovely presence did not seem to do the trick." She dipped low, going into her fighting position, and holding her blade up, thrust outward and parallel to the ground. "*En garde.*"

"With no fencing gear or protective buttons on our blades?"

"I thought you knew I liked to live dangerously," she drawled, her eyes sparkling, then she darted forward.

An inexplicable feeling he could not name welled within Simon. He slashed his blade up in a parry to her attack, the *clang* of steel ringing in the room. A wicked pulse of anticipation throbbed within him, and he allowed the thrill of the fight to flow through his veins. They danced around each other with fast-paced and graceful attacks, counters, and counter-riposte. They fought for a long time, even until his damn arms started to ache, and she kept pace with him, giving him the full measure of her skill and defiance.

A worthy opponent indeed.

Mina Crawford was a brilliant fighter.

When they ended, the point of her rapier was pressed against his chest, right over his heart. He dropped his sword with a clatter.

"It did not work," he murmured, stepping forward, pressing the tip of the sword to his skin.

With a gasp, she drew back the rapier, clearly afraid that his move had allowed the point to pierce his skin. Simon prowled toward her, watching her eyes widen and a flush blossom across her cheeks as she read his intention. She did not release the sword, holding it to her side like a fair damsel about to defend her virtue from a ravaging predator. Mina stepped away from him until her back came upon the wall and she could retreat no more.

She dropped the rapier, her chest lifting on a rapid breath.

"Remove the trousers."

The command hissed from him as a dark tide of lust crested throughout his entire body to settle hot and heavy against his cock. Mina tried to undo the buttons, then stopped, resting her head against the wall. "My fingers are trembling too much."

Simon stooped before her on his haunches, reached out, and undid the trousers, removing the pants and her drawers, baring her cunny to his greedy gaze. Well-curved thighs were revealed in creamy, sensual splendor. The soft curls peeking from beneath the shirt and protecting her sex from him were as red as her hair. He leaned forward, pushed up his shirt, and kissed the lower part of her belly right above her mound. She quivered in his hands as he savored the silky feel of her skin on his lips.

He widened her legs, and she pressed the palm of her hands against the walls as if bracing herself for his anticipated onslaught. Simon wasted no time with small, seductive moves. He parted through her silky curves with his fingers, opening her sex, leaned forward, and licked her, the taste of her heady and lush. Mina made a hoarse sound in her throat, halfway between objection and surrender, her thighs now trembling.

He ran his tongue over her plump folds up to her clitoris. Her hand flew to his hair and gripped as she moaned her delight. Her fingers combed through his hair almost frantically, before she gripped the strands in a death grip when he repeated his motions over and over. Simon gripped her buttocks and moved his mouth over her clitoris and sucked the bud into his mouth.

Mina gasped hoarsely, her thighs trembling even more.

Simon held her under the lash of his tongue, not relenting in his carnal ministrations, not until she convulsed, crying out her pleasure as she climaxed. His belly tightened and his cock flexed hard against his trousers. He needed to be in her this very moment before she fully came down from her orgasm.

He shot to his feet and peered into her eyes, lust, pleasure, desire, and passion looking back at him. He spun her around and was greeted by well-rounded buttocks that tempted him with their firm lushness. He cradled her into his arms, reaching between them to free his desperately aching cock. Placing one hand over her sex, he reached down and stroked her nub, then used his other hand to hug her midsection from beneath the shirt to fondle her breast.

Simon buried his face into the crook of her shoulder to lavish kisses on her neck, pinching and stroking her clitoris with greater carnal intent. He marveled at the silky feel of her skin, the wonderful taste of her body. Stooping slightly, he positioned his cock at her slick entrance, then surged forward and was met by scalding heat and tight resistance, her convulsing muscles as she orgasmed once more with a wild gasp.

Her release flowed over his cock, pulling a deep groan from him. Simon wanted to chase his own pleasure, but this moment had to be savored, had to be delighted in. He withdrew and pistoned back into her, then retreated slowly again while working her clitoris. Mina sobbed her pleasure, and her quim clenched around his cock, the hot, wet rippling sensation of her cunny on his cock twisting his gut into knots.

"Brace your hands on the wall," he growled.

She obeyed, and he worked his cock inside her in a slow and deep, relentless rhythm that built his orgasm to a gradual peak. His Mina was perfect in her wild and passionate response, and the low, aroused way she murmured his name wrapped itself around his body. A lustful whisper of satisfaction ghosted over his body, racking him with pleasure. She reached her hand over her shoulder to his hair, her hips arching into his thrusts. Fire rippled over his cock and settled in his balls with an aching need. He bit into the curve of her shoulder, his hips snapping now in an uninhibited rhythm, dragging another release from her body. Simon barely managed to keep his promise of protecting her from falling with child as he pulled from her and shot his release on the curve of her derriere.

The pleasure still rocked his body, making him damn well tremble and with a groan against her throat, he held her to him until she stopped shaking. He felt drained, his mind emptied and calm, only filled with…Mina. "Have I told you that you are something wonderful, Miss Crawford?"

She shook her head, a light laugh leaving her throat. "No."

"You are damn wonderful."

Mina turned in the cage of his arms, stumbling. He caught her against his chest and gently held her in his arms.

"Now it is my knees that tremble," she said, wrinkling her nose.

"Spend the night with me." Her eyes widened and something flickered in her eyes that had him frowning down at her. "What is it?"

"I want to, but I do not think it is wise."

Simon held himself still as he considered the flush rising in her cheeks. While he did not understand it fully, whatever her reasons, he would respect them. "Very well." He hauled her into his arms and swallowed her startled gasp in a kiss. Lifting his head, he slipped his fingers over her cheeks, cupping her face between his palms. "Take a bath with me before you go."

Smiling against his mouth, she nodded before kissing him back with the sweetest passion. "You make me ache for so much, Simon."

"Tell me what you want, and I will give it to you."

She stilled in his arms, and he could feel her rapidly beating heart against his chest. Mina lifted her eyes and let her gaze lock with his, then moved her fingers to Simon's mouth, tracing the curve of his lips with her forefinger. "I can see that you are entirely serious."

He bent toward her, his mouth barely touching the corner of her lips. *I want to lay the world at your feet.* But he did not say the words, thinking them a bit outrageous. Finally, he murmured, "Of course I am."

She took a tremulous breath, shook her head wordlessly, before slipping her hands around his neck to fiercely hug him. Simon returned her embrace, wondering at the rapid beating of his own heart and the feeling of certainty rising inside that he never wanted to let go of Mina Crawford.

CHAPTER FOURTEEN

Mina wanted adventures. To be free to fly and soar as high as her wild heart would take her yet remain safe to do so. She brimmed with an energy that captivated Simon's soul and enchanted him. He wanted to show Mina more of the Town. He offered her an off day in the week to call upon old friends should she wish it, and with a polite smile, she declined. When he probed, a faraway look had entered her lovely eyes and she'd murmured, "I think all my old friends are...gone."

He'd felt an inexplicable urge to draw her into his arms and hold her tight against him. The echoes of loneliness in those soft words had twisted his gut into knots, and they had stayed with him for days, distracting him from work, a feat he had not thought possible. He wanted to give her a better understanding of London life, for her to feel the pulse of life in the city, to experience it how he experienced it.

He leaned back in his chair, letters from reformers forgotten as he mulled over the idea of taking her about himself. He smiled, thinking of how titillated she would be by the idea of touring the metropolis with him. Simon had always been methodical and precise, and planning to take Mina out was planned with the same care.

Simon summoned his housekeeper, Mrs. Basil. She presented herself nervously and bobbed a curtsy. "You sent for me, my lord, how can I assist you?"

"I would like a tape measure, Mrs. Basil—is one available?"

"Several, my lord. I shall fetch one at once. Is there anything else I can do for you?"

"No, I think that is all for now, I shall deal with the rest myself."

The tape measure was fetched and that evening before Mina left his town house, he locked the door to his office and asked that she undress to her chemise and drawers.

In the act of shuffling several sheaves of paper together, she lifted her head up, a small frown between her brows. "Undress?"

"Hmm," Simon said with an air of distraction as he ruffled about for a piece of paper to note the measurement.

"My lord, I know you loathe repeating yourself, but did you truly ask me to undress?"

"Your ears did not deceive you, Miss Crawford. The door is closed, we are assured of privacy."

"Certainly, " she said after a small pause and with a wrinkle of her nose.

She looked rather bemused when he brought the tape and started taking her measurements and carefully writing them down on the piece of paper. He started by sizing the crown of her head, then the width of her neck and she snuggled into him as he measured other parts of her body.

"What are you up to, Simon?" she asked, her eyes already twinkling with anticipation. "I sense a mystery afoot, and I suspect you know I have a very inquisitive nature."

He kissed the tip of her nose. "It's a surprise, Mina, now be a good girl and try and stop wriggling at least until I finish…"

She leaned forward and kissed him. "I quite like surprises."

"Good, you will enjoy it."

Her eyes lit with delighted anticipation. "Perhaps a small clue?"

"No."

Her stroking fingers slid to linger on his jaw. "Simon—"

"Behave yourself," he growled.

With a laugh, she nibbled at the corner of his mouth. "Half a clue?"

He gave a brisk shake of his head, fearing that the hoarseness of his voice would reveal how much he desperately wanted her.

The temptation to take her whispered in his mind and arrowed down to his cock. "You shall not distract me from my purpose, woman."

"I like a challenge even more," she breathed. Her face was alight with mischievous teasing.

She made to go around him, and Simon turned with her, caught her as she moved. "Be still, Miss Crawford."

He felt her tremble against him as he trapped her back against his chest. Reaching around, he measured over her breasts, loving her breathy inhalation. He bowed his face to the curve of her throat, touching his mouth against the soft skin just below her ear.

A little aching sound came from her throat. Lazily drifting his hands lower, he created the barest space between their bodies so he could measure her waist. He did not move to record this, not wanting to be away from her, but kept the numbers in his mind. Simon allowed his hands to linger on the soft of her belly, nuzzling her throat and inhaling her sweet scent into his lungs. She was so much smaller than he, in spite of her lush figure. And delicate and feminine and soft.

Stepping back from her, Simon turned her to face him. Holding her eyes, he stooped. A burning flush rose in her cheeks.

"I need to measure your inseams."

"My inseam?"

Tender amusement rushed through him. "From your crotch down to your ankles."

Her eyes widened and her lips parted but no sound emerged.

"Place your hand on my shoulder and balance yourself, Miss Crawford," he murmured huskily.

She complied, and he lifted one foot then the other, removing her boots. Her stocking-clad toes curled into the carpet when he glided his fingers from her ankle up to her shin, over her knees and high up on her inner thighs. The heat of her quim reached through her drawers, tempting him to behave wickedly. Still, he restrained the urge and carefully measured her, even if at one point he allowed his knuckles to brush with sensual deliberateness over the scrap of cloth that covered her cunny.

The silence in the room was only filled with the rustle of clothing and their breathing. Surely she could hear the harsh thump of his heart. He went to measure the other leg.

"Surely the measurements are the same!"

He smiled at the quaver in her voice. "I've read most people don't know one leg is longer than the other."

A choked sound came from her. He shaped the

round curve of her thighs, aware of the slight tremble of her frame.

Breathing raggedly, she cried, "You teasing wretch!"

With a laugh Simon rose to his feet. As he finished up with her hips and thighs, he was vaguely startled to feel the prickling of heat rushing through his veins. Mina clung to his shoulders and pressed her mouth to his. Barely managing to finish his task in between her desperate kisses, he dropped the tape to the carpet and hauled her into his arms.

"*Shh*," he murmured against her laughing mouth, kissing away that sweet, unfettered sound and swallowing it into his being.

Simon bore her down to the carpet. Mina was soon gasping and writhing underneath him on the carpet, breathlessly murmuring his name as he drove her wild with pleasure. Several minutes later, they lay beside each other, staring up at the ceiling.

"That was…"

"Remarkable," he ended.

Mina smiled at him as if they shared some amusing secret. "How long have you been planning this?"

"I assure you, loving you was a madness conceived spontaneously."

She regarded him for a moment beneath arched eyebrows. Then that mischievous twinkle appeared in her eyes. "I am happy I also drive you mad with wanting."

"Come here, Mina."

She rolled into his arms, resting her head on his chest. He breathed deeply of her scent and closed his eyes.

"Are you about to sleep on the floor of your office?"

"Perhaps."

Another laugh and in that moment, he knew he would never tire of the sound.

They stayed like that for several minutes, until her even breathing informed Simon that she soundly slept. He lay there, hating the thought of getting up and going to dine alone. He wanted Mina to stay right here beside him for the night. And still be here the next day and the next day. Simon did not want snatches. He wanted it all.

He stilled, absorbing that feeling swelling inside of him with imperative hunger. A soft breath shuddered from him, and she murmured, shifting closer. He held her against him, let her head tuck against his neck. The power she held over him was profound, nor was it purely physical. She called to something deep inside of him that he had no answer for, and Simon only sensed that he might never be able to let her go.

• • •

The following day, Mina arrived promptly and got down to work. She wondered what Simon was up to, because he had been plotting something the night before and she still could not see why he needed her measurements. It was a puzzle she could not figure out and she wondered where he was today, as he had given no explanation of who or where he was visiting. However, when she went to the office door to ask for a pot of tea, she noticed two footmen with their arms full of parcels which they were carrying upstairs.

So, it appeared that Simon had gone shopping, there was no mystery to that. Having ordered her tea, Mina returned to the pile of letters which had arrived

that morning. Most were only invitations to some society affair, and she sorted them as she thought
suitable. She wrote short notes declining most of
them, placing the draft letters with each invite. Then
she examined his diary and decided whether those she
thought Simon might wish to attend would fit in with
his schedule. She penciled in the possible new entries
before she wrote letters of acceptance and placed
them in another pile.

That greatly reduced his correspondence, and she
went through the other letters drafting replies that she
thought Simon might find suitable, while he usually
scanned the other letters and signed or directed the
opposite response, these he would go through and edit
as he thought fit. Mina was relieved that he was usually fairly satisfied with them and altered them less
than when she had begun acting as his secretary.

She drank her tea and enjoyed some of the short-
bread biscuits that the cook had sent up as she
worked. Simon was prompt at noon and asked her to
take dictation before going through her work and
signing the letters. Further parcels were delivered during the afternoon, but Simon simply ordered them to
be carried to the blue bedroom.

When the clock chimed six, Simon put down the
papers he was reading and stood. "Mina?"

"Hmm?" She lowered the quill and glanced up.

"Would you come out with me tonight?"

Her heart leaped. "I was not aware you accepted
an invitation for a ball tonight."

A small smile touched his mouth. "It isn't a ball."

She stood, leaning her hips on the edge of the
desk. "You are acting rather mysterious."

"Tonight we'll go about town as gentlemen."

Her heart lurched. "As gentlemen?"

"Yes."

For a moment, she stared at him with incomprehension. "I am to be in disguise?"

"Yes."

Good heavens! Her heart trembling and delight blossoming though her, Mina laughed and hurled herself toward him, clasping his jaw between her hands and kissing his mouth with great exuberance.

"We are going out at seven, Mina. Get changed—your clothes are laid out for you in the blue bedroom," he said once she released his mouth.

"Yes, my lord," Mina said, giving him a curtsy and then leaving the room, heading upstairs and searching out the blue bedroom. On the bed lay a full set of male clothing which looked like they had been made for her. Now she understood his measurements. Someone knocked and she bid enter.

"My lord said I was to help you change, Miss," Mary, the maid she had been provided with, declared.

Mary helped her out of her work gown and corsets and Mina soon found herself dressed in clothes suitable for a young man about town. The dark trousers and jacket, brightened by a green waistcoat which almost matched her eyes. Mina had no problem with tying a cravat, although the modern ones were simpler than those worn by her father as a young man, as he had often told her. Her hair was taken down and pinned close to her head, and Mary very skillfully covered it with a light brown wig.

Mina thought it was a fairly effective disguise but as she picked up her gloves, hat, coat, and silver topped cane, she remembered to lengthen her stride and move her feet more apart as she walked. She descended the stairs taking them two at a time, something which had been both difficult and forbidden for her as a lady to do, and she reveled in the freedom. Pure unguarded joy and warmth burst inside her chest.

Simon was waiting at the bottom of the stairs and chuckled at her antics.

"Good, kind sir. You're punctual. The carriage awaits."

They discussed some of the problems of their day's endeavors while the carriage trotted along the London streets. Mina could barely contain her delight, frequently brushing aside the carriage curtains to peek outside. Soon they were pulling up in the Strand and getting out.

"I thought you might enjoy visiting a coffeehouse."

"I have always wondered what inside one might be like. I would imagine playwrights, poets, actors, politicians all gathered in a smoky and lively atmosphere drinking and arguing late into the night." A sigh of anticipation left Mina. "I even read about a floating coffeehouse, the Folly of the Thames, and how disreputable it had been."

Simpson's Grand Cigar Divan at 101-102 the Strand was a fascinating building. Upon entering through the glazed doors, she noticed a huge window, where one could watch the world go by or acknowledge one's friends. It had a lamp above the glass bearing the legend Grand Cigar Divan. Mina straightened her shoulders, following Simon into the fairly noisy coffeehouse.

He paid the attendant two shillings, which was their entry fee. The price included coffee and a cigar, all the day's newspapers, and the opportunity to play chess. The attendant showed them to an empty table and went to order their coffee. All around them, men were talking, some of them loudly, most of them about the plans to reform. Opinions were heated, with strong feelings on both sides of the discussion.

A waiter brought them coffee and cigars. Simon tipped him with a small coin. "Could you bring us a chess set?"

"At once, my lord," the servant said, bowing.

Mina sipped her coffee and watched Simon as he rolled the cigar in his fingers and then tapped it against the table. When the chess set appeared, she set up the pieces, glancing nervously at her own cigar.

"Here, shall I trim the end for you?" Simon said, smirking and bringing out a silver cigar cutter.

"I've never smoked before, my lord, but I suppose there's a first time for everything," she said, smiling.

"You smile far too prettily for a lad, Mr. Crawford."

Mina dipped her head to hide her reaction. When she was assured that she had control over her smiles, she met Simon's gaze. "Why did you think of this?"

"Are you exhilarated?"

"Most assuredly," she murmured.

"Then my aim is met." A shadow touched his eyes. "The next time you climb a tree and dream, I want you to remember tonight and all your moments with me."

That sweet ache inside her chest intensified even as she was reminded that all of this had an ending. "They will keep me company, always."

Simon cut the cigar end and then lit it for her.

"We are living dangerously tonight," Mina drawled.

"That we are," he said with a small smile that hit her right in the heart.

She sucked in the smoke from the lit cigar and choked, coughing and spluttering. "It is ghastly!"

He chuckled. "Perhaps, you had best not. You're only a bantling, after all. I will smoke it and keep this one for later." So saying, he tucked the spare cigar into his breast pocket and took the offending cigar from her.

They set to playing chess, and some of the other men hovered and watched. The first game was over swiftly, with Mina taking Simon's king with considerable ease and panache. By now nearly all the men in the coffeehouse had clustered around them to watch, because Simon was not known to have ever lost a game of chess before. They were setting up the pieces for a second game when Mina noticed the hush in the crowd, and a man wearing spectacles in the corner furiously scribbling in a journal.

"What is happening?" she asked, careful to keep her tone low and scratchy.

"They are in awe that you had me pinned down for over thirty minutes. That man is a journalist, and tomorrow all of society will read about our match."

Mina was astonished. "We are not playing against time!"

"I am that good," he said with roguish arrogance. "Come, my good sir, are you up for another?"

She lifted her chin. "I love a good challenge."

Pleasure burned his eyes brightly, and Mina loved that he saw her as a worthy opponent. Leaning over to study the newly set-up board with fierce concentration, she tried to drown out the soft mutters abounding about whether Creswick could actually lose two matches in a row, with others suggesting that before he had merely been indulgent. There were some bets placed and a little teasing over the earl having met his match. Mina blushed as she was congratulated on beating the earl previously. This time, Simon's concentration was as intense as hers. She felt awed and proud that he thought she was worth his complete focus. Determined to play the best match, she leaned forward and gave it her all.

Almost an hour later, Simon conceded to a draw, and the crowd around them cheered, with even a few clapping her on the shoulders. Simon grinned and discreetly winked at her, and Mina flushed with pleasure.

Some of the gentlemen present fell to discussing the war in Abyssinia. The conversation got heated again, as many of the group believed the British army should punish the Abyssinian Empire and thrash them soundly.

They settled down to a third game, but this time Simon's moves were too good for her, and she lost with her queen and king taken. Having decided to move on, the two spilled out into the night air, and Mina lifted her face to the sky.

"The evening has been glorious, my lord! Where do we go next?"

He arched a brow. "You are not tired?"

"There is too much excitement in my veins. I have read about gambling dens. I admit I have always wanted to peek inside one, and is there a better time than tonight?"

She held her breath for him to deny her, but his mouth only curved into a sensual smile.

"Then away we shall go."

Mina stared at him, speechless. As she stared, a searing flash of awareness burned through her. She couldn't possibly crave anything in life as much as she desired to be with Simon always.

"What are you thinking, Mina?" he demanded gruffly, stepping far too close to her, considering they were pretending to be gentlemen.

"That I...I..." Her throat closed over the words. *That I do not want this to ever end.*

He smiled knowingly, and her belly fluttered with nerves and a sense of shock. What did that smile mean?

The earl lifted his hand for his carriage, and once they were settled in the vehicle, it drove away. She gripped the edges of the seat, almost desperate to question him but afraid to ruin a night that felt perfect.

The carriage ride was shorter than expected, and only a few minutes later, Mina was almost breathless with anticipation when they strolled inside the Asylum, a gambling den that had been notorious and well received for the last several years and was considered one of the golden halls, and in the caliber of Brooks or White's.

She pressed a hand over her chest and laughed. "Oh my."

The interior had been decorated with the aim to dazzle the senses and tempted one to sin and decadence. A twenty-set orchestra was on a raised dais, and they played the Venetian waltz. Several couples danced, the ladies twirling in their lavish ball gowns and face masks and the men fashionably dressed. To the left of the dancing couples were a large, organized sprawl of tables where men sat with cigars in one hand and cards in the other. At several tables, cards were sliced and shuffled with artistic expertise, or dice danced between the roulette wheels, several players waiting with evident anticipation to see which way their luck ran.

"This is the first floor. There is a second and third floor with more gambling," Simon said. "You could find a pretty lady to invite to the dance floor or take a risk and gamble."

Her heart pounded. "I could play faro."

"Are you good?"

"I've only ever played Anthony," she admitted with a wrinkle of her nose.

Simon grinned. "I shall spot you a hundred pounds for you to test your mettle at any table."

"A hundred pounds to gamble with," she choked out. "All with the possibility I might lose? I do not believe I shall be playing, my lord. I will observe."

He cast her an amused glance. "Men make fortunes at these tables and lose entire estates."

A lady passed by with a silver slaver of champagne and Mina plucked two glasses and held out one to the earl. A wicked kind of daring went through her, and she grinned. "Perhaps I might use five pounds."

He chuckled and led her through the crowd. Mina ended up using three hundred pounds and winning ten thousand. Still giddy from her wins and the four glasses of champagne, Mina asked him to walk for a few minutes instead of riding in the carriage.

"I still cannot believe I won such an astronomical sum. I shall not sleep a wink tonight! Anthony will not know what to do with himself when I inform him of this."

"I sense you are already making plans for how to spend your fortune," Simon said. "I can see those wheels spinning."

Mina laughed. "I am. We'll settle some of Anthony's debt of course. Then I shall shop until my feet hurt. The children will be so delighted."

The earl had stopped in the shadows of a gas lamp on St. James Street. "The children?"

She glanced over her shoulders. "Charlie, Oliver, Thomas, Susan, Mary, Nathaniel, Matthew, Annabelle, Agatha, Elizabeth, Edward, Harriette, and Sarah."

"Your thirteen students."

"Yes. I'll buy each a new coat, shoes, and parcels of sweets. Perhaps some chocolate bars. The local vicar had plans to build a school, and it has been postponed several times. I will discuss it with Anthony, because I am certain he will agree that this fortune can be shared so a proper school is done."

Mina's smile faltered when she noted the way Simon stared at her. "What is it? Do I have a spot on my face?"

"What will you purchase for yourself?"

Her heart jolted and she stopped, peering up at him. "I…I have no desire for anything…perhaps except you." The words spilled unplanned from her, and Mina froze. She had felt unbalanced since the first time she kissed this brilliant man before her; now looking into his eyes, she felt steadied. Unafraid of admitting that she was falling in love with him.

He drew her into the pocket of shadows with him and took her mouth in a kiss that filled her with burning desire.

"I shall build the school for you," he murmured against her mouth.

"You shall do no such thing!"

"How do you plan to stop me?" This demand was said with an arrogant lift of his brow, then the dratted man walked away.

Mina growled, ran after him, and jumped onto his back, laughing at the sheer impulsiveness and sense of play which had propelled her.

"I am at a loss as to what you are doing, Miss Crawford."

"Ah, Miss Crawford. How I miss hearing you call me so."

"Are you fully aware you are on my back?" Yet instead of urging her down, he hooked his arms under her legs and hoisted her farther up.

"It is almost three in the morning, the street is dark and empty, the area shrouded by fog and mystery. There is no one to see us. Best of all, we are dressed as gentlemen."

"Therein lies the problem," he said drily. "We are as men and should we be seen, it—"

His words vanished when a carriage clattered to a stop right at their feet. Before Mina had the presence of mind to jump from his back, the small carriage window shoved open, and the dowager countess's face appeared.

"Creswick?"

Her tone suggested she observed a scene she had little chance of ever comprehending.

"Grandmother," he said in a tone coated with cultivated boredom. "How are you?"

A strangled sound came from Lady Creswick, and she clearly took several moments to compose herself. Mina kept her head down, but there could be no mistaking the feel of his grandmother's eyes upon her. *Oh God.* How could they have been so caught up in their bantering that she'd not heard the approaching equipage? It was evident to Mina the dowager countess returned home from a ball. A bit early since most of the *haut ton* partied to the wee hours of the morning.

"Shall I offer you a ride, Creswick?" the dowager countess demanded sharply. "And your...companion?"

"I am content with walking, madam. I shall bid you a pleasant journey home."

The dowager countess seemed unsure what to make of the entire affair but kept her counsel. She withdrew, closing the window with a decided *snick*. The carriage rolled away.

"Hurry, let me down!"

Mina paused when she realized the earl's shoulders were shaking, and rich laughter poured from him. She wiggled and he let her down, with no effort to contain his amusement. She stared at him, her heart pounding, thinking his laugh was the loveliest thing she had ever heard. The ridiculousness of the entire matter struck her. Mina smiled, and then she too started to laugh. It felt the most natural thing in the world for them to stand there laughing for several moments.

He reached out and touched her cheek. "I love laughing with you."

Such simple words, yet they slammed into her heart with the force of a hammer, for it sounded like he'd never had reason to laugh before. Mina quickly tipped onto her toes and brushed a kiss across his mouth, then stepped back. "I love laughing with you, too, Simon."

They stared at each other, his eyes gleaming with dangerous sensuality.

"Why do I feel we are not only talking about laughter," she whispered, feeling the promise in his stare.

"Well done, Miss Crawford," he murmured and held out his hand. "Well done."

Her heart shook fiercely, and Mina felt that if she took his hand, she was responding to that silent question in his eyes, that demand for more…for perhaps always. She took his hand, and though he squeezed her fingers gently through the gloves, they did not speak, but continued walking, even when it started to rain.

CHAPTER FIFTEEN

Over the course of the next few weeks, the fashionable capital of London came alive as the weather warmed, spring announced itself in a bright burst of colors and sunshine, and more support for reform grew. Tension ran unchecked through England, and each week it seemed as if the earl received a report of some protest from Manchester, Leeds, or Edinburgh. A few times the earl would call for his carriage to visit these places, and the newspapers would mention the eloquent speech Lord Creswick had given to settle the crowd and that the working people were awed that he would take the time to even speak with them. Below stairs, servants gossiped with an air of anticipation and expectation about how reform would impact their lives and their extended families'.

Lords and ladies planned their lavish balls, dinner and card parties, charity balls, galas, musicales, outings, and grand picnics. Mina had kept busy answering piles of social correspondence and letters for the earl, and at times helping him to draft speeches. It seemed as if all the hostesses wanted Lord Creswick either in their dining room, drawing room, or ballroom. The man was immensely popular, yet he was indifferent to it all.

Her chest ached at the thought of him, and she lowered the book she'd been reading, *The Undying One* by Caroline Norton, and rested her head against the headrest of the sofa. The worst thing she could do was feel enough for Simon to ache for him, yet it was also the best thing. Mina peered sightlessly into the fireplace. She was falling deeper and deeper into loving him, a thing she knew would only bring her heartache. Yet she could not prevent herself from her continual tumble. Each night in his arms filled her with more delight and equal despair.

Only an hour ago, the earl had taken her with a slow, thorough wickedness in his office atop his desk, and his gaze had quiet depth, filled with things she did not want to see. Things that made her heart leap with wonder, awe, and tenderness. That this man would even think to start falling for her…because that was what it felt like with each day spent in his office working together and nights spent wrapped up in each other. More frequently of late, they would break off to play chess or to just indulge in idle chatter as if to do away with the tension building in the city resulting from the speeches in the House of Commons. Then there were the days they fenced together, and then the times when he loved her with such intensity, it was almost frightening. All of that…felt like the beginning of love.

Or perhaps we are beyond that.

The door opened and she rose as the dowager countess entered with a most beautiful lady who affected some surprise at seeing Mina in the drawing room.

"Your Ladyship," Mina said, dipping into a quick curtsy.

The dowager countess gave her a tight smile. Mina suspected the lady had come to believe that it was because of her presence the earl had not taken the time to accept a call from the lady Mina believed was Lady Cassandra, the lady the earl was supposed to marry. Mina had heard enough urgings from his grandmother to make time in his busy schedule to meet the lady, but the earl had always declined.

Mina had to admit that Lady Cassandra was a real beauty, slender but with ample curves, her clear complexion the perfect strawberries-and-cream of the ideal English belle. Her gown was simple, with few embellishments in excellent taste, and a sweet but subtle perfume floated around her. Her raven locks, carefully arranged in plump ringlets, shone and bounced as she moved, and from every angle she looked the very picture of winsome elegance.

The earl entered the drawing room, his attention on the papers in his hands. "Miss Crawford, I received a most urgent letter from—" He simply stopped when he saw the other ladies inside the room.

"Grandmother," he said drily. "I never knew you were coming."

"Of course, I could not announce it," she said with a touch of asperity. "I've not had the pleasure to sit and converse with you for the last month."

"I am busy."

"*Bah*, you are an earl. You will always be busy. Allow me to present to you, Lady Cassandra Farcoun, daughter of Lord Gilmanton. Lady Cassandra, this is my grandson, Simon, Lord of Creswick."

The lady hurriedly dipped into a graceful curtsy and the earl bowed. The dowager countess almost grudgingly introduced Mina, who curtsied to Lady Cassandra.

"A lady secretary," she said brightly. "The idea sounds novel and vastly entertaining. I do admire women who are not able to marry and do not hesitate to seek honest employment."

Mina detected no spite in the girl's tone, just an open friendliness.

"It has been eye-opening and refreshing," she said with a small smile.

"If you ladies will excuse me," the earl began, only to be interrupted by his grandmother's cry that he must sit with them for a spell.

He cast his grandmother an indifferent glance but acquiesced to sitting in a wingback chair a small distance away from everyone, his expression aloof and bored. Mina was surprised when the invitation was extended to her, and she graciously accepted, careful to not glance at the earl. The dowager rang for tea and cakes, then settled her gaze on Mina—a look she did not like. It was…cold and assessing.

Lady Cassandra aimed a polite smile at her. "What book do you read, Miss Crawford?"

"It is *The Undying One* by Caroline Norton. It is a delightful read—"

The outraged gasp of the dowager countess strangled the rest of Mina's words.

"You would read that woman's work and claim it to be delightful?"

"Forgive me," Mina said, "I was not aware Caroline Norton was an objectionable character, nor that her work was considered so."

"Is she not the lady who had an affair with Lord Melbourne who was then sued for criminal conversation by Mr. Norton? A stunt that almost brought down the government and to this day is a taint against the earl's great legacy."

Lady Cassandra gasped. "Permit me to ask, what is

criminal conversation?"

"In simple terms, adultery," Mina murmured, a piercing disquiet settling heavily on her chest.

The dowager countess's lips flattened. "That you would read such a woman's work is questionable of your character, Miss Crawford, and—"

"Is it?" the earl asked with an icy air of boredom.

"Creswick—" his grandmother began.

"There is nothing questionable about Miss Crawford's character, and I'll not suffer anyone who suggests otherwise."

Lady Cassandra had stiffened, staring at her with a frown, then back at the earl.

Mina curled her finger over the book. "Thank you, your lordship, but I am quite able to defend myself, not that I believe I must. However, Your Ladyship, please allow me to say that Lord Melbourne's testimony in court was that Mrs. Norton's husband was abusive and she only fled to him as a friend, for she had not the temper to manage her husband's own. Nothing else was proven, certainly not an affair. I admire Miss Norton because she was denied the right to see her children by her husband from sheer malice and spite, but she was not defeated in her spirit," Mina said softly. "She proved herself a woman of courage by becoming involved in promoting laws to achieve social justice, especially those granting rights to married and divorced women. I find her to be a woman of courage and unfailing strength."

"*Bah*!" The dowager duchess said with disdain. "That woman almost ruined a great man, and it saddens me to think that the scandal of being sued over that ghastly affair is what is mostly remembered about

Lord Melbourne, even years later after that debacle. And it is for that reason I must ask you, Miss Crawford, why don't you answer to the name Mrs. Petretti? I would hate for my grandson to be so similarly sued and dragged before the courts."

Shock scattered her thoughts, and a soft breath shuddered from between her lips. Mina's heart was beating so hard, she felt sure that her voice must shake. "I…" Truly, she could not say anything.

Simon had grown so still, it was as if he were made of marble, and a quick glance in his eyes only revealed an expression of chilling indifference.

"If you have something to say, grandmother, please say it," he murmured.

"I merely recalled that Miss Crawford eloped a number of years ago. An acquaintance of mine ran into her husband only last year in Glasgow. I simply wondered why she does not mention him. Is Mr. Petretti not in town, Mrs. Petretti?"

Mina swallowed down the tight feeling of dread. "I do not go by that name, Your Ladyship, and I have no knowledge of Mr. Petretti's whereabouts, as he does not answer to me, nor I to him. We live our lives separately and have done so since our marriage."

Mina took a sip of her tea, determined to remain unflappable even as she wept inside. She had known the affair with Simon would have ended one day, she had just never imagined that it could in this manner.

The dowager countess narrowed her eyes at Mina's affected calm, then looked at her grandson. He was in turn staring at Mina, his expression inscrutable, but his eyes burned with emotions. Lowering her head, she stared down into the curling smoke lifting off the tea, hating that tears obscured her vision.

"Never say you did not know of it, Creswick," his grandmother said coyly. "I am certain you understand why I had to bring it up, given the topic of discourse."

"What I understand is that the topic proved useful for your agenda. How you must have silently cheered when you saw the book Miss Crawford read," he said with biting softness.

"Creswick! I had Miss Crawford investigated only for your sake. You hired a woman with a past scandal without doing your due diligence. We can only hope Mr. Petretti will not surface to embroil you in a dreadful scandal by taking you before the courts! That has been my great fear since I discovered you cavorting with her about town dressed as a gentleman! Did you not think I recognized Miss Crawford?"

Lady Cassandra gasped, for his grandmother's words were all but an accusation that she believed they had both committed adultery. *Oh God*! Mina had not even considered the risk to the earl. Yet the worry of it now lodged in her heart with the force of a battering ram.

"If you will excuse me, grandmother, Lady Cassandra, I have tarried long enough from work and I have urgent reports to attend. Miss Crawford, if you will join me, you are needed for dictation."

Mina rose, and it was with jangled emotions and a twisting pain low in her belly, she made her excuses to both ladies and exited through the door the earl held open for her. She could feel the dowager countess's stare on their retreating backs. The earl closed the door and walked beside her down the hallway.

"Simon," she began.

"Do not speak, Mina."

She flinched and gripped the edges of her skirts until her knuckles pained her. His words had been mild, but they had stung with a raw undertone of indefinable emotions. The tears came, impossible to stop, but thankfully they were silent ones. Mina did not want to cry about something she had no hope of changing, yet the tears fell, and pain felt as if it pricked all over her body.

• • •

Simon held himself still as Mina faced him, her eyes and cheeks damp with tears, but her chin lifted. That icy knot in his gut only grew colder at the evidence of her misery.

"Are you married?" The sound of his voice was oddly disjointed to his ears.

Mina closed her eyes, torment etched on her face. "Simon, I—"

"Answer me!"

She flinched. "Yes."

"To a man who is alive?"

Vulnerability glittered in her eyes. "Yes. I…that is my secret, my lord. But let me say I am not married in my heart or in my actions."

Those soft words sucked the air from his lungs and burned him with a raw feeling of denial and rage. Simon held himself still, ruthlessly suppressing the feelings until he was numb, until his heart was immovable. It took immeasurable effort, for everything about Mina Crawford moved him, especially the tears that now coursed down her cheeks. "Tell me about it."

She lifted trembling fingers to tuck a few wisps of hair behind her ears. "When we... When we eloped to Scotland, we got married."

"Who is the gentleman in 'we,' Mina?"

She appeared disconcerted for a minute, tucking the strands of her hair behind her ears with shaking fingers. "Leonardo Petretti. He was...my fencing tutor. He was young and dashing and I thought he was... amazing."

"How old were you?"

"I was fourteen when he started teaching me and Anthony and...and a little over seventeen when we eloped." She closed her eyes as if pained by the memory. "My father did not fight my assurances that I wanted to marry Mr. Petretti. You see, he was a man who believed in love and loved my mother greatly."

The damn fool, Simon thought viciously of the man he had admired. When he should have been protecting her from the man's advances, instead he had damn well cossetted and indulged her.

"My father had been urging me to accept an offer from Viscount Deerling, a man who was wealthy and would not mind my dowry only to be a thousand pounds. I railed against this and even confessed to Leonardo that my father was encouraging me to marry another. He... He convinced me to elope with him instead, and I was so foolish and certain of my feelings and that I was embarking on a grand adventure, I was persuaded into eloping by my own reckless heart. Though I felt I made a mistake almost as soon as we were away, I realized it was too late to turn back. We were married as soon as we reached Scotland."

She took a bracing breath and leaned against the

wall. "On our wedding night while I waited for him to come to me, I grew so nervous about what to expect that I decided to go downstairs in the inn and ask for a drink. As I passed a door, I heard female laughter and a man's voice. It sounded so much like him that I paused to listen, and so certain it was he, I opened the door. He was... He was with another woman in bed, and they were naked."

His fingers tightened on his glass. "The rotten bastard."

"I thought so myself and told him as much before rushing to my room. I had started to pack when he entered and said I was being silly. She was just his mistress and all men had mistresses, surely I knew that was the way of the world. I was so astonished that I laughed. I called him vermin and said I could only blame myself for thinking I might love him one day, and even with the promise of adventurously traveling, I preferred to return home. And he slapped me."

Simon grew cold, and in that moment he knew he would find the man who laid his hands on her and gut him.

"That even shocked me more and...well, I slapped him back."

Good girl. Still, what she had revealed about the man's character made Simon close his eyes, almost afraid to hear the rest of the sordid tale.

"He..." Mina's breath caught at the memory and her voice trailed away. "He hurt me."

The soft words were devoid of feelings but her green eyes swirled with them—remembered pain and shame and such unflinching defiance.

"How did he hurt you?"

"He hit me several times," she said quietly. "I had known that I made a foolish decision when I saw him with that lady. I was greatly deceived of his character and the affection he claimed to have for me. But when he slapped me over and over, even against my stomach dropping me to the floor, I knew he was a monster I would never forgive. I was so filled with rage and pain, I...I grabbed the chamber pot and hit him over the head with all my strength. He crashed to the floor, and to ensure he did not get up and chase me, I hit him twice more. I feared I had killed him. I packed what little I had traveled with and ran."

Ah, Mina. Simon could not have imagined the courage it must have taken for her to fight back in a world where women had no rights when under the power of a husband. Worse, she had been a naïve girl of seventeen years whose only fault had been to dream of adventure.

Her eyes were large and wounded as she held his stare. "I tried to return to England. I had no money. I was so determined to leave Scotland, I started walking. Lord Kittredge and his countess picked me up and were kind enough to deliver me home."

"Such a kindness that the countess had to spread what she saw."

Mina had no reply and stared at him in silent misery. "She suspected an elopement and pried, but I gave her no confirmation. I unburdened myself to my father once I was home and he set out to find Mr. Petretti. I am not sure what Papa intended but he never found him. The scandal that I was found alone, coming back from a clear elopement, was all over town in a few days and even followed us to the countryside. My reputation was then irretrievably ruined."

Simon recalled reading about it and dismissing the entire thing as frivolous and beneath his notice. "And this man has never reached out to you over the years?"

"No."

"Was the wedding over the anvil?"

His gut clenched as he waited for her answer. *Please, God*, he thought, and Simon was not much of a praying man. *Let it be a simple Gretna Green marriage with a blacksmith*.

"No. You see he had planned ahead, and the banns had been called in the local Kirk weeks before. He explained it as a surprise, and I did not mind it. All I truly imagined was the adventure of traveling the continent."

He flinched before he could prevent himself.

"It was before a local priest in a kirk and there is a marriage register."

Simon felt as if he had been kicked in the chest. Miss Mina Crawford was well and fucking truly married. Except the marriage had not been consummated. He held on to that thought, his mind whirling, the hollow ache inside his chest intensifying.

"What would you do should he present himself in your life demanding his husbandly rights? There is no law to protect you."

"I always have an empty chamber pot at the ready," she said lightly, but he saw the fright in her eyes. "And there are no laws yet. Every day I feel more hope that one day things will change and then I might be free of my mistake. But I would never live with that man, share a home with him, or go where he goes, even if he tries to drag me with him. I would fight him, and I would fight the law."

Simon nodded, scrubbing a hand over his face. Mina did not love this blackguard and never had, yet she was bound to him with no way to be free. There was nothing for them beyond an affair. Seeing the fright and tears in her eyes, a feeling he could not defend against—a brutal, aching need to slay those fears—wrenched through him with shocking intensity. "Mina," he said gruffly. "Come here."

Her eyes widened and a harsh sob escaped her. "Where?"

"Into my arms."

There was a little upward tilt of her chin, a slight parting of her lips. "Still?"

"Always."

With a harsh cry, she hurtled herself against him and he held her to his chest as she sobbed. "I am sorry I did not tell you. I meant it to be a secret until we parted because there was simply no purpose to say it and I was... I was afraid to tell you how much you mean to me and the feelings I own for you in my heart because I knew... I knew it was impossible for us..." The words died away as her voice broke.

"You were under no obligations to share your secrets, Mina. I have mine, too."

That I am falling in love with you, and I cannot stop it any more than I can expect water to flow uphill. A thing perhaps he would never speak aloud. For what would be the purpose of it? There was no future for them. That place he wanted to harden inside himself suffered its first crack.

Mina's fingers clutched at his jacket. "Am I still

your secretary?" Her words were muffled against his chest.

"Yes."

Am I still your lover? Those words lingered unspoken, but he felt them.

The door opened, and his grandmother's eyes widened, her lips parting in shock. Simon returned her stare, his expression inscrutable. "You should learn to knock, Your Ladyship," he said.

Mina stiffened in his arms before gently extracting herself. She dipped into a curtsy. "Your Ladyship, I was overcome with emotions and—"

Simon cut her off. "Under this roof, you owe no explanation to anyone but me, Miss Crawford."

Her eyes were intense as she watched him, proud and yet vulnerable. "Thank you."

"If you'll excuse me, Miss Crawford, I will meet with my grandmother. Please avail yourself of the library, read and…and simply be free with your thoughts." Simon turned around and with measured steps followed his grandmother to the smaller office that he did not use.

His grandmother whirled around as he closed the door, every line of her slim figure vibrating with indignation. "The scene I just witnessed is beyond the pale, Simon. That you would leave me and Lady Cassandra alone to comfort that woman is…it is shockingly insupportable."

"What is insupportable was that you had her investigated, knowing it might stir her scandal," he said with tempered steel. "She is under my protection and for some baffling reason, you did not keep that in mind when you acted."

Silence fell and his grandmother appeared unusually flustered. "I had to know the nature of her elopement."

"You did not. It is no one's business but her own."

Her gaze sharpened. "Do you mean to keep this Miss Crawford as your mistress?"

"That, madam, is not your concern." He considered her. "Miss Crawford is my friend and will always be my friend."

An incredulous laugh came from her. "Do you think I do not see how you look at her, my boy? Like a ravenous wolf, surely for all of London to see! You took her to a coffeehouse only last week and sat there and discussed politics with her as if she were a peer. It was mentioned in the scandal sheets. Surely you saw them wondering that you own to having a female secretary whom you've publicly praised for her shrewdness and wit. A friendship with that woman cannot be supported—"

"You dare to tell me how to live my life?" he said with a harsh bite. "I had thought you a different woman, Grandmother, but I now see I erred in my judgment."

Her eyes flashed. "And what do you mean by that?"

"Do you know of Miss Crawford's wit and intelligence? Of her bravery, and kindness, and loyalty? What do you know of her character that would permit you to stand in judgment of her like the many idle fools who pepper the *haut ton*, only puffed up with their own vanity and ruthless selfishness? You dare judge one of the best ladies I have ever known and on what grounds? You made deliberate and callous insinuations today in front of Lady Cassandra, knowing the possibility that she might make unflattering remarks to her set or spread idle gossip. Rein her in," he hissed with biting coldness. "I promise I shall crush anyone who dares malign Miss Crawford in the *haut ton*."

"You mistake the matter," his grandmother said tightly. "Lady Cassandra will not spread such rumors because they also link your name to Miss Crawford."

"Do not play the fool. Men are never reviled in a supposed affair. It is the women who are always ground beneath the collective boots of society. You very well know it and it is that you played and hoped upon."

Her mouth tightened wryly and she had the grace to at least appear guilty, if only for a brief moment.

Simon allowed his lips to curve into a smile he only gave his political opponents. "See that you never act against Miss Crawford in such a manner again, Grandmother. I will not forgive it a second time."

He walked away from her with silent assurance, calling for his horse to be prepared as he left the office. Simon did not want to see Mina right now—or anyone for that matter. He simply wanted to ride and close himself away from the chaotic dissonance scything through his mind, and the raw agony that seemed to stab at his chest. It was an inevitable conclusion for him to realize he had lost her before he had even gotten a chance to make her his.

CHAPTER SIXTEEN

The very next morning, a team of the best lawyers and barristers in London were crowded into Simon's library, responding to his summons for they were eager to procure the business of The Earl of Creswick.

"I fear an annulment may prove to be impossible," Mr. Drummond, lead solicitor of the firm Drummond & Peel said. "This marriage took place in Scotland. Though they are a bit more flexible with their marriage laws than England and Wales, there is no justification in existence for an annulment."

Hell. "Tell me more," Simon said from where he sat behind the large oak desk. "Are you certain?"

Everyone remained silent, as if afraid to be the bearer of bad news.

Finally, a junior barrister said, "Yes, your lordship. It can only be a divorce. And it is certain this was not a Gretna Green marriage?"

"It was not done with an anvil priest but in a local kirk, and there is a marriage register. There was no consummation of this marriage and they have not lived as man and wife for over six years. Divorces are allowed in Scotland and the woman is allowed to sue."

A few of the solicitors shared glances. It was Drummond himself who said, "A petition will have to be put before The Court of Session in Edinburgh. They will only grant a divorce on the grounds of adultery and on the grounds of desertion."

"It will be desertion, as the wife was not provided

for in any respect by the husband as was his duty to undertake, and the man has publicly traveled with a mistress in Glasgow and even farther abroad," he said icily. "I want to know about every man that sits on that court. I want to know their lives from infancy. I want to know their weaknesses, and who is susceptible to threats and bribery."

He met the stare of each man, allowing them to see his ruthless resolve. "No expenses must be spared. I also want a deep investigation into that…Leonardo Petretti. Everything about the man I want to know, including his location."

"Yes, your lordship," several voices caroused before they stood, and one after the other left his townhouse.

Simon sat in his study for several minutes, one forgotten drink in his hand, his eyes staring unseeing into the empty fireplace. Then he stood and went down to the drawing room where his grandmother awaited him.

She regally nodded her head when he entered. "I received your rather vague summons earlier. What is this that you must discuss that you could not have said in that note?"

"I have never broken my word to you before, Grandmother, and I beg your forgiveness that I must do so now."

His grandmother stilled. "I am listening, Creswick."

"I will not be making an offer for Lady Cassandra Farcoun, nor can I allow you to select the woman I am to make my countess."

His grandmother waited a few beats before saying, "You have not given Lady Cassandra a chance or even attempted to court her."

"The lady is certainly beautiful, but I am not interested in her."

His grandmother sighed. "I had my hopes rested on her."

"I know you did. However, I must consider someone else."

"What exactly is your objection to Lady Cassandra?"

"I do not feel anything for her, while I feel…everything for another. I made that vow as a boy, and I understand why you asked it of me. However it is no longer necessary. It would not be fair or honorable to marry one woman while I love another."

His grandmother looked startled, then her face creased in a delighted smile. "My boy, I never imagined to hear words of love from you one day. I am very heartened to hear it. Who is this lady? Is it the Duke of Vernon's daughter? You made a very pretty picture when you danced with her last evening."

She said this with a hopeful air and a wary look in her eyes. Simon suspected his grandmother full well knew the lady with whom he had fallen in love.

"It is Miss Crawford."

His grandmother froze. "*Miss Crawford*?"

How aghast she sounded.

"Yes."

"She is a married woman with a husband who is very much alive. The man was last seen gallivanting around Glasgow with his mistress." She sucked in a harsh breath. "You *must* marry. If you must have her, discreetly take her to be your mistress after you've married. Do not look at me so, it is what is done, and has been done by gentlemen for centuries. In everything you do, never forget that she would not be a mistress like most others, for she is married!" his grandmother reaffirmed stridently. "Should society get wind of it, that husband can sue you for adultery and vilify your good name in the courts."

There went that clawing tearing through his heart again. "Miss Crawford would be no man's mistress, nor would I dishonor any vows I made to my wife," he said icily. "It is also of little consequence that she is married. I mean to see her free from those shackles."

"What are you saying, Creswick?"

"I mean to procure her a divorce."

His grandmother slowly stood, looking ready to faint. "A *divorce*?"

"Yes."

"You cannot mean it," she began faintly.

"I do. It has been done before. Several times." He stood and walked over to the windows. "Then after I have freed her from that vile pond scum, I shall marry her."

His grandmother sat so abruptly, it was if someone had pushed her. "Have you lost your good senses? You would associate yourself with a woman with such low moral rectitude and—"

"Be careful, Grandmother," he warned, turning slightly to meet her fiery gaze. "I shall suffer no insult toward Miss Crawford."

"Creswick," she said sharply. "You are not thinking. You must not marry her."

"I am not a man who is easily muddled in thought. I explained myself to you, and only to you, Grandmother, because I love and respect you."

She jolted, her eyes widening, and it sunk into his

bones then that he had never used such words with her before. Not in all the years she had tried to cuddle him close as a lad, or even as a youth when she spoke words of affections to him. He had always shied away for he was not an emotional boy, and he had never returned her grandmotherly sentiments.

"Before I met Miss Crawford, love was simply a word. Now I understand what the word conveys," he said, his tone low and measured. "Trust. Loyalty. Courage in the face of hardship. Laughter. Admiration. Passion. I do not take the word lightly and never will. I love Miss Crawford, and she will be the only woman I'll ever love."

His grandmother stood, her expression lined with regret. "You will be socially humiliated if it becomes known you married a divorced woman."

"There will be no scandal. I will bury it and anyone who tries to create one," he said confidently, an implacable will filling his veins. He had too much to lose if he could not suppress all murmurings. Mina's happiness, other influential lords' respect, and support that he would need for future votes, especially for the Reform Bill.

"You are not thinking," she hissed.

"I am very clear in my thinking."

She waved her hand. "In recent years, every time a divorce bill has been introduced in England it was voted out against, with words such as 'disgusting and demoralizing' the main points of discussion. It was even proposed that a divorced woman should not be allowed to ever remarry, and many believe Scotland by giving women the right to divorce means they are a country without morals!"

"The hypocrites," he said cuttingly. "What need have I to fear hypocrites?"

Her eyes flashed. "Society will see Miss Crawford as *immoral*! And to think that…that she would be allowed to marry *you*, a beloved peer of the realm? My boy, it would be political suicide. You may love Miss Crawford, but you must never marry her."

He walked over to her. "Miss Crawford will be the only woman I'll marry because it is her I love. Only her."

•••

You must never marry her.

Mina stood in the doorway, staring at the earl and the dowager countess locked in battle. So cold and raw were their arguments they had not heard her open the door.

It is her I love. Only her.

Mina was destroyed. Simon wanted to marry her? Why did she let it hurt like this? She hadn't expected love or loyalty. But how she had wanted it. But though it hovered within her reach, she would be the most selfish creature to claim anything from Simon.

His grandmother looked over his shoulder, and whatever she saw in Mina's expression made her close her eyes with a heavy sigh of regret. When the dowager countess looked at her again, there was an odd glint of respect in her eyes, as if she understood what Mina was about.

Simon turned to her. "I was not aware you had entered, Mina."

"I… I did not mean to interrupt. I knocked and no one answered. There is a solicitor in your office…I…" Mina let out a long breath and her words blew away like ashes in the wind.

Simon Loughton, the Earl of Creswick loved her.

He walked over to her, his expression serious and intent. Uncaring that his grandmother was still in the room, he stopped in front of her, staring down at her with hungry shadows in his eyes. He took her chin in his hand. "Tell me why you look so afraid."

"For you will slay the cause of it," she whispered.

"Yes."

Mina stared at him, seeing the truth in his expression. "I love you," she said in a cracked voice, unable to find any long speech about why she did. "I love you so much, I…" Her voice trailed off. She put her fist to her mouth.

His eyes gleamed and that sensual smile touched his mouth.

"I love you so much, I cannot bear the idea of never being in your life," she said hoarsely.

"Good, for I—"

She pressed her fingers over his mouth, halting the words. "But Simon, I would never consent to marry you in this lifetime."

Stillness flowed over him, transforming him into marble right before her eyes.

Mina couldn't breathe. Oh God. It hurt.

"Do you not believe I can procure your divorce?"

"Oh, I believe it," she said, uncaring that the dowager countess watched them with unchecked inquisitiveness "I *believe* it."

"Then if you have such faith in me, why do you hesitate in stepping forward with me?"

"*Because* I love you," she said again. "More than I have ever loved anyone in my entire life."

"Mina—"

"I would be a *divorced* woman, Simon. That you would dare to marry me after that would see you vilified and judged by your peers and all of society. Yes, women have made great strides and there are a few who have successfully been divorced in England. But surely you know that none of them are about in society. They were all cut from its ranks."

A harsh, forbidding grimace settled on his face, but how his eyes burned with untamed emotions. "I would not think you would be afraid of this. Do you for a second believe this scares me, Mina? Do you not know me at all?"

"I am afraid that they might cut you, destroy you and everything you have ever worked for."

"I am Creswick," he said with chilling arrogance. "They can try."

As she stared at him, a searing flash of awareness burned through her. "They would dare!" she cried. "Because you are so much more than a lord about town. You are also a voice of the people who do so much for them. Many might not know it, but those powerful lords who sit with you in the House, those gentlemen who sit in the Commons, all who see you as an enemy will use this divorce and society as the weapon they need to bring you down. You are known and respected for your influential voice in world affairs, and political battles across the realm. What reputation will they allow you to

have should you marry a divorced woman? Any
hint of a scandal may very well lose you the support
you need of your peers for the reform bill. Do you
not see it?"

The silence between them felt brittle and desperate. His grandmother started to walk away, as if
realizing the moment was too private to intrude
upon.

"I would give it all up," he said quietly.

The dowager countess stumbled, and Mina faltered into stillness. Those simple words destroyed
her, rendered her speechless, and stripped her of all
defenses.

Mina stood in the center of the room, staring at
him with silent tears rolling down her cheeks to wet
the collar of her shirt. Mina closed her eyes tightly
and shook her head without a word. She wanted to
reach for him and say, *hang it all*. Mina opened her
eyes, her gaze blurring with the tears that ran from
their corners. She saw the truth in his beautiful eyes.
He would give up his reputation, the legacy they
would try and tarnish, the good he might accomplish
in the future, because he loved her. She couldn't bear
the hurt.

For a moment, profound regret and sadness lined
the dowager countess's face before she squared her
shoulders and walked out of the room with jerky motions.

"Say you'll marry me when it is all done, Mina."

Her throat thickened in that desperate, aching way
that said she was afraid, afraid she might falter and
say yes. Afraid that she would be the cause of his ruin
and disgrace. Afraid that this brilliant, lovely man

would be made less because of her.

Mina was terribly afraid because she loved him more than she had ever thought possible to love. Unable to suppress the emotions tearing through her heart, she shook her head, unable to stop the tears rolling down her cheeks. "I'll be your lover, your mistress even," she said in a choked whisper. "But I'll not marry you, Simon."

Something elusive pooled in his gaze. "You have no faith in me, yet you say you love me."

She almost cried out at that flat, indifferent tone. They stared at each other in the silence that blanketed the drawing room. All she could hear was the sound of her own ragged breathing and her pounding heart.

"Very well, Miss Crawford, we shall return to work."

A jolt of shock went through her. She had always been astonished by his mercurial moods and brilliant nature, but the cloak of polite civility that he now pulled around himself, while she stood there vulnerable and shattered, almost felled her. Mina drew up on her resolve and struggled for equanimity.

"Very well, your lordship," she said hoarsely.

"I will still see you free," he said politely. "That way, I know you have the freedom to be more than just a girl who hid away in the country for fear from a brute and society's censure. You'll be free to travel, perhaps marry in a foreign country and fill your arms with children. Do you wish for that?"

She gripped her fingers until they hurt. Mina wanted to tell him that she would never marry another or love another, but the words were trapped in her throat. Instead, she said, "Yes."

And with that soft whisper, she felt as if the thread which had connected them had been severed.

Mina tried to work and found that she could barely see through the tears she shed. Pushing herself to her feet, she said, "Forgive me, my lord, I find that... I find that I am unable to continue working today."

"You may leave," he murmured without lifting his attention from the sheaf of papers in his hand.

She held on to her composure for the carriage ride to her home. Though she fought it valiantly, once she was inside, a harsh sob tore from her, and she ran down the hallway.

"Mina," Anthony said, opening the door to the drawing room. "I hoped that was you. Cousin Jocelyn has come to call. I was certain you would be most pleased to see her after so long...." He lowered his hand from the latch. "You look ghastly. What happened?"

She stared at him in silent misery. "Jocelyn is here?"

"Yes. She is to be married and heard we were in town. I know you have missed her these last few years."

"I... I cannot see her just yet, Anthony, I cannot."

Acting decisively, he stepped forward and closed the door behind him. "Did something happen with Creswick?"

Just the sound of his name created gaping wounds inside her heart. "Yes. I promise I shall explain it all later. Please convey my apologies to our cousin and I shall call upon her soon."

Then Mina turned around and dashed up the staircase for her bedchamber. Once there, she flung herself onto the bed. The memory of the first time she had met him, their duel, their first kiss, and the way he had laughed that night he took her out and about wrapped around her. Mina missed him already. She felt the pain of losing him inside her like a savage hook.

Enclosed in the privacy of her room, Mina sobbed, her entire body trembling and allowing all the tearing pain and loss out into her pillow.

CHAPTER SEVENTEEN

Simon peered down at the laughing crowd, aloof from the excitement which pulsed in the air at the midnight ball. His grandmother was in attendance and had signaled that she wanted him to attend her, but he had not yet gone over to her. She stood in a small circle with Lady Cassandra and her parents, Lord and Lady Gilmanton.

His grandmother was still hopeful that he might change his mind in regard to the lady. A few days ago, his grandmother had sent him a list of ladies, all from fine families, with suitable dowries, impeccable bloodlines, and without any stain or scandal attached to their names. He had burned it in the fireplace and sat in his library brooding and restless for hours.

Several days had passed since he discovered Mina was married. More than a week since she vowed never to marry him even after he freed her from that man. A week without her kisses or laughter or sparkling wit. A week in which she diligently did her work but cast him such somber stares. She would quickly glance away whenever he looked at her, and arduously attend to her task before bidding him good evening, then hurrying to his carriage to be whisked away to her brother's townhouse.

Simon did not reach for her in the days, and she did not reach for him. The awareness of the distance growing between them left him feeling unmoored—a sensation that was the very antithesis of his character. A feeling of loss haunted his sleep and prevented him from resting. There was a part of him that had felt removed from the world and its idiosyncrasies even apart from emotion, as if it had been frozen all his life. For a time, he had been considerably puzzled as to the nature of his own malaise, before Simon had accepted it as his natural state. Then her. Surely, it was the very first moment he'd met Miss Mina Crawford he had started to thaw without even realizing it. She had shaken his entire existence, and the revelation that she was possibly forever lost to him continually shattered his heart.

Simon breathed deeply, never imagining it was possible to feel such an agony that was not physical. Each day he saw that same pain and loss mirrored in Mina's gaze. God, he could never hate her for holding on to her secret, not when he respected her privacy so much. But he fucking hated that a part of him had been awoken because of her, and he had no idea how to put it back to sleep.

Then this morning, he had sharply started to rebuild himself to the man he had been before Mina Crawford, determined to once more be indifferent to the temptation to linger over her features, to yearn to touch the softness of her skin, and to take that lush mouth with his and become drunk on her kisses.

Pushing her from his thoughts, he descended from the upper balcony and into the lower floors, wading a path to his grandmother. A few gentlemen snagged his attention, and they discussed politics briefly, before he excused himself and carried on.

Prowling over to Lady Cassandra, whom he had

been publicly introduced to earlier, he requested her hand in a dance. The lady exchanged a small smile with her mother before accepting. He spied the relief in his grandmother's eyes. Simon led her out to the dance floor, aware of the many stares of society upon them, and the whispers already making the rounds that they made the perfect couple.

How tedious and predictable.

Several couples joined the dancefloor for the polka, and while it was a partnered dance, the fast tempo of the accompanying music lessened the intimacy and the need for conversation. Unlike the waltz, the couples' bodies were not closely held together as they skipped through the distinctive three steps and a hop, which repeated to the tempo of the music. It was lively and energetic, leaving all the participants warm and flushed with the exercise.

Lady Cassandra glowed, her beauty truly radiant, yet no desire or temptation curled through Simon. Her lilac silk gown clung to her delightful curves, displaying her English rose charms, but although many of the gentlemen looked on the earl with envy, she did not warm his blood. The dance lasted for several minutes and when it ended, the lady laughed, and her joy pulled a small smile to his mouth. Simon led her toward her parents and his grandmother who watched them with evident approval.

"You are a wonderful dancer, Lady Cassandra," he declared.

Her entire face lit with her smile. "Thank you, your lordship. You were a rather graceful partner." The lady cast him a few glances below her lashes, perhaps a bid to be flirtatious, but only that peculiar dissonance plucked its chord within. He relinquished her to her parents, bowed, and walked away. At his request, a footman brought him a glass of champagne and Simon stood by the terrace windows, observing the throng, boredom settling over him like a suffocating blanket.

The sparkling ladies in the ballroom fluttered around like brilliant butterflies, all except one—Miss Mina Crawford. She stood by one of the columns, looking painfully lonely. Her brother was by her side, and even the young viscount seemed discomfited, at times tugging at his cravat as if it choked him. The viscount stiffened when a pretty young lady came into view, and that lady also appeared to glow when she saw him. They clearly had a *tendre*. The viscount said something to his sister, who nodded and smiled. He then hastened through the crowd toward the young lady.

Simon did not take his gaze away from Mina. He had always thought her lovely, yet dressed in the heights of fashion in a gown of chartreuse, the lady was stunningly beautiful. Dark red ringlets curled on her forehead and nape, softening her loveliness. He noted that several gentlemen sent her covetous stares, and Simon smiled at the aloof look of politeness she returned.

Inexplicably, he lingered over her features. The stark yearning on her face struck him hard.

Whatever are you thinking, Mina?

He observed that she had no friends who came over to speak with her, and though it was clear a few ladies recognized Mina, none approached her. Simon could not imagine such loneliness, for he always had something of interest to occupy his thoughts, even friends when he was of the mind to entertain. She'd had no one, buried in the country for so long, and since her return to town, not once had she revealed in their long conversations that ladies of society called upon her.

Simon felt as if he wanted to slay the world for her.

"An elopement? Are you certain?" a voice too close to him said in a hushed whisper.

"Yes, we heard it from Lady Barclay herself, who heard it from Lady Kittredge. It is a sad mess, for Miss Crawford had been the toast of the season once, even giving my daughter competition for Lord Salisbury's hand."

"Who was this man?"

"No one knows, but it is rather easy to deduce he was not a man of consequence as he was not brought up to scratch and she vanished from society for a number of years after…"

Her words ended on a gasp as Simon leveled his gaze on the ladies to his left. They hurriedly dipped into curtsies, looking suitably mortified. When they greeted him, he did not return the courtesy, which was observed by many, and a few titters broke out.

Ignoring them, he glanced back at Mina. A flash of fire seared his chest, and he embraced the sensation instead of killing it with his will. Simon wanted…connection. Something deeper than duty. Something…Someone.

He felt a sudden hot longing for Mina and when their gazes collided, all the edgy restlessness quieted. Awareness of her flooded his entire body. She touched him in places that had been obscured even to himself, a connection he truly thought not even death might sever. Dark amusement washed over him at that touch of whimsy.

Emptying the glass, he handed it to a passing footman. Simon walked over to Mina, who watched his approach with a wariness in her eyes that scraped at his chest.

• • •

"What a lovely couple they made," a lady unknown to Mina said from behind her fan, her avaricious gaze on the earl.

Her companion replied, "There are many predictions Lord Creswick and Lady Cassandra will be the match of the season."

That excited chattering pierced Mina's heart with pain, but she flicked it aside, refusing to linger on the hollowness that had resided in her heart for the last several days. In truth, the only thing she could not dismiss from her awareness was the earl as he prowled in her direction, his stroll that of a man confident of his power and his place in the world.

"He is coming this way!"

"Perhaps he means to ask you to dance, Anna! Drop your handkerchief at his feet. He will stop and pick it up and you must do your best to snare his attentions," came that excited sage advice.

Mina ought to leave. Her feet would not obey, though, and she watched his advance with a helpless feeling of agony clawing at her insides. The lady dared to drop her lace handkerchief, and he faltered, his gaze tracking the wisp of cloth that settled atop his boots. The ladies present held their breaths. A sardonic half smile touched his mouth, and her heart hitched. The man was truly, appallingly beautiful.

He picked up the scrap of cloth and handed it to the lady, who flushed and sweetly thanked him. Simon did not linger but moved on, drifting even closer to Mina. He seemed to have cloaked himself in a mask of civility and chilling elegance, and Mina hated that his indifference petrified her.

Then he stopped before her and peered down. The very air around them went remarkably still. "Will you dance tonight?" he asked, a savage glitter in his blue gaze which had first seemed deep and impenetrable.

A sweet shot of delight pierced low in her belly, and something tentative unfurled inside her chest. A petal opening to the first rays of the sun. "Only if you ask me."

He held out his hand silently and she placed hers in his, allowing him to walk her out onto the dance floor. The twenty-piece orchestra started the Viennese Waltz, and many ladies and gentlemen took to the dance floor. Mina was the third lady he danced with tonight, but the weight of the throng's eyes upon them felt heavier. She lifted her chin and met his gaze, unable to look anywhere but at the earl.

His hands upon her shoulder burned. His scent invaded her senses. They danced the Viennese Waltz, gliding and twirling to the sensuous notes in silence. When it ended, he moved her through the crowd, and deposited her beside her brother.

"Lord Creswick," her brother greeted.

He made introductions to Miss Rebecca Ashley

and her parents who had hurried over. They preened and seemed delighted to meet a man of the earl's reputation and status, and were even more impressed by her brother's association with him. The earl indulged in some small conversation with Mr. Ashley, even praising the man's business investments on England's soil as it provided much needed employment for the working class.

Mina pled a headache and told her brother she would return home early. She curtsied to Simon and made her way from the ballroom, requesting that their carriage be summoned to collect her. The butler assisted her into her cloak and held open the door for her. Music and laughter and the *clink* of glasses followed her outside into the cold night air.

She felt him, and Mina closed her eyes as his wall of warmth came up behind her. Simon did not speak, and her throat would not work. The carriage clattered to a stop before her, and the tiger hopped down and lowered the steps. Simon took her elbow and assisted her inside, his presence dwarfing the confines of the carriage.

He sat opposite her, leaning back against the squabs, his gaze hooded. Her heart was a tattoo against her breastbone, and she folded her hands in her lap. The drive home was only a few minutes, but it felt as if it took hours. Driven by an intense need to be closer to him, Mina rose and sat beside him. No reaction came from him, and they continued to sit there in silence. Once the carriage stopped, it was almost a relief to descend once again into the cool night air.

Simon walked her to the door. "Good evening, Miss Crawford."

"Good evening, my lord."

Mina used the key and let herself in, leaning against the door. She couldn't say how long she stayed like that, the breath trembling from her body, her belly knotted in an agony of hope and fear and such aching love. Minutes passed as the hallway clock ticked and she did not move.

"Let me in, Mina."

She closed her eyes, trapping the tears behind her lids that were so desperate to fall. He had not left.

Turning around, she opened it. The faint moonlit sky fell across Simon framed in the doorway, painting him in dark shadows and beautiful moonbeams. She stepped back and he entered, closing the door behind him. They stared at each other in the darkness of the foyer. No words were spoken, and she turned around and padded down the hallway, aware of the stillness of the townhouse.

She held onto the banister as she headed up the stairs, aware of his footfalls behind her. Mina entered her chamber, relieved to see that a fire had been left in the hearth. The room was warm if not brightly lit. He acted as her maid, helping her to remove the bows from the gown, before unbuttoning the dozens of pearl buttons at the back. His motions as he rid her of the gown, corset, a three-layered petticoat, and the wire bustle were efficient without any hint of carnality.

It was a wonderful ache that had been building low in her belly. He trailed his fingers up the length of her leg, and over her silken stockings, before stooping to remove them along with her satin shoes.

He stripped her until she stood naked in the

room, yet she could not face him. Mina was afraid. Afraid that she would look into his eyes and only see indifference and cold lust without tenderness. Rustles and whispers rode the air as he removed his boots and clothes, tossing them on the chaise in the far corner. When Simon was done, he remained silent, and an unbearable ache welled inside her chest. A movement from behind her, and then his hands clasped her hips and drew her against him, so her back was flushed to his chest. Her eyes fluttered closed in pleasure as his hands stroked through her hair.

She felt soft and shaky against him.

"I love you," he said right at her ear.

A sob left Mina and she turned in the cage of his arms. "I was afraid...I was..."

"That I could stop loving you? Do not hold such little faith in me," he hissed, that savage expression settling in his eyes, rendering him hard and almost forbidding. His hands pulled her closer, tangling in her hair, knocking the loose pins free as he took her mouth in a desperate kiss. Mina's cry was muffled against the sensual assault, and she clung to his kiss, matching his passion and fervor.

Simon feathered kisses which drifted down her cheek and jaw. Her head fell back, and her breath came harshly. He kissed her exposed throat, licked the skin down to her breast. He laved her nipple with his tongue, drawing a sharp breath from her throat, then a whimper when he sucked that tender pebble into his mouth with sensual greed. A hungry moan broke from her throat as he repeated the caress with her other breast.

They tumbled to the bed, and he sat on the edge, drawing her into his lap so that she straddled him, her knees bracketing his hips. He took her mouth in another bruising kiss, stirring her hunger. Simon held her hips and dragged her onto his cock. The sensation was exquisite, the heavy, stretching penetration of his body joining hers. As was the passion that burst over her, shattering and throbbing through her body in waves.

His husky laugh of satisfaction whispered over her heated skin. "Tonight, I am going to wring every drop of pleasure from you that your body has to give."

She shivered at the almost harsh sensual promise. Then he started to move her atop of him, and her body wept with pleasure for him. Mina struggled to take control, kissing his mouth to toss him off balance, and took control of their movements. Instead of Simon rocking her onto his length, she rode him. She took him. She thought of a word he had so carnally whispered to her once as he took her to devastating heights of pleasure…tonight it was she who fucked him.

He kissed her all along the curve of her throat and shoulder, kissed and nipped and sucked at her skin, as she rode him. Then it was her turn. Mina licked the line of his throat, tasting salt and heat, and the man himself. She trailed kisses up the side of his throat, up to his jawline, and over his lips. Sweet kisses, so innocently at odds with how she rolled her hips and lowered herself onto his throbbing manhood in a driving rhythm.

His groan as it echoed in the chamber was harsh and desperate. His fingers as they dug into her arse would surely leave bruises, but Mina did not care. She already felt bruised everywhere, especially inside her heart. He turned his head and tried to kiss her mouth, but she buried her face in his shoulder, holding him close as she rode him with deep, sultry movements.

His bare skin felt hot beneath her hands. His taste invaded her senses, and in that moment, Mina knew she would never be able to free her heart of him.

She loved him too much.

Hot tears slid down her cheeks to mingle with his sweat. He made a rough sound near her ear. They slid against each other, skin to skin, his heartbeat sounding as hers. Simon spun with her, pressing her down on the bed. Her back slid up against the sheets and he came down heavy, burying himself even deeper within her body, a full and hot possession that dragged a whimper from Mina. It hurt, but deliciously so. Once he was deep inside her, she wanted nothing more than to feel him moving, filling with pleasure, comfort, love, and a whisper of what life forever in his arms could be like.

Simon took her in a fierce driving rhythm of deep, pounding thrusts that broke her apart with pleasure. He rode her even harder through her climax as he chased his own release. Agonizing pleasure seared through Mina's body once more, and with a muffled cry, a powerful orgasm washed over her. Simon found his own pleasure, pulling from her and splaying his warm seed atop her quivering mound.

He kissed her chin and throat. "The first time I saw you under the soft glow of lamp light in my library, you looked so fierce and defiant, you stirred me. You tempted something to awake inside me, and I came alive for you, Mina. I love you beyond thoughts of scandal and consequences."

Her resolve quivered and she had to fiercely remind herself all that he stood to lose.

He held her against him, kissing the curve of her shoulder, inhaling her fragrance. "Don't you know who I am?"

"The Earl of Creswick," she whispered.

"I will be the shelter for the storm over our heads, Mina, you need not fear what I might lose. What I know I cannot lose is you."

Mina's throat closed over the desperate ache rising inside her chest. "I cannot be your lover forever. The threat is real that…that…he might surface and sue you. If only to go after your wealth."

She smoothed her hands down his bare back, hugging him gently. Simon was an intelligent and astute politician, and nothing in his character and reputation must diminish. His good opinion carried immense weight within the realm, and for any sort of scandal to be attached to him would cause irreparable damage to that influence which was much needed as he fought for those who had no power.

This was a man who believed the poorer classes needed more wealth, education, better housing, and health care. He believed women should have more choices together with social and economic power. He believed every man should have the right to vote and have a say in their own futures instead of having its direction decided for them. The earl was a powerful force, and if she chose to love him, marry him, she would be the greatest hammer to topple his brilliant power. Everything inside of her reached for him, hungered to hold him to her and never let him go.

I'll also be your shelter from the storm.

Mina felt bruised inside. Unable to bear the sense of loss anymore, she pushed from the bed and from his arms to slip on her robe. She hurried from the room and went down to the library below stairs, ignoring the cold that seemed to seep into her bones and turn her body brittle. Once in the library, she did not make it over to any of the sofas.

She sat down abruptly on the carpet and ducked her head between her knees. Powerful arms wrapped around her from behind and held her. With a ragged sigh, she leaned against him, her slender figure shaking from the cold and the pain. Simon said nothing, and Mina knew he understood the truth of their situation.

They could either burn in selfish passion and desire, damning everything else, or he could let her go.

We shall be friends always, she wanted to promise but could not bring herself to say so. How could she bear it when he got married and had children? How could she bear to stare at him across the street, knowing that they would never laugh or play chess again, never share a flask of whisky, never discuss politics or books nor eat ice cream together. Their mouths would never again meet in passion, and she would never feel his arms like this around her.

"Mina?"

"Yes," she whispered.

"You are fired," he said almost tenderly, yet the underlying thread of steel told her he was most assuredly serious.

"No."

A low sound came from him, almost like a chuckle. "Yes."

And she understood. It was already unbearable seeing each other daily, the heat and want there but unable to bask in it or admit their love.

Papa, I am indeed unable to bear the consequences of my folly.

CHAPTER EIGHTEEN

A few days later, a soft knock came on the door before it opened and Mina briskly walked inside, dressed in a buttoned up rose-colored gown, a hat perched jauntily atop her red curls.

"Miss Crawford?"

She cast him a small smile of amusement, even though the light in her gaze remained dimmed. "I decided to unfire myself until…well, until I am ready."

Simon choked on the air. "Woman, you are shameless."

She went perfectly still. "Do you wish me to leave?"

"No," he admitted gruffly.

"Very well, I shall start working immediately." Then she sat before her desk, carefully not meeting his eyes, her head lowered.

"Mina."

He observed her take a deep breath and then she looked up, her beautiful eyes glittering with tears.

"I missed you, too, most painfully."

Her throat worked on a tight swallow. "Are you also unable to sleep in the night?" she asked hoarsely, "And does it feel like you are haunted at the memory of everything?"

"Yes."

Her lips trembled. "Good. I decided since I shall be tormented no matter what, it is best to occupy my mind with work."

"Of course," Simon said, wanting to go over and drag her into his arms. "I still might fire you at six."

She laughed lightly, and the warm tinkling sound filled every crevice of his soul. They stood that way for several minutes before he decided to share a plan he had been working on. "We leave for Scotland in a few days."

Mina's head snapped up, and her fingers tightened around the quill. Her throat worked on a swallow, but then she nodded in acquiescence. "Is it wise for you to leave with so much going on with the reform bill?"

Simon closed the journal he'd been reading. "This is more important."

"It cannot be," she said, stricken.

"It is, and we will travel to secure your divorce."

"What if the courts deny my petition to void the marriage?"

Ice congealed in his gut. "I will not allow it."

Her lips parted and fire snapped in her eyes. "Simon, you must do nothing that will threaten your—"

"I will free you from that marriage," he said with implacable softness. "There is no use protesting this, Mina. You will have your freedom and what you do with it afterward is up to you, but you will damn well be free."

I'll be your lover, your mistress even...

How those words had been haunting him since their last night of untamed loving. Simon could not envision he would let her go in this lifetime. But by God it had to be done. For she deserved much more than to be hidden away in secret as anyone's mistress. Wilhelmina Crawford deserved to be loved and adored completely, with her extraordinary eyes glowing with happiness and no hint of shame or bleakness.

Simon suspected it might be an uphill battle to convince the court to void the marriage, and he was willing to use bribery and threats if necessary. He did not inform Mina of that, for if she knew he was willing to be that ruthless and to compromise his honor to see it done, Mina would protest and run from him.

For she loved him.

He saw it in every lingering look she cast at him when she thought him occupied. He had felt it that night in how she touched, kissed, and loved him for the night. Mina had allowed him to take her until they wilted from exhaustion, and when she thought he slept she would weep, kissing his chest and shoulders, hugging him close with her slim arms as they trembled.

Simon had not held her to him since or even kissed her mouth, for he had discovered something about himself that had shocked him to the core. He was bendable. He was breakable. He was corruptible. He would do anything for her. If he could get his hands on that bounder she had married, he would joyfully throttle the bastard.

Simon's heart could be shattered in the face of her pain. He had felt himself bend under the onslaught of loss which twisted his guts into knots whenever he thought about no longer having her in his arms. And he could, without compunction, tarnish his honor and morals to set her free. He could kill his honor and reputation to call her his forever.

A knock sounded at the door, and he rose and

went to collect the two bowls of strawberry ice cream from his butler. Taking the silver tray over to her desk, he set it down. He handed her a bowl and sat in the high wingback chair close to her and took up his bowl. Simon did not speak as he started to eat his treat. Mina stared down at her bowl for several seconds and when she lifted her face to his, she gave him a bright, glorious smile, though her eyes glittered with unshed tears. They ate their ice creams in companionable silence, with Simon wondering if she would eventually kill that love he spied in her gaze when she discovered the ruthless way he planned to fight for her and to chain her to his side.

Secure the divorce. If not, find the bounder and kill him.

Marry her over the anvil.

Get her with child.

Then marry her properly in the church.

If she had the withal to refuse to marry him, then Simon would simply have to be more ruthlessly persuasive by kidnapping her. Though he knew he might never be able to force or deceive her in any manner. Simon tried to keep his face impassive, to hide the monstrous agony that seemed to live and breathe inside his chest. Mina glanced at him, and a slight frown touched her brows. He allowed his mouth to curve into a smile and wariness flickered in her eyes. Her lashes lowered, and her fingers, as she lifted the spoon to her mouth, trembled. A tear held suspended on one of her thick, long lashes before it fell on her suddenly pale cheeks.

Yes, Mina mine, you understand it very well. I am not letting you go.

• • •

Mina arrived with Simon in the town of Carlisle after three days of traveling in his largest country carriage. Nerves and tension made her feel brittle as a portly woman with a kind face escorted them up the stairs of the hotel in the center of the town, to their best room. They would only stay for a few days, then they would travel on to Edinburgh where the earl had a home, and where they would make their petitions to the court to void her marriage to Leonardo Petretti.

A team of some of the best lawyers and investigators had traveled ahead of their arrival, and as they entered the room, Mina cast a quick sideways glance at Simon. He went over to the window and stared down into the courtyard, an aura of almost dangerous energy emanating from him. His eyes were dark with mysterious intent.

That energy made her unaccountably nervous. Perhaps even a bit petrified. Each step closer to their destination seemed to stamp a harsh resolve on his handsome features that she did not understand. Each step closer also reminded her that she would lose him soon, and the tearing wound ripping apart her heart would never heal.

The court might take weeks, or even months to decide her case, and she knew Simon would stay with her for the duration. And then after…

The bed beckoned, and she went over and lowered herself into its warm confines fully dressed. Mina hugged a pillow to her chest, closing her eyes, only to dream of what their life might be. The life they would have if she fought the fear of society which would condemn him if she said yes to a marriage between them.

A surge of breathless want went through her. To be his wife. To have children with him. To have such happiness and fulfillment had been a dream she had long given up on. To have his love and protection until they were old. Then in the next lifetime, should such a thing be real, they would meet again and fall hopelessly in love a second time. It was impossible that they would perfectly recall they had loved each other fiercely and endlessly, but still she hoped their love would endure.

It was a beautiful fantasy, but it might be the death of the much needed reform and would mean many would continue in abject, cruel poverty.

I will be the shelter for the storm over our heads.

His weight came down behind her, and his arms slipped around her waist. "I can feel you thinking."

"I am weakening," she confessed. "And I hate myself for it."

"You speak like that about yourself ever again, I will be most displeased," he hissed.

"I want to reach for you, Simon. I want to reach for all of it."

"Ah God, Mina, then reach for it. I could not want another woman the way I want you. I could not love another woman the way I love you." He lowered his head and whispered the words at her ear. "It is simply impossible. I will stand before the fallout of the scandal and squash it before it can be manifested. Have faith in me."

She could not speak, and they reposed like that for several minutes. A knock sounded at the door, but she did not stir herself to look when he slipped from the bed and padded to the door. Mina closed her eyes and allowed the call of sleep to drag her close. The terrifying future loomed before her, one that was bleak, cold, and empty.

Or she could have the faith in Simon that he demanded, hold his hand and step forward together, and fight the storm together. She thought of everything she knew about him, his energy, brilliance, purpose, and knew he would never let down her heart. The steadiness in his gaze when he stared at her. The love she felt was the same reflected inside him, and that was not a thing to run from, but something to embrace. Mina needed to be strong, to trust in their love, his strength and in hers.

The Earl of Creswick was not a man who could ever be conquered by scandal or gossip. He was too indomitable. Raw hope unfurled inside her chest like the petals of a flower and Mina pushed from the bed to a sitting position. "Simon?"

When he made no answer, she turned around and stilled. He was no longer in the room, nor had she heard him leave. Mina rose and padded to the door, opened it and glanced down the hallway. He was nowhere in sight. She hurried down the hallway and into the lobby of the small hotel. The earl was nowhere to be seen, and worry curled through her. She went outside, and after seeing his coachman, she hurried over.

"Mr. Jefferies, have you seen his lordship?"

He dusted off his hat and bowed. "His lordship

collected his stallion and raced away with another gentleman, Miss Crawford."

Mina went inside and checked with the front staff if he had left her any messages. Her belly knotted with anxiety as she waited. Mina paced in the comfortable and well-situated common room, with worry eating at her insides. Each moment she thought about the look in Simon's eyes, her anxiety grew, until fear sat heavy inside her stomach. She paced until she grew dizzy and had to sit on a small well-padded sofa. A waiter offered her coffee or tea which she declined.

Oh, Simon where are you? It was so unlike him to not communicate his thoughts to her, she could not help thinking something had prevented him from returning to her. Something ghastly.

Mina went to bed that night and succumbed to a restless sleep. The following day, she woke late in the afternoon after a restless night of tossing and turning alone in the large bed. A quick check below stairs revealed the earl still had not returned to the hotel, nor had he sent a message for her.

The fear ebbed and she seethed with anger. "Does he not know I have been torn asunder with worry!"

Determined to not idly wait, she called for the maid who rested in the next room to help her change. Mina donned the boy's evening clothes she had carried on a whim and secured the hat firmly onto her head, hiding most of her wild curls. The maid said nothing at her scandalous get up, only looking mildly surprised when Mina withdrew a cane that clearly held a hidden rapier and marched from the bedchamber.

Mina went outside, inhaling the brisk air into her lungs. She lingered in the courtyard for several minutes, until evening fell in beautiful shades of lavender, a pale moon already adorning the night sky. She would certainly give him a piece of her mind to leave her to worry so!

As she was about to return inside to the warmth of the hotel, a horse in the distance made her still. Mina could tell it was the earl from the confident way he sat upon the large stallion. She raced toward him with all the courage she owned gripped tightly inside her heart.

He drew on the reins sharply, bringing his stallion to a stop, and peered down at her. Shock and relief blasted through her. He was safe even though his clothes were dusty, the lines about his mouth grim and his eyes holding that savage glitter. "What has happened, Simon?" she cried, fear piercing her heart. "Are you hurt?"

"I was coming for you." He held out a hand and she reached up and allowed him to haul her up to sit before him astride. Wrapping his arms around her waist, he held her firmly to him and gathered the reins, wheeling the horse around.

"You were gone for hours," she said, hating the quaver in her tone.

"There is a reason we did not head straight for Edinburgh."

Her heart jolted. "And what reason is that?"

"The investigator I sent ahead believed he found Leonardo Petretti."

Mina contained her flinch and tried to breathe evenly. She gripped her hands into tight fists, kneading them onto her thighs. He drew her against him, tucking her head below his chin. "Relax. I can feel the brittleness inside your body."

As if she had needed that assurance to release the tension that gripped her, she softened against him. "Simon?"

"Yes?"

"I will marry you," she croaked. "It may not be a month after the divorce, or even a year, but I swear I will marry only you in this lifetime. I will have faith in you, my love. Faith that you will be the shelter from the storm."

"Then why do you cry?" he gruffly said.

"Because I am still afraid that I am selfish in my desperate love for you. I want to take your hand and step forward, face the cruelty of the world with you, and also face the joys; even if I am hurt and heartbroken, I'll not let go, Simon."

His hands tightened around her waist until she felt as if she could not breathe. "I am no less selfish in mine for you, my Mina. I am willing to slay the world to have the privilege to call you my wife."

"That sounds ominous," she whispered.

His chuckle held no humor, and Mina accepted she was petrified to ask him what it meant. Somehow exhaustion overtook her, and she fell asleep in his arms. Until a soft brush against her cheek jolted Mina awake. She looked around, her heart climbing into her throat. "We are in a cemetery?"

"Yes."

"Simon, why are we in a cemetery?"

He assisted her from the horse, and she winced, her derriere and thighs tender for having been in the saddle for so long. He grabbed her hand and led her to a spot where the dirt was recently overturned. She stared down at it in shock, the awful truth slamming into her like a derailed train. She snapped her gaze to him.

"Leonardo Petretti is buried here, and—"

"You killed him," she breathed, fisting her hands at her sides. "Oh God, you killed him."

He stared at her for a moment. "And what if I had, Mina?"

"Then we must hide the body carefully," she instantly replied. "No one must ever trace this back to you. Is it even wise that you buried him here, Simon? Will it not lead back to us?"

He smiled, a tenderness entering his eyes. "You would help me hide the body, hmm?"

She stared at him, astonished. "Of course."

He reached into his pocket and handed her a folded piece of paper. Mina opened it and frowned. "This is…this is my marriage certificate."

Simon held out another piece of paper and though she glared at him, for being filled with too much anxiety while he smiled, she took it. "It is a death record," she gasped.

"Do you agree the names are identically the same?"

Mina moved her gaze between both papers. "Yes. Mr. Leonardo Petretti."

"Good, now look at the dates."

Mina arched the papers more to the gas lamp that burned, noting the date she got married, and then the date on the death record.

"This says Mr. Leonardo Petretti died of a wasting

illness in August of 1866," she whispered.

"Yes."

She snapped her gaze to his. "I...I do not understand, you did not kill him?"

"No. I did a thorough investigation, and this man is the only Leonardo Petretti known in the area, and with tracking his movement without a doubt he is the same bounder you ran from."

Relief trembled through her, and Mina's throat burned with the ache of tears. "So he is dead, and you did not do it," she whispered, smiling up at him. "I am glad to know it, Simon."

Simon smiled and lightly touched her chin. "I am heartened to know you've quite the murderous heart *and* would have helped me hide the body. What an incredible woman you are."

"Simon! Now is not the time to jest!"

He gently touched the tip of her nose. "You were a widow when we met, Mina mine."

"Oh!" Mina drew in a breath. She pressed the papers over her chest and stared at him wordlessly, her mouth trembling. "You knave! You *wretch*! Why did you not tell me as soon as you knew?"

He held out his arms and she flew into his embrace, clutching at him, laughing and sobbing at the same time. "I knew you would have still been worried," he said. "I also needed to ascertain it myself before I brought you false news."

"I meant just now on the horse!"

He cupped her cheeks, lifted her face to his, and pressed a kiss of violent tenderness to her mouth.

"This is rather macabre," she murmured against his lips. "We are standing in a cemetery. Kissing."

"I wanted you to see his grave and know that it is done and release all the fears in your heart. I love you, Mina."

His austere male beauty peered down at her, and she once again felt that sheer awe that this man loved her. "I love you," she said, burying her face against his chest. "I love you so much."

Soon they were on the horse, sedately riding back to the inn. "I cannot believe I have been a widow all this time. Thank you, Simon, for encouraging me to come here."

"You are welcome. Now let's find a blacksmith to marry us."

She laughed. "I think not. I want to be wed in spectacular fashion for all of London to see and envy."

"Then it shall be done."

Mina leaned back against his chest, happiness blossoming through her entire body. This man would forever take her care into his keeping and grant her the things she desired. The awareness of it burrowed deep inside her heart. "I've changed my mind. I do believe I would prefer a quiet ceremony in the village, and the schoolchildren shall attend."

"As you wish."

"Do you have any wants for the day?"

"Just you, Mina mine."

She laughed, happiness surging through her veins. "We are so lucky I dueled in Anthony's stead."

He nudged the side of her face, kissing the corner of her mouth. "I am certain we would have met regardless, because I was waiting for you."

Mina blew out a soundless breath, awe and love expanding her chest. Simon nipped her neck again and with a sigh of contentment, Mina leaned into him and closed her eyes.

But right before she drifted to sleep, she heard him once again say her name. "Mina?"

She stirred, breathing in his wonderful scent. "Hmm?"

"For the final time, my love, you are fired."

EPILOGUE

"*En garde*," Mina murmured, dancing forward with careful steps to cross her swords with her partner.

He skillfully countered her strike, advanced, and thrust.

"Wonderful!" Mina cried and dipped into a bow.

"Mama!" Percival George Lambton, Viscount Bollinger, and the future Earl of Creswick cried, dropping his wooden fencing sword and rushing over to her. "I was great!"

Mina laughed, stooped down, and swept him into her arms, pressing a soft kiss to his gently rounded cheeks. "Your form was wonderful, my dear boy. In no time, you will be an even greater fencing master than your mother."

His blue eyes, a brilliant reflection of his father's, lit up with pride, and he beamed. "I must tell Papa!"

Percy wiggled, and she set him down, watching with a smile and love bursting inside her chest as he ran toward his father in the distance. Simon held their two-year-old daughter in his arms, pointing at the swoop of birds dancing in the sky. Their daughter, Charlotte, pointed upward, and even from where she stood, Mina could see the delight on her face.

"Your family is wonderful," a voice gruffly said from behind her.

Whirling around, Mina smiled up at Anthony. "You've arrived early!"

His letter had stated they should be in Hertfordshire sometime after five in the evening. It was not yet noon.

"We took an earlier train," he said with his familiar lopsided smile. "I've missed you, Mina."

An ache of emotions crowded her throat. A few weeks after she and Simon had gotten married in a beautiful and private ceremony in the chapel of this estate, Anthony had set sail on a ship with his fiancée. They had gotten married in New York a year later, and due to her pregnancy, Mina had not been able to visit for the wedding.

Still, he had sent her a long letter and a portrait of himself and his new bride. They had frequently corresponded these last few years, but this was the first time Anthony had returned to England's shore since he left. He was now nine and twenty and owned to a disreputable air, what with how he wore his hair long and held it back in a queue. His lean frame seemed more powerful, and though he cloaked himself in fashionable clothes, he did not have the appearance of a dandy but of a gentleman confident of his stature and position in society.

Peeking behind him, she spied Rebecca, Viscountess Crawford, pushing a perambulator across the lawns with their sleeping daughter tucked inside.

"How long are you staying for?"

His grin widened. "We have returned for good."

She gasped and clasped him in a brief and fierce hug. "Mrs. Bell will be happy to hear that. Though I have offered her a lovely retirement package with her very own cottage, she refuses to leave your manor." Mina smiled. "It has been restored most splendidly, Anthony. Papa and Mama would be so proud of you."

"Of us," he said, emotions gleaming in his eyes. "You are a countess, Mina, and from what I heard in town, a popular one who is vocal yet delicate in her support of women's rights. It is said Creswick is a man in love, and he is not afraid to show it to the world. He has found his perfect match."

She grinned. "I am his perfect match."

"He loves you."

"Shamelessly," she drawled. "And I love him with my whole soul, Anthony. Every day I think how lucky I am to have raced off to face him in that duel."

Her brother chuckled. "It is you Papa would be most proud of, poppet."

They shared a smile, and Mina couldn't help thinking about the last five years with Simon. Their marriage had hardly caused any ripples in society, and whatever rumors had tried to stir about her previous elopement, the dowager countess, who was delighted Mina had proved to be a widow and that her grandson was finally in love, had used her considerable influence to squash them.

It had been a good year, with the Reform Bill winning a majority vote, and the act came into full power in 1869, allowing all male heads of households the right to vote and to many working-class men. Since then, her husband had worked to ensure women received more rights. Simon had been instrumental in passing the Married Women's Property Act 1870, which allowed married women to be the legal owners of the money they earned and the right to inherit property.

Anthony glanced over his shoulder at his wife, and his face softened into pure love. That unguarded expression had her shifting her attention to her family. Her two babies were now chasing three puppies while their father looked on indulgently.

"Yes," she said softly, staring after her loves. "Papa would have been most proud."

• • •

That night, Mina was wrapped in Simon's arms, her legs entwined around his hips as he made love with her. Her husband kissed her with slow, easy possession, a perfect mimicry of the way he moved inside her body. Sweat slicked their skin, and that pressure low in her belly built with each thrust, which deepened as they reached a pinnacle together.

He made her weak and desperate. Ripping her mouth from his, she nipped his chin and laved the sting with a kiss. "Simon," she moaned, clasping his shoulders. Each stroke carried her higher, and she chased the hovering ecstasy until she caught it, and pleasure shattered her into a thousand pieces. The sensations that poured through her were wild and pulsating as Simon hugged her even tighter to him and chased his own release to empty deep inside her body.

He rolled from her, taking her with him to tuck her against his chest, her head under his chin.

I am bound to you, always.

Mina loved him so much, there were days the feeling was almost frightening. Then she would smile, and that fright would blossom into intense love and certainty that they would be together, in this lifetime and the next.

"I love you, Mina, mine."

She lightly kissed his throat. "I love you, too."

ACKNOWLEDGMENTS

I thank God every day for loving me with such depth and breadth.

To my husband, Du'Sean, you are so damn wonderful. Your feedback and support are invaluable. I could not do this without you.

Thank you to my wonderful friend and critique partner Giselle Marks. Without you, I would be lost.

Thank you to Stacy Abrams for being an amazing, wonderful, and super-stupendous editor.

To my wonderful readers, thank you for reading *A Matter of Temptation*. I hope you enjoyed Mina and Simon's journey to love and happily-ever-after as much as I enjoyed writing it.

Special THANK YOU to the Historical Hellions who always root for me and everyone who leaves a review—bloggers, fans, and friends. I have always said reviews to authors are like a pot of gold to leprechauns. Thank you all for adding to my rainbow one review at a time.

THE DUKE'S
SHOTGUN
WEDDING

USA TODAY BESTSELLING AUTHOR
STACY REID

CHAPTER ONE

Lady Jocelyn Rathbourne's hand did not waver as she pointed the derringer at the Duke of Calydon. Eyes that were the color of winter blue, colder than the wind that whistled through the open windows, stared at her penetratingly. Jocelyn gritted her teeth and desperately hoped that he did not hear the pounding of her heart, or sensed her fear. He was reputed to be ruthless, and have one of the shrewdest minds in all London. But then, Jocelyn's papa had always called her his little Napoleon.

Long elegant fingers coolly caressed the card that she had presented to his butler to gain entrance, and those ice-blue eyes flicked to the note she had written. "I must assume that the house and name on this card are as fabricated as this dire situation your note hinted at?"

Jocelyn flushed as the husky rasp of his voice stirred deep within her. She was taken aback by how sinfully attractive he was.

She squinted at him as rage flared through her, scorching in its intensity. She was not about to be taken in by the man. Not ever again by a pretty face and prettier lies. Not that she could call the duke pretty. He was more raw and masculine, possibly handsome—if not for the rapier scar that had flayed his left cheek. But he was certainly compelling with his midnight black hair and mesmerizing eyes. His appearance was everything a powerful duke's should be as he sat behind his massive oak desk intricately carved with designs of dragons—dark, sensual, handsome, with just a hint of danger.

She gave an involuntary shiver, then scowled as his lips turned up as he noted her body's reaction. Thank goodness he could not see past her veil.

"My name is most certainly not fabricated, Your Grace," she said, and straightened her stance. "I am Lady Jocelyn, the daughter of the Earl of Waverham, and your brother has perpetrated the most heinous crimes upon my person and must be brought to justice!"

He relaxed in his chair as if she were not a serious threat. She gritted her teeth and ignored the cold flint that entered his eyes as she raised the gun a little higher, in line with his chest.

"Well, in that case, please take a seat." He gestured at the high-backed chair she was standing next to. His expression didn't waver.

She didn't want to give him the satisfaction of following his orders. But her knees were shaking so badly she thought it might be best. She sat gingerly on the edge of the chair.

"Now. What heinous crime has Anthony perpetrated that has you invading my country home and committing a crime that will certainly see you to the gallows?" His voice had gone flat and hard.

She leaned forward and slapped a copy of the *London Gazette* on his oak desk, sending it skidding across the polished surface, tumbling the inkwell. "The society page reports his engagement to Miss Phillipa Peppiwell of the Boston Peppiwells." Jocelyn's lips curled in derision as she spat the woman's name at him like it was one of her bullets.

"And this distresses you…how?"

Her hands wavered slightly as the duke leaned forward, resting his chin in his hands, studying her as if she were a fascinating bug.

She drew herself up. "He seduced me!"

The crackling of the fireplace hushed as if waiting for an explosion, but her hand did not waver. Not even when the elegant royal blue drapes billowed under a sharp gust of the winter wind.

"I beg your pardon?" His voice was so low she was not sure if he'd really spoken, or if she'd simply imagined a response. He gazed steadily at her, his expression betraying not the slightest flicker of reaction.

She swallowed. "He seduced me, promised me marriage, and even gave me this as a token of his affection. An *engagement* token."

She sent the locket skidding across the desk to be halted by a finger. The chain of the necklace slid through his hands slowly. A muscle ticked in his forehead as he glanced at the golden locket.

"Anthony gifted this to you?" His voice was chillingly polite, but his eyes had gone from wintery to glacial as he tracked her movements, missing nothing.

"Yes, as a promise of his commitment to me," she assured him. "Yet now I read that he is engaged to be married in fewer than three weeks." She shifted in the high-backed chair, straining to keep her hand from trembling as she aimed the derringer.

He cocked his head as he considered her, and she desperately wished to have just an inkling of his thoughts.

"Could this, by chance, be a desperate ploy by the impoverished Earl of Waverham?"

Jocelyn flinched at the soft question and forced herself to hold steady under the ruthless intelligence that shone in his eyes as he studied her carefully. Again she was grateful her eyes were covered by the veil. Her hair was also hidden, completely stuffed under her top hat, giving her partial anonymity, albeit useless since she'd told him her name. She fought not to squirm under his stare. "My father might be impoverished, Your Grace, but he does not plot, nor is he desperate," she said, lifting the gun for a better aim. "Is this *your* desperate ploy—to lay the abominable behavior of your brother at my father's doorstep?"

His brows flickered.

"Despite my weapon's fragile appearance, Your Grace, it is not easy to aim a derringer at a man this long. My hand tires...I may accidentally pull the trigger."

"Ah, so it is not your intention to shoot me, Miss Rathbourne?"

She ignored the eyes that roved over her. "It's *Lady Jocelyn*. And most assuredly, my intention to shoot you is genuine, if I do not receive justice. I would hate for my shot to be accidental. It will be done very deliberately when I choose to fire."

The duke unlocked his hands from under his chin and leaned back in his chair. He drummed his fingers on his desk with a *click clack* sound, possibly hoping to unnerve her as he studied her. She had to admit she was slightly intimidated by the glare from his eyes.

Despite being an earl's daughter, due to their dire financial straits she had not received the chance to have her season, her foray into society. Today was the first she'd laid eyes on the formidable duke, knowing him only by reputation and Anthony's recounts.

"Are you with child?" he asked evenly.

She spluttered, a wave of heat blossoming on her entire body at his unexpected question. Mortified, she gazed at his expressionless face, uncertain how to answer.

"A seduction does not necessarily result in a child, Your Grace." At the slow raise of his eyebrows, she hazarded a guess that what Anthony had told her was correct. "As you are a man of the world, I am sure you are aware that the outcome of a child can be prevented?" She posed the question, and her lips tightened in a moue as she awaited his answer with heart pounding.

"You may lower your weapon, Miss Rathbourne. And do not presume to correct me of your title, as a *lady* would not barge into my home under false pretense and threaten me at the point of a gun." His fingers halted their drumming. "Indeed, I am uncertain as to what you require of me."

Her eyes narrowed at the insult of him referring to her as *Miss*. A scathing reply formed on her lips, but she had to remind herself of what her aim was. After a brief hesitation, she lowered her arms, but she did it slowly, and rested the derringer in her lap, continuing to point it directly at him. For some unfathomable reason, she liked the amused twitch of his mouth as his wintry gaze thawed. He shifted, his jacket stretching over his very broad shoulders. His blue waistcoat was the finest she had ever seen.

"I have no pretenses, Your Grace, and everything I said in my note is the absolute truth."

He looked skeptical. "Your note claimed a dire situation of grave misfortune that threatens scandal and *death* for my family—namely my wicked brother Anthony Williamson Thornton."

"Despite what polite society would have many believe, a seduction does not have only one perpetrator, Lady Jocelyn. Now, let's get down to business. What is it you want? Money? A house?"

Affront flared through Jocelyn and she raised her weapon with such speed he froze in the act of opening his top drawer.

"How *dare* you!" She breathed deeply to contain the rage that burned through her. "Do you not have a sister enjoying her first season? If a cad had used her, enticing her with promises of love and marriage, then abandoned her, what recompense would *you* demand? Money? A house? A duel? Or a marriage?"

"Only death would suffice."

She flinched at his unwavering response, the derringer jerking in her clasp. "I do not desire Anthony's death." Her stomach churned at the mere thought of it. "It discredits you to speak so easily of your brother's demise."

Once more, amusement twisted his sensual mouth, infuriating her.

"I spoke to the demise of a hypothetical cad who had seduced and abandoned my sister. Not of my brother, Lady Jocelyn."

"But it was your *brother* who seduced and abandoned me. I demand marriage!" she said, trying to keep her voice from trembling.

"Request denied."

She felt her back go ramrod straight and she vibrated with rage. "I beg your pardon?"

He held up a hand. "I do not deliberately stoke your scorned woman's wrath, but I am afraid Anthony is already married."

She darted a gaze to the *Gazette* with a frown. "You lie!"

The smile that twisted his lips at her slander was not one of amusement.

She flushed and swallowed. *No*. It couldn't be true. "I—"

"Let me be clear. Money is all that will be offered. Do I believe my brother seduced you? Frankly, yes. Only a madwoman would storm my estate with such an elaborate story that can be so easily verified. And make no mistake, it will be verified." The muscle in his forehead ticked again. "However, Anthony and Miss Peppiwell had the brilliant notion to abscond to Gretna Green with a special license two weeks past. Ergo, they are now married and she may be enceinte. Thus the reaffirmation of vows in three weeks that will appear to polite society as their actual marriage."

Jocelyn blanched, lowering the gun as her mind sifted through her options with dizzying speed. Despair made her voice hoarse when she responded. "I will need proof."

It was the Duke of Calydon's turn to throw a paper onto his desk, one he pulled from the top drawer. She reached for it, and gasped as she read the document. Dear God, it was true. *Anthony was married*. Pain squeezed her chest tight and her hands trembled as she lowered the paper. She slid it back across the desk with infinite slowness.

"One hundred thousand pounds is my first and

final offer." He rose from his chair and stalked around the desk toward her. She scrambled up from her seat and her reticule fell from her lap, spilling its contents on the lavender Aubusson carpet.

"Come no farther!" she cried, the words echoing off the library walls. She pressed her back against the bookshelves that lined them and stared at him with wide eyes. She did not like the duke's smile as he detoured to the sideboard and poured ruby liquor from a decanter into two glasses.

The crumbled ruin that was her father's estate flashed in her head. A hundred thousand pounds would put him on the path of removing the unrelenting burden of debt that was entailed with his property, and possibly give him a fighting chance.

She almost took it.

But then the voices of her sisters rushed in, crowding her mind.

Do you think I will ever have a season, Jocelyn? Her beautiful younger sister Victoria.

I wish not to be so cold all the time, but I think I would prefer to have pretty dresses like Lady Elizabeth. Don't you wish for pretty things, Jocelyn? Her twelve year old sister Emily, more bookish and enraptured by Latin, Plutarch, and Socrates—as was Jocelyn—but sometimes wholly feminine in her desire for dresses and pretty trinkets.

Jocelyn's throat tightened as the voices that affected her most blared in her head. *I wish for warm milk on Christmas morning. Loevnia says every Christmas her mama and papa give her presents under a Christmas tree. They eat roast duckling! Pudding! And Christmas punch! Yum! If we could only have such things…* The eight year old twins Emma and William had danced together as they fantasized, yet Emma's voice had rung hollow for someone so young. But it was William's sad smile as he said, *I would be so happy if you were warm, Emma*, which had decided everything for Jocelyn.

The raise of the derringer to Calydon's chest was slow and deliberate, as was the cool smoothness of her voice as she said, "If Anthony is unavailable for marriage, Your Grace, an offer from you will do. That is the only thing that can atone for your brother's reprehensible conduct."

CHAPTER TWO

Ah, yes. She would do.

Sebastian Jackson Thornton, the twelfth Duke of Calydon, Marquess of Hastings, and Earl of Blaydon had decided on Lady Jocelyn Rathbourne the instant she drew the derringer from her reticule and pointed it at him so determinedly. Or it could have been when his butler Thomas announced her entry. Her walk had been militant yet provocative and graceful, stirring something that had withered to a cold nothing over the years. He doubted those qualities were natural, as chits like her were trained from the schoolroom how to walk, talk, and entice a man to marriage.

Even though, Sebastian had to admit, she did not appear like many of the simpering misses and ladies of the *ton* who thought they had only to bat an eyelash and wield their fan to be captivating.

"Marriage?" he asked blandly, as his eyes tracked the pulse that beat so frantically at her throat.

He held out the glass of sherry. "Drink," he commanded, expecting her to obey without question. He suppressed an impulse to smile as her lips flattened, and from the slight spasm of her jaw he surmised she was gritting her teeth. She would make a poor gambler.

He wondered at her eyes—their color and shape. The dark veil that covered them was a source of irritation he meant to remedy. Her hand trembled as she pressed her back closer into the shelves that lined his library walls, filled with thousands of books and tomes.

He hoped her bravado was not failing her. It would not do for him to turn around and offer marriage so easily.

"Yes, marriage." Her voice was a hiss as she straightened her spine and took a tentative step forward. "And I do not desire refreshment."

Ah, there it was. The spirit that had stoked his intrigue, the sheer boldness that had rushed from her as she confronted him with Anthony's folly, so different from the simpering flowers the mamas of the *ton* had been throwing in his path over the years. She vibrated with passion and fire.

"Very well."

Her gaze slashed from his to the glass of sherry he placed on the desk. His chuckle when it rumbled from his throat surprised even him. The unthinkable deed that he had been contemplating with part rage and sometimes icy detachment suddenly seemed intriguing as he studied her. Slowly, he closed the distance between them.

"Come no farther!"

He halted inches from her, the barrel tip of the derringer brushing against his waistcoat. He ignored her gasp as he reached out deliberately and drew the hat from her head.

"What are you doing?" she demanded, grabbing for it. He held it behind his back.

He liked that her voice did not lose its husky timber even though she appeared rattled, so unlike the high-pitched nasal tone of the many debutantes of the summer season.

He was even more relieved that her voice was not pure throaty seductiveness, or else his disgust would have been instant. Stripped of its veil, her delicate face had blushed crimson, and her gray eyes were like saucers. He feared she may be in danger of fainting.

"It is normal, Lady Jocelyn, for a man to fully gaze upon his intended before committing to marriage, especially under such unorthodox circumstances."

She took several breaths and lowered the weapon slightly, in line with his waist. He circled her neck with his hand, his thumb teasing the pulse that fluttered at her throat. Her tongue peeked out and moistened her lips. His nostril flared, but he ruthlessly ignored the sudden desire that burned him. She had dressed for their meeting in her riding habit: a green, high-collared shirt with matching skirts that molded her petite but voluptuous figure. From the nerve-racking tutelage he had received from his sister, Constance, about the current season's fashion, Sebastian determined that she was wearing last season's habit.

She inhaled sharply as he stepped in close enough to her that she was forced to lower her weapon completely or shoot him. Her eyes widened even further, and Sebastian realized he'd done her an injustice when he'd thought of them as merely gray. They were the color of storm clouds, full and raging with emotion.

"Your Grace, you presume too much!"

"Do I?" Sebastian chuckled as the click of the gun echoed like the crack of a whip. "Brave little thing, aren't you?"

"You will address me as Lady Jocelyn." She lifted the derringer again, and pressed it to his ribs. "Unhand me, and summon your solicitor at once. I require him to procure a special license and prepare our marriage contract."

"Ah." He reached past her and set her hat and veil on the bookshelf. "In that case, I fear I must insist on first sampling the wares you so boldly offer, Miss... *Lady* Jocelyne."

She froze. "*Sample?* I am not a common doxy!"

"No you are not...nor are you a lady." He traced his thumb along her jaw. "I have yet to figure out what you are, Jocelyn."

"Oomph—"

He swallowed her reply in a kiss, an action meant to shock the sensibilities she obviously possessed. But instead, it completely floored him.

The flavor of her lips was like the finest wine, the texture sublime, and her taste could intoxicate even the most jaded rake. She went rigid against him. He clasped her face with both hands and tilted her back, sinking in for a more thorough kiss. She shuddered, and parted her lips on a soft gasp which he took immediate advantage of, dipping his tongue into heaven.

The stab of his own arousal stunned him, yet what he tasted from her infuriated him, sending rage through his blood like poison.

For he tasted innocence.

It was there in the hesitant dart of her tongue as it met his, in the soft moan, the hand that fluttered to his shoulder, clasping him tightly as he deepened the kiss, and her shiver as he slanted his lips over hers. But it was the guileless hunger she responded with that bespoke her innocence. There was no artifice, no seduction...and no expertise behind her natural response. It was pure and unguarded, and it drew him under as nothing else could.

He kissed her with scorching proficiency, drawing her pleasure as an artist with a brush. His tongue plunged into the warm recess of her mouth, tasting nectar, eliciting a fractured moan. His hunger grew, and he licked and engaged her tongue in a feast of the senses. Her body arched, and he groaned as her moans roused the full length of his cock. Too much, and too soon for the innocence he tasted, for as he molded her body to his, curving her shape and pillowing her breast to his chest, she tore her mouth from his. Horrified by his boldness, or by her own response, he wasn't certain. But he could guess.

"How *dare* you!" she choked out.

The storm clouds of her eyes appeared about to crack, unleashing torrents of rage. Her lips glistened, the high flush on her cheeks spread to her neck and lower, her petite frame held taut with outrage.

She was magnificent in her fury.

• • •

"You take liberties, Your Grace! Your actions are of an unspeakable cad!" Jocelyn spluttered, and darted sideways away from Calydon, lest she shoot him and unravel all that she had plotted for.

He tilted his head and regarded her. "It seems your shrewish tongue is the offset to such angelic beauty, Lady Jocelyn."

"And you are a libertine!" She had not been in his library thirty minutes and he had accosted her. Her hands trembled and her heart pounded in shock.

Mostly at the startling pleasure of his kiss.

His actions had surprised her so much she had

responded with a wantonness not in her nature. How had he wrought such a change in her?

The man was more dangerous than she'd ever imagined.

Heat burned in her entire body as she remembered how the duke had crushed her to him and plundered her mouth as though he had every right.

With an unreadable mien, he turned to watch her, graceful and panther-like in his movements. Her hand itched to shoot him for his arrogance, so much so that she clasped both hands over the derringer in fear she might actually pull the trigger.

His brows arched at her action. "Do you still intend to shoot me, Lady Jocelyn?" he drawled, seemingly unconcerned that she held a gun in her shaking hand.

"I can see where Anthony received his propensity for disgraceful, ungentlemanly behavior."

His lip curled. "You mistook me for a gentleman? How naïve. For I am still trying to determine if I will take you before you leave."

She could only gape at him in stupefied amazement. She searched his face, and what she saw shook her to the core. Her hand stilled, and all tremors left her body as her mind endeavored to understand.

He was coldly furious.

She was sure of it. The curve of his lips, and the ease with which he leaned against his oak desk suggested otherwise. But his eyes gave him away. They burned with an intensity she did not understand. *She* was the wronged party, not him.

She belatedly realized that Calydon was nothing like Anthony, or the few other noblemen who had graced her home in Lincolnshire. He was not like the earnest suitors her father maneuvered her way hoping they would be ensnared by her beauty and title despite the lack of a dowry. This man was not amiable, easily spoken, nor, indeed, a gentleman. He would not be led nor easily deceived. He was a lord, through and through.

Rich, powerful, and ruthless, and Jocelyn feared she was far out of her league, even if her papa claimed her Napoleonic mind had no match.

Restrained strength emanated from him, and a dark sensuality stamped his features. Despite the smile that teased his lips, his eyes remained cold, distant, and aloof.

She rocked back on her heels, and tipped her head to search his face. His reputation for shrewdness and ruthlessness extended to more than business acumen. Apparently it was well-earned. She was not dealing with a rich fop of the revered *ton* as she had believed.

"You are angry," she observed, her heart pounding.

She watched his face for signs that she may be wrong. And did her best to block what he had said about taking her. Visions of true ruin had been pummeling her since he'd uttered those threatening words. If he did, she would be more than impoverished, she would be disgraced and cast from society. If not worse. Should he decide to force her, she doubted she could shoot him and remain a free woman. Images of her swinging from the gallows had her paling.

"Because I detest liars." His voice whipped contempt.

Jocelyn swept down her lashes, shuttering her gaze. "I am telling the truth." In all that mattered...

"Anthony did *not* seduce you. And if so, he did a piss poor job at it."

Her eyes flew open at his crude remarks. "You persist in thinking me a simpleton! I demand satisfaction. I swear on my honor that your brother took liberties and promised me marriage."

She did not fidget under his cold assessment, despite the riotous emotions that boiled inside her.

"Women have no honor." His tone was positively glacial, devoid of anything but disdain.

She struggled for a reply, but could say nothing under the judgment that lashed out from his eyes. Fire burned in her cheeks.

"Ah, she blushes. Mortification at being revealed?"

"Blushing is the color of virtue, Your Grace," she snapped.

"A gun-toting woman who quotes the philosopher Diogenes. Tell me, Lady Jocelyn, what other talents lie beneath such a beautiful face and glorious body? Do you paint water colors or play the pianoforte, perhaps?"

She cursed the weakness that filled her limbs as he slowly perused the length of her, from the tendrils of curls on her forehead, over her breasts, where he lingered a moment, then all the way down to her black boots.

She drew herself up and met his derision with pride. "No. But I do read and write in fluent English, French, and Latin. I don't know all the great philosophers, only those who had something interesting to say. I am apt in managing a household, and have served as both chatelaine and steward for my father's estate for years. I swim, I ride, and I hunt. And I shoot very, very well."

He strolled to the bell and rang it, ignoring her passionate outburst. The butler instantly appeared, as if he had been stationed outside the door all along.

She gaped in humiliation.

The butler bowed. "Yes, Your Grace?"

"Summon the vicar," Calydon ordered. "And have the cook prepare luncheon for me and my future duchess."

The room swam around Jocelyn at his pronouncement. She dropped abruptly onto the chair and reached for the glass of sherry on his desk. She drank it in three unladylike gulps.

She had to admire the butler's aplomb. He betrayed neither dismay nor pleasure at the duke's announcement. "Yes, Your Grace." He bowed again, and exited.

She took a steadying breath. "Your Grace, I—"

"Sebastian, please. Now we are on intimate terms, let's dispense with the titles, Jocelyn."

A shiver went through her at the way he said her name, rolling it slowly over his tongue as if tasting and savoring the syllables. She frowned, disoriented and overwhelmed. He was so mercurial. She knew rage had held him in its grip a few moments ago, darkening his eyes to deep blue. Now he was smiling at her with lazy sensuality, all trace of rage suppressed behind shuttered eyes.

"You are marrying me?" She was still disbelieving of what she'd heard.

"Was that not your demand? I cannot give you the satisfaction of Anthony's hand, nor can I meet you on the field of honor at dawn. And I certainly do not wish to be shot in my own library. I thought you said I would do?"

"I… I am merely startled by the ease of your capitulation, Your Gr…Sebastian. I feared I would at least have to shoot you in the arm for my intentions not to be doubted." She glanced uncertainly at the closed door. "You sent for the vicar."

"Yes… He will marry us upon his arrival."

Jocelyn laughed, the sound thin and high. "You jest, I'm sure."

"Do I detect unwillingness? Is there a chance I mistook your meaning when you demanded satisfaction?"

She surged to her feet. "No, you did not."

She paced the library in a daze, unable to stay still. "The scandal of wedding so quickly without my family present, or a courting period of a few weeks at least—"

"Denied."

"I beg your pardon?" She plucked up her veil and top hat, and clutched them to her chest.

"I do not bow to the conventions of society, Jocelyn. Nor did I imagine that you did, after the way you stormed my estate waving your derringer."

Her feet sank into the thick carpet as she resumed pacing. The duke leaned against the bookshelf and watched her.

"I cannot credit that you would have us wed so soon. It's impossible. The banns will need to be read and—"

"I will procure a special license and we will wed tomorrow morning at nine."

She gaped at him. "I do not think it possible to

obtain a license so soon, Sebastian."

"I am the Duke of Calydon. It will be done."

She blinked at him owlishly, unsure if she could even scoff at his arrogance.

A slow, devastating smile slashed his features and she swallowed at the strange flutter it caused inside her.

"Are you at least twenty-one, Jocelyn?"

"Yes."

"Then I will have my solicitor visit Doctor's Common and procure a special license for us."

A disconcerting thrill went through Jocelyn at his words. He was willing to marry her.

Disbelief and a deep excitement unfurled within her. She stopped her pacing abruptly, staring at him with wide eyes. He prowled over to her as myriad emotions tumbled through her—doubt, fear, relief, followed by unguarded joy. Her family was saved.

But it didn't take long for the fear and uncertainty to return. Could she really do this? "I…"

"Yes, Jocelyn?"

"My father will object to such a short notice. I fear he may—"

"You will spend the night here at Sherring Cross and we will wed in the morning. There is no need for you to return home to face his objections."

Jocelyn stared at him, scandalized. She had not forgotten what he'd said about taking her. Even if he provided a paragon with the most virtuous of sensibilities as a chaperon, she would not spend a night under his roof. "Please disabuse yourself of such a ludicrous notion. I have a cousin who resides in Cringleford. I could visit her, and send a note informing my father of my decision," she ventured carefully.

"Does that mean you consent to marrying me tomorrow?"

She had no choice. She must, for her sisters. To give them all a chance at happiness. That had been the plan all along.

Taking a deep breath, she said the most momentous words of her life. "Yes, I will marry you tomorrow, Your Grace."

She didn't dare analyze the shadow of primitive satisfaction that swept across his face.

Nor did she have time, since he quickly angled his head down, gently fitting his lips against hers, sealing their agreement.

And as she melted into his too-tempting kiss, she just hoped those words would not also prove the most calamitous of her life.

CHAPTER THREE

Jocelyn's capitulation had ignited a fire in Sebastian's cock and he could still taste her on his tongue. After taking luncheon with her and conferring with his lawyer, he had used the remainder of the day to draft their marriage contract. He'd spent the night restless, wondering if she would return to Sherring Cross. This morning, he dared not analyze the feeling of pleasure and satisfaction that permeated every cell in his body when his butler announced her promptly at eight o'clock.

She was dressed in her freshly laundered riding habit with her hair pulled back in a severe bun. Sebastian thought she looked delectable.

She graciously consented to break her fast with him despite her apparent nervousness. Conversation for the following hour was very stilted, but Sebastian did not mind. He felt contented observing her and envisioning the upcoming night.

He suppressed a flare of need as he watched her eat the last morsel on her plate. She darted her tongue to capture a crumble of cake from the corner of her mouth. Her lips had a lush sexuality, and he swallowed a groan at the mental image of her tongue caressing his thick shaft. He doubted he'd ever anticipated being deep inside someone as he had her.

The emotions that stirred as he'd watched her for the past hour were not welcome. And yet, her boldness pulled him, and the mirrored need in her gaze intrigued him as she watched him covertly and with a soft hunger. He wasn't given to fanciful notions, but if he was not careful, he could find himself steadily craving her. A state he would never welcome.

Despite her innocence, given her easy capitulation to his brother's charms, Sebastian fully expected her to be unfaithful in marriage. Wasn't that what women did? They couldn't be trusted. He'd learned that the hard way from the two women he had loved and given his trust.

A savage surge of denial filled him at the thought that she might betray him to such an extent. His fingers clenched tight around his knife. He forced himself to release it, and leaned back in his chair. He would not suffer disloyalty or betrayal from her.

Her nervousness grew notably when his butler announced the vicar's arrival. Her gaze flitted around the room, glancing everywhere but at him.

He rose and sauntered toward her, enjoying her discomfort. Next time, perhaps she would be more cautious in her demands.

"Come. The vicar awaits us in the library." She scraped back her chair and came to her feet without waiting for him to assist her. She walked before him with short, easy strides, graceful yet determined, and the rounded curve of her backside had arousal teasing him once more. Thrusting his hands in his trouser pockets, he wondered how best to deal with her. He knew full well she was only marrying him for his wealth. Not that he cared. He did not know if there had ever been a time when marriage had been about something other than money.

A sensual smile curved his lips. Though, indeed, marriage did have certain other benefits. He would ensure the lady had no time even to think of taking a lover, if that was her wont. He would keep her—and himself—well pleasured, day and night, riding her long, slow, and deep. If she then still had the withal to find a lover, he would either tip his hat to her or banish her.

She swept into the parlor and halted when she saw the two young ladies who waited. She glanced at him.

"These are Vicar Primrose's wife and daughter, Miss Alicia and Mrs. Felicity Primrose. They are our witnesses," he explained.

They rose to their feet, twin blond heads bobbing to greet them.

Jocelyn nodded mutely in acknowledgement, and he signaled the baffled vicar to begin.

He wondered fleetingly if he should halt the proceedings to grant her a courtship period and a wedding that befitted a duchess. Was he denying her a dream that he could easily accede to? Constance, his sister, reminded him every so often that it was an atrocity not to be married in a wedding gown fashioned by Worth from Paris. But he dismissed the notion immediately. This was a business arrangement. She wanted his money, and he wanted an heir. Dreams didn't enter into it.

The vicar cleared his throat and asked them to face each other. Satisfaction rushed through Sebastian when she squared her shoulders, lifted her chin a notch, and met his eyes unflinchingly.

As the vicar's voice droned on, he only partially listened to the words of affirmation and commitment. He responded when needed, a smile quirking his lips whenever he noted the wild fluttering at Jocelyn's throat that belied her serene expression. He couldn't help but admire her aplomb.

"Your Grace, the ring."

He withdrew it from his pocket and her hand shook when he slid the turquoise encrusted, rose-cut diamond ring on her finger. He could feel her surprise at it, no doubt wondering how he had come to procure such a beautiful ring so quickly.

A light sheen of disbelief then glazed her eyes as he tightened his fingers on hers, and said, "I thee wed, Jocelyn Virginia Charlotte Rathbourne."

Vicar Primrose asked her to repeat her vows. She complied, voice smooth and sure, holding his eyes captive the entire time.

The final words of the vicar binding them together resounded through the library. "Those whom God hath joined together, let no man put asunder."

Gratified, he listened to the vicar pronounce them man and wife. That had gone better than expected.

"Your Grace," he drawled, and slid his left arm about her waist, drawing her close. He took her mouth with deliberate gentleness, aware of their audience. Her lips parted, and her taste, hot and sweet, sank into him. And slowly the kiss became deeper, hungrier. Only the discomfited squeaks of the vicar's wife and daughter pulled him from his bride.

He lifted his head, drinking in her beauty, anticipating the upcoming night. A blush reddened her cheeks, but her eyes glittered with heat. He felt like he was holding fire in his arms, and he wanted her with a ferocity that stunned him.

Not good. This was the way of folly. The path to losing one's heart, only to have it broken.

He stepped away from her, hardening himself

against such treacherous emotions. She was a means to an heir, and a willing body to sate his needs, nothing more.

• • •

She was the Duchess of Calydon.

The lush countryside, the fresh bite of air did nothing to soothe Jocelyn's shattered nerves. She was still a little confused at what had happened in the library. The powerful Duke of Calydon had married her.

Her heart thumped in fright as she wondered for a moment if the marriage was legitimate, or if he had somehow seized a winning hand about which she knew nothing. She dismissed the notion as a product of the stress of the day. What could that possibly serve him?

When she had demanded marriage from him, it had been sheer recklessness that had driven her—and the bitter taste of failure. Never had she expected Sebastian to summon the vicar and actually wed her. She had been hoping to drive a harder bargain and have him offer two hundred thousand pounds. She still could not believe she went along with a marriage. In his many recounts of his brother, Anthony had repeatedly stressed how much the duke hated scandal, and how withdrawn he was from the glittering throng of society. Jocelyn had prayed for strength and hoped on that account he would affiance her to Anthony. She had also logically realized he would most likely offer monetary compensation in lieu of that, but while making the cold morning trip from Lincolnshire to his ducal estate in Norfolk, Jocelyn had been quite determined to secure marriage—to Anthony. Her family needed more than money. She needed Anthony's connections, a sponsor into society, if she had any hopes of giving her three sisters a semblance of a future away from the genteel poverty they had all been living in.

But to Calydon himself? The thought had never entered her mind. Not until the moment it had blurted out of her mouth. Last night she had visited her cousin, Rosamund, in Cringleford, and it had been difficult for her to partake in conversation and tea. She'd felt certain he was playing some cruel jest and had braced herself for disappointment when she arrived at Sherring Cross this morning. She'd been both elated and scared witless that he really intended to wed her.

The elegant Calydon chaise rumbled and rocked along the rough country path, the horses' whinnying jarring her from her thoughts. The carriage was pulled by a magnificent team of six. She knew the duke owned one of the finest stud farms in England, and the sleek, powerful grace of his horses mesmerized her. She leaned forward, peering out the windows as her home—*former* home—came into view. As usual, her breath caught at its majestic grace, and a smile pure and joyous came to her face for the first time in days.

Somehow, she really had done it!

Not only was her family truly saved, but her childhood home had been saved, as well.

Even though a grand manor with sixty-seven rooms, Stonehaven, with its rustic design, paled in comparison to the duke's country home. The grounds of Sherring Cross, Sebastian's palatial estate, were stunning. The rolling lawns, the rings of gardens, and the several lakes her carriage had rumbled past had taken her breath. The land had been softly dotted with snow, and the many gardens made up of blood-red roses against the snowy backdrop had made Jocelyn feel as if she were in a fairytale land. But it was the sheer size of the estate that had amazed her. Anthony had boasted it had one hundred and fifty rooms and sat on over forty thousand acres of land.

And she would be its duchess.

Jocelyn hugged herself and grinned. And refused to let the thought that tonight she must dance to Sebastian's tune mar her joy.

I am looking forward to our wedding night.

She swallowed, recalling the parting words he had whispered against her lips. She had been so nervous when the vicar had made the final pronouncement that bound them together for life. For some reason she had pictured Sebastian whisking her off and ravishing her right then and there. She had been so relieved when he acquiesced to her request to return to Lincolnshire immediately to inform her family.

The only thing he had been unbending about was that she must return tonight. Then he had summoned one of the most beautiful carriages she had ever seen, and unceremoniously loaded her in it, uttering those compelling parting words. Anticipation? Or a warning…?

She forced her thoughts from her new husband, and let her plans for restoring Stonehaven occupy her mind. Only a skeleton staff operated the estate and had done so for years. She relished filling it with the full staff that was sorely needed. Her father had faced the looming threat of debtor prison, but no more. Joyous relief pulsed through her once more, overshadowing the worry that she must soon return to Sherring Cross.

The chaise rumbled into Stonehaven's courtyard, and she flew out the door as Flemings, the manor's sole footman, opened it for her. "Welcome back, Lady Jocelyn."

She smiled warmly at Flemings then hurried inside the massive oak door already held open by their butler, Cromwell.

"Welcome back, milady." He took her coat and smiled back—a rare thing. Her happiness must have been contagious.

"Where is my father, Cromwell? I am most anxious to speak with him."

"He is anxious to speak with ye as well, milady. He has been awaitin' your return in the green parlor."

Her steps faltered when she saw Cromwell's wrinkled forehead. His brown, rheumy eyes gazed at her with concern.

Oh, dear. "My father knows of my journey to Norfolk?" she asked.

"I believe so, milady."

"I see. Have Mrs. Winthrop bring tea and cake."

"Yes, milady."

She smiled tightly and hurried to the parlor. She blew into the room and saw her father, Archibald Grayson Rathbourne, the seventh Earl of Waverham staring out the window pensively at the east gardens, gardens that her mother had tended so lovingly. It was why Jocelyn had ensured they always had a gardener to maintain the exquisitely designed grounds that her mother had poured so much loving energy into, and to furnish her grave with fresh flowers at all times.

Her father was a portly man, more scholarly than physical. His hair had just begun to pepper with gray, and glasses were perched on his aquiline nose. He rose at her entrance and his eyes, so much like her own, lost their worried expression.

"You're back, my dear! Now tell me where have you been since yesterday? I was concerned when you didn't appear for breakfast, and have been gone all these long hours. I received your note that you would spend the night with Cousin Rosamund, but it all sounded so mysterious and unexpected."

"Oh, Father." She rushed over and threw herself into his arms, hugging him tightly.

"You are trembling, Jocelyn."

She did not lift her face from the crook of his neck as the door opened. She listened to the footfalls of Mrs. Winthrop and the *clanks* of the china as she laid out the tea and cakes.

"Come, come. Let us sit down."

He led her to the sofa that was in desperate need of upholstery, its green color faded and discolored. She gratefully sank into its depth and smiled tenderly at the sight of her father pouring her tea and arranging her favorite sweet cakes on a plate. It bespoke how worried he must have been. She gratefully accepted the teacup, curling her hands around it, loving the warmth that flowed into her.

The sofa creaked as he sat. "Now tell me, my dear, what has happened to put such a strange glint in your eyes?"

Jocelyn did not hesitate. The words tumbled from

her lips, unstoppable as she poured out the day's events to her father. She paused several times to compose herself, and at last she met his gaze as she ended her tale. Her father's expression could only be described as flummoxed.

"Are you saying, my dear child, that you are now the Duchess of Calydon?"

"Yes, Father."

He stared at her in disbelief. "You are married to the Duke of Calydon, Sebastian Jackson Thornton?"

"Yes, Father!"

She fidgeted under his intense scrutiny.

Then his shoulders slumped. "My God. I have failed you."

With a gasp of distress, she leapt to sit beside him and clasped his hands. "You have not failed me, Father. Please do not say such a thing."

"You are obviously unaware of the reputation of the Duke of Calydon. He is very powerful, and Sherring Cross is one of the richest estates in the realm. But there were rumors that circulated about him years ago. Rumors of stunning depravity, of a duel, and of him killing his mistress."

Jocelyn recoiled in shock, withdrawing her hands from his. "What utter rubbish! The duke has never been embroiled in a scandal. Even so removed in the country, we would have heard about it."

She surged to her feet with sudden restless energy. She stalked to the windows and stared down at the flowers dotted with fine flakes of snow, trying to find some comfort from the uncertainty that flooded through her. She did not turn as he draped his hands over her shoulders.

"Think, my dear. He did not marry you because you waved a derringer at him. We're talking about the powerful Duke of Calydon, with direct familial connection to the prince regent. He is known to me, even here. If he hadn't wanted to wed, he wouldn't have done so."

"But—"

He squeezed her shoulders. "I say I have failed you because of my unwise investments and choices. I am ashamed because you felt you had to lie and deceive in order to wed. You are only twenty-one. You could still have had a season. With your charm and beauty, you would have received many offers. My foolish ways denied you the opportunity every young girl of society should have."

She twisted to face him. "No, Father. I have no regrets over something I have never experienced. There is more to life than balls and soirees, and I have attended many here in the country and in Devonshire."

He gave a wan smile. "Hardly the same thing."

She placed a finger on his lips, silencing him. "As Duchess of Calydon—" She inhaled as the words resounded in her. She continued shakily, "As the duchess, I will have many opportunities to take London and the glittering throng by storm, as you would say. I did not start out my rash scheme to entrap the duke, but Lord Anthony. Never did I imagine that Anthony would already be married, nor that the duke would respond favorably to my impetuous demand."

He gently brushed a stray lock of her hair that fell forward, and tucked it behind her ear. "But how could he resist such a catch?"

She gave a soft laugh. "I must admit that I, too, am at a loss as to why he wed me. I felt the entire time that he was the one in control and he was directing me toward his own agenda. But that could not be. We had never met until I entered his library."

"Perhaps Lord Anthony spoke about you?"

"I doubt it. I now realize that the few weeks Anthony spent here in Lincolnshire was merely to gain perspective on Miss Peppiwell. There was a problem he often talked about, one that clouded his eyes with doubt. It must have been her."

"Were you hurt by Lord Anthony's defection?"

She considered. "No I am not. I had a grand time with him. He was witty and charming, and he danced beautifully. He did kiss me a few times, too, which was nice."

"Jocelyn!"

She laughed at the indignation on his face. "I now know they were very chaste kisses, Papa. But I was not so much angry that he made promises then broke them, as I was in despair. Because I had hung all my hopes for my family on marrying him. Not because I loved him."

"How do you know they were chaste kisses, Jocelyn?" The frost in his voice did not escape her. Heat blossomed in her cheeks, and she turned away.

Too late. He scowled as embarrassment swept through her. "Jocelyn?"

"Calydon— He kissed me. More than once."

Her father's jaw worked. "And you did not think *they* were chaste?"

She cleared her throat. "No, Father."

Something swept through his gray eyes that she

could not decipher. "Did he kiss you before or after the wedding?"

"Before and after."

"Ah."

She did not understand his soft chuckle. "What, Papa?"

"Did you enjoy his attentions, child?"

"Father!" Her eyes widened. She swallowed as he patiently waited for her response. "I— I have never felt anything like it. Not even while racing Wind Dancer or dancing a waltz. I burned, yet I felt so alive," she whispered.

This time it was his eyes that widened, then he fussed with his tea cup. "You are deplorably honest, my dear. I pray you are not quite as guileless with the duke." He straightened and met her eyes. "You will, however, make him an excellent duchess. Your mother, bless her heart, ensured that you possess all the social grace and polish to walk beside him. I have no doubts you will succeed brilliantly at your new station in life."

Jocelyn smiled at her father. Thank goodness he did not condemn her for her actions. Her heart beat with enough trepidation already—that the duke would hold her in contempt after their wedding night. After all, if she had been seduced as she'd sworn, the matter of her virginity should not be a problem anymore. She wondered if he would be able to tell. She frowned thoughtfully. Could men tell? They must be able to. It would be foolhardy for the men of society to value a thing so greatly, and have no way of proving if the value is still intact. She could not ask her father, she was already mortified by discussing a simple kiss with him.

"I worry for you, my dear. I do not believe the duke is a man to trifle with. He has the power to crush you if you are not careful. His reputation may just be a rumor… It has been years since I've heard him spoken of, other than regarding his miraculous touch with investments."

"What have you heard, father? Back when the scandal happened." At his hesitation, she implored, "I return to him tonight. Please do not let me go in doubt."

After the deepest of sighs, he answered, "Rumors circulated of a duel, of a mistress that he strangled with his bare hands, and of the duke himself being murdered. The fact that he is clearly still alive could well mean they were all just foul rumors."

The room spun around her as a sick feeling roiled in her stomach. "Oh."

"It is an uncertain future that you have bound yourself to, my child," he said, his gaze filled with concern. "Just be careful."

"I will." She eased out the breath that had backed up in her lungs. "To know that Victoria, Emily, and Emma will all have seasons and dowries, that Stonehaven will be made solvent for William…" Her smile wobbled as her father tenderly cupped her cheeks with his hands.

"You take too much upon yourself."

"Oh, Papa, to know that my little loves and you will now be safe and happy, that all makes it much more palatable to have married a man who may or may not have been involved in murder." She gripped his hands so fiercely that her father laughed, pulled her close, and hugged her tightly.

"My sweet child."

"What's done is done. You mustn't worry. I will not let rumors of the past affect me, and I will resolve to be as happy as I can be with my new husband."

A sharp pang went through her heart. She could only hope the man she married would feel the same about her when he learned the truth.

CHAPTER FOUR

Snow crunched beneath Jocelyn's boot heels as she alighted from the chaise.

Only a few lamps were lit in the courtyard, and they barely pierced the gray fog that blanketed the night. She almost stumbled at the line of servants that had assembled on the steps to greet her. The wind howled, and even through her winter coat, the cold bit at her bones. She shivered and pulled the cloak tighter, warding off the icy chill. She knew it was customary for the servants to be introduced to their new mistress, now the lady of the house, but she thought it unnecessary that they were lined up in the cold waiting for her.

Calydon appeared like a specter from the mist and stalked toward her. Images of a murdered mistress floated suddenly in her mind, and she tried to banish her dark thoughts. Without success.

A strange kind of dread gripped her, and she was barely aware when he introduced her to his staff as his new duchess. Her smile was wooden, and she went through the motions with a loud thundering in her head. It was only when she was swept through the massive hall that she realized it was her heartbeat pounding in her ears.

"Have you dined?" Sebastian asked politely.

She jumped, betraying her nervousness. "I did, Your Grace."

"Ah."

She felt compelled to fill the silence that pressed

on so ominously. "I am sorry I'm a bit late in arriving...home. I needed to spend some time with my family preparing them for my sudden absence. My sisters are quite attached to me, even though I must admit they vibrated with excitement over the happy circumstances."

His only response was a grunt.

Her knees weakened as they started to climb the winding staircase. She glanced wildly behind her, but nary a servant was in sight. Did he mean to escort her straight to the bedding chamber? It was impossible to slow her racing heart. She was not sure what emotion filled her most at the thought of being ravished—dread or curiosity.

I am looking forward to our wedding night.

Since she hoped that meant he was prepared to enjoy it, she decided on curiosity.

She would not believe a gentleman would lead her straight to the event after travelling for hours in the chaise. Not without time to ready herself.

But then, he was not a gentleman, as proclaimed by his own words.

She was nervous, even though she had nearly convinced herself there was nothing to be afraid about.

Nearly.

She gulped as heat rushed through her at the memory of her father's talk. He had tried to tell her what to expect. She had been amazed, then stupefied as he had taken a seat before her, his complexion florid, and wheezing like a bellows. She had thought he was on the verge of a heart attack. Unfortunately, the only words he managed to utter did not reveal much about the act itself.

"Be brave," he'd said. "Be brave."

Then Mrs. Winthrop had not helped at all by telling her that she must not gainsay her husband, even if he wanted to do wicked and immoral things to her. Jocelyn could not imagine what could go on in a bed chamber that was wicked and immoral. She had rolled her eyes and said as much.

Mrs. Winthrop had then warned her in the most ominous voice, "Beware the devil's trap, girl."

She hadn't known that Mrs. Winthrop had it in her to be so dark and gloomy.

She and Sebastian reached the landing without him speaking. He seemed lost in thought…possibly plotting the wicked and immoral things he would do to her. The idea sent an unbidden curl of excitement through her body.

He stopped at a massive oak door carved with an intricate design of a dragon. "Your lady's maid will be here shortly to assist you."

Without another word he spun around to leave.

"Wait!"

"Yes, Jocelyn?"

"Will you…um— Will we…?"

The sensual smile that creased his handsome face was her answer.

She inhaled shakily, wrenched open the door, and stumbled hastily into the room.

Immediately, her gaze zeroed in on the bed. Good lord. She had never seen a bed so massive. Fashioned of the finest exotic woods, it was raised on a dais, and surrounded by dark blue and silver drapes hung from a high wooden frame and gathered at the corners with silver cords.

She blinked as she studied the room. The sheer size of it was boggling, but the design exquisite. Persian carpets covered the floor and all the furniture was oak with the strange dragon motif emblazoned on them. The colors of the decor, from the carpet, the billowing drapes, and sofas, were shades of deep blue with silver. The elegance of the room awed her.

But— Surely this was not her chamber. She walked over to the bed and flushed at the garment splayed in its center. She lifted the pale blue chiffon peignoir and swallowed at its sheerness. She dropped it and stepped away from the bed.

She spun as the door opened and a maid swept in with a curtsy. "Yer Grace, I am Rose, your lady's maid."

"Hello Rose." She smiled warmly, and started to unpin her hair as Rose hurried over to start unpacking her valise, which had somehow appeared.

"Would ye like a bath, Yer Grace?"

She gave her a tired nod, and sank into one of the sofas in the room. A moan slipped from her lips at the wonderful feel of the deep, soft cushions. Rose bustled with a jaunty kind of efficiency, disappearing several times into the adjoining room to prepare her bath.

"Are all the rooms this large, Rose?" Jocelyn called.

"No, Yer Grace, Mrs. Dudley says His Grace had this room specially designed."

"Oh? Is the duke's room just as large?"

She paused in rubbing the tightness from her neck at the bird-like look of inquiry that Rose threw her way.

"This is His Grace's room, Yer Grace."

Jocelyn surged to her feet, nervously searching the walls around her. "I do not see a connecting door to my own chamber."

"There is no duchess's chamber, Yer Grace."

"I beg your pardon?" The look on Jocelyn's face must have betrayed her shock.

Rose rushed to explain. "Mrs. Dudley says on account o' His Grace's parents' cold marriage with lots o' closed doors, he tore down the wall separatin' the duchess chambers from this one, so they made one big room. Mrs. Dudley says it must be on account o' the duke not wantin' such a cold marriage."

Trepidation surged through Jocelyn at this bit of information. "I see." She remained quiet as Rose undressed her and led her to the bath chamber. "Oh, my!"

"It's a beauty ain't it? His Grace had it fixed up with the latest modern plumbin' a few years ago."

Jocelyn hastily stripped off her dressing gown, stepped into the marble Grecian bathtub, and sank into the welcome heat of the water. She rubbed the scented jasmine soap over her arms, neck, and chest, her mind swirling with the idea that Sebastian did not want a cold marriage with separate chambers from his wife. Still, it was never prudent to listen to servants' gossip. For all she knew, he'd removed the walls and connecting door for some completely unrelated reason.

She sank deep into the tub, all but purring in enjoyment as the heat of the water soothed the tenseness from her body, and she savored the luxurious bath to its fullest.

She refused to dwell with fear on the coming night,

when her new husband would return to the chamber...to do wicked and immoral things to her.

• • •

He'd acquired a duchess.

Standing at the open library window, Sebastian dipped his hand in his trouser pocket, touching the locket that Anthony had given her. A wry smile twisted his lips and he raised his glass in a mock toast to his mother and drank.

His mother had given Sebastian the locket several years ago, telling him to bequeath it to his duchess for a future daughter, as it had belonged to the first born females in her family for several generations. As turned off by the notion of marriage as he was, he had gifted it to a reluctant Anthony for his first born daughter, instead.

When the locket had clattered across his desk to him, Sebastian had been stunned to realize the feeling that powered through him at the sight of it was relief. The necklace was back in his possession. It had never occurred that the heirloom meant so much to him.

He had sworn never to marry, comfortable to pass his several entailments to Anthony, even though Sebastian knew that wasn't a burden his brother wanted. Anthony wanted to live free, sail the oceans, and visit the Americas and the Caribbean with his Miss Peppiwell. He continually expounded to Sebastian that he wanted to be unencumbered, to live his life as he wished, not be shackled to a handful of family piles containing only bad memories.

Unfortunately, Sebastian shared the sentiment.

The clock in the library chimed, signaling the midnight hour. He wondered if Jocelyn had fallen into slumber. He had secluded himself in the room where he felt most comfortable, to give her time to prepare, and had become lost in his thoughts for at least an hour. Was she waiting on him with virginal anxiety clothed in the provocative peignoir he'd had his lawyer acquire for him in London? Or had she fallen asleep, too exhausted from the day's events to care about her wedding night?

His mouth curled in disdain.

A virgin.

He took a healthy swallow of the whisky that burned all the way down, filling him with the warmth that was desperately needed in the library. He stood with the tall windows open, the chilly air whistling in, deep and biting. He could never understand why he liked the cold so much. The fireplace that roared behind him did little to dull the ache that filled his bones, its only purpose to shed light into the room. The wind howled, and flecks of snow blew in, stinging his face and neck.

Jocelyn had lied about Anthony seducing her. Sebastian detested liars. He took some comfort from the fact that she was completely transparent with her emotions. Indeed, he did not doubt that Anthony had teased and flirted with her, and even made promises of marriage. The necklace being in her possession showed that his brother had, at least momentarily, questioned the depth of his affections for Miss Peppiwell. But he had not bedded Jocelyn.

He might well have gone far enough for her to be deemed wholly compromised by society. But clearly, he had not even kissed her properly.

Sebastian muttered a curse as his cock came to life, and his grip on the whiskey glass tightened at the memory of the taste of her lips and her passionate response.

He understood Anthony's slight defection from Miss Peppiwell. Jocelyn's dark beauty was astonishing. Her skin was smooth and flawless, though her cheeks had been kissed by the sun, showing him she spent a lot of time outdoors. Her luxurious mane of raven hair with her storm-cloud eyes had a stunning effect on his senses. Yet, it was not her beauty that intrigued him. There were too many beauties in London, eager to been seen with him at balls and operas and desperate to be in his bed, for him to be enchanted by appearance. Beauty alone had never piqued his interest.

Jocelyn fascinated him. It was her fiery temperament that drew him most. He already knew she wasn't a simpering fool. He had no time for the vain and frivolous women of society. He viewed the sweet-tempered, pliable young misses straight from the schoolroom with disdain. None would dare storm his estate and point a derringer at him, a duke, demanding the stain on her honor be satisfied.

The *ton* would be titillated to know that was how the arrogant Duke of Calydon had wed. The scandal would roar like an unquenchable fire.

Distaste curled his stomach at the fickleness of society. The scandal would die under the onslaught of his undeniable power. For he controlled the purse strings of many families through his investments. Days later, they would all simper to be seen with her, and be invited to the balls she would come to host. She would probably be declared "an original" for how she had snared him, where a less fortunate woman would be an outcast for life.

He pulled the locket from his pocket and held it up in the glow of the fire and moonlight, despising the relief he felt to have back what she'd gifted to him.

His father had died in a carriage accident several years past, and his mother, Margaret Abigail Jackson, the dowager Duchess of Calydon, had not even honored the appropriate mourning period before wedding her lifelong lover. She had not suffered the condemnation of society overly much, either.

Her eldest son, on the other hand, had long harbored a fathomless disdain for her because of her illicit affair and complete disregard for his father. A contempt so deep Sebastian had hardly deigned to speak with her. After he came into the title, he had wasted no time in banishing her to the dowager house and cutting off her allowance, ignoring her pleas, cold and indifferent to the perfidious female's tears and machinations.

A few months back the family solicitor had hand-delivered her secret cache of diaries, written over the years of his childhood. His father had held them in his possession and left instruction for them to be handed to Sebastian at a certain time. He glanced at the packet of bound journals on his desk still awaiting him to read them fully. His parents had endured a cold marriage, never kissing or touching. He barely remembered any words or gestures of affection at all, only the perfunctory kiss his father normally placed on her forehead, unable to do more in the face of her revulsion for him. Sebastian had hated her after discovering her in the garden with her lover at the tender age of six, furious at realizing the cause of the constant arguments which had resulted in the nearly total absence of his father from his life.

All because she had a lover whom she could not relinquish.

Two things he learned from the couple of diaries he'd read thus far: his unfaithful bitch of a mother loved her paramour unashamedly and unreservedly, and she'd abhorred the touch of his father, who worshipped the ground she walked on. Sebastian had suspected what he would find, but had still found it difficult to read the words of a woman he had once loved. She had hardly found it fit to love him in return, too busy with her lover. The pain he felt reading her words had been too real, so he had yet to read the remainder.

Her journals also brought home another inescapable fact. That he needed an heir. His father had not been lying in the letters he left for him. When he wrote about Anthony not being his son, Sebastian had thought it bitter ranting. However, her diaries revealed Anthony and Constance to be the children of her lover. His father had proof of this as he had not been in her bed for years, and he also had one of her journals as irrevocable evidence. His father hated his wife's perfidy so much that he had promised to use the journal to renounce Anthony and Constance, if Sebastian did not marry and obtain an heir for himself.

Sebastian had told Anthony, and let him read the damning letter his father left him. The pain that had flared in his brother's eyes had punched Sebastian deep. He had seen right through the laughter and quip that Anthony now understood why their father had always been so cold with him.

Sebastian had promised to fight the provisions their father had implemented with the lawyer. But Anthony had refused, fearing how scandal would devastate their sister and mother. And it was possible that even now Anthony's nemesis was hinting of his illegitimacy, and the rumors were being whispered, already tainting Constance, diminishing her chances of marrying well. Sebastian had seen the profound relief in his brother at being freed of the unwanted responsibility of their father's titles. So he knew he had no choice in the matter.

He could not bear the idea of his titles and lands passing to strangers, or worse, reverting to the crown. The estates, the tenants, the responsibilities of nobility that he had learned at his father's knee, the things that had bound them together in respect and a common purpose from the day he was born, were his to shoulder, and his alone.

Except—

Marriage had always left a sour taste in his mouth, and until the fateful day he had learned otherwise, he had always believed women served but one purpose.

But then, at thirty, he found himself suddenly resolved to the idea of a wife. He had duly composed a list of eligible females. The chore had left the most God-awful taste in his mouth. And just as he'd been about to resign himself to the worst fate imaginable, something miraculous had happened.

Jocelyn had crashed into his life pointing a gun right at his jaded heart.

Disbelief and fascination had held him immobile in his chair as she had pointed the laughable weapon at him. He could have easily relieved her of it anytime he wished, but he had been too riveted by the drama unfolding before his eyes.

He'd known in an instant he had to possess her.

And so, in the space of one brief meeting, he found himself a married man, with his tempting duchess awaiting him in their chambers. A wife who would brighten his life, and share his burdens. He knew it was all right there for him to reach out and take.

But he also knew he could never relent and trust his wife completely.

CHAPTER FIVE

Jocelyn's slender, graceful back was turned to Sebastian, and he could see the fine tremors that sifted along her frame at his entrance.

He closed the door with a soft *snick,* but she did not turn to face him from where she stood in front of the windows gazing into the bright starlit night.

He had thought she might be hiding under the covers, or at least pretending to be asleep. A pleased smile curved his lips as he observed her. He should have known she would confront things head on, despite her fears. Hadn't she done that very thing this morning?

He did not have to wait long for the familiar rush of desire that hardened his cock. He paused in removing his dinner jacket, startled by how visceral the need to hold her was. She still did not stir. She had no clue that he was removing every stitch of his clothes. Or perhaps she did. With every rustle and noise he made undressing, her frame tensed and shook with even more tremors. Her hands, held at her sides, clasped and unclasped, moved to form a tight ball at her front.

Suddenly she spun around to face him, her glorious mane of hair that had been loosely pinned tumbling to her back and shoulders. He met her eyes and a shock of surprise pulsed through him.

His intrepid duchess was not trembling from nervousness or anxiety, after all. The storm clouds that had gathered in her eyes, threatening to break any second, were tempestuous ones. He expected to see a flash of lightning and hear the crash of thunder any moment now.

His beautiful duchess was enraged.

He smiled with satisfaction, and his cock swelled in anticipation.

This…should prove interesting.

• • •

Jocelyn's rage was so intense she felt like a bowstring drawn to the verge of snapping.

"Do you realize you've had me waiting for almost two hours? With no consideration for the uncertainty I may be feeling?"

His head tilted insolently. "Have I?"

Her rage burned brighter at the complete lack of remorse reflected in his wintry blues.

She had been pampered and scented, her hair brushed for what felt like a thousand strokes, and then dressed in the peignoir he had gifted her. It was so sheer her heart still palpitated at the thought. All for his bloody pleasure. And the conceited cad had kept her waiting. Two miserable hours.

"Why, you conceited bas—"

The rest of the words strangled in her throat as he dropped the garment he had been holding loosely in front of him.

In a shocked daze, her eyes tracked its fall to the carpet and scanned the pieces of clothing strewn about haphazardly—his jacket, waistcoat, his pants, boots, and assorted unmentionables.

She gasped and snapped her head up, and her eyes popped as she beheld her husband standing there.

Gloriously naked.

My God. He was splendid.

She drank in the sight of him, from his slashing brows to his chiseled jaw and sensual lips, down his powerful body. He was tall and sleek with a broad chest, wide, athletic shoulders, and thighs and calves that were hard with muscle. Everything about him was hard, strong, and proud. She had never imagined the male body could be so…beautiful.

Her hands fluttered to her throat as she stared at the part of him that jutted out toward her, so hard and rigid. And huge.

Good heavens.

She snapped her gaze up and met his eyes. They smoldered with something primitive and predatory that took her breath away.

In two strides he was directly in front of her. Then he reached out, hauled her into his arms. And he took.

His fingers locked into the thick coils of her hair as he angled his head and crushed his lips over hers. He was not slow and seductive as he'd been earlier, instead he devoured. The intensity of his kiss shook her enough that fear once again slammed through her stuttering her heart.

She gasped into his mouth, and his tongue plundered, entwining with hers, lashing her with unexpected pleasure. She moaned as that same unfamiliar fire swept through her body. A strange buzzing whipped through her and she whimpered as he pressed her back into the icy cold wall. Need pulsed between her legs, melting her and creating sensations there that left her weak and stunned.

She felt as if everything was happening too fast. A

sharp rip sounded, and her sheer nightgown parted down the middle. She let out a yelp as he hoisted her, and she instinctively wrapped her legs around his waist. She felt hot and restless, her skin painfully sensitive. His hands moved over her, caressing her buttocks, then cupping her breasts. He dragged his thumb across her nipple, and the rough caress slammed pleasure directly to her core. His kisses and nips stroked over her lips, her throat, her collar bone, and she arched in a stinging ache of pleasure as his mouth clamped over her nipple and sucked. She gripped his dark head tight as he pulled strongly with his mouth, destroying her with the electric sensations he sent flooding through her entire body.

The hand not pinning her to the wall sent flames of heat streaking up her thighs and between her legs. Shock and excitement vied for equal attention when he parted her curls and ran his fingers though her slit. She was mortifyingly wet there, and she desperately wondered if she should be. Her thoughts derailed as he plunged a long finger inside her while circling his thumb just above, touching a knot of agonizing pleasure.

She splintered.

Her scream was muffled as he captured her lips, kissing her in time to the fingers that continued to torment her between her legs. She felt delirious with the unbearably hot desires twisting within her. She shook with the pleasure, the lightning that struck her, and the fever that invaded her limbs, too wrapped in the overwhelming physical sensations to care about the liquid that wetted his hands and slickness that ran between her thighs.

He plunged a second finger inside, and she cried out at the bite of pain. He did not give her time to adjust to the invasion before he continued thrusting. Sweat slicked her skin and she was dazedly grateful, for it seemed to cool the fire that burned so hotly in her veins. The room spun as he tumbled her down on the bed.

His lips left hers and created a wake of scalding heat as he licked down to her breasts, dipped in her navel, and continued down.

Shocked embarrassment stormed through her as he replaced his wet fingers with his mouth and tongue. She shrieked, her back bowing under the riotous sensations that gripped her. His tongue speared inside her and fiery tingles coursed through her body. She gripped a fistful of his hair and yanked. She was surprised when he came up easily, his muscled frame poised over hers as he stared down at her, his eyes glittering with heat.

She gasped raggedly and stared back at him with her heart jerking and thundering painfully.

She could not stop the tremors that shook her, try as she might.

"Ah, Jocelyn." The softest of kisses brushed her swollen lips. "I have not lost so much control since I was an untried boy." His lips gentled even further as he kissed her cheeks, her eyelids, and back to softly fluttering over her lips.

Instead of his hands burning her with pleasure, they now ran languidly over her, gentle and teasing, but with a focused intensity that wrung soft moans and gasps from her. The sharp, desperate edgy feeling eased, replaced by languorous pleasure.

"It surely must be wicked and immoral to feel so good," she moaned against his lips, her focus blurring at the feel of his skin rubbing sensually against hers.

He chuckled softly. "We haven't even begun to be wicked and immoral yet, my duchess."

The edgy uncertainty and fear she had felt earlier fled completely, and a tentative trust formed, allowing her to relax into the pleasure he bestowed upon her body. She trusted him wholly when he eased her over so that she lay on her stomach, and she could only purr deep in her throat as he kissed and nibbled her neck, over her shoulder blades, and down her back, stopping at her buttocks. He nipped sharply. Her hips rolled and arched up, loving the heat of his tongue as it soothed the sting. She purred, squirming under his sensual touch. His chuckle vibrated against her, and his crooning words of encouragement as he licked a sensitive spot behind her knees had almost as strong an effect as the fingers that continued to thrust so steadily inside her.

She shivered, moaning weakly, helplessly craving the pleasure he tormented her with. His powerful hands gripped her hips and spun her to face him. She swallowed at the dark sensuality that marked his features. Without breaking their gazes, he drew her under him, lifting her legs to hook at his hips.

She ran her hands over his arms and chest, reveling in his strength and power. Her hands drifted down his roped abdomen, then hesitated.

His breath fanned over her lips as he exhaled. "Touch me, my duchess. Do not shy away now."

He gritted his teeth and groaned as she circled his hard length with her fingers. He felt like hot iron.

"*Sebastian*." Her moan was an entreaty to fill the emptiness that clawed at her.

He growled in answer.

His movements were rough when he parted her thighs and started to push into her. His lips captured hers, claiming her tongue in a teasing foray as he slowly thrust, deeper and deeper. A burning pleasure-pain consumed her, bowing her back, and had her bucking and moaning in his mouth. He held himself taut above her, his body shaking as he waited for her to adjust.

She felt stretched, wonderfully full, and excited by what was happening. An excitement that tunneled into amazed wonder at the sensations that gripped her as he started a powerful lunge and retreat.

The sharp pain had been fleeting, and now the sweetest pleasure she had ever felt spiraled from her center and ignited within her. Her hips instinctively arched, undulating to the rhythm of his powerful thrusts. She could not contain her moans or the strength with which she clutched him as sensual pleasure held her in a vise. She wrapped her legs higher around his waist and was rewarded as he plunged deeper. She screamed as the pleasure roared through her, fierce and sweet, and she exploded in a conflagration of delight. Sebastian's harsh groan rumbled against her lips as he kissed her, plunging with increased power and speed until the pleasure overtook him, too.

"Bloody hell," she whispered against his lips long moments later, her frame still trembling from the mind-numbing pleasure.

"I should have known that cursing was part of your repertoire," he mumbled with a chuckle.

He rolled with her so that she splayed on top of him. She reared up to look at him, searching his face. She followed the scar that ran from his temple and across his cheeks so savagely. Instead of giving him a grisly mien, it hinted at rakish danger. She smiled at her thoughts.

"Not many see my scar and smile, Duchess." His voice was still husky from their lovemaking, and an answering thrill surged through her.

"I like it." When his eyes shuttered, she lowered her face so less than an inch separated their lips, and asked, "Disappointed? Did you expect me to scream or cry?"

A warning growl rumbled from his chest. "I have had young ladies faint at the sight of my visage, Duchess."

"I find you devastatingly handsome, and I simply don't believe anyone fainted from this little scratch." She brushed her lips across his scar, trailing soft kisses over the crescent shape. She halted her movements when she realized how still he had become. The hands that had been loosely wrapped around her waist had tightened painfully. But she did not protest. She raised up, observing his expressionless face. "What?"

"Being hidden away from society, you obviously have not had a chance to look upon many handsome faces to judge accurately, Duchess."

Even though said with a smile playing at his lips, she had a feeling he was not amused. The curve of his mouth held no warmth, and she could glean nothing from his cool gaze.

"I disagree," she said quietly.

Suddenly she wished for the privacy of her own chambers, unsure how to deal with her husband's changeable moods. Especially while splayed over him, naked. Heat rushed through her and her discomfort grew.

"You're blushing, Duchess. I believe I would give you one of my finest studs for your thoughts right now."

"Indeed?" She raised skeptical brows. "Many would only offer a penny."

"I did not think a penny would entice you to reveal the unladylike thoughts that have you blushing so becomingly and averting your eyes from mine."

She smiled hesitantly, heating even more. "In truth, I was thinking of all the wicked and immoral things we just did."

Laughter burst from him. "Ah, Duchess, you have much to learn. We have done nothing wicked or immoral. Yet," he added with a sinful smile.

She sucked in a breath. "Show me." The words came out as more of a moan than the demand she had meant it to be.

His hands had cupped the curve of her backside and one slipped lower, his fingers teasing her wetness. "My pleasure, my incorrigible duchess. My pleasure."

• • •

The early fog that rolled in through the windows Sebastian had opened sometime during the night obscured the soft rays of the rising sun.

He shifted in the bed, the unfamiliar feel of a female body curved so trustingly into his side startling him for a moment. He had bedded many women, but never had he slept through the night with one. Not even Marissa, his only mistress, as she had belonged to another.

His gut tightened as he recalled the many ways Jocelyn had surrendered to him, over and over through the night. She made love as she did everything else, with boldness and fire. If he had not breached her maidenhead himself, he probably would have doubted her innocence. After the first wave of loving, her unguarded responses had almost bewitched him. She was a fast pupil, and at one point he had felt as though he was the student and she the teacher as she licked and caressed him with a natural sensuality that had drowned him in sensations he had never felt before.

A derisive smile curved his lips and he grunted softy. A simple memory of her hot mouth over his cock had him forgetting how perfidious women were. He must take care with this woman. She could so easily make him want to let down his guard.

He gently eased her head from his shoulder, moving silently to stand before the windows. He drew open the drapes that were only slightly parted. The fog rolled over the hills, casting gray shadows over the land. A soft moan came from the bed and he turned to observe her. She wriggled, murmuring in her sleep. His gut clenched when his name whispered from her lips on a loving sigh, then she settled into deeper slumber.

He was annoyed that he wanted to join her. Instead, he forced himself to turn away, and opened the door to his dressing room. He could not admit his valet to dress him—not with his duchess splayed so wantonly on the sheets. He had not given a thought to how tearing down the walls that separated the two master chambers would affect the logistics of daily life. He only knew he'd wanted no closed doors between him and his future wife. His mother had used the connecting doors like an ice fortress his father had been unable to breach. He'd sworn he would never allow himself to be in such a situation if he were to ever marry. A locked bedchamber would not become a weapon between him and his duchess, ever. And if that meant dressing themselves, so be it. He wanted no other eyes but his on Jocelyn in her present state of undress.

He did not choose to analyze the feeling. He also ignored the yearning to return to the bed and wrap himself around her. He did not possess one of the biggest fortunes in England because he lay abed. He had much to do. His solicitor should be on his way with documents outlining the settlement that would be paid to her father, the sum that he would settle as dowries on his new sisters-in-law, accounts to be opened for Jocelyn at the milliners and modistes, and an amount set for her allowance.

There was no time for idle pleasures.

No matter how much he wanted to return to the unexpected warmth of his new bride's arms.

CHAPTER SIX

When Jocelyn awoke, she was certain she was in love. The chill in the bedchamber could not daunt her spirits as she untangled her limbs from the linens. The massive drapes were drawn, and the sun poured its rays through the several windows. The panes were closed, but she saw that the fireplace had died to low embers, accounting for the chill in the air.

She felt the most glorious smile lift her lips along with her spirits. Sebastian had been magnificent. She could not fathom why her father told her to be brave, or why Mrs. Winthrop thought anything could be immoral.

But it was true, Jocelyn certainly felt wicked.

The feelings Sebastian roused in her were a surprise, to say the least, but she welcomed them. He was sinfully sensuous, and all hers.

She laughed as she jumped from the bed, ringing the bell for her lady's maid. She did not have to wait long for Rose, and she bathed and dressed with her assistance. Jocelyn did not want her hair pinned up, but instead she left it uncoiled, brushing against her hips with every sway. She dressed in her very finest yellow muslin morning dress. It was from last season, but it complemented her complexion and the dark luster of her hair.

Curious about the household, she went in search of her husband.

Within a few hours, Jocelyn was sure of two things. First, she doubted that the glow she'd had when she awoke was love. The feeling had burned away too quickly in her disappointment and anger.

She breakfasted alone in the morning room, having learned that the duke had eaten much earlier and was now ensconced in his library dealing with business matters. She had been undaunted after being warned by the housekeeper, and had entered his private domain without invitation. He had been so cold and remote at her simple query as to how he fared that morning, that she had been completely flummoxed. He had summarily dismissed her, indicating the depth of work he had waiting, and that he would see her for supper.

Supper!

Where had the teasing lover of last night gone? She felt miffed, and more than a little hurt that he had not deigned to speak with her after the wonderful experiences they had shared on their wedding night. Their *wedding night*. If this was an indication of things to come, things were bound to get tumultuous, for she could not accept such coldness after their firestorm of passion.

She paused on the way to the parlor as a shocking thought occurred to her. What if feeling those incredible things was a common occurrence to the duke, nothing to be in awe and amazement over?

She banished the thought, hating the ugly jealousy that griped her at the mere notion. After a tour of the large, stately manor and speaking with Mrs. Otterbsy, the head housekeeper, Jocelyn realized that the estate ran with a grim efficiency that needed little to no input from her. Everything Mrs. Otterbsy presented to her had been in proper order, and she could find no fault.

The second thing Jocelyn realized was that she was completely and utterly bored. The concept so stunned her that for a few minutes she did not know what to do. She was always occupied at full tilt running Stonehaven, so to now be a duchess who sat on a luxurious cushion with her thumbs twiddling and nothing else to do—it would soon drive her mad.

When she could stand it no longer, she had launched into motion, ordering up the carriage.

She now stood in front of her old home.

The door flew open before she had a chance to ring the knocker. "Milady." Cromwell did not look surprised to see her.

She sailed inside, loving the feeling that swept through her as Emma and William spied her from the parlor. Their shrieks rang joyously in her ears as they tumbled into her arms.

"Come now," she said, laughing. "Have you turned into little barbarians after only a day?"

"I fear they have, Jocelyn."

She glanced up at the teasing reply of her sister, Victoria. Only a year separated them, and Victoria was her dearest friend. She could see the concern in her sister's eyes, and Jocelyn smiled at her in reassurance.

"Where is Papa? I will see him first, then visit with you," she said, shooing the twins.

Victoria went with her as they strolled toward the library. "Are you truly well?"

Jocelyn glanced up to see her searching her face with her expressive hazel eyes—eyes that reminded her so much of their mama. "Yes, I am truly well."

There was a slight pause and then her sister asked,

"Were you brave?"

The surprised laughter that spilled from Jocelyn had Victoria laughing with her. "Oh, goodness, Vicki."

"You must tell me, sister dear." Victoria gulped. "Please do not fear for my delicate sensibilities. I must know what happened."

"Oh, I fear your sensibilities are in for a treat. It was glorious!"

"Was it wicked and immoral?" The question was spoken in a hushed whisper.

Their gales of laughter were cut short by her father opening the library door. He arched his bushy brows at her. "I see you have suffered no ill effects from your evening trek to Norfolk, my dear." Her father brushed his lips against her forehead in greeting.

"I will have Mrs. Winthrop bring tea and cake, Papa," Victoria said. "And I will tell Emily you are here, Jocelyn. She has been ensconced in the school-room all morning with some medieval text, completely enraptured." She hurried away, leaving Jocelyn alone with her father.

Jocelyn groaned as she sank into the library sofa. She turned toward her father, loving that he sat beside her instead of behind his desk.

"I had not expected you to visit so soon."

She let out a breath. "I was dreadfully bored, with little to do, Papa. The estate is run with frightening efficiency, and I fear I am at a loss with a day of complete leisure."

The corners of his eyes crinkled as he chuckled. "Your life will doubtless be much different. You must now host balls, soirees, and luncheons. And attend operas and masquerades with His Grace. You have been running this household for a very long time, my girl, ensuring all our needs are met. You must now do so for your own home, albeit in a different way. Victoria and I will manage splendidly in your absence."

She sighed gustily. "I wanted to see Sebastian this morning, Papa, to discuss the renovation of Stonehaven. But when I left at noon he was *still* secluded in his library, working."

"No, no. That won't be necessary."

"Papa?"

"The Duke's solicitor paid me a visit this morning. It is all settled."

"Oh?"

She shifted to fully face her father. She barely glanced at Victoria when she came in with Mrs. Winthrop and the refreshments. Her father was silent as he waited for the housekeeper to serve them.

Jocelyn tapped her foot impatiently. "What do you mean his solicitor visited this morning?" she burst out after Mrs. Winthrop had departed. "Sebastian did not mention such a thing to me."

"Sit down, dear," he said to Victoria. "This interests you, as well."

Jocelyn bit her lip, glowering at her father. Then she sat stunned as her father told them the details of the solicitor's visit.

Well, she thought in astonishment when he was finished. It seemed she must have pleased her husband, after all.

• • •

"Are you very disappointed that he did not share the financial settlements with you?"

Jocelyn glanced up from a bench in her mama's favorite garden. Its dark, luxurious beauty dotted with snow had done little to soothe her. She had visited with the twins and Emily, an occasion that had put her unease at bay for a while. But it had flared to life the minute she was alone. She had come outside to clear her head, feeling suffocated under the curious stares of her father and sister.

Her smile was strained. "Not really. I do feel odd that he wouldn't discuss something so important with me. But I realize I do not know him. He may not have thought it necessary to discuss it with me. I must remember we've only been wed for one day."

Victoria clasped her hand as she sat beside her. "Oh, Jocelyn, I could scarcely believe what Papa was saying. His Grace bestowed one hundred thousand pounds upon Papa for your hand! And Emily, Emma, and I are practically heiresses! Why do you think he provided dowries for us, or allowed Papa to partake in his latest investment scheme?"

Jocelyn was just as mystified. "I do not know. I had planned to speak with him today about restoring Stonehaven. We hardly had time for any discussions yesterday. Everything happened in such a whirlwind."

"Not even when you returned?"

"Especially then!" Jocelyn giggled at the scandalized gape that Victoria gave her. "I am so grateful to him. I came to him with no dowry but he made such generous settlements. Now I won't have to worry about any of you. And, Victoria, you can have a wonderful season! And I will be there as Duchess of

Calydon to sponsor you into society."

"What will be the first event you will host, Jocelyn?" her sister asked, gripping Jocelyn's hands and practically vibrating with excitement.

"At first I thought of a winter ball. But I am unsure where to start planning a grand event like that. Then I realized that Christmas is only four weeks away. I would love for us all to be under one roof as a family. So, I've decided I will hold a family dinner."

Victoria squealed, clapping her hands with glee. "That would be wonderful, to dine at the magnificent Sherring Cross. The twins and Emily will be so excited to have a magnificent Christmas dinner."

They looked wistfully around the gardens, sharing the same thought—a memory of their last Christmas dinner with their mother. They had never had another since, and it was something they had both always yearned for.

"Oh, Jocelyn," Victoria breathed. "It will be a beautiful holiday."

"I believe it will be, sister." Jocelyn kept smiling through a twinge of unbidden foreboding. "I truly hope it will be."

• • •

Jocelyn arrived back at Sherring Cross in time for the evening meal. The journey home had taken a couple of hours, though it had seemed much shorter with the riot of thoughts that had consumed her the whole way home.

She dressed for dinner in her finest evening gown that had a low waist and bared the rounded slopes of her breasts. Rose had done up her hair in an intricate Grecian knot, saying it highlighted the graceful arch of Her Grace's neck.

Jocelyn was gratified to see the glitter in Sebastian's eyes as they sat down to dine. Pigeon soup, roasted duck in butter almond sauce, and wild rice with leeks was the first course.

They ate in silence for a few minutes before she spoke. "I visited my father today."

"Mrs. Otterbsy informed me of your journey." He arched a brow in question, and Jocelyn plowed ahead.

"He told me of the settlements you bestowed, and I wanted to thank you."

Sebastian waved it off. "It is my duty to see to my family's welfare."

She stared at him uneasily, and cut into the pigeon. She chewed slowly, watching him as he watched her. A tingle unfurled inside her. From the intensity of his stare, she knew exactly what he was thinking about. A blush heated her cheeks, and she reached for her glass of wine.

"Why did you not discuss with me your decisions?" she asked.

He lowered his fork and regarded her. "It did not concern you."

"Of course it did. It was about me and my family."

"I will make a note of that for future reference," he said coolly.

His tone rang of finality, and she glared at him, stabbing the pigeon with her fork.

"I have sent in an announcement to the papers that we are wed. You can expect droves of callers, and even more invitations. Accept or reject them as you will. Oh, and a modiste from London will be visiting to outfit you with the latest fashions."

Her back went ramrod straight. "Indeed? I would appreciate that you at least include me in decisions that involve me directly, Sebastian."

"Do you object to the modiste's visit, or the announcement of our marriage?"

"No, of course not," she all but growled at him.

"Then I fail to understand your pique." He seemed genuinely puzzled.

The man was maddening! "It's what a married couple does," she said frostily. "They communicate, and learn to share, and make decisions together."

"I see." He lowered his fork completely. "You have been married before, to come by your knowledge?"

She took a sip of her wine, holding his gaze steadily. "No, I have not been married before. Nor have you. But I feel that to be happy and form a genuine attachment with mutual respect for one another, we must learn to speak openly. It is in the same spirit as your belief that we should have no closed doors between our bedchambers."

The smile that formed on his lips could have been one of admiration, but she was not completely sure.

"I concede, then. I will strive to be more open with you."

She cleared her throat. "And I *also* believe that we should endeavor to be in each other's company for at least one hour every day."

He leaned back in the elegantly carved dining chair. "I am confident you will expound on that with little prodding from me."

She inhaled deeply. "Our first night together was

incredible." Heat suffused her face, but she refused to break eye contact. "It's something I will always remember. But then today, you shut yourself away from me without a word, even pushing me out when I came to say good morning. I found your behavior baffling and hurtful."

His jaw worked. "I see."

She feared if she stopped now she would never get it all out, and her marriage would be doomed, so she plunged on. "It will not do for us to ignore each other during the day, each busy with some task or other, then fall into pleasure at night. Our marriage would not be based on anything of real substance, don't you agree? I think an hour is not too much to ask of you."

His gaze was completely shuttered by the time she finished. The seconds stretched out so long in such total silence that she worried she had made a dreadful mistake.

Her breath eased out in relief when he lifted his wineglass to her with a smile on his lips. "Come here Jocelyn."

He dismissed the footmen with a glance. She went over to him, slightly nervous. She squeaked when he pulled her into his lap.

"Sebastian," she whispered, scandalized.

He seared her lips with a kiss and she melted in his embrace.

"An hour a day," he conceded between hard presses of kiss. "Then in the night when you tumble into my arms you will burn. There are times when I will be rough, riding you hard and quick."

She moaned as he took her mouth in a drugging kiss.

Pleasure deepened his voice. "And then there will be the unhurried nights, when I take you slow and leisurely."

"Don't forget the days," she murmured against his lips.

His laugh rumbled through her. "The days will be sinful, too, Duchess."

A thrill skittered through her, terrifying and exhilarating. An overwhelming desire to make him need her as much as she feared she was beginning to burn for him swept through her. She sank into his kiss, her tongue loving his.

And she ignored the insidious little voice that whispered it was all a lie, and that she was leading her foolish heart straight to a wealth of pain.

CHAPTER SEVEN

"We do not celebrate Christmas in this family." Sebastian's tone was so forbidding that Jocelyn hesitated to speak further.

She rolled over on her side, taking in his magnificent form as he gazed out the window at the rolling planes of his estate.

"Why not?" she asked, her voice soft, her body sated. "The holiday season is magical. The laughter, the gathering of families and friends, and the gifts. It's a beautiful time to grow closer, Sebastian. My sisters and I have longed for such a gathering, the last one we experienced was before our mother's passing. The twins have never enjoyed such a festive occasion," she said wistfully.

She waited patiently for his reply, too boneless to join him by the windows. The past two weeks had passed in stunning pleasure. Especially their nights. But in fact, the days held nearly the same enthrallment.

The hour each day that she had demanded had gradually lengthened to two hours, then three, which they spent either on a picnic, visiting his tenants, fishing through the ice holes on his lakes, or racing horses. Even though she loved their outdoor activities, their evenings of seclusion in the library, where they played chess or read in companionable silence, were the hours she treasured most. The nights left her weak and craving, filled with intense loving and passionate embraces. Those were the times she felt closest to him, and where he lost the reins of control that he held onto so tightly during the days.

In the night he was her lover in all ways—playful, gentle, demanding, fierce, and always intense. She fluffed several of the pillows and lazed her back against them. She furrowed her brows as she waited for him at least to acknowledge her wishes. His reaction had surprised her. Tonight was the first time she had mentioned the idea of a family gathering on Christmas to him. Victoria had visited several times, and they had been having tremendous fun organizing with Mrs. Otterbsy.

She saw the muscle in his jaw jump several times, a sure sign she had struck some kind of nerve with him.

"If you insist on having such a gathering," he ground out, "you will strike the Dowager Duchess from the guest list."

"Sebastian!" She scrambled from the bed, drawing on her silk robe to stand beside him. "She's your mother. Please explain."

He turned to her, and her heart lurched at his closed, hard face. She had not seen that shuttered expression in his eyes for more than a week. His guardedness had disappeared after the first week, and she had reveled in his relaxed manner. It made her think he might truly be happy with her.

"The subject is closed, Jocelyn. Anthony and the Peppiwells are welcome. But you *will* remove the Dowager Duchess from the list, do you hear me?"

She heaved a rebellious sigh. "Sebastian, I insist…"

"You…*insist?*"

Her heart thumped painfully against her ribcage. The look of warning he gave her sent a rash of goose bumps rippling over her arms. His eyes were as filled with ice as the winter lakes.

"Sebastian," she murmured shakily, "please tell me. I can see whatever it is upse—"

"The subject of the Dowager Duchess is closed, Jocelyn," he gritted out. "You will never mention her name in this house again, and you are forbidden from having any contact with her whatsoever. Do you understand me?"

"You cannot forbid me this without an explanation, Sebastian. Make me understand."

"You will obey me in this matter, Jocelyn," he ordered.

She gaped at him. "You are being insufferable. I will not listen to such nonsense without an explanation. She is a part of our family, Sebastian."

His hands reached out for her, but he halted himself and only choked the air with a furious expression on his face. Jocelyn's eyes widened, she could not help feel as if he would dearly love to have his hands around her neck. He seemed to rein in his emotions and his hand circled her neck, his thumb caressing her lower lip. His touch was gentle, but there was steel behind it.

"It is not wise to willfully disobey my wishes, my duchess."

Ire spiked through her. "Do you plan to strangle me, then, as you did your mistress, if I do not obey?" she spat out, angered that he was not willing to talk to her.

Regret sliced through her the instant she released the words. He dropped his hands as if he had been stung, which she supposed he had. She flinched from the look in his eyes. She had thought him cold and remote before, but it was as if he became the very god of ice and snow.

"Forgive me!" she rasped.

She waited in the tense silence for him to apologize in return. Or say something. Anything.

But he ignored her completely as he methodically dressed and reached for his cloak.

"Are you leaving?" she cried.

Shame burned through her. How *could* she have thrown that foul rumor in his face? It was unconscionable, even if he had upset her with his barely veiled commands.

She grasped his arm. "Sebastian, please let us talk."

He offered nothing, no assurances or explanations, merely yanked his arm free from her grasp.

A sick feeling grew in the pit of her stomach as he pivoted and stalked out, slamming the door behind him without uttering another word.

• • •

The arctic chill at Sherring Cross had more to do with the total silence between Jocelyn and Sebastian than the winter snow that fell so steadily outside.

She did not know how to reach him. He had withdrawn completely, brooding and spending his entire days locked in his study. What tormented her even more was that he did not respond to her overtures of peace, nor did he take her in his arms at night. She had slept restlessly for the past week, desperately wanting him, helpless against his wall of distant reserve. Nothing thawed him. He was chillingly polite when he spoke. Their conversations were confined to the mundane, and Jocelyn despaired of ever finding a way to breach his solid wall. The aloof courtesy he treated her with left her baffled.

Desperate to distract herself from her unhappiness, lest she go mad, she had thrown all her energy into planning the holiday dinner.

Within days, she had turned the mausoleum of an estate into a cozy home. Rooms where Sebastian had forbidden the fireplaces to be lighted, she had ordered to be cleaned, and now they smelled of fresh lemons and pine. Fires roared and crackled, and the cold, dank feel of the place gradually warmed under her careful ministrations and strict orders.

Miniature incandescent lamps dotted the mantels, and were used to light the towering Christmas tree in the great room. Red drapes were added to the silver ones. Pine cones, evergreens, and mistletoe decorated nearly every room. Slowly the mansion transcended beauty under her touch. She was awed as she toured the rooms with Mrs. Otterbsy, admiring the fruit of their days of relentless work.

Restless energy ate at Jocelyn. Several of her gowns had already arrived from London, along with the gifts she had ordered for her family. The milliner in the village had been in rapture when she came in and opened an account, ordering several gifts for the twins and her sisters. She had ordered Sebastian's special gift from Mr. Wallaby, at a shop in upper Lincolnshire that specialized in antiquities. When she had first seen the green jade dragon it had reminded her of Sebastian. She hoped he would love it, but most of all she prayed that the silence between them would end before their Christmas dinner—just seven days away.

The worst was, she feared she was in love with him. A bleak smile played over her lips. It was irrational to feel fear upon realizing that she loved someone other than her sisters, brother, and father. That she loved her husband. It was such a different kind of love, intense and deep, filling her with a longing to be with him always.

She knew she would tell him, and soon. She wanted only honesty between them, even though her heart ached with the knowledge that he could not possibly feel the same about her. If he did, he would not be shutting her out, hiding from her whatever it was that tormented him so.

She had seen the flash of rage just before he closed himself off when she mentioned his mother the first time, though there were times when she wondered if she had only imagined it. She despaired even more as she recalled his response to her blunder about a mistress.

She wrung her hands, frantic to find a way to break the silence. A thought stormed through her.

What if she revealed her feelings to him?

Would he then be more open? What if he was so withdrawn only because he thought she believed the rumors?

She swallowed and made up her mind. She was not afraid to confess her love. And what could it hurt? She hurried to his study, knocked, and entered before he bid her go away.

He glanced up at her intrusion, and his raw beauty warmed her as always. Garbed in gray trousers with a snow white shirt with the sleeves rolled up to his elbow, he appeared relaxed and at home. Unfortunately, he seemed so cold and frighteningly unapproachable that he scared her.

"How may I assist you, Jocelyn?"

His polite inquiry was so bland she almost changed

her mind. The vulnerability felt terrible. But she took a breath and stated the truth.

"I am in love with you."

She met his gaze, and leaned against the closed door. Her hands were clasped so tightly around the handle that she knew she'd have welts on her palm.

When he did not respond, only stared at her with his icy blues, she repeated, "I am in love with you, Sebastian. I love you. Your warmth, your generosity with your tenants, your intensity…your passion. Your—"

"Enough, madam!" he bit out.

She could feel his fury pouring over her in waves. What had she said to make his eyes fill with such anger?

"I neither want nor require your love, Jocelyn. Do not speak such things." His admonishment whipped over her, stinging and flaying.

"You are angry because I love you?" She did not think it possible for his expression to become more closed off, but it did.

"Did you not hear when I just ordered you not to speak to me of such things?" His voice had grown so forbidding she hesitated, her natural boldness squelched under the utter disdain that flowed from him.

"I love you, Sebastian. You not wanting to hear it won't stop it from being true. I am not asking you to return the sentiment. I will not say it again if that is your desire, but know that every time I look at you, touch you, kiss you, and when you are deep inside me and I am calling out your name, I am saying I love you. That is, if you ever return to our bed."

She did not wait for a response, or even watch his reaction. She whirled and jerked the door open, and stalked from the room.

She feared he would never come back to her, no matter how hard she tried.

. . .

Sebastian was rooted to his chair. Her words washed over him and punched into a deep, cold recess in his heart. He felt a crack, and hardened himself at the rush of feelings. It could not have been easy for her to declare herself in the face of his indifference.

"I do not believe Jocelyn was aware that I was in the room."

At Anthony's amazed remark, Sebastian swiveled in his chair to face his brother. He had arrived early for the Christmas gathering, and Sebastian had yet to inform her.

"I don't think I have ever seen you looking quite so at a loss, Sebastian." Anthony grinned at the scowl that Sebastian sent him.

"Shut up, damn it," he snapped, and prowled over to the decanter to pour two whiskeys. "How is Phillipa?" he asked as he handed one to his brother.

"Very happy and contented. She will journey down with her sisters and parents in a couple of days." Anthony took a healthy swallow of his drink. "I thought someone was playing a prank when I read in *The Times* that you had wed Lady Jocelyn Rathbourne. Then I realized it must be true, because who would dare?"

Sebastian grunted, and stalked to the windows. He opened them a crack, letting in the chill.

"Bloody hell, Sebastian, you and the damn cold!" Anthony rose and joined him, gazing out at the landscape that was blanketed white with snow. "How on earth did it come about that you married Lady Jocelyn?"

Sebastian ground his teeth. "She barged in here with a derringer, claiming you had taken advantage of her and demanding satisfaction."

"The hell you say!"

Sebastian broke down and chuckled as amusement trickled through him. "She was quite amazing. And I thought that instead of choosing one of the vapid, shallow misses who pepper the *ton*, a bold and adventurous woman would be preferable. Although I've come to realize that my days would be far more peaceful with a more biddable wife."

He glanced at his brother, and they both roared with laughter. It was the first time he'd cracked a smile in days.

"I don't think I have ever seen you this surprised, Anthony."

"Lord. I knew the woman was fearless, but I never thought she would appear on your doorstep with a gun, Sebastian! Good God, man!" Anthony thrust his hands through the blond hair that fell in wild disarray, so different from the severe cut he normally wore.

"I was a bit taken aback myself," he admitted with a reluctant grin.

Green eyes so different from his own assessed him. "And then you wed her without knowing if I had been with her as she'd claimed?"

Sebastian heard the undisguised shock in his brother's question. "Whatever you are, Anthony, you're not the libertine she claimed. I knew something must have happened or she would not have had Mother's locket in her possession. But I did not believe you capable of betraying Phillipa so completely—not when you had been making such an ass of yourself." Sebastian sipped his whiskey.

Anthony winced. "Bloody hell."

Sebastian said nothing, just downed the rest of his whiskey.

His brother jetted out a breath. "I went to Lincolnshire to gain some perspective, and Jocelyn came out of nowhere. I thought I desired her, and kissed her a few times, but nothing beyond that, Sebastian. Her beauty was so different from Phillipa's, and her character, as well. I became enchanted. And of course there was her pedigree— I believed I was making the right decision."

"Why did you change your mind?" Sebastian asked, and waited patiently while Anthony poured another whiskey.

"She scared me."

Sebastian gave a bark of laughter.

"It's no laughing matter, Sebastian." Anthony grimaced in chagrin. "She rode her horse astride, her skills with her bow surpassed any I had ever seen. She *hunted*, Sebastian. And I don't mean for fox. After a few weeks, I realized how different she was from the women of the *ton*. She made no effort to be demure, and her energy left me dizzy. It had enticed me to think she would make a bloody awesome bed partner—" He broke off at the glare Sebastian sent him, and shrugged. "I'm just telling you my thoughts at the time. But it was mostly the lure of Phillipa that drew me away."

"Just take care," Sebastian said evenly. "Did you propose?"

"No," Anthony said softly. "But I meant for my

actions to be interpreted as such. Phillipa had rejected my offer of marriage and I was reeling. Jocelyn and I became friends and I knew she needed to make her estate solvent. I left the locket with her and returned to London to ensure Phillipa was not with child before I made any concrete decisions in relation to her. You know all that happened after."

"I see," Sebastian said.

Anthony jerked his chin at the study door. "What was that all about? Her comment about you being absent from her bed?"

Sebastian related the gist of their fight in a cold, clipped voice.

Anthony lifted a bemused brow. "She has heard the rumors about Marissa? Have you explained?"

"What is there to explain?" Sebastian ground out. "I have no desire to dredge up my past mistakes."

"Jocelyn is your duchess, Sebastian. Do you think the old rumors won't surface upon her first foray to London? Don't be blind, man. Many will flock to her side wanting to be associated with you, and there will always be those who thrive on gossip and innuendo, if not outright lies. And really, it is hardly fair to expect her to obey you about Mother without questioning your reasons."

Sebastian stared at him intently. "Are you saying Phillipa would gainsay your wishes?"

Anthony gazed out at the falling snow. "No, but, I assure you, their temperaments are very different. Besides, I tell my wife the reasons behind my decisions."

Sebastian threw back the rest of his whiskey. "I do not speak of our mother."

"Will you ever forgive her? She longs for you,

Sebastian, she—"

"Enough!" Sebastian gritted his teeth and slowly unclenched his hands from his glass, fearing it will crack. "I said I will not discuss our mother. Not even with you, Anthony. I do not give a damn what she longs for," he snarled, and prowled the study with restless energy. "And when my duchess enters society, I have no fear that she will handle herself brilliantly."

"She will. Even in the short time we have been acquainted, I know her to be fearless and poised."

Sebastian grunted in agreement.

"Have you read the remainder of Mother's journals?"

"You know I have not," he ground out. "I will not discuss her further, Anthony."

"I read them in one sitting, Sebastian, and you refuse to hear about its contents from me. I believe if you were to read all twelve volumes you would not feel such disdain for her."

Sebastian glanced at his brother with blank eyes. "I will not discuss this further, Anthony."

"Well, then," Anthony murmured, stuck his hand in his trouser pocket, and bounced on his toes a couple of times. The seconds drew out until he said, "So, I see Jocelyn has been busy decorating for the festive season. The place fairly glows."

"I noticed," Sebastian clipped out as he rolled down his sleeves and reached for his riding jacket. "Let's visit the stables. Further talk of Jocelyn's avowal and our mother are off limits."

He ignored his brother's taunting chuckle as they strode outside into the bracing cold. He hoped the cold would help harden him against the rush of emotions he had been feeling since Jocelyn's heartfelt declaration.

He had not let himself be open to love for years. Not since Marissa's perfidy. Sweet words and coyly delivered promises of love sickened him.

As he stalked toward the stables, he thought about how his wife had declared herself. There had been nothing sweet, or shy, or remotely coy about it.

His duchess had been bold and unflinching, true to her temperament.

And he had been a complete bastard.

• • •

JUNE 19TH 1864

Today is Sebastian's twelfth birthday celebration. I have been ordered to not be there. I deeply wish I could, but I know that Clement will execute his threat to banish me from Sherring Cross if I do not adhere to his demands. There are times I think banishment would be preferable to the cold silence I must endure. I have tried in so many ways to connect with my beautiful boy but he only stares at me with hatred. How I wish I could hug him to me, and tell him how much I love him, and how proud I am of him. My heart shattered as I—

Sebastian closed the journal softly and leaned back in the sofa, his heart squeezing.

After deeply contemplating Anthony's stance on how Sebastian treated his duchess and their mother, he had approached reading the rest of his mother's diaries with a calm stoicism he had not expected himself to possess.

Slowly, as he'd read the heart-wrenching words of

his young mother, his hatred had tempered and his condemnation thawed. Some semblance of regret had sliced through him, deep and painful. He'd then felt consumed with the need to learn everything about her. Hours passed as he absorbed her words, the crackling of the fire the only sound in the library.

It was through the lines of her diaries, absorbing the passion, the love, the unending need and warmth she derived from her lover, which caused the first pulse of need for more in his life to flare within Sebastian. He had been utterly shocked to realize that he was lonely. He realized how cold and withdrawn he was from everything around him, especially from Jocelyn. He had shuttered himself away from his wife in the same manner his father had done with his mother, and yet, Jocelyn deserved none of his anger.

He was grateful for the small measure of peace he found from the hurt and betrayals of his childhood. He understood some of the pain she'd had to endure being kept away from him. He had always thought she'd chosen to stay away, being too consumed with her lover. But it had been his father's way of punishing her for her unfaithfulness. Had he known he was punishing Sebastian, as well?

He glanced down at the volume gripped in his hand. She'd written that she loved him wholeheartedly. Her accounts of his many accomplishments and her overwhelming pride in him were unmistakable, even to his biased eyes.

He had six more journals to read. He knew Jocelyn needed to understand his refusal to have his mother at Sherring Cross, and he would explain. But Sebastian still doubted he could have his mother's presence in his home so soon. He understood her need for her lover, but he still had not forgiven her for it.

His mind shifted to Jocelyn, and his heart became quiet. He thought about the words his duchess had so passionately declared, and an ache settled deep inside him. He could imagine what his silence and coldness must have done to her. He could not escape the knowledge that the past few weeks with her had been the most blissful time of his life.

She loved him. But did he love her? He still doubted he had the capacity to accept and give love. Love was something he had banished from his life years ago out of necessity, but she made him yearn to be loved. That passion his mother wrote about. The need to share, to be comforted, and the joys that are found in laughter. He found it all in Jocelyn. The days of silence had been hell, and he admired the strength it had taken for her to admit that she loved him. The ache in his chest was almost unbearable.

He had the urge to go to her and explain his actions, but he repressed the feelings for now. He himself did not fully understand. He had much to atone for with his duchess, but allowing his mother to visit so soon, Sebastian could not grant her. His wound felt too raw. She would have to allow him to reconcile in his own time. His headstrong duchess would have to concede to his wishes on this, at least.

CHAPTER EIGHT

I thank you, Your Grace, for your warm greetings. Viscount Radcliffe and I are much honored to accept your invitation to Christmas dinner. I am so very thankful that Sebastian is happy to have us in his home, although I confess to being a bit surprised. But most pleasantly so, I assure you. I am looking forward to making your acquaintance.

Yours,
Margaret, Lady Radcliffe

Sebastian's mother.

Jocelyn had blatantly disobeyed him and invited the woman to the Christmas gathering.

The rage that gripped him unnerved even Sebastian himself.

He read the note for the fifth time, still in disbelief. It had been by pure chance that he had stumbled upon it. He had seen the seal and recognized it as his mother's lover's seal. So he had opened it, despite its being addressed to Jocelyn. He could not believe the nerve of the woman.

He realized that he had been too soft on his wife, allowing her far too much latitude. Something had to be done.

He summoned her to his study, and sat down to wait.

She swept into his domain looking glorious as usual, and he girded himself against the desire that flooded through him. Her hair was upswept in the most severe fashion, but the tendrils that curled loosely over her forehead softened the effect. The purple tea gown she wore bared the creamy swell of her breasts and Sebastian itched to pull her into his lap and have his way with them.

"You summoned me, Your Grace?"

He could see the wariness in her eyes. Three days had passed since her declaration of love and he had ignored her completely, not even dining with her. He had needed the distance so he could think clearly. So he could come to peace with all he'd learned about his mother, and unravel why Jocelyn's words would affect him so. And then this.

She did not understand the full extent of the trouble she was in.

He smiled, but not pleasantly. "Do you have something to tell me, Jocelyn?" He kept his voice deliberately bland, lest he bellow his rage.

"I do not, Sebastian."

He surged to his feet and stalked around his desk to lean against it. "I detest liars. Have I not made myself clear on that regard?"

Puzzlement shadowed her face as she took two halting steps forward. "I have not lied to you, Sebastian."

"Then how would you explain this, madam?" He pushed the note forward, and it fluttered to the ground.

She stooped to pick it up. "Oh!" She gasped as she read the contents. Sebastian blinked in disbelief when she had the nerve to smile broadly at him. "I was not sure if she would respond."

He wondered if she was daft. "How is it that you fail to understand your precarious position..." he murmured softly. Then roared, "You defied me!"

Her body jumped, startled at his anger. "You gave me no choice," she snapped. "I had no way of reaching you, Sebastian. There has been tension between us for ten bloody days. I have tried in so many ways to mend my thoughtless remark, to explain my feelings, but you have shut me out completely."

"So you sought to manipulate me by inviting my mother after I have forbidden it?" he asked incredulously. "You have not comprehended your folly, madam. As you so indelicately pointed out, the last woman that tried to manipulate me is dead."

"I did not try to manipulate you!" She clutched her hands and glared at him. "I wanted to provoke a reaction from you. And I succeeded. Your anger is better by far than the icy detachment you have thus far treated me to."

"Do you believe so, madam?" he said with chilling softness. "You will retract your invitation, Jocelyn, and you will do so immediately."

She glared at him mutinously. "I will not. If you will but hear me out—"

"There is nothing to hear, Jocelyn. Retract the invitation immediately."

"I will not!"

He clenched his teeth, debating how to deal with this…this…flagrant insubordination. It wasn't so much the invitation that infuriated him as her blatant, willful defiance of his orders. "Where have you been living, Jocelyn?"

"What do you mean?" She sent him a baffled glance.

"Where have you been residing for the past twenty years? Has it been in Lincolnshire, England?"

"I do not understand what your questions have to do with our discussion, but yes."

"Let me educate you, then. You are my wife. Thus, my property. I am well within my rights to beat you if I so desire, or banish you from my sight. I am trying to understand how you thought you could so blatantly defy me and go unpunished. I believe the best punishment will be to banish you. To Devonshire. And it would be an injustice if I did not beat you first."

Her jaw dropped in outrage. "You arrogant, egotistical, unfeeling *beast*!"

She launched herself at him.

Her actions so surprised him, he did not brace to check her momentum.

"*Oomph*."

Her muffled scream as she slammed into him had him letting out a laugh in amazed disbelief. But it was quickly wiped away as her palm swung and caught him solidly on the cheek.

Good God. He had truly enraged his duchess. Was she really not aware that he would never beat her? He doubted he had the heart to banish her from his sight, either.

"You do not display much prudence, do you, wife?"

Her breaths heaved, making the swell of her breasts rise precariously above the gown. Her eyes darkened to almost black as they glared a furious dare at him.

Just that quickly, he wanted her. A fierce need to possess her surged through him. And not in the slow and languid way of their nights of loving before their falling out.

He needed her. And he wanted her to burn.

• • •

Sebastian's mouth crashed down on Jocelyn's, stunning her at the abrupt turn of his mood.

The intensity of his mouth as it captured hers sent shocks of desire through her whole body. She responded with complete hunger, gripping his dark head tightly to her.

"Oh, yes!" she gasped as he roughly yanked down the bodice of her gown, as though its low cut had been fashioned exactly for his ravishment. His lips covered her pebbled nipple.

"Sebastian," she cried out.

He stalked backward with her, whipping up the hem of her dress and petticoats, pushing the layers of fabric upward as he trailed his hands up her legs. She gasped into the mouth that kissed her as the back of her knees hit his oak desk. Papers and objects flew, and he lifted her bottom onto the desk. His breath was ragged as he withdrew his mouth from hers and stepped between her thighs, wedging them apart and hoisting her legs to his waist. Then his fingers deftly parted her bloomers, exposing her to the chilly air.

That, and the scalding look of passion on his face sent erotic shivers dancing up her spine.

"You infuriate me," he growled. "I do not know if I should beat you, strangle you, or kiss you."

"Do I have a say?" she managed breathily.

His jaw worked as he pulled his member from his trousers. "No."

Then he angled her hips up and slammed into her in one powerful movement.

The desk jerked. Her scream of pleasure-pain rang in the library. He kissed her brutally before withdrawing and forging home again, slower, but just as powerfully.

"You also drive me mad," he all but snarled as he gripped her hair, then feasted on her lips again.

Jocelyn reeled with pleasure at the intensity of his lovemaking. It had never been like this before, his control shattered. Weakness infused her limbs, and dark, wanton need seared through her. She tried to rise to meet his thrusts, but with the powerful grip he had on her hips she couldn't move. She could only submit to his powerful strokes and the merciless pleasure that he rained upon her. He buried his face in the curve of her neck as his hips plunged faster, driving into her over and over, hard and relentless, sending deep shards of pleasure to her very core. She felt his teeth at her shoulder, scraping against her skin, nipping her with erotic bites. Burning ecstasy speared her body, and she came apart in a thousand pieces.

He plunged once more into her convulsing body, and with a harsh roar he tumbled with her, emptying his essence into her.

"My God, Sebastian," she gasped long moments later, still trembling from the aftershocks of such violent pleasure.

He groaned against her lips before capturing them in a kiss that only served to make her mindless. "I cannot believe I have been absent from your bed for ten days."

Hope surged through Jocelyn.

"Does that mean I will not be beaten or banished?" she asked breathlessly as he lifted and carried her, still impaled, over to the sofa. She moaned at the sensations that traveled through her at the feel of him hardening inside her again. He sat on the sofa with her straddling him, the skirt of her gown spilling backward over his knees, his morning coat crushed beneath her folded legs and bunched-up petticoats.

"You infuriate me, Jocelyn, but know that I would never lift a hand to hurt you in any way."

"Banishment, then?"

He grunted and her heart raced at his intent regard.

"I do not have a pleasant relationship with my mother," he said without preamble. "It has been so since I found her with her lover in the gardens when I was six."

Jocelyn stiffened in shock. "Oh, Sebastian, I'm—"

He shook his head to cut her off. "The rift only got worse after she married her lover, Lord Radcliffe, only three months after my father's passing."

Regret flooded through her, as it dawned what she had done by sending that invitation. No wonder he was furious. "Oh, husband, I am so sorry. If I'd known—"

"I had planned on explaining everything to you tonight. I realized what an ass I have been for not speaking to you as I tried to come to grips with how you make me feel. It was wrong, and I'm sorry for that."

She blinked, her heart stalling with dread. "H-how do I make you feel?"

"Be silent and listen, Jocelyn." He nipped at her lips. "You came into my life and completely turned it upside down, when all I wanted was a biddable wife to give me an heir."

All the hope she'd felt a moment ago fled in an instant, and a noise of anguish escaped her throat.

He didn't love her. He would get her with child, and then he would banish her, just as he'd threatened. Oh, God, what had she done?

•••

Sebastian cursed as Jocelyn stiffened, her muscles tightening, sending shards of pleasure running along his cock, still buried deep inside her. Then she squirmed, attempting to climb off him and get away.

"Be still!" he rasped, his fingers digging into her hips.

"No! I—"

He gave her a shake. "Just listen, damn you!"

He groaned as she wriggled, settling closer on his lap, loving the rush of liquid heat from her, telling him how much she wanted him.

But he needed to finish this conversation before giving in to the arousal. He gripped her hips and gently eased her off him. He grunted at the sensations that travelled through him as her tight clasp reluctantly released him. He tucked himself back into his trousers and drew her down on his lap. He held her chin gently and titled her face up to meet his gaze.

She froze, her eyes questioning, and he went on before she could move. "When you stormed my library, so fearless and demanding, I knew immediately. It was you I wanted, not some vapid miss without a thought in her head."

He felt her rigid muscles relax a little.

"Truthfully, never did I expect you to enthrall me as you have. The days I spent with you only carried me further and further into my feelings for you, and I began to fear your lure. I withdrew, uncomfortable with the intensity of my emotions. The last time I felt anything close to this, I fought a duel over a married woman...whom society still believes I murdered."

"Oh!" Her uncertain gaze shifted to disconcerted.

"But what I feel for you is wholly different. You make me burn with life, and yearn to set aside my cold and distant, solitary ways."

"Oh, Sebastian." Her eyes softened with love, and she tenderly kissed his face and his lips.

"I am not finished, Jocelyn," he murmured between kisses. "We will not have this conversation again, so I implore you to be attentive."

She gave him a radiant smile and stilled.

"I had already decided to break the silence with my mother after reading a series of her journals. I may not fully understand what she did, but I can empathize with her plight, and the agony she felt over her decisions. But reaching out to her was something I wanted to do on my own terms."

Jocelyn lowered her eyes, toying with the buttons of his shirt. "Can you ever forgive me? I—"

"I know you are not repentant, Jocelyn," he said wryly.

Her contrite expression melted into a mischievous smile, and Sebastian embraced the notion that for some mysterious reason, her disobedience no longer bothered him.

"When you foray into society as my duchess you

will hear many things whispered, and I do not want you to be ambushed. Marissa was my lover both before and after she was married. In a bid to force my hand, she accepted the offer from an earl, hoping that jealously would bring me up to scratch. It did not."

He grimaced. He had been determined never to marry. Ironically, that had led him into exactly the same situation for which he'd always condemned his mother. He just hadn't seen that until now.

"I foolishly continued the affair," he went on. "Marissa wanted me badly enough that she told me lies of her husband's brutal beatings, hoping I would call him out and kill him." He swallowed, hating the memories of that time. "As proof, she showed me horrible bruises, which I later learned were self-inflicted. And I fell for it. I challenged her husband to a duel, which he accepted eagerly." Sebastian traced a finger over the scar on his cheek. "He gave me this, and I almost killed him."

Jocelyn's eyes were wide with dismay. "That's awful," she murmured.

"As he lay wounded and cursing, I realized he believed it was me abusing his wife so viciously. She'd been lying to both of us. I confronted her, and she confessed she'd done it to be free to wed me. She implored me to actually kill him so we could be together. Of course I wouldn't, and ended our association. She threatened to kill herself because she loved me so desperately. When I ignored her threats, she later hanged herself. Then the foul rumors surfaced that I strangled her."

Jocelyn's face went ashen. "Little wonder you do not want to hear my words of love."

He gently captured her lips. "No, you're wrong. I've changed. Because of you. I want the kind of marriage you once described to me. To communicate, and share, and make decisions together."

Slowly, her face cleared, and her lips parted. "I do believe you love me, Sebastian," she said, her eyes filled with wonder.

Warmth unfurled through his whole body, and intense love filled his heart to bursting.

He gripped her hips, spinning and tumbling her into the depths of the sofa. He settled between her thighs and kissed her lips with tenderness. "I believe I do, my duchess. I do believe I love you."

• • •

CHRISTMAS DAY

Fierce pride and joy filled Jocelyn as she looked around the massive dining table. It was perfect. Everyone had arrived, and laughter and merriment spilled through the halls of Sherring Cross.

The parlor rang with excited chatter from her father, brother and sisters, Anthony and Phillipa, Phillipa's sister and parents, and the dowager Duchess Margaret, Sebastian's mother, with her lord, and Sebastian's sister Constance. Jocelyn had expected the dowager to be cold and forbidding, but the dainty creature that looked up at her long-lost son with such wide, imploring eyes had surprised her. Sebastian had not disappointed, and Margaret and Jocelyn both had been pleased with their first tentative conversation.

She and Victoria had been gratified and a little

bemused at the twins' shrieks of joy to be dining at the table with the adults. They had all crooned over the roast ducks, turkeys, stuffed pigeons, and roasted pork. Not to mention the Christmas pudding and punch.

Jocelyn could not have asked for a more perfect day.

She thought of her mama, and emotions tightened her throat. How she wished Mama could be here! How she would have loved it all.

Sebastian's gaze met hers, and she gave him a smile and a subtle signal, then swept out of the room, away from the bustle. She went into the library, the room she thought of as their special place. All the things that brought them together so deliciously had happened there.

She stood at his favorite window, staring out at the snow falling steadily over the estate that she had come to love as home. Excitement bubbled through her.

His strong hands curved around her waist and he held her from behind. "Do you wish to retire?" he murmured, kissing her nape.

"I doubt they would forgive us." She smiled at his reflection in the frosty window pane. "I have a gift for you."

His brows went up, but he looked pleased. "Another?"

"Yes, I thought I should tell you tonight, considering the multitude of generous gifts that you have showered on me."

"Tell me what?"

She spun in the circle of his strong arms, glowing

with joy and contentment. "Our child will be here in the summer."

"Our—"

The stunned look of elation on his face made her heart overflow with love. "Merry Christmas, my love."

Sebastian wrapped her in his arms and held her tight. "And Merry Christmas to you, my sweet duchess. You've made me the happiest man in the world."